LADY HELLGATE • BOOK FIVE

GREG DRAGON

STEEL-WINGED VALKYRIE

This is a work of fiction. Names, characters, organizations, places, events, and incidents are either of the author's imagination or used fictitiously.

Copyright © 2021

Thirsty Bird Productions
All rights reserved

No part of this book may be reproduced, stored in retrieval systems, or transmitted without the publisher's written permission.

Cover Art by Tom Edwards

For more books by the author
GREGDRAGON.COM

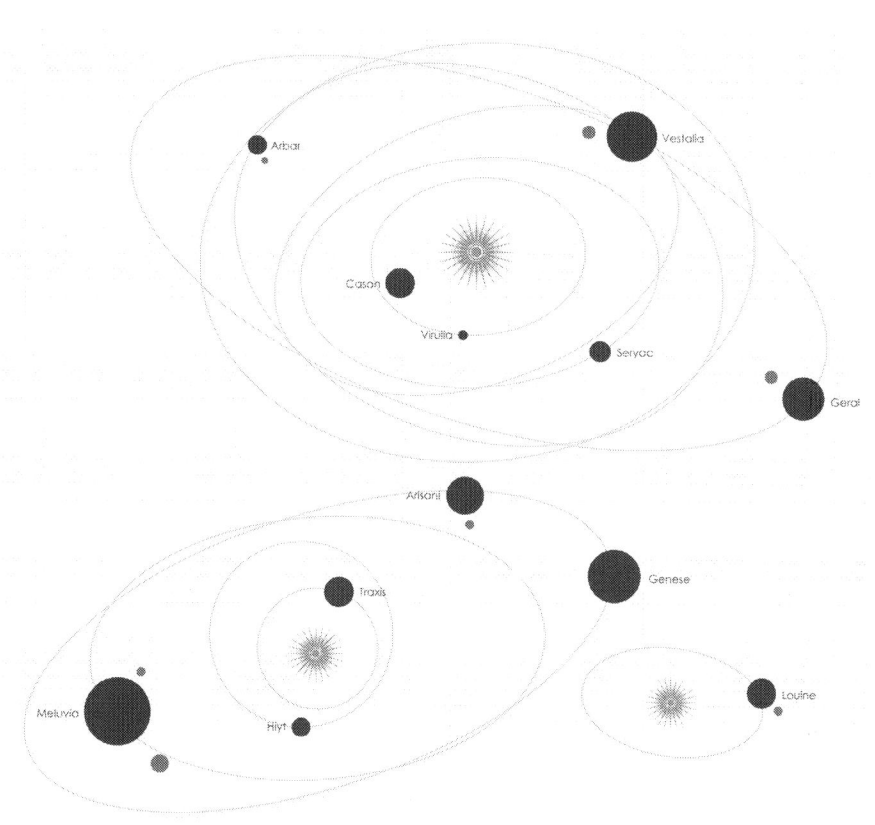

The Galaxy of Anstractor

1

Fio Doro ran her fingers over the leather seat next to her, taking in the texture and scent, relishing and wishing that she could afford a transport like the one she was seated in. For an up-and-coming fortune-runner of Basce City, this was one of those moments that either became a common occurrence from scoring the bigger jobs, or a once in a lifetime view of the ceiling, the one job that would pay enough credits to change her life for the better.

The Cel-toc in the driver's seat hadn't spoken to her since they made their introductions. She had been scanned for weapons and contraband, then ushered into the back of the aircar. Here she waited for her mysterious contact, who had hired her through "the company," so this was to be the first and only time they would see each other.

Reaching out to touch the square glass panel in the seat's headrest in front of her, Fio changed its display to become a mirror, touching up the black around her eyes. She scrutinized her appearance, trying to imagine how she would appear to a stranger looking to hire a smuggler. Did she look reliable, seasoned enough, or would this be yet another client lost due to her youthful appearance?

The front door popped out with a loud sound before sliding backwards to open as a dark form slid into the front seat. "Drive," he commanded, in a deep baritone, accented with the rolling r's of a Virulian. The door slid shut before the interior of the vehicle became awash with light. Fio felt the ground drop from below them as the aircar took off into the sky.

"You have ten minutes to convince me that I'm not wasting my time," the deep voice said, still not giving her the courtesy of an about-face, a name, or direct acknowledgment.

"I'm Fio, and I'm the best at this, which is why you took this meeting," she responded confidently. "I know Basce City like the back of my hand, and have the support of four of the six major clans. Those relationships give me access to zones where your product can be transported quickly and discreetly. I may look young to you, but I've been doing this since I was sixteen, running with the Lords. I've got runners, gunners, and transports, all ready to haul your cargo."

"Ever move living cargo?" the mysterious man asked.

"Living cargo?" Fio knitted her brow, frustrated. There were lines one shouldn't cross as a fortune-runner, and actions that could black line a smuggler's reputation forever. "Are we talking livestock, prisoners of war, or do we mean slaves? Can you turn around and face me? I feel like I'm talking to the back of your seat and it's unnerving."

The passenger seat made a hum, tilted forward, and then shifted towards the door, rotating slowly until the mysterious man was facing her. He was everything she imagined he would be, a suited, manicured, elitist with power. His low-cut curls were black but for the sides, which showed snowy white patches, patterned to favor snowflakes, blowing from his face to the back of his scalp.

While he could be considered handsome, even without the trimmed beard and mustache, his piercing brown eyes were off-putting, reminding her that beyond the money and costume, what sat before her was a ruthless predator. She held his gaze without showing fear, a practice mastered from a truncated youth filled with many powerful men questioning her usefulness.

"Is this better?" he asked, spreading his arms for effect.

"Much better," Fio agreed. "As to your question, I will need details. I'm not in the habit of transporting slaves, captures, or soon-to-be prisoners. No offense, but if that is what this is all about, I am not the smuggler you're looking for."

"You're not what I expected," he admitted, "Can you even fight? Or should I say, have you won any fights? That's a right nasty scar there by your ear."

Fio thought of the dagger tucked away in her sleeve, and wondered if the poison would be potent enough to stop this man if he tried to test her physically. "Look, man, I don't care what you expected," she said coolly, "Either detail me the job, or you can land this junker and let me on my way to find a client with some actual professionalism."

"You're icy, that's good," he allowed, reaching into his pocket to pull out a holo-card bearing the image of a man. "Know this fellow here?"

Fio leaned in closer, though she instantly recognized the face. It was a local gangster, a man with a wicked reputation that stretched back over twenty years. "He's a heavy-duty runner, practically a legend. What? He was busy, so you had to come down to the stocks to get one of us up-and-comers?"

"Not quite," he countered quickly, nearly cutting her off. "This man has something of mine I'd like returned. The job is simple. This thief, this fatheaded thug, stole a suitcase with my belongings in order to contact me, looking for ransom. Luckily there was nothing compromising in that luggage, though there is an important set of documents for my work. One-of-a-kind documents, the type the city doesn't want on the black market, you understand?"

"He stole your luggage then, and I am supposed to, what? Take him on somehow, and get it back?" Fio didn't like where this was going. She was quick and had connections, sure, and there was access to arms, but she knew better than to mix up with the gangs.

"Not proud to admit this, but I contacted the thug and we came to an agreement on a price for my luggage. Now, your part is easy, I will give you an address and a time to retrieve my luggage from where he's supposed to drop it off. Bring it back to me, and you get 500 credits," he said, whispering the words as if the number was astronomical for such a "simple" job.

Fio nearly laughed. "500 credits, really? All this secrecy, and bringing me up here for this chat, all to offer me a pittance for risking my life? 1,500 credits."

"750, and I will refer you to my colleagues who need smuggling," he countered, looking away from her to stare out at the rooftops. He was trying to be stoic, but Fio had seen his eyes when she countered, and knew he was bartering out of principle. This was a desperate man, and he was aware of who she was and that she would take the job. Why else would he have given her so much detail?

Fio thought hard on how she should answer. 750 was enough to purchase a hover, or pay rent for half a year. Standing on principle the way he was could have her back on the street that night with no credits and no job. She had been out of options until tonight, and here was this man offering the type of credits that she and other runners only speculated on.

Agreeing could mean the difference between remaining a small-time go-between, or riding expensive aircars to high-rise levels above Basce City. But something inside of her despised the thought of compromise. Not with a robe-wearing serpent like the one sitting in front of her, slithering to the poor section to offer a pittance to any fool willing to take the job.

3

If all I wanted was to survive, I'd be hawking loose supplies and trinkets, not sitting here about to be ripped off, Fio decided. Looking up from the floor, where she had sat thinking with her elbows resting on her knees, she met his eyes bravely. "1,500 credits is my price. You deposit 500 now, I pick up your luggage, show you the evidence, and you deposit another 500 for me to drop it off at the address. Once business is concluded, you pay me the final 500, and we can do this again. Agreed?"

The older man grinned, a wolfish smile, one of acknowledgment and respect, before handing her a paper to write down her bank information. He let her off by the wet docks with an address for the pickup and a contact for arranging the drop-off. The night air held a chill that forced her to pull her cloak close, and she regretted that she hadn't forced him to drop her off near the tenements where she could run to her apartment.

It started to rain, so she ducked into the closest door, which turned out to be a ticketing station. It was dark and smelled of rusty metal, mold, and something else foul, but it provided her some shelter and privacy. Her cloak was heavy with rain, so she hung it up on a bit of metal jutting out from one of the stations. She hugged herself tightly and rubbed at her arms, trying in vain to warm herself up.

"This is *schtill*," she shouted, frustrated with the weather, but this soon passed when it dawned on her the number of credits she was about to earn. Fumbling for her smart-comms, she placed it to her lips and asked it to bring up her credit account, and search for any pending deposits. The disk-shaped device vibrated and emitted several running lights, and a set of holographic numbers hovered above it, which made Fio smile with satisfaction.

At least this will pay well just to make the drop-off, she thought, trying to imagine a future where she had her own transport and could upgrade her apartment. "Something stinks," she decided out loud, remembering how calm he was. She hadn't even gotten his name, but he had deposited a third of the credits. *Is he setting me up for a fall?* She wondered if this was a trap being set for her arrest from an enemy, possibly a rival?

No, that wouldn't make any sense, she decided. This was Basce City, and if it were an enemy, they would have just had her shot. Closing out the finances, she cupped the small disk in her hands and held it up to eye-level, thinking about who she should call for advice.

"Call Pops," she announced, and the device came to life, cycling through a myriad of cards bearing faces and names. It's shuffling stopped on an older, smooth-faced man with a scar running from one glassy, dead eye to the left corner of his mouth. His card glowed and came to life, replaced by the actual man. He didn't appear happy to see her.

"You have thirty seconds, Runner, and if it's not about my credits, I'm gone. You know the rules, and you're one day out. What have you got for me?" he practically growled, violating the silence of the rundown ticket station, with only a well-timed echo of thunder to drown him out.

"I have your credits, but I need some help, Pops, not as a runner but as your daughter," Fio offered, biting the inside of her lip, hoping that her play on his sentimental side would soften him up.

"Daughter?" he guffawed. "You have some nerve, Fio Doro, I'll give you that. You were my best student, but that was a lifetime ago, and the woman on the call is not my child, but a *thyping* psychopath."

"Can we not bring that up now, Djesu? This isn't a trick, I may be in trouble, and like it or not you're all that I have," Fio pressed, already sure he would crack. "Got a job, but it's likely dirty. A ransomed recovery for a politician who tried to rip me but I stood my ground. Threatened to cut him and he was soft, so he allowed me to carve him up. Tune of three times the going rate, had him make a deposit, like you taught me. That stack of credits is yours."

"Politician, you say?" Djesu seemed intrigued, "Are we talking about William Vray, Fio? Or should I say the so-called consul since he's as crooked as the BasPol bruisers?"

"One in the same, but how should I play it?" Fio said, shivering now and rubbing her palms together to try and summon some warmth.

"That one has no honor, little Fio, you should have cut him when you had him alone," Djesu said, rubbing at his chin. "The entire Basce City underworld would love you, and the rest of the consul as well. What're you running?"

"He said government documents. Scarred Roan ripped him when he landed at the shuttle port. Cruta stuck a *thyping* councilman, can you believe it? Then he goes and pays for it, the sucker. There's bound to be spice in that package, or some sort of weird sexual deviance. Who knows?"

5

"Can't trust the BasPol for justice, Fio. A mark this big if he decides not to pay, nothing much can be done short of threatening his family," Djesu said, still rubbing away at his chin. "This your first time running for Vray? Yeah? Who made the rec then?"

"Gaius referred me," Fio replied. "I was quite shocked, to be honest. Thought he wanted nothing to do with me."

"Gaius?" Djesu practically shouted. "Didn't he get picked up?"

"Yeah, for running spice out of Stardust's," Fio admitted.

"The minimum detainment for spice is a week inside, Fio Doro. Selling it gets you three months hard labor, scrubbing out grime from the barges, or buffing old metal down at the yards. Smuggling though, girlie, you should know well the risks we take being runners. Smuggling comes with a fine and a lengthy stay in the Municipal Rehabilitation Center."

Fio wasn't sure what to say to that, but her memory of the Municipal Rehabilitation Center sent shivers down to her toes. "He knows my past then," she said, standing up to grab the disk and pace about to get the blood flowing. "Is that what you're thinking, he's got a stash of spice?"

"Not likely," Djesu replied. "But these ransom jobs are always crooked. Either you won't be paid or he'll call BasPol, telling them that you were the one who stole it."

"So what am I to do, Pops? Just go through with it, get arrested and thrown into one of those five hundred cells with the rest of them? I would sooner join the outlaws before I subject myself to that."

"Easy now, girl, we'll think of something," Djesu urged, and she could see that his protective ice had all but melted. He stopped rubbing at his chin and stared directly at her, as if they were really together, and not his holographic representative. "It's the eve of the grand committee, Fio, the time of year these politicians come knocking. They will use us for their blackmails, kidnappings, anything. Why not? They won't be the ones losing their lives over it. There is no limit to their conniving. Tell you what, Fio, when you get the package, take it out of the city and look inside. When you learn what it is, you decide for yourself what to do with its contents."

2

Static, rust on the bulkheads—wait, not rust, but something sticky, like clay or wet mud, thrown against it. An endless passageway of horrors, drifting past the young woman in this relative blackness. No alarms, which was the norm whenever there was a loss of atmosphere. Helga Ate, lieutenant (junior grade), was pulling herself along using handholds conveniently built into the bulkhead at the end of every third panel.

The low light made it hard to determine just how much farther she had to go, and at the twentieth handhold, she stopped to consider whether or not it was futile. A gauge at the corner of her mask's HUD revealed the amount of oxygen left in her reservoir. Five minutes was the countdown, but still, she didn't panic, though anxiety had her hands shaking uncontrollably as she held on to that metal rung.

This isn't good, she finally admitted to herself, *and why am I shaking? I'm normally stronger than this. What am I going through?*

Placing the toe of her boot inside another rung, she squatted as deep as she could go, then pushed off suddenly, propelling herself forward past a thousand motes of light and a ... human head? Whatever cool she had left in dealing with her plight was immediately shattered when she focused on the decapitated helmet bearing its grim visage.

Three minutes passed, and she was still pulling herself along by the handholds, floating at a steady pace. *Which passageway is this, and how am I here?* she kept thinking, probing the dark for answers. Nothing eased her thoughts or provided clarity, only more bulkhead, holds, and dead spacers drifting past.

Time felt ambiguous, which made no sense to her. Being so close to dying—familiar territory to a Nighthawk—yet accepting of it, somehow? No, this wasn't her. Not when all her life, she had fought hard to survive. Anticipating her demise, Helga looked for her oxygen gauge to see if it was depleted.

With the lack of any alarms coming from the helmet's comms, she reasoned that there was a malfunction with the sound. Why else would her Nighthawks ignore her calls, and why was there no alarms warning her of her doom, which was standard when your oxygen was depleted?

Now there was no gauge, no readouts, and thinking that the display too had decided to die, Helga reached up to touch the glass, finding nothing there. The icy fingertips of her Powered Armor Suit's gloves made contact with her bare face, sending a chill of panic through her body, causing her to sit up suddenly, inhaling a big gulp of air.

Recognizing that it had all been a nightmare, the frightened Nighthawk exhaled a long sigh of relief and looked about her dark compartment. She tried to recall what she had dreamed about and why it had her heart racing, but all she came up with was blank, leaving her confused more than anything else. A faint memory of a dark passageway was all she could recall, and she eventually gave up on trying when the details refused to resurface.

Helga swung her legs off the side of the rack and stared off into the darkness. Waking up with the sweats in this tiny compartment made her miss Joy Valance, who always knew what to say to her when she was alone and feeling foolish.

Before Joy's promotion to CAG of the infiltrator *Soulspur*, Helga would look forward to spending time with her, drinking, arguing, and getting into mischief. Having those long talks into the night, with each of them bearing their soul. Even monotonous patrols were a riot when they involved Joy. Her sister, rival, mentor, and drinking partner, all bundled up in an imposing figure of beauty, brains, and short temper.

Never before had Helga felt as alone as she had since returning to *Rendron*. Every Nighthawk had resumed their former lives, including Cilas, who, in her opinion, was too busy traipsing after the captain to give her any attention. Even Raileo Lei, who had grown closer to her in their last mission, spent all his time with his girlfriend, Cleia Rai'to.

Quentin was hard to catch up with since he trained so much, and Sun So-Jung, their resident Jumper, had taken a shuttle to Virulia and hadn't returned, leaving her to worry that she would never see him again. The thought of him being gone without a proper goodbye weighed heavily on her conscience. Cilas was supposed to be her man, and Joy was her sister, but Sun So-Jung, who they called Sunny, had become much like a mentor to her.

Being miserable, Helga had counted down the cycles until the Nighthawks could return to the *Ursula*. Rough night, but this was it, the day when the old girl would be finished with all her upgrades and refitting. Helga glanced over at a glowing hologram hovering above the bowl-shaped entertainment device she had purchased a cycle before. It rotated past a few previews of upcoming shows and a series of news feeds from Alliance central before finally displaying the time.

It was thirty minutes into the first shift, so Helga sprung up, showered, and dressed as fast as she could before donning a skintight 3B-XO suit and pulling on some coveralls. On the way out of her compartment, she grabbed a ration bar and scarfed it down as she ran the length of the passageway towards the hangar.

"Helga," she heard Cilas call, and felt a mixture of surprise and annoyance at him disturbing her rush to see the new vessel. She stopped and collected herself: as an officer being hailed by a superior, not a taken-for-granted girlfriend. Turning to regard him slowly, she placed both hands in the small of her back, and held her chin high like that of a cadet. All of this she did methodically, knowing how much it would annoy him. When she finally faced him, however, her jaw grew slack when she saw that he wasn't alone.

"Captain Sho," Helga croaked before snapping to attention and slamming her fist against her chest. "Commander," she drawled, letting the title out slowly to let Cilas know she didn't appreciate the ambush, but regretted it immediately when Retzo Sho gave her a knowing look.

"Off to see the *Ursula*, Lieutenant Ate?" the captain said, which amused her, since as a former pilot and owner of the corvette, he would have been just as excited to see *Ursula* as she was. It was no secret that the Nighthawks were one of Retzo Sho's obsessions, and he was grooming Cilas personally to take command of the vessel.

Helga felt herself smiling, and pursed her lips to hide it, pretending to reach up and shift a stray lock from her brow. "Yes sir," she said quickly. "My curiosity got the better of me and I wanted to get a quick look at her."

"Seems we are of the same mind," Retzo admitted. "It's not very often we get to remodel and redesign a vessel on our own. This is a monumental occasion. A chance to show those Genesian master builders that we can hold our own when it's necessary, especially out here keeping the lizards off our trade routes."

"Redesign, Captain?" Helga stood buggy-eyed, nearing her limit of holding in her excitement.

"It was Commander Nam's idea," Cilas said, grinning at her as if it was a gift for her that he was now showing off. "When I told him of our fight with the lizards and those Arisani pirates, Commander Nam suggested we commit to making the *Ursula* into a proper warship, something like a cruiser, but keeping the stealth and scout features from the former program."

"Making a vessel that is in itself a Nighthawk," the captain added, deadpan to mask his excitement. "Stealth will allow it to close undetected, and the torpedoes and tracers allows it to take on even a destroyer class lizard ship."

"Maker," Helga whispered. It was the very idea she and Cilas had discussed before returning to *Rendron*.

"Told you she would freak, sir," Cilas said, all but nudging his captain.

Retzo Sho smiled, still composed, but internally jumping with so much joy, Helga could feel it in his ambiance.

"Well, let us all go together," Retzo Sho suggested, already starting to stride down the passageway, the crewmen touching their hats to acknowledge the officers and giving a wide berth so the trio could make their way through.

Had she made it to the hangar on her own, Helga would've climbed a ladder to a narrow shaft that was meant for a handful of dock workers assigned to service and repair the officer's personal vessels. It would have given her a bird's-eye view of *Ursula*, which would have been enough to make a good guess at what new weapons and tech had been newly fitted.

Being with Retzo Sho, however, led to them walking through the main entrance, and two steps in and she was looking up at the nose of a vessel she barely recognized as the *Ursula*. The first thing that struck her was how much the once sleek scout-class now favored a wicked bird of prey. Her nose was tilted down, presenting her cockpit, bordered by twin dock entry ports, large enough to accommodate fighters, assault class ships, and every variety of dropship.

"Two docks now?" Helga turned to Cilas, thinking he would know since he had been in on the plans, which she felt more than a little miffed at him keeping it a secret.

The commander held up three fingers, smirking. "Three entry ports, leading to the one dock we know. Oh, the third would be the main hatch on her belly, for the Thundercat and any other bulky vessels that we take in."

"She's a miniature-sized infiltrator," Helga whispered, walking up to place a palm on the foremost extension of the landing gear. The metal was pleasantly warm where her fingers touched. She'd expected it to be cold since the hangar was freezing. Helga scrutinized the vessel with a mixture of awe and something akin to love, since she believed that the warmth was the *Ursula's* way of letting her know she was happy.

Looking towards her stern, Helga noticed the thrusters, which had been upgraded from the first-generation FTL to a multipurpose titan engine, meant for battle cruisers, sloops, and warships. Now they could truly joust with the enemy instead of just circling about them.

Thinking of their past fights, Helga ran out from below the belly to examine her port side to see if the tracers had been upgraded. She was disappointed to find the old ones remained, but was happy to see three additional torpedo launchers had been installed next to the lower dock hatch.

Seeing the sides, Helga noticed the hull had the same sleek, glassy sheen from before, which was another positive. It was too much ship to take in from the dock floor, but she didn't want to be rude and run off to view it from the service entrance.

"Jenny?" the captain suddenly announced, causing Helga to look in his direction, only to find that he was on comms. "Keep him distracted, I will be there in five. Good enough?" He marched towards the exit doors then stopped, raising his free hand to give the Nighthawks a friendly wave.

No breaks for the top man either, Helga thought, his sudden departure a reminder that they were still on the *Rendron*, and Retzo Sho was a busy man.

"Does the captain get a cycle off, ever?" she asked, though she knew the answer already.

"When he needs one, he can." Cilas shrugged. "But would you take a break if every time you do, something blows up in engineering? The little experience I had on this bird taught me that even when your team is reliable, something always finds a way to break, or lizards pop up out of nowhere, forcing you to cancel the off-cycle to jump into action. The void of space is a demanding mistress, Hel. She plays quiet and coy, but if you relax, she will go out of her way to rouse you."

"*Thype*, you sound like a captain now more than ever," Helga muttered, still wondering if Retzo Sho's lectures had managed to remove all of the fun she had worked at pulling out of her stoic and handsome commander.

Strong arms found her waist, and she held her breath in disbelief at Cilas's actions there inside the captain's private hangar. "The captain knows, Hel, he just pretends to be clueless. Genevieve would never call him this early, not for some minor gripe on the bridge." He laughed out loud. "He unlocked the hangar to allow us entry, left us alone, and I know for a fact that no dockworkers are scheduled to work this cycle."

She felt his chest against the back of her skull, his left hand on her abdomen as his right teased a stray lock near her ear. Turning, she threw her hands up behind his neck and pulled him down for a kiss, nipping his bottom lip hard, but not hard enough to draw blood. *That's for making me wait so long*, she thought, hoping he would get the message.

Cilas lifted her off her feet and sat her up on a portion of the landing gear tall enough to function as a stool. He kissed her hungrily, and started working his way down to her neck and shoulders. Helga was on fire, but still too nervous to commit to whatever he was planning to do. All manner of thoughts flooded her mind then, fear and lust having a twelve-round bout inside her brain.

What if the captain forgot something and came back into the hangar to find his young commander and lieutenant breaking protocol with their tryst? What if Commander Jit Nam was to come in too? Surely, he had access to the hangar, and would also be curious. Did he too suspect them being together, and was willing to blindly allow it?

The zipper on her coveralls was already down, and Cilas cursed when he saw that underneath it was a 3B-XO suit. Getting that off was always a chore, and what he planned wouldn't allow for that amount of time. He stepped back from her and sighed, his face showing a rare expression of surrender that Helga only would ever witness when she turned him down. This time, however, she wanted it more than he could ever know. This was their final cycle on *Rendron*, and with the new crew on *Ursula*, sneaking off would take days of planning, if he was even game to continue.

Retzo Sho was a seasoned operator, and as observant as they all were, so she expected he had read into their interactions to know they were secretly a couple. The crew, however, expected their commander and lieutenant to follow the same rules they followed, and a superior and his subordinates should have a line, so it would be sneaking around or risk corroding the chain of command.

Helga peeled off the remainder of her coveralls, put it under an arm, and then took Cilas's hand and led him up one of the access ramps where she placed her palm against the panel to command it to open. A hatch collapsed inward and slid to the side with a "pop," followed by a loud hissing sound. She pulled herself up inside a small cargo hold with its bulkheads lined with stores.

Cilas followed her up and closed the hatch, and while she worked on peeling off her suit, he embraced her again from the back. "I missed you so much," he whispered hotly into her neck, his adventurous fingers roaming to regions that he knew well would set her off. A wiggle of the hips and some rhythmic steps and Helga escaped the 3B-XO suit, her feet relishing the warmth of the deck.

"Missed me so much, eh?" she smirked. "You sure have a funny way of showing it."

Naked but for her underpants, too hot inside to notice the chilliness in the air, Helga stepped backwards between Cilas's legs, threw a hip into his abdomen and took him to the floor with a violent twist. The commander, being a hand-to-hand expert, chose not to defend it, landing in an arch to protect his back, but eventually lowering his hips to allow her to mount him.

"Decisions, decisions," she teased, pinning his hands down, as she pressed her groin into his, seeing his face betray his impatience. "How does it feel to be made to wait, Commander Mec? You have a lot to make up for, are you aware?"

"More than you know, Lieutenant Ate, but you see where I was. Still, I accept this challenge and look to setting things right from this cycle forward," he promised, and she could see from his face that he was being sincere.

"This place may be filthy and inconvenient, but we're finally together, so I'll table my rage for now," she relented, though she kept his hands pinned as she continued teasing him with her heat. Part of her wanted to keep this up, to see if he could keep himself under control. "Want to dock in my entry port, Commander? These shields won't retract until I hear the right words."

"Lieutenant." Cilas chose his words carefully. "The captain knows, as far as I can tell, and we are both still Nighthawks, so all my fears are gone. You've been patient, which I know is a challenge for you." This earned him a slap on his bare chest before she quickly reclaimed his hand. "Ouch, wait," he pleaded before she followed up her salvo. "Rather than words, why don't you let me demonstrate how much I have missed you, Lady Hellgate."

3

The air was thick, but not enough to make breathing difficult, though a myriad of new scents now violated the space. It had been nearly a Vestalian month's time since Cilas had held her like this, and for a lonely girl on a capital starship, it had felt like a whole year to the young Nighthawk.

Now they lay in the afterglow, silent, but for the *Ursula's* core, which would purr, squeak, and whisper at random times. Helga's mind was on her nightmare, remembering the floating head, and wondering if it had truly happened, or if this was her brain adding extra horrors to keep her away from replaying it. She stared up at the overhead, blankly, enjoying the coldness of the deck, which was a contrast to Cilas's heat where their skin still touched.

Eventually he spoke. "Hel, are you still upset with me?" he said, and she turned to meet his eyes, wondering if he was serious.

"That's a yes, I take it." He nodded slowly. "May I ask why?"

Helga sat up and teased at her hair, massaging the shaved areas above her ears before reaching for the 3B-suit to start dressing. "You don't get to pay off the neglect with sex, Cilas Mec. You're not that *qual*," she said, pulling the tight material onto her legs, then standing to work on her arms. "One comm call, every cycle, that's what I got from you, and even when you weren't with the captain, nothing. How do you think that made me feel?"

"I had no way of knowing, Hel. This whole time, I thought you were out having fun," he admitted, sitting up to look into her eyes. "Is this about those *crutas* who made your life hard when you were a cadet? They're eating Vysen dung now that you rank all of them. And you're actually famous, about as famous as an active operator can get. Even the ones who didn't forget how much *schtill* they gave you likely look up to you now. *Rendron* loves Lady Hellgate."

"With all due respect, Cilas. *Thype* you and all the other human male officers, who presume to know the pain of being an alien woman serving on a Vestalian warship. You don't know what I felt being a cadet here, or what I continue to feel as a Nighthawk. Stick to what you know, because this, you can't begin to understand. I swear, you all do the same *schtill*, as if we're either too emotional or dense to qualify our rage."

"Whoa." Cilas threw up a hand. "My intent wasn't to minimize your feelings. You should know I'm better than that. What gives? All I want to do is help, and if saying what I did evokes—you know what? Never mind. I'll seal my hatch, alright? And for the record, I'm yours this whole cycle. I am taking some personal time off to spend it with you. I've been—"

"A bastard?" Helga said, glowering.

"Don't like that word much," he said softly, easing back up on his elbows to stare at the overhead. "None of us are bastards, Helga, we're 'heroes.'" He threw up air quotes as if to reinforce his distaste with the Alliance calling them heroes. "I'm not big on words, you know that. It's one of the things that makes this work. I can be myself with you, Helga, not the commander, and not the so-called hero. Duty makes me an imperfect partner, but I want you to know that it isn't intentional."

Helga suddenly felt bad for speaking so harshly before, but not enough to apologize or show that she no longer harbored hard feelings. It was all so heavy she wanted to explode. Why couldn't he have just reached out more so she knew that he cared? Retzo Sho wasn't with him every minute of the cycle, so why couldn't he have given her that? Surely it wasn't asking too much.

"This morning, when I saw the time," she said. "I felt a sort of happiness I haven't felt since the time you sent me the invitation to become the newest recruit for the Nighthawks. I was happy because today, this cycle, which I have had marked on my calendar since coming aboard. Today meant that we would be leaving soon. That I can return to the helm of the *Ursula* with the brothers I trust, feeling wanted, being useful."

"Oh," Cilas whispered, "I see."

"But do you, Cilas?" She turned on him again. "Do you know that I've had nothing but nightmares since coming back to *Rendron*? All of the salutes, fake smiles, and 'Lady Hellgate' cannot fix that. The pain runs deep here, deeper than Dyn, and much deeper than any of the other *thyped* up *schtill* the Alliance has had us do." Helga exhaled slowly and closed her eyes to push the anger down the way that Sunny had taught her during their meditation sessions.

"So, what could I do, Helga?" Cilas said, "The captain had me under his wing for months, and it was very much like school. When he wasn't teaching me, Commander Nam was, and when the two of them were busy, they would assign me reading, vids, and all sorts of other material. *Ursula's* remodeling came with a requirement, you see, which was for me to become a true captain in the eyes of the Alliance. They put you all on ice to catch me up. But had it not been done, they would have been forced to turn over *Ursula's* command to another officer."

"Got a promotion coming with all that learning?" Helga teased, leaning back against the bulkhead, kicking playfully at his feet.

"They do that, and I would likely be killed in my sleep by one of the many glory-chasers already jealous of who I am," Cilas groaned. "Helga, I don't take you for granted, and you really did hurt me just now, making me out to not care. I am not using you. Just the thought of that sickens me to the core. The two of us have been through so much together. Surely you see that I care for you beyond anything physical?"

"You sure have a funny way of showing it, Cilas, and I'm about at the end of the line with people treating me like *schtill*. Especially someone I am intimate with. *Thype*, when in the worlds did I sink this low?" She rolled her head back and stared up at the overhead.

"Again, ouch, but you have been heard," Cilas said. "I will just have to prove it to you, won't I?" He settled back down to the deck then, using his clothes for a cushion as he closed his eyes and went still as if he'd fallen asleep. "I held you long enough from the *Ursula*, and I know seeing her will cheer you up. Why don't you go explore the interior, and when you're done, I will be here, dreaming of you."

"Oh enough, Mr. I'm-no-good-with-words," she said, cutting her eyes at him, annoyed that she had let him break through. "Be back in a few then," she said, stepping towards a door and giving him a long, measuring look before entering.

The hold opened up to the *Ursula's* dock, which looked a little different than what Helga remembered. The already expansive space had gotten bigger, and where there were once stacked cages against the bulkhead for cargo, there now were open compartments with shielded entryways to protect the inhabitants from any loss of atmosphere during a launch. Two machine loaders stood powered down, like iron sentinels asleep until they received their orders.

Towards the stern sat the R60 Thundercat, whose mass took up a third of the landing space, her hull practically twinkling below the overhead lights. On the other side, lined up wing to wing facing one of the launch ports, was her Vestalian Classic, and a new Phantom fighter, though Helga hadn't heard of another qualified pilot joining the team.

"Always good to have backups, I guess," she muttered, though she still wondered who, aside from her, would be piloting a fighter if the need arose. "Loaders mean we intend to capture prizes, and there is more than enough space left for a cruiser or merchant class. Hmm, this will be helpful for the next time we're sent on a reclamation or rescue mission."

Fearful her Vestalian Classic had been tampered with, Helga spent several minutes scrutinizing her ship. Knowing the engineers on *Rendron*, and how eager they were to please Captain Retzo Sho, she expected to find the Classic outfitted with a new console and Phantom engine, her worst nightmare realized after years of fighting to keep her ship outdated the way she liked it. The Classic was what she had learned to fly on, and if they tampered with its controls, she would go ballistic.

After getting into the cockpit, powering it on and playing with the controls, Helga made a sigh of relief when she saw that it was still her old ship, through and through. The seats had been swapped out, and that was annoying, but there was nothing added, merely replaced, and that was good enough. Next, she checked the Thundercat, whose upgrades wouldn't bother her as much, but she was pleased to find that it too hadn't been touched.

The new compartments on the dock floor were cozy, and she was happy to find that Quentin's supply cage and Raileo's gun range simulation had been converted over. New installations, clean smell, but they were still the old docks that she remembered. This, more than even the official mess hall that was above deck, had been the Nighthawk's primary hangout during their downtime.

Walking towards the stern where a wide passageway linked the docks to the Nighthawk's berths, Helga saw that it too had been expanded, adding a fourth door on the port side next to hers. Every door had an access panel which required contact with the owner's palm, but this fourth opened on approach, and Helga stepped in to find the crew's new living quarters.

The space seemed cozy, and well thought out, holding twenty-four bunks, but strategically placed to give their inhabitants some space and privacy, which was more than they would have received on a starship. Helga counted six separate berthing blocks, each holding four bunks connected by a ladder and power-lift. Built into the bulkhead of every bunk was a storage cabinet and locker, a personal air-controller, and a noise-proof privacy shield.

Every section of the bulkhead not occupied by berths had something for the crew that would keep them entertained, educated, and comfortable. In the center was a low table installed on the deck, with a food processing unit for snacks, surrounded by an assortment of cards and games. Helga whistled. "Now every spacer's going to want to serve on our ship. Look at you *Ursula*, all dressed up and beautiful on the inside and out."

Curious about her own compartment, Helga decided she'd seen enough, and walked over to her own door, where a new plaque had been installed with her callsign "Hellgate" engraved on it. Running her fingers across it, she was surprised to find it truly etched in, practically permanent. Something about this brought her to tears, which she blinked away quickly, feeling foolish for having reacted that way, though hers was the only door with a plaque and name.

There was a tiny message on the bottom, "Dedicated to heroine Helga of the Revenants, who defended our home against Geralos invasion," signed, Nova Han, Secretary, Meluvian Alliance.

Where seeing her name had stirred those emotions, the message and the memory of that battle overwhelmed Helga. Perhaps it wasn't just seeing this; it was everything leading up to this moment where she was here, back on *Ursula*. Taking a breath, she touched the panel and the door opened up to her old compartment. All of her personal affects had been stacked neatly into a small crate, which was the first thing she noticed.

Ready to explode over the violation, Helga stood in the doorway, frozen, glaring at the contents, trying not to panic at the thought of something missing, broken, or spoiled. Some of those items were priceless, one-of-a-kind souvenirs from former ships, moons, and people who had passed on. Especially her most prized possession, an old Revenant helmet, gifted to her by the squadron Joy Valance commanded, most of which had died in the same conflict the plaque on her door honored her for.

Looking up to see what had been done to the compartment itself, Helga understood why they needed to box everything up. While she hadn't noticed any new windows earlier when she examined the *Ursula's* hull, she now saw across from her door a large round window. The shields were down, so the glass was opaque, though it would offer a breathtaking view of whatever planet or moon they were in close proximity of in the future.

Helga was a small woman, only 160 cm, but the overhead too seemed taller, making the space feel twice the size, though she was sure it was the same compartment she'd always had. Gone was the cozy bunk, replaced by a rack twice its size. *Another Meluvian gift?* she wondered. Across from it, against the bulkhead was a pair of giant lockers, and a multi-functional screen that displayed the ship's statistics when it wasn't pretending to be a mirror.

To the left of the entrance was her desk and PAS suit on its mannequin, next to a closet lined with uniforms and equipment. She took a step inside and sniffed at her underarms, feeling suddenly filthy within the *Ursula's* sterile environment. A meal and a shower would be in order, then putting her compartment back together, before taking a tour of the bridge to see what new war toys would be available for them to use against the Geralos.

She thought about Cilas, still in the cargo hold, waiting, and considered inviting him in to accompany her on seeing the rest of the *Ursula*. "Nope," she thought out loud, as she crossed to the window and retracted the shields, revealing the captain's dock. "I've been waiting several cycles, and now its his turn. Now, let's see if we have any of that rowcut tea left over from Meluvia."

4

Fio Doro stood on a lonely elbow of the East Central monorail, staring out at the ocean. Black waves sparkled, reflecting light from a passing shuttle whose probing beacons illuminated the cloudy night sky. Surprisingly, there were no ships out on the ocean, though the wind picking up made her wonder if a storm was coming in.

The air was chilly and smelled of fish, chemicals, and something else familiar that she just couldn't place. She inhaled it all, deeply, and closed her eyes, thinking this could be her last time visiting the shore. There had been tougher jobs in the past, challenging hauls in which she competed with some of the more desperate of the Runners, who did whatever it took to win.

This time it was simple, a pick-up and drop, but the job felt dirty, and every fiber of her being knew that it was a setup for her to take a fall. She had made the one mistake her mentor, Djesu had warned her about. She had allowed credits to blind her to a gig that could have her locked away or shot.

Still, she reasoned, if there was any scene to choose as her final one, going out in a blaze while running a package on the shores might be it. A better moment and place didn't exist, not for a homegrown of the dockside tenement stocks. Basce City had been a cold mother, favoring the strong, and accepting of only those lucky enough to score a fortune in credits to book a shuttle out past her walls.

There was a saying often repeated by the elders: "leave before you find yourself loving the wickedness." Basce City was wicked, and for Fio Doro having been on both sides of that wickedness, she sometimes wondered if it was too late for her. If the job was to go through smoothly, and the balance made to her account, would life allow her to escape the tenements without a knife finding its way into her throat?

Her eyes roamed the skies until they settled on a long line of streamers, multicolored traces against the clouds. Hellcats on hacked hovers, racing for props at break-neck speeds between the spires of the towers spanning the city.

Seeing them go made Fio smile, the memory of a past love coming to mind for one sweet moment. Her first ride above the clouds on a rusty hover, screaming her lungs out, for never wanting it to end. Something caught her eye then, something below her on the sands, and she saw a slow, lumbering figure making his way across to the pier.

Fio stepped back into the shadows, watching him go, occasionally looking in the direction of the tracks, just in case someone had followed her up. *I hope that's him,* she thought, watching the figure shambling onward. He was carrying a case and looking none too concerned for his personal welfare, which let Fio know that he was well-armed. *Scar Roan the Blade, if what I hear about him has any parts that are true, then I better stay out of sight from that cruta.*

She looked back to where he had come, surprised that he'd do this alone. Something flickered in the darkness, a bit of glass reflecting the light. Fio ducked down quickly behind the metal railing, adrenaline surging to prepare her for a fight. A near-numb, trembling hand fumbled for the sidearm that she had worn beneath her jacket.

Gripping it tightly, Fio brought the weapon up to her face, and took several breaths to calm her nerves. When her nerves became tolerable, she chanced a glance over the railing, seeing that the large man was now returning back to where he had come. Waiting was a transport, a two-seater that she hadn't noticed before. Inside it was a driver, waiting patiently for his boss, and as the man stepped into the vehicle, the driver looked straight at Fio, and that was when she knew it was him that she had seen below the boardwalk.

Despite this validation that they knew she was there, Fio dared not reveal herself until they drove off, and even when they did she remained still for several minutes. When she was sure the coast was clear, she scrambled down a support beam and sprinted across the sand towards the boardwalk to where Scar Roan was to leave the luggage. She found it half-buried in the sand, with a busted lock and obscenities scratched into the surface.

I hope the inside of this thing had better luck with that animal and his goons, she thought, *or all of this was for nothing, and Vray got doubly robbed.* The thought of that pleased her before she realized it would mean that Vray would be less likely then to pay.

Fio scanned the skies for a flo-bot, reaper drone, or any sort of surveillance that could come back to haunt her. The skies were cloudy, but clear of anything short of stars and aircars, so she grabbed the suitcase handle and hoisted it, pleased to find that it was light. She felt a vibration in her front pocket from the communicator, and though she hoped it would be Djesu, the timing was concerning.

She plucked the disc out and placed it over her ear, depressing the center. "This is Fio Doro," she answered.

"Did you get the package?" Djesu said.

"Literally just grabbed it, Pops. Let me buzz you back." Fio stopped and looked around to make sure she was still alone.

"Fio Doro," Djesu whispered sharply, "You need to run like the wind, girl. I just got off a call with Fiona Brightstar, and she says that BasPol was just tipped off on a runner making a pick-up by the docks."

"*Schtill!*" Fio cursed and cut the call off. Djesu would understand and now she needed to focus, or she would end up inside The Brick or worse, dead from a gunshot. She sprinted down the boardwalk, then ran onto the beach, back below the tracks, where she ducked below a triad of clogged sewer pipes. This she did to get on the west side of the pier, where she could find her way back to her apartment.

The smell was suffocating, the pipes were broken here but clogged from the frozen spillage, which had the appearance of being caramelized in the rain. Where Fio emerged was a broad expanse of beach, with refuse littering the sands, from bottles, boxes, discarded clothing, the occasional Cel-toc body part, and a particularly disturbing doll's head.

Fio ran past it all to a thick crop of bushes, which opened up to a road, paved with small, round lights. She slowed to a walk, hugging the suitcase close, holding her chin low to slow the rain running into her eyes. She eventually found a parking lot, barely occupied, though she could see people seated inside a shuttle. Not wanting to take the chance with them being BasPol, or Scar Roan's men, Fio ducked between two transports to stay out of sight.

The transport on her left was a hover, luxury built, which made it nearly impossible to crack and steal. The one on her right was a one-person town-car, a model she knew well from joy rides in her younger years. Pumping a fist at her fortune, Fio used her knife to pry off the door's handle, made a twist and it came unlocked.

Once inside with the console pried off, and the dashboard's face open and completely hers, Fio allowed herself a second to relax. In the distance she could hear the BasPol sirens, and saw new lights from the direction of the beach. Despite it raining, her footprints from running were bound to stand out in the sand, and she felt disappointed with herself for not anticipating that. She expected that at any moment they would spill out into the parking lot, guns raised.

Fio jammed her thumb into the open faceplate and pumped the accelerator to bring it to life. She triggered the manual override to unlock the driving functions and watched the power gauge fill itself up before releasing the brake to start her drive. The old town-car shook to life, nearly choking Fio with fumes that she assumed meant a break in the regulator.

"I just need you to get to Jun Street, beautiful. Be a treat, will yeah?" Fio urged, tightly gripping the yoke and pushing it forward ever so slowly. The lights flicked on, and the engine revved. It was as if it heard her words and decided to betray its true master and assist the thief with her escape. Fio maneuvered past the hover, then around the shuttle, and was out in traffic less than a minute after leaving the parking lot.

Traffic was congested on the roads, forcing Fio to slip in and out of lanes with her smaller transport. Above them the lucky owners of hovers flew on unobstructed, slipping into launch pipes that would rocket them over to the far side of the city where she wanted to go. *Wish I'd snagged a hover*, she thought, nearly breaking her neck to follow one as it dipped low, banked, and performed a skillful U-turn.

"Hey, watch that junker," someone shouted at her when she nearly collided with a shuttle that had suddenly braked. A last-minute twist and pulling of the yoke, however, slowed her enough to slip off to its right and avoid running into it, which would have surely crushed her. Shaken, though more annoyed than flustered, Fio took a moment to collect herself before pushing in the yoke again to pick up speed and weave her way through traffic.

Several BasPol drones littered the night sky, their blue and white trackers lasing the highway, scanning for the package sitting next to Fio Doro. To avoid being scanned, she pulled in between two larger cars, and sat sandwiched in between them until one exited the highway, leaving her exposed. Worried that she had come all this way just to be captured, Fio stuck her head out into the wet air, craned her neck to look above her and was happy to see the drones flying off.

Pumping her fist excitedly, she wanted to scream, but inhaled the crisp air into her lungs and held it, exhaling it slowly until her head was swimming. *That was too close*, she thought, *and stupid going in with a half-cocked plan.* She hated being alone on a job like this, but being at large meant she couldn't involve Emma Rhone or Flavia who were usual partners in getting contraband smuggles out to the space port.

Pulling off onto a narrow ramp, Fio coasted the town car onto a side road leading out into Bitcrest Algae Farms, a set of looming white domes arranged into a grid spanning 150 hectares of wetlands, far from the city. A few kilometers in and she chanced stopping to check on the package, pulling off onto a dry patch of land where the only light was from her headlights, which she cut and sat in silence, ready for anything.

Her right hand reached down to grip the handle of her gun, and brought it up to her chest, where she cradled it against her racing heart while she waited. Five minutes passed like hours, but Fio knew better than to think they were enough, and when nerves finally won out against patience, she exited the transport and looked around for any drones.

When nothing showed, she reentered the town car, grabbed the case and examined the lock, wondering how likely it was that it was rigged to harm her. *That wouldn't make sense if he planned to entrap me*, she thought. *No, there's something in here that's likely dangerous, but not to me.* She brought out a flashlight, and placed it on the floor, positioning it so the light was just enough for her to see what she was doing.

"Now let's see what we have here," she whispered through teeth clenched tight against the growing fear.

She popped the lock, sliding the cover open to reveal a crumpled suit and other personal effects along with a stack of papers covered in grease stains. Reaching for these, she placed them to the side and continued searching the suitcase. The only other item of note was a data tablet, pre-hacked, but all it had was a number of starmaps.

On the paper was a seal Fio recognized as the Anstractor Alliance, which made her go white with fear at the thought of having them in her possession should she end up caught. Basce City's law enforcement offices had no patience for smugglers, who they saw as pariahs, transporting poison. She was already in their system for several offenses ranging from theft to smuggling spice. The last time she was before the mandate, she'd been made to promise to keep a clean slate.

"*Harridan*: Alliance infiltrator class," she read out loud. "Formal report: to undergo repairs in Louine space." The line ended in a series of glyphs that Fio recognized but couldn't understand. Picking up the tablet, she pulled up one of the starmaps and saw a similar glyph with a line pointing to a space outside Genese.

Fio flipped through several diagrams, searching for the glyph that was printed on that line. She found it on a map for the Louine system which made her wonder why someone would print this instead of sending it through encrypted intelligence waves. Surely the Navy had better means of communication than singular printouts and an unlocked tablet. It all felt wrong and possibly dangerous.

These are from someone working for the Alliance, she thought. *Why does Vray have them?* She kept on reading, pausing occasionally to scan the perimeter. It was all silence out there on the algae farm, though she found it unnerving, since she had lived all her life around trains and tenement homes.

For over an hour Fio pored over the documents, her fascination with the contents overriding her worry and fear. Ship names, models, locations, and details were outlined with no real intention of concealing any of it. To find Alliance documents there was unheard of, especially within Basce City where the war was little more than a thought.

Part of her obsession was the thought of a reward for bringing the information to the local recruitment offices for the Alliance. She had never been inside that building before but had known people with children drafted onto starships to begin their careers as Alliance cadets. Some had even returned on occasion, taking their shore leave to visit with family and friends.

One of the ships she recognized immediately, *Scythe*, a name she had always liked, and so it stuck out in her memory from seeing it on one of the news feeds a younger Djesu would watch. This expose was to some sort of enemy, she reasoned, maybe even the terrible Geralos that invaded Vestalia and terrorized the system, making trips off-planet a privilege of only those who could afford Alliance bodyguards.

Fio's parents were Vestalian, and Djesu made it a point to make her never forget her heritage. Credits were the only goal for a street runner, but here she saw an opportunity to play the part of hero while taking down a parasite of the slums.

She cut the lights and sat in the darkness, outlining a roadmap in her mind of how she would expose this without risking her life or freedom at the hands of the corrupt BasPol organization. Pops will have the answers, she reasoned but hesitated, knowing his patriotism would overtake his greed, and she could gain nothing from this incriminating haul. He, however, had the experience, and the Alliance connections necessary to help her get out.

"Let's just get to it then," Fio groaned. "The longer I wait the more chances I have of flubbing this up."

Reaching up to her ear where the communicator still hung, she plucked it off and sat it on a clear area of the console. She twisted it once, resulting in a holographic logo above it, floating in a washed-out display of blue and white lights. It transitioned into a scene of a forest, with the wind blowing gently through the trees. "Call Pops," she said, and collected the documents, stacking them neatly onto her lap.

Djesu's image appeared, full-bodied, his holographic presence still imposing despite his 53 years. "Fio Doro, where have you been?" he said wearily, looking off to his right and gesturing for someone to be quiet. "Frida and I have been sitting here waiting for you, thinking the worst may have happened."

"Reapers chased me for a while and the highway was borked due to the elections, but I managed to make it to the algae farms. Never mind all that though, Pops, I took your advice and looked inside the package," she said, whispering loudly as if she wasn't alone. "Take a look here." She held up one of the papers. "See the seal? It's Alliance, and if I'm not mistaken, this is information being sold by Vray and his cronies."

"That traitorous *schtill*," Djesu cursed. "I will call my friend at the recruitment office. If we can get him a copy of those documents, he can alert the Alliances, and we'll get a reward."

"But this is my leverage," Fio argued, running a hand through her damp blue hair. "You show the Alliance and Vray gets arrested. No amount of reward could match the credits that he owes. Pops, you know the drill. We have him by the low ones, don't you see? We can demand 10,000 credits and he would have no choice but to cough it up. This is our chance, Djesu."

"Fio Doro," Djesu said, gripping the arm of his chair. "This isn't spice or kidnapping, this is something dangerous that could affect the war, and us. Need I remind you where we come from, girl? What's the use of 10,000 credits if the Geralos were to come and take over the port? No, we need to be smart about this and inform the Alliance. Do you understand what I'm saying to you?"

"For Vestalia," Fio Doro recited. "Go ahead then and call your friend. While you're doing that I am going to squeeze him for another third of the credits since I managed to make the pickup. He won't know that his arrest is imminent, so I will threaten to expose him if he doesn't make a hefty deposit. We can be heroes to the Alliance, and I will be rich and on the next shuttle off to the pleasure coast."

5

Nero deck was the title given to a section of the *Rendron*, near engineering, accessible only by a rarely used passageway. It was one of those decks where asking a random spacer for directions would elicit an, "uh, what deck?" unless it was someone who went out of their way to study the blueprints. For this reason, it became the Nighthawks headquarters, gifted to them by Captain Retzo Sho.

Whenever they were on *Rendron*, this was where they berthed, and in their absence, it was where the Nighthawk hopefuls were housed. The thought that was while Cilas and team were deployed, the officers could nominate recruits for special operations. Qualified spacers would be sent off for BLAST training, only earning access to Nero if they graduated in the top five.

Two cycles after visiting the newly fitted *Ursula*, Helga received a formal summons to Nero deck. She, like Cilas, had retained her officer's berthing, so she decided to visit him early so they could both head down to see what the XO wanted. They took their time walking together, talking and laughing as if they had never been at odds.

This didn't go unnoticed by Helga, who only wished Cilas would have come to her thirty cycles prior. They could have had more time together until the inevitable call to get back out there for a mission. His career had taken off, and while she was happy for him, she knew it would eventually drive them apart.

Helga had been through so much already, things that 99 out of 100 spacers couldn't imagine, let alone say they had seen or done. This was something new to her, the juggling of duty with being a young woman in a relationship with her commander, and knowing their relationship was doomed. It frightened her, not because she was new to a broken heart, but because she wasn't sure it would be the last thread to eventually pull her apart.

Some of the worst situations in the field had shown her what she was capable of doing. She had seen the leader Helga, the compassionate Helga, and the relentless, "Lady Hellgate" that was not only effective but terrible. Becoming that when the bullets were flying was something she had forced herself to accept. Becoming that and unable to return to herself, however, she worried that would be her fate if she gave up.

They made it down to Nero and a short passage took them to a large set of double doors with the Nighthawks emblem engraved in the center of it. The doors split open on their approach, each door sliding into an adjacent bulkhead. A loud "whoosh" caused the two Nighthawks to react, Helga hopping back into the passageway to avoid whatever it was.

Above them, several meters in the air, hovered Raileo Lei and Quentin Tutt. They all were wearing their Powered Armor Suits, which was the source of the noise that had startled them. Raileo Lei, who had performed a dive at the ill-timed moment when they had come in, was apologizing profusely to Cilas Mec, who stood frozen with his hands balled-up into fists.

Helga was annoyed at being startled and felt somewhat offended that they hadn't thought to invite her to whatever this was. Nero deck was large enough to house a cruiser, and with the berths being built into the bulkhead, it made the ideal arena for PAS training. Helga wondered why she, being the resident pilot, hadn't thought of this.

"How long have you all been training here, using your armor?" she inquired, looking directly at Raileo Lei.

"We do every fifth cycle, in the first shift," Raileo said, landing softly in front of them and saluting before removing his helmet.

"This is what you do instead of taking personal time?" Cilas seemed dumbfounded. "You know, I can't let this go on, men. Personal time is for personal time, not for squeezing in training, especially here. I'm impressed you all haven't trashed the place."

Quentin landed next to his commander, still a little clumsy but leagues better than the last time Helga had seen him fly. "Commander, Ray did it as a favor to me and Sunny, see. We're not the best at controlling the PAS, so we've been using our time to plan a bit of a ... *thype* ... Actually, you ruined our surprise, Lieutenant," he said turning to face her. "We wanted to see how long you'd take to notice, the next time we had a chance."

Helga put a hand on her chest to still her heart and grinned from ear to ear. She wanted to melt, and to think she was annoyed with them for leaving her out. "Oh, Q," she said, reaching up to grip both his and Raileo's shoulders. "Here I thought you all saw me as a fussy nag, but you really were listening, weren't you? Thank you."

"Oh, here it is," said a cheerful voice, and Helga turned to see Ina Reysor leading a party of three strange spacers.

"Ah, Ina, you made it," Cilas said, thawing Helga from her momentary stasis.

Ina rushed forward to give her a hug, and Helga returned it readily, happy to see a familiar face. The hug had so much behind it that she found herself emotional, and was forced to break it off quickly.

"Ina Reysor." Helga smiled, still holding her hands when they separated to take each other in. "The commander didn't tell me that you agreed to come. This is exciting. I can't wait for you to see the *Ursula*. Oh, you and I are going to need to catch up."

"Of course," Ina said, practically bouncing with excitement before her face grew suddenly grave. She stood up straight and gestured towards the men who had come in with her. "Commander Mec, here are some of your crew members. As you were, men, introduce yourself to *Ursula's* captain and his first mate."

The first man was Cilas's height but stocky, with massive muscles and a warm, genuine smile. He was darker than Sundown and looked every part the Marine. Stepping towards them, he saluted crisply. "Commander, Lieutenant, Nighthawks, I'm Chief Faruq Mas-Umbra, Culinary Specialist, reporting from the Starship *Missio-Tral*. Thank you for having me serve with you on the *Ursula*."

"Welcome aboard, Sarge," Cilas said casually. "It said in your records that you did a drop on Meluvia right out of cadet academy. Is that right?"

"Yes sir," Faruq said, proudly, his chest seeming to grow bigger when he confirmed. "Did a year with Orion Company, Marines of the 275th."

"Sambe," Quentin said suddenly, recognizing a fellow planet-buster. "Doing it all. Cooking lizards by day and feeding the boys at night." This earned him a look of curiosity from Mas-Umbra, who grinned in recognition of the joke.

"Welcome, Marine." Cilas smiled, entertained by the exchange, before shifting his focus to the gaunt figure behind Mas-Umbra. What made this man stick out, besides his height, was that he seemed more machine than human, the lower half of his face and arms being cybernetic constructs with exposed wiring and circuitry where his uniform didn't cover.

A 3B XO suit below his coveralls would cage those wires nicely, if he cares, Helga thought as she examined him, trying her best not to stare. *Something to suggest to him later, perhaps.*

"Alon Weinstar." The cyborg introduced himself in a voice just as mechanical as his cybernetic arm. "A pleasure, Commander. *Ursula*, well met, I am Chief Engineer Alon Weinstar. I have served on several ships throughout my career, the lengthiest station being on *Scythe* for approximately fifteen years."

"A pleasure to finally meet you, Mr. Weinstar," Cilas said. "You come highly recommended. I look forward to your calibrations."

Helga found nothing particularly interesting about the cyborg. He was older, Vestalian, with flat gray eyes. Outside of the cybernetics he was not particularly interesting, and she wondered if he would find it difficult fitting in with a crew half his age. The last man was the complete opposite. He was of average height with a youthful face, and blond hair cut low like that of a graduate fresh from the cadet academy. He waited patiently for Weinstar to finish his introduction, then stepped forward to salute Cilas Mec.

"Commander," he said in a voice which was about as average in tone as his appearance. "Chief Petty Officer, Anders Stratus." He then turned to Helga and saluted crisply, who in turn nodded her acknowledgment before sizing him up.

"You're our Nighthawk?" she asked him, curious that out of all their potentials, this Vestalian was the one chosen for the post. She had expected another character like Raileo Lei or Quentin Tutt, but this man lacked the presence or swagger.

"New Nighthawk?" Raileo's interest was piqued, and he showed it by stepping forward to glare at Anders. "Says who?"

Helga made to react and tear into him for being out of line, but Cilas placed a hand on her arm to tell her to let it play out. The young man stood his ground, but something changed in his demeanor; it reminded Helga of the cadet academy when a new child would show up and the bullies would start in with them only to learn that they could fight like cornered cats.

Every child on an Alliance ship went through the cadet academy and all of the schoolyard antics that came along with it. Anders reacted in much the same way she'd seen others react who wound up fighting back against the bullies. She had been the same, though were it her being questioned by Ray, and not knowing who he was, she would have been tearing into him with insults and calling him to the floor for a one-on-one.

"I am your new Nighthawk, Lieutenant Ate, " he said to Helga, as if Raileo had been but an annoying gnat, swatted and flicked to the deck for landing on his skin mid-conversation.

"Welcome to the team, Chief Stratus," Commander Jit Nam said, surprising them all as he walked into the compartment. "Gather around now, I have a few things to say."

Together, the Nighthawks and the new crew members bunched up to face the XO, with Cilas and Helga in the forefront, holding fists to their chest in a salute. Raileo, somewhat embarrassed that the second most powerful man on the *Rendron* had witnessed him "seasoning" a recruit, went five shades paler as he faded to the back to stand next to an amused Ina Reysor.

Jit Nam, a stickler for presentation, stopped to survey the space and nodded with satisfaction. He then faced the Nighthawks to continue.

"By first shift, you will be underway to Genesian space, where you rendezvous with the 501st Guardian Task Force to assist them with the defense. This will give you a little under a full cycle to make your goodbyes and collect your necessaries for your deployment. We cannot estimate how long you will be gone, Nighthawks and crew, but expect this op to be lengthy. Genese is under pressure from the lizards, and the council has asked us to bolster their defense. Now, many of you have never been to the planet before, so let me quickly educate you on what to expect. There are no less than 5,000 stations scattered about the space, most being colonies owned and operated by private organizations.

"We have a small fleet there to deter lizard invasion, but most of the defense is handled by the Genesian Guard, the planet's elite Special Forces. With the uptick in action above Meluvia, Arisani, and even Louine, our presence is thin on the planet. I don't have to stress to you the importance of Genese, and industry being allowed to continue uninterrupted. This isn't about force; we lack the numbers. What we need here is finesse, and a team like yours looking into why the lizards have become bold all of a sudden. It may mean visiting a few of the colonies to ask around, or communicating with the guard, whatever it takes. The Alliance council is looking for answers."

"The pirates we neutralized above Arisani wanted a newer ship from Genese as part of their ransom," Raileo added from the back. "They were in cahoots with the lizards waiting somewhere near Genesian space to collect. Do we know if that was related, Commander?"

"That is what we'd like to find out," Jit Nam replied. "Jump out to their vector, swap a trace, and poke your nose around those colonies to see what you can find out. Any other questions? This could very well be the last time we see one another for quite some time."

"With us shoving off tomorrow, Commander, what will happen to Sunny?" Helga said. She wanted off the *Rendron*, but one of the things she was hoping with *Ursula* was to spend more time training with the man they called Sundown, or Sunny, to master the things he had shown her, and learn more about Seekers and Jumpers. Having him absent would be felt, and not only by her. Sundown was unmatched in combat, and with this new crew she worried that this could be a nightmare deployment.

"Sun So-Jung is with his agency, Ate, undergoing a necessary trial from what I understood from the correspondence," Jit Nam said. "The length and outcome is something they were not able to share, but if he is successful at whatever it is, he will be taken to a station by shuttle, and you can rendezvous with him."

Helga became worried when she heard those words. They were neutral and practical, but knowing the commander, it could very well mean that Sundown would be detained for much longer than she expected. He had violated the rules of his order, and had been summoned to Virulia for court. Jit Nam wouldn't say this in front of the Nighthawk recruit and rates, but the Nighthawks all knew it, and she saw the same concern reflected across all their faces.

"Sunny survived Sanctuary, he can survive anything, let alone a trial, so I believe we'll be seeing him in a few cycles," Helga said with some confidence. "Thank you, Commander."

Jit Nam angled his head and nodded, then surveyed the other faces, looking for additional questions that weren't coming.

"Alright, Nighthawks, take the cycle, make your goodbyes, eat your favorite meals, and until the next time we meet, maker's speed. Cilas," Jit Nam said, stepping forward to grip his shoulder in a Vestalian sign of friendship. "Congratulations on your new command, she is the pride of the *Rendron*. What a beauty. I was surprised the captain didn't give you an infiltrator and kept her for himself," he joked, revealing a sense of humor that Helga didn't know existed until this instance.

"She's the newborn baby taking her first step into the black," Cilas said. "She's in good hands, Commander. We may bring her back a little dirty, but she will have earned her place as the star of this mighty ship."

Jit Nam regarded everyone in the space, his long face reverting to a hard mask of determination. "That I don't doubt," he said, and then turned and abruptly walked out.

"Was that a joke from Commander Nam just now?" Raileo said, once he was sure that the older man had left the deck.

"You heard the man, get out of here," Cilas said. "Go kiss your partners, stuff your faces, and pack your gear—only time I'm going to remind you. Get your personals to the dock before 1:110 or you will have to make do with what we give you."

Helga sidled over to Quentin and jabbed him playfully in the abdomen. "Looks like you get to see your home planet after all," she whispered, and he looked down at her to reveal the emotions he was struggling with. He squeezed her shoulder to show his gratitude and she trapped his arm to play at breaking it.

"Ate," Quentin finally said. "I haven't seen you this happy in a while. Tell me, are you really good with this?"

"Good with what?" Helga said, stopping her tugging at his arm to regard him, puzzling through what should be bothering her.

"New crew and only one of our recruits making it to get some time on the op. Weren't there supposed to be six? Anders is it, really? And no Sunny? While I know there's a reason we haven't learned yet, it still makes me feel queasy rushing out. Mind, I'm happy to go home, to see Genese once more in my lifetime, but how is this different from Sanctuary or Meluvia? I thought the whole point of us coming back to *Rendron* was to leave with a full complement."

Helga made a face. "It's a *schtill* salad. Wouldn't be Special Operations if it wasn't. May as well be cheerful about it."

"You, cheerful? Now I know you're blowing smoke up my thrust. Lieutenant Ate doesn't do cheerful, she does 'sarcastic.'" That earned him the yank of an arm over an outstretched leg, which he gracefully avoided to walk off, laughing.

Helga watched him clasp forearms with Cilas and then Raileo, the three of them glancing in her direction, a subtle invitation to come and join them. She felt a wave of emotion, bringing with it flashes from the past, and the many near-misses where she almost lost them all. Cilas on Dyn, Raileo on Sanctuary, and Quentin on a derelict dreadnought by himself. She too had faced death, only to be saved at different times by the three of them.

Sundown's first meeting with her had been as a hero, saving her with his immaculate aim. They had seen fire, and it tempered them, both individually and as a team, and through that temperance they were deadly effective. So what if they were missing Sundown and were short a handful of recruits? Whatever came, as always, they would be ready for it, and while *Rendron* had kept her miserably grounded, here was a chance for them to spread their wings.

6

The Alliance Corvette, *Ursula*, newly updated and refitted for covert operations, slid silently along on a translucent blue line of the holographic starmap above Helga's console. Unlike the return to *Rendron* those 186 cycles prior, there was no crowd to wish them off, and no speeches from the captain. There wasn't even a mission, just an order to get geared up and ready to shove off at the top of the first shift.

Helga was elated to have Ina with her in the cockpit of the bridge, as their reunion had been cut short by the commander's visit. They had to launch under the cover of cloak, and as with most stealthy launches, everyone was forced to be quiet, the silence only breaking when they had jumped to light speed and *Rendron* was a countless kms in the distance.

"Think we're good to come out of restraints?" came Ina's voice from her right, where she sat in her own cozy pilot's seat.

"Yeah, we can let them go," Helga said, still in disbelief that she was not only back helming the *Ursula*, but had Ina Reysor on board, a woman who she could trust to leave in charge of everything. Ina was a ranked pilot, an Ace even, but Helga had never seen her fly a fighter or an assault ship. She would have been vetted stringently as all their new crew was, since this was Captain Retzo Sho's personal ship. This made it even more unbelievable for Helga. Not only were there four women on *Ursula*, but one was someone that she actually knew.

"*Ursula* crew, you're free to move about now. We'll be traveling at supercruise for approximately two cycles, so keep all hatches and blast windows sealed," Ina announced, in a voice that could best be described as strong and sweet.

Helga hated the intercom, and would let *Ursula's* computer or the Cel-toc Zan do the announcing while she shouted out orders to the rates in her vicinity. Ina, however, had a gift, and didn't seem to mind doing it. Ina removed her finger from the intercom activation link and exhaled heavily before staring forward. Helga watched her go through the motions, wondering if she had read her wrong in her rush to relieve herself of announcements.

The red-headed pilot worked at her restraints, slender fingers going through the practiced motions of popping the lock and pulling the straps from her shoulders, then finishing with a lurch forward to tease and throw back her hair. When she sat up, she turned to Helga, who was still watching while removing her own restraints. She let out another heavy sigh before rolling her eyes. "Don't you hate launches?" she asked quietly so only Helga could hear.

"Sometimes." Helga laughed. It wasn't something she expected to hear from a fellow Ace. "Had a bad one before, I'm guessing?"

"Yes, and I relive it every single time I hear that alarm before we're cleared." Ina fanned herself, forcing a smile, which brightened up her face. "Won't affect my duties, Lieutenant. Don't you go worrying about me and launches."

Helga shrugged. "Since we're sharing, I feel the same about breaking atmosphere when we go on drops. Talk about a spike to the chest with every mission, but I'm working on getting over that reaction. I told you about Dyn, didn't I?"

"You did, back when you and the commander saved me, right after going through all that you did. *Thype*. Guess it comes with the territory, eh? I can bet that every spacer on this ship who's seen action has their own personal tick that sets them off," Ina said.

"Everyone here does, and just like us, they do what they can to get over it. Let me know what you need to help, Ina. Zan is more than capable of handling a launch, really. She's fully synced with *Ursula's* system. All we would need is just to ask, but you know that."

"Thanks for looking out, Helga, but I got this." Ina winked. "You brought me on to take care of our lady, and I'm a hands-on type of girl. Even after my situations, I've been through no less than twenty to twenty-five launches. It's not the act of doing it that stresses me out, it's the restraints, the alarm, and the movement. One thing that does make it easier is when I am the one pulling the landing gear, engaging thrust, and punching in the nav points."

"Control does help." Helga nodded. "Same for me, which is why I won't let another spacer do our drops. Last mission to Meluvia, we had an Ace named Mika take us in. Thought I would die, not because of her flying—girl had skills, but every shudder brought me back to our Britz being perforated over Dyn, and ever rattle from the bulkhead came with memories of my mentor slumped over in his chair. Whew, what a mess. Took just about all my will to get through it."

"Feels like ten cycles have passed since you saved my life, Helga." Ina reached over and gripped her shoulder. "I've never forgotten that day. I just knew I was dead, and you stood up for me without us even exchanging words. I never asked you why you trusted me, but I need you to know that I'm eternally grateful. You know how I feel about the Navy, after—"

"Ina, you don't have to," Helga tried to assure her when she saw how much the woman was struggling.

"No, let me say this, because I've been wanting to tell you for years, and in here is the only time we're alone. I really need to get this off my chest," Ina said. "Helga Ate, I need you to know that when I received the invitation to try out for this job, I only considered it because of you and Commander Mec. There's an element of debt owed, a big one, because I wouldn't be alive if you hadn't stopped to check on me in that passageway."

"And I wouldn't be alive if the commander hadn't pulled me and Brise out of stasis," Helga said, reaching up to put a hand over Ina's, which remained on her shoulder. "You don't owe me anything. Girl, if there's anything I can tell you about the Nighthawks, it's that we all have pulled each other out of the fire at some point. No one is keeping count of that stuff. We take care of our own. Now on to more important topics. What happened to Brise Sol?"

Ina laughed and pulled back her hand, sinking lower into her seat as she rolled her eyes and stared up at the overhead. "Brise Sol, where to start, eh? The last time you saw him was *Inginus*, correct? When we both got our discharge?" Helga nodded in affirmation, and Ina's brown, freckled face suddenly became serious. "He was in love with you, and never reconciled it. That, and he really hated the commander; all that man ever did was complain about how unfairly he had been treated. Damn shame too. I thought he was cute, but for an Alliance spacer to be so *thyping* negative, it made me dislike him. Tried to convince him to move on, since he was obviously skilled and talented, having passed BLAST, and formerly a Nighthawk, not to mention his work as an engineer. He would be an asset to any station or planet. Even from an Alliance standpoint, after discharge he could aid the effort. He didn't want to hear any of it, he was a failure, and that was that."

"Did he remain on your ship as part of the crew?" Helga leaned sideways in her seat to glance back through the doorway to see if any of the rates were close enough to eavesdrop.

"No, he had me drop him off at Ilvercom Station, which in my opinion is a glorified *schtill*-pit," Ina rejoined. "Handsome man, naturally kind, but broken from all you went through in that Geralos prison. The pragmatist in me believes he's still there, now a member of that little hub, building crate berthing for the refugees and using that big brain to make life better for them."

"Sounds like Brise." Helga smiled. "I just wish that I could talk to him again. I never agreed with the way we threw him out when what he really needed was a psych and some therapy. I was still such a child, and afraid of speaking up. Not to mention, I was going through my own brand of *schtill*. I do hope he found a new life that comes with some healing."

"That would take a girlfriend, and one with the patience to put up with his incessant wining." Ida stood up and stretched as if to signal to Helga that the conversation had become boring. "Have you met the crew yet, Helga?"

"The way they threw us off *Rendron*, when would I have had time?" Helga complained in a much lower voice. "By the time I blinked out the last bit of sleep, I was seated here next to you prepping for launch."

"Um, yeah, they did that didn't they?" Ida laughed, and reached for Helga's hand to help her out of her seat. Having spent so much time on *Rendron*, the gravity felt strange, and it made her wonder if something was different now that they had a full ship's complement, not counting the Nighthawks.

"*Ursula* crew, this is your captain," came a loud voice, cutting Helga off before she could say anything else. "Meet below deck at 1:640. Assemble near the nose of the dropship. This goes for everyone, Nighthawks as well." The two women exchanged looks before checking the time, which at the moment was 1:610.

"This our brief?" Ina inquired.

"Not likely," Helga replied. "I'm going with formal introductions and preliminary orders, knowing Cilas." She reached past Ina to pluck her coat from the hook on the back of her chair and slipped it on in one fluid motion. "Funny, you made to take me around and boom, we get summoned to a meeting."

"Think the commander is eavesdropping?" Ina whispered, provocatively, and the way she said it made Helga wonder if she too knew of their relationship.

Helga cleared her throat and reached over to touch Zan, who was powered down and staring forward like a focused pilot in her chair. The Cel-toc's eyes fluttered open, and her pale skin flashed red before settling on her normal shade of beige. She smiled welcomely, a part of her program meant for owners and friends. "Lieutenant Ate, a pleasure to see you. How may I serve?"

"Zan, this is Lieutenant Ina Reysor. She is our *Ursula* pilot, reporting to me and then Commander Mec in that order. Do you understand?" Helga said, to which the Cel-toc made a formal bow towards Ina. "You should find her clearances are similar to mine, with the exception of certain commands pertaining to the Nighthawks. You are to afford her the same respect that you have shown me since we first met." At this she smiled, and Zan began to blush in the most convincingly human way.

"Lieutenant Reysor," Helga continued, "This is Zan, a Cel-toc assistant assigned to *Ursula*, but on this tiny deck of ours, she's one of us. Zan has been my wingman for multiple contacts, and has shown her quality."

"Okay, charmed, Zan," Ina said, somewhat sarcastically, which didn't surprise or offend Helga, who knew that most spacers viewed Cel-tocs as tools, smart enough to replicate human behavior when they weren't playing chauffeur or servant.

"The cockpit is yours, Zan. Steer us straight, and communicate with me directly if there's an emergency," Helga said as she stepped down from the half-moon pilot's deck onto the incline of the control center, which took her up past Cilas's chair. Two strangers she hadn't noticed before stood at attention by the entrance, saluting the two of them as they walked past. They wore the battle dress uniform of Marines, and carried sidearms.

"You know you're official when you have stationed guards on your bridge," Ina complained.

"Better get used to it, girl, it's no longer just a Nighthawk ship," Helga explained. "This is now the *ACS Ursula*, a new class of fighting, Alliance Combat Ship."

"You were always funny." Ina laughed. "Good to see they haven't blunted your edge."

"Wasn't for lack of trying, but what's the point of life if we aren't able to laugh and sing?" Helga said, surprised at herself for sounding optimistic for once, as they descended the nearest lift to the lower decks.

As the metal shaft cleared to reveal the open space of the hangar, Helga leaned against the guardrail to scan the new faces that gathered there. It was a collection of archetypes, as if Cilas had been focused on nothing but diversity. *Rendron* was a Vestalian ship, with a small community of aliens, but even before her refit, *Ursula* had a Traxian doctor, a half-Casanian Nighthawk in Helga, and a Virulian Jumper in Sunny.

They stepped off to shouts of acknowledgment, salutes, and gestures of respect, but it didn't go unnoticed to Helga that her youth and alien features prompted the occasional look of surprise and wonderment. Twenty years of life—twelve of which were with the Alliance—and Helga had become used to it. Her looks would never live up to the legend of "Hellgate from the *Rendron*."

There were so many stories going around and false rumors spread. Half she suspected came from Raileo, who delighted in pranking her whenever they were off the clock. Much of it was true; she was a rock star, used on posters to recruit female hopefuls into Special Operations.

Two very active years with her Nighthawks had afforded her somewhat of an infamous reputation, which she learned quickly on the *Rendron,* when the rates all but carried her away on their shoulders upon their return. Those who only heard of her, expected her to be bigger, even physically imposing like Quentin Tutt. It was always the same, that look of surprise and poorly veiled disappointment, when the giant "Lady Hellgate" turned out to be a tiny, effeminate woman.

She approached them, exchanging greetings and settled in between Raileo and Quentin, who would normally give her a bear hug, but kept up appearances by offering a nod. Giving him a wink, she jabbed his arm playfully, then turned to face forward when she felt the tension in the air. Cilas had just descended his own lift, and was bordered by the two Marines from the bridge.

Everyone faced him as he walked towards them, his suit as sharp as a las-sword, and his boots so clean they practically gleamed under the lights. He seemed different in this moment, something much more than their team leader, something powerful. Gone was the star operator playing at helming a warship, replaced by a captain, not only capable, but having accepted his responsibilities and position.

Every step of his was confidence, so much so that Helga couldn't look away. Their eyes met for just a moment, and what she saw there left her embarrassed from practically beaming with pride. "Who here hails from *Rendron*?" he asked, stopping in front of them to await their response. Several hands went up, while the others looked concerned for his intentions with that question. Helga tried hard not to let this bother her, as this was the typical response from a crew to its new captain.

"That's what I thought," Cilas said, pacing. "Many of you hail from other starships, stations, and even planets. Welcome, Nolan," he said to one of the Marines, and the big man nodded, barely able to restrain a smile. "Some of us hail from dreadful places, others wonderful, and you probably miss it. The act of service is at its base, sacrifice. The sacrifice of our time, our comforts, and even our lives," he said, stopping for impact, though Helga had picked up on the pain behind his words. "But without service, we Vestalians would be an extinct race, victims of the Geralos, whose destruction would have moved on to another planet, possibly Hiyt, whose brilliance we see glowing through that window."

He stopped to look out through one of the dock's bay windows where Meluvia was visible, though only as a ball of light no bigger than a ball made for catching. "When we all signed on, we took an oath. Serve the Alliance, and rid the galaxy of the Geralos. A tremendous goal, it's in an enormous galaxy," he shouted, evoking laughter from his audience. "Which makes it easy to forget, it's so enormous, but I'm telling you right now that here, you will not be afforded the luxury of forgetting. We are at war, *Ursula*, with an enemy that sees us as food; no, less than food, since they don't even bother to consume us. They want our brains to bite, in hopes of pulling out some mystical power that they believe exists."

And you don't? Helga wondered, stunned that Cilas, her Cilas, not believing in the Vestalian Seeker gene, which she, the woman with whom he had shared so much had flowing inside her veins. *All this time and you don't believe*, Helga thought, wondering if this was a sign that it was time for her to tell him.

"As you all know," Cilas continued, "This is a unique vessel, first of its kind, a warship with specific outfitting and ordnance for stealth and neutralizing. *Ursula* is a Nighthawk, so in a way, so are the lot of you, and as your captain, I will demand the same commitment to the fight that I demand from my team. Here, there is no option but to go max thrust with everything you do for this team, and as your captain, I vow to be fair. The Alliance comes first but the next in that order is this crew."

He kept on speaking, running through quick introductions that Helga could barely keep up with. *Ursula* before refit had been crewed and run by the Nighthawks, all serving double-duty, fitting in where they could to keep the vessel floating. Now there were thirty-five crewmembers, some who she hadn't seen until now, now that they were forced back together.

Helga mentally checked out, finding it hard to focus. Her mind kept going back to Cilas, and how stunned she was at the revelation that he didn't believe in the Seekers. For someone to question so big a legacy of their heritage as Vestalians meant that he saw the Geralos as fanatics, committing genocide in search of something that didn't exist.

She wanted to approach him and ask him if the Seekers weren't real, how was it that she could do the things she could inside a cockpit? If he argued that, she could bring up her isolation during their capture, when the Geralos segregated her in order to chemically split her Casanian blood from the Vestalian, which they needed. It was all so disappointing to her, she couldn't contain it, so when the introductions were done and everyone made to disperse she approached him directly.

"Great speech, Commander," she said, and meant it. "That bit about the Seekers though, you had me at a loss. Am I to believe that you, Commander Cilas Mec, do not believe that our Vestalian women can be born with the Seeker gene?"

She expected him to go on the defensive, but he merely shrugged. "Of course I believe in Seekers, Hel. Which part of my speech would have you thinking I'm doubting our powers?" he said, putting her on the defensive suddenly. "Wait, so you did think that. I knew there was something bothering you the way that you were glowering. Helga, come on, I know our history, and you should know that."

"Hence my surprise, Ci—I mean, Commander, but for once, where you're concerned, I'm actually relieved to be wrong."

7

It had been raining for three days since Fio Doro opened the luggage and saw the details of those Alliance vessels. Following Djesu's instructions, she had gathered her closest belongings into a pack and paid the apartment's rent forward in case she would need to be gone for several months. Retreating back to her old room in Djesu's house, she had stayed out of sight while he set up a meeting with the friend he had working in the recruitment station.

The plan was to meet him outside of the starport, since the Alliance recruitment office was in the same general area. He would meet them when he got off work, and assured them that the place would be empty since he was normally the last one leaving there. Djesu made them take a taxi out there, informing Fio that his friend, Garson, intended to give them a ride back home, while speaking to them about the documents.

Once they made the drop-off, Garson would contact the Alliance and the Genesian Guard, who had authority over the local police agency. They would arrest Vray and question him, and both Fio and Djesu would receive rewards from the Alliance. On their way over Djesu was like a child en route to getting a much-wanted toy. "We're going to be heroes, Fio," he said. "This could be our way out. That reward will be generous, and we may get titles."

She had never seen him so happy, so she had allowed him to ramble on, uninterrupted. When they made it to the steps of the recruitment office, he had finally run out of suppositions, and was on to being annoying with his anticipation.

"Since you're of a mood, Pops, mind if we have a talk?" Fio said, crossing her arms.

She kept her eyes on the dark glass of the offices, which reflected the courtyard of trees behind them, their branches casting long shadows from the plaza's floodlights. She had her doubts about Garson being inside the building. They were locked and showed no signs of life, all of the workers from the day long gone. In the neighboring lot where the taxi had dropped them off, the transports had been sparse and with nothing resembling a government vehicle.

"Let me guess. Something I said to you ages ago has been digging at you something fierce, and now we're alone you want me to explain myself?" Djesu posited, tilting his head back to catch some of the rain on his face.

"You called me a psychopath," Fio nearly shouted.

"That is what you're sour about?" Djesu seemed legitimately surprised. "I didn't mean anything by it, but you do go to the extremes sometimes, Fio."

"This is about Alana, isn't it?" Fio looked at him with disbelief. "Pops, she was a thief. Siphoning credits when she thought we were sleeping. I caught her red-handed, but you wouldn't believe, so I had to do what you wouldn't. How does that make me a psychopath?"

"You were barely 13, it wasn't your call, and I don't want to have this conversation right now."

"It was her that called BasPol on me when I stole that cab. Did you know that?" Fio pressed. "Do you know what they put me through in there? I could have died."

"After the way you beat her, Fio, it was her way of getting back at you, and it was foolish. She didn't mean for any of that to happen. We talked, and she was apologetic. That isn't why I called you what I did; I didn't mean anything by it. A joke was my intention, but you obviously want to get this off your chest." Djesu turned and made to sit down on the wet stones, then thought better of it and leaned against a post instead. "I sure wish Garson would hurry up."

"You let me down, Pops. You chose her over me," Fio said. "It's why I left. I didn't think I could trust you, and what did she do? Take everything from you, and now she's on the north side, living like a *thyping* queen, and we're in the rain."

"I probably deserve that," Djesu said. "If you haven't loved, you wouldn't understand what made me make those bad decisions." He turned to face her and spread his arms. "Now that you've got it out of your system, and Alana has left me and gone, will you find room in your heart to forgive?"

"Whatever," was all Fio could manage as she stared out into the dark. "*Cruta* ruined my life."

"Did she though, daughter?" Djesu sighed, his face seeming pained. "You've had it rough since birth when your mother abandoned you to these foul Basce City streets. You came into my life, angry and resentful, but that was your survival. You had that spark, and I knew all you needed was support to grow into the light. It's not easy to raise a child here, Fio, and I admit, I played the role with you at first because I saw an apprentice I could train to help me amass the credits needed to get out. Aye, but you were so much more, learning fast, and never a disappointment outside of your spats with the neighborhood tramps.

"You were more daughter to me than I could have hoped for, even if you were my own, but Alana filled a gap in my life that even you, as special as you were, could not close. When you left, I was angry with you, and looking back, I had no right, but things were moving so fast, I didn't know. Yeah, Alana played me, I was a fool, and by the time I was wise, you were out there with an apartment of your own and running goods uptown. I tell you." He laughed. "Fio Doro, I couldn't have been prouder."

Fio didn't know what to say to that. She was happy to hear that he really hadn't abandoned her, but still felt the sting of betrayal from those early days. "I've been in love, I get it," she said, "though I wasn't fool enough to allow that individual to blindly rob me. What would you say now, if I propose that once this meeting is settled, we take a transport uptown and take back what is ours? That should mend some wounds."

"Would it though, Fio? It's likely she has a family now, which involves small tykes, and a clueless husband," Djesu countered, his voice revealing that the wound hadn't been healed from his past relationship with Alana.

"Wasn't being serious, Pops, I'm just helping the time pass. Is your friend really coming? The rain is picking up, and this—" Fio heard a noise from the direction of the trees, and she looked over at Djesu to see if he too had heard it. "Are you positive that we're safe here, Pops? Vray knew enough of my background to know that you and I are linked."

The noise came again after a second had passed and Fio knew it wasn't her imagination. It was a slight sloshing sound, similar to the blowing rain, but distinct enough for her to know it wasn't natural. An invisible hand gripped her heart, squeezing it, forcing her to catch her breath, and as she turned to her left to see what it was, a bullet tore through her neck, not hitting vitals but searing a bloody hot gash right below her chin.

In the distance standing amidst the trees she saw a trio of men dressed in black tactical gear. They appeared to be BasPol spice-breakers, but their helmets were different, and they were firing assault weapons unlike any she had ever seen. "Your man isn't coming, but we arranged another meeting for you to deliver those stolen documents," one of them shouted, his voice a deep rasp, frightening, revealing no mirth or sarcasm. It was as if he was stating facts.

Another hit her chest, striking the communications disc, and it exploded on impact, knocking her back against the stairs. Djesu was down, and she didn't know how and when. Fio scrambled to get up, reached for the suitcase, but a high-pitched whine made her retreat from it and scramble up the stairs. The suitcase exploded into cinders, the traces of the laser still visible in the night air.

Fio was up and running now, certain that if she lived, she would quickly regret that she hadn't been killed. Djesu was dead, and the pain was an expanding balloon stuck in the bottom of her throat. She didn't know where she was going, what she would do, and how she would survive the night. Her only focus was to push past the pain, get out of the port, and find her way back to the stocks.

A whistling bullet zipped past her ear as she ran through the arc that separated the offices from the starport's entrance. A long line of buses had pulled in, their passengers spilling out into the parking lot, and Fio darted into their midst, swimming against the current as they made their way towards the starport. Her appearance caused some confusion, particularly from people who saw the wound on her neck.

Fio slowed down, and as her adrenaline waned, she began to really feel the pain. The intense burning in her chest, the soreness of her eyes from crying in the freezing rain, and the numbing pain in her shoulder from the shot. Unsure, confused, and paranoid that at any moment now one of her pursuers would jump out and sink a knife into her, Fio hurried through the oncoming rushers until an unimpressed mother stood her ground and shoved her into the pavement.

Suddenly, a hand shot down, grabbing her wrist and pulled her back up to her feet, where it began dragging her the other way. Fio made to yank back her hand and reach for her gun, but she recognized who it was from the galactic map tattooed on her wrist. Looking up in disbelief from that hand which she knew too well, Fio couldn't believe her luck. "Zulia?" she asked, unsure if her condition was having her imagine things.

"Fio, you're bleeding," the woman whispered accusingly, not breaking her stride as she dragged her along to the crowded starport's entrance.

"Don't worry about me," Fio managed, but then an alarm from the intercom drowned out all sound to alert them of an incoming announcement.

"Attention, travelers, welcome to Basce City Adventures," came a woman's voice, loud enough to grab the attention of the buzzing crowd. "Please have your tickets out and be ready to present them to our Cel-toc agents at the entry port. Additionally, I must inform you that we've been temporarily listed as code red. Gunfire has been recorded close by and the Basce City Police are on their way."

Zulia stopped and looked over Fio, her violet eyes reflecting a look of disappointment. "Those gunshots, were they for you?"

"Yes, and I need to go before they find me. I owe you big time, Zulia, and I will make it up to you. Whatever you want, just buzz me later and—"

The tall, slender woman took her hand and placed a ticket inside her palm. "You need to disappear for a while, right?" she said, and when Fio nodded she pulled her along to one of the entry ports. "Perfect, then you're coming with me to Neroka Station. There's an extra bunk since Cheyenne's on leave having her baby, and you could have time to heal and reset. What do you say, Fio? It's a chance you may never get again. Take me up on it this time? Please?"

Fio was beginning to feel weak, and as dreadful as serving drinks sounded, it meant safety and some time to process everything that happened. "Sure, Zu ... but I don't want you to think—"

"What? That because we share a room, that things will revert to what it was last year? Don't flatter yourself girl, and right now, the only thing you should be worrying about is getting some medical help. Come with me." She dragged her into a restroom, where she opened her bag and pulled out a medkit. She cleaned the wound on Fio's neck and placed a bandage on it, then rubbed her chest with a numbing cream to lessen the pain.

Fio Doro wanted to thank her but couldn't bring herself to act. On the outside she looked tired, drawn, and on the verge of losing consciousness. Inside she was falling, rapidly, past herself into a void where the guilt of Djesu's passing threatened to bury her deep enough to where she too could be dead. If there were any more tears to cry out, they would have been streaming, but all she felt was pain.

Now that her wounds were treated, Zulia went into a booth and emerged wearing a uniform and a hat tilted on her short, curly hair. "Here, put these on," she said, handing Fio a bundle. "They're a little wet from outside, and the pants won't fit, but with my top and coat on, nobody should recognize you as we make our way onto the ship."

Fio nodded and began to undress, not missing the look of sheer horror that crossed Zulia's face as she saw more and more of her bruised and battered body. She let out a nervous laugh, nearly delirious. "Had some adventures since our junior cadet days, girlfriend. You should see your face." She started to laugh even though it aggravated her chest. She let herself have it, for if she didn't laugh, she was likely to break down crying instead.

She pulled on the shirt, popped the collar, and pulled it in close to conceal the bandages. At first she declined the coat due to it putting weight on the shoulder, but Zulia insisted, so she wore it. In the mirror, outside of her blue mop and running mascara, she did look the part of the working-class hustler on her way up to do a shift on the station.

"Ever been off-planet?" Zulia asked, turning to dispose the bloody garments into the disposal.

"Never," Fio admitted.

"Oh, this is exciting, I get to experience your first flight. I bet when we make it up to the station, you won't want to leave there. It's not as terrible as you think, Fio. There were plenty rumors misleading you. It's a job I love, and if you're willing to help, you can stay with me as long as you need until you find your footing. Just one stipulation before we go. I want the whole story of how you wound up shot, and bleeding out here of all places. Fair?"

"Fair," Fio nearly shouted, ready to be seated on the space shuttle, restrained, and finally able to rest. Djesu was gone, and so were the credits, her apartment, and all of the things she'd been collecting since her childhood. *I'll be back for them*, she promised herself, knowing deep down it was a dream that wouldn't happen. "Leave before you find yourself loving the wickedness," she recited.

"That one of Djesu's old sayings?" Zulia asked.

"It was," Fio replied, and when she met her eyes she was surprised to see understanding and regret.

8

"Hoo." Helga gasped for air after ripping off the headset for the simulator. The small compartment slowly faded into focus, and her brain did the rest of the work to remind her that what occurred hadn't been real. She patted herself down out of habit, searching for wounds that wouldn't be there, and when her hands found her face, she suddenly felt foolish for her actions. It had only been a simulation, yet she was having difficulty accepting it.

"Good run there at the end, Ate," Quentin said, rubbing at his eyes as he placed his headgear back onto its charging station.

"Yeah, that was intense. Reminded me of Meluvia," Helga managed, her mind still reeling from the experience.

"No way I got shot inside that transport," Raileo whined from another station closer to the door. There were six stations total inside each of the four simulation booths, installed specifically for these exercises, though most would remain untouched until there were more than five Nighthawks.

"You got shot, hero, deal with it," Quentin quipped, gripping him by the shoulder as he stepped out from his own simulation booth.

The new recruit, Anders, observed them quietly from his own, though his face betrayed a smile of satisfaction. Unlike Raileo and Quentin, he had managed to survive the exercise, even assisting his lieutenant, Helga Ate. Helga gave him a cursory nod to show her gratitude, but he wasn't paying attention, so she took the opportunity to get a good look at his stature.

At 170cm in height, he was shorter than the other two men. Small in frame, with large hands and feet, he owned a set of brooding dark eyes below short blond hair worn high and tight, the Marine way. He did have a good smile, and better manners, but this remained hidden behind a rehearsed wall of stoicism. Helga didn't have a real opinion of him just yet, so she decided that now would be a good time to learn more.

"Way to keep your head in there, Stratus," she announced, which got his attention. "You operated like this wasn't your first time. Run a lot of simulations back on *Aqnaqak*?"

"Thanks, Lieutenant, and no, not many sims, but I do have some experience. Before BLAST, I was stationed on *Starlance*. It's one of our infiltrators. *Aqnaqak*, I mean. *Starlance* is one of *Aqnaqak's* infiltrator," he informed her as they walked out to the center of the hangar where Quentin and Raileo were changing.

Helga wanted to laugh at this new recruit giving her lessons on one of the more popular infiltrators in the fleet. "I know the *Starlance*," she said. "Were you there under Captain Hyde?"

"Oh no," he quickly recalled. "I was still a cadet, but I was there before graduation. My team placed first out of all others on the Ubari trials. Four of us were rewarded with berthing on *Starlance* until we reached Vasylik Station."

"The Vasylik Station?" Helga couldn't believe what she was hearing.

"The one and only," Anders rejoined. "We didn't learn until it was too late that we were headed to a warzone. The Alliance had been warned, but by that time *Starlance* had already jumped beyond the range of FTL communication. Our dropship was intercepted by a cloaked lizard cruiser, and we were forced to land in what turned out to be an occupied station. Sergeant Cashe, our chaperon, ordered his Marines to arm us to help fight back when the hatches opened."

"Maker. How many of you were there?" Helga was dumbfounded.

"Many of whom?" Quentin chimed in as he approached them, wanting in on the tale.

"Anders here is a veteran," Helga informed him with a smirk. "Seems he's been through it in the past and killed his share of lizards as a green cadet. He's giving me the details. Sounds like quite an adventure."

"You've killed lizards?" Quentin seemed skeptical. "Lizards with an S. Where?" he asked, his face becoming hard.

"On Vasylik Station, Sarge, but to be fair, our Marines did most of the killing, I—we just fired where they told us, and covered their assault. We cleared the hangar, but the lizards rallied and—"

"Vasylik." Quentin's eyes widened at the mention of the station. "You're from *Aqnaqak*?"

"Yes, sir, under Captain Tara Cor."

"Surviving Vasylik was likely how they discovered Anders was ESO material," Raileo added, stepping up to place a supporting hand on the young man's shoulder. "Everyone knows what happened on that station. Is it necessary to have the rook relive it just to explain that he belongs?"

Rich coming from you, Helga thought. *Aren't you the one always giving him schtill with the childish hazing?* She looked over at Anders who had gone silent, his demeanor becoming one of discomfort. Dark eyes stared lasers into the deck. The memory had been triggered, and she could tell that he was still in the moment. "You make a good point, Ray," Helga quickly added, feeling guilty for being the one to have started questioning him. "We all had our Vasyliks, and none of us wants to run through the memories of them. I know I don't. Right, Q?" She punched the big man in his arm.

"Oh, he's cold, I have no doubt," Quentin added. "I saw what I needed inside of the sim. This man shows promise, but we'll learn soon enough how he does in the real."

"Are we to conduct a rescue operation then?" Anders asked.

"Hell if I know." Quentin shrugged. "The only person who knows would be the commander, and perhaps Lady Hellgate, though she is forbidden to speak on it. Right Lieutenant?" Now it was his turn to jab her in the arm for the well-timed dig.

"Next time you drop from one of my vessels, Tutt, you may experience a bit of turbulence, I don't know," Helga mused. "You know how it is. Any number of things can go wrong on those drops, depending on the atmosphere. If, or should I say, when something goes wrong, just remember who has your life in her hands."

Anders stared at her, measuring the threat, not knowing whether she meant it, since her face was stoic. "Good to see that everyone here gets on so well," he added.

Helga stopped to place her hand on his arm. "You did well today, Stratus, but despite your history, when we get deployed it is going to be a *schtill* show, so don't expect it to go as neatly as a simulation. People get hurt, and there will be times when you won't know if you'll even make it. All we have is each other, and trust is everything. Don't take our praise as an excuse to get cocky, or feel you've already made it. You will be tested, but it will make you into a Nighthawk. Am I clear?"

"Yes, ma'am. I won't ever forget why I'm here, you have my word on that," he said, straightening his back and meeting their eyes directly. "Thank you for the advice."

"You got it," Helga said. "Now go hit the showers and head up to the galley. You look exhausted." Helga gently shoved him towards the door, and he feigned tripping over his own feet before heading off to their berthing.

"I'll admit I didn't see Vasylik-survivor-turned-BLAST-graduate in our recruit there," Raileo admitted.

"You can never tell who has it in them," Quentin commented. "Not by appearances. Just look at yourself, Ray. If someone was to meet you without knowing your history, would they know what you're truly capable of?"

"What are you trying to say?" Raileo became defensive.

"I'm saying that for all your dancing and flirting on *Rendron's* decks, outside of a PAS suit the rates wouldn't know that you were a coldblooded killer." Quentin grinned.

Helga made to add her own dig but stopped short when she heard a change in *Ursula's* engine. The droning sound coming from the ship's generator had begun to stutter. It was a sound she knew well, that of the tracers coming online to pull energy from the reserves. She wondered if any of the other men had noticed. "Do you all not hear that?" She studied their faces, but both Quentin and Raileo shook their heads.

"All I hear is my stomach crying out in protest," Raileo complained, placing his hand over his abdomen.

"Tracers are online," Helga announced. "Didn't hear an 'all hands,' or warning, so it's probably Ina running through our ordnance, calibrating timing, and making sure that we're prepared for any contact. I'm surprised at you lot. Really. We've been here before on numerous cycles. What gives? It would be good to familiarize yourselves with these sounds. It is important."

They all exchanged their farewells, with Quentin and Raileo suggesting they continue the banter over chow within the next few minutes. Tired, sore, and struggling internally with relinquishing control of *Ursula* to her new pilot and friend, Helga spent the next half hour showering before changing into her formal Navy blues to take her watch on the upper deck.

Time to play at officer now, she thought sarcastically. *Check in on Ina, and then a quick perusal of our decks.* She looked at the time and the third shift had barely started, which meant a clutch of the crew would be in the galley, eating and conversing loudly as they wound down from their dailies. It would be the optimum time to visit Cilas alone inside his cabin, or to do as he had suggested some cycles before, and engage with the rates to get to know them.

A chime snapped her out of her hemming and hawing, and she nearly ran to the door, hoping it was Cilas. It was Chief Alon Weinstar's face that appeared when she powered on the door's monitor, and while he was still technically a stranger, Helga was happy for the distraction.

Reaching down to collect her discarded 3B-XO suit and deposit it into the refresher, Helga opened the door expectantly, and upon seeing Alon Weinstar and not her commander she tried to hide her disappointment. She beckoned him in, noting how tall the older man was, his 196cm dwarfing her in that instance. The chief engineer stepped inside her compartment, saluted crisply, and kept the fist over his heart until she gave him a nod of acknowledgment.

"Lieutenant Ate, apologies." He tilted his head. "I was told by the commander that this was the best time to catch you."

"It is," Helga said coolly, as she walked over to her desk, and placed her buttocks against the edge, not quite sitting, and not quite leaning, though it took the strain off her sore quadriceps. It dawned on her no sooner had she done it that this was the exact same thing that Captain Retzo Sho would do whenever she would visit his cabin. The only thing missing in her version was a glass of brandy, or something exotic in a glass.

"Yes well, I came to deliver this," the older man offered, coming to life. "It's a new comms accessory to replace the one you all wear on your wrists." He held up a box, which was small enough to fit inside her palm. "It's a new design donated from the Genese Trade Federation, ma'am. Experimental for the Alliance, and approved by Captain Sho for our detail." He grinned, revealing a top row of neat white teeth, and a lower set of a mechanical variety, glinting below the lights.

"*Xi'so*," Helga said, surprised, using a Traxian expression she had picked up from the ship's physician, Cleia Rai'to.

"*Xi'so*, ma'am?" Weinstar seemed confused.

"I'm just excited. Please do continue," Helga said.

Weinstar chuckled. "As I was saying, it's new tech, lighter, and much better. Will you give it a try, please, Lieutenant? It is my duty to not only deliver it, but to make sure that it is working for you." The man held so much strained anticipation in his face that even if Helga wanted to decline, she would have found it difficult.

Weinstar stuck a hand out towards her, palm turned up, long, thin, part metallic fingers holding a small coffin-shaped box with three small items inside. Helga accepted it, taking a step backward away from him, and plucked one of the items from the box.

"You know, this is highly unusual, Mr. Weinstar. Popping in the way you did to ambush me with technology," Helga teased, but nearly lost her composure when she saw the older man's face flush red. "Not being serious," she said, smiling quickly. "Am I supposed to wear these?" She picked out a small transparent container from the box that held a pair of red-rimmed contact lenses.

"Ah." Weinstar cleared his throat, embarrassed now that she had managed to get a joke over on him. "Yes, those are cornea shields with a holographic HUD display which connects to an activator."

She scrutinized the contents, wondering if she was his first victim, and if so, why? Everything inside the container looked factory-made, and the case did bear the Alliance's seal.

"And this other piece, the 'activator,' as you call it. Does that go inside my ear?" Helga held up a miniature disc with spikes on one side, giving it an eerie resemblance to a spider.

"That is the activation node. It serves two roles, one for comms, the other for powering on the interface. When installed, you would merely need to touch an area behind your right ear." Weinstar reached up to his ear to demonstrate his meaning. "A holographic interface will appear, allowing you to perform several functions, mostly for communicating with the ship and crew. Oh, and there are separate options for covert operations, concerning members of your team. It's a computer, so it can be programmed to do more. No more need for clunky headsets and ear clips. Isn't technology fascinating?"

Helga shot him a wary look. "The teeth on this disc. I'm assuming they break flesh to secure it to the back of my ear, similar to Genesian jewelry?"

"Yes ma'am. The hardware and intelligence are housed inside that tiny button. All you would need to do is press it against the back of your ear and it will secure itself. One small pinch and after a few minutes, you won't remember that it's even there."

"We'll see about that," Helga said, skeptically. "Who else is rigged up with this?"

"Commander Mec had his installed last shift, and I intend to visit Sergeant Tutt, and Chief Raileo Lei once I'm done here," he said, looking more than a bit put off by her distrust.

Helga was surprised. Cilas hadn't said anything. "Can I put it on myself when I'm ready, or is there something else I would need from you?"

"Just wanted to tell you about the contact lenses. They are biodegradable, and once in place should not irritate your eyes," he instructed. "If they do, remove them immediately, and give either me or Dr. Cleia Rai'to a call. They can be worn for up to a Vestalian month, but really you can wear them for three. Extended use could damage your eyes, so be careful. I would advise you to only wear them when you intend to use the holographic interface."

"Oh, I see," Helga said. "Without the lenses, the ear nodes can be used normally for communication, without having to speak into our wrists. Neat. This will make things a lot easier. Thank you, Mr. Weinstar, I think I've got it now." Helga replaced the items in the box before sliding it into one of the many pockets on her coveralls. "How do you like it?"

Weinstar's face revealed a look of surprise at her question. "It's an absolute game-changer, in my opinion. This will allow you to be fully independent of your armor. Even more, with this being available to all the Alliance, the engineers who build the powered armor suits will modify the helmet's interface to sync with the new comms, possibly enhancing them. For me, as a man with enough tech fused to his organs to know the beauty of untethered synchronization, I'm excited for you all to experience it yourselves."

"Wow, you're really passionate about this, Mr. Weinstar," Helga said. "Are you synced right now?"

"I am," he replied, showing her the silver head of the node clipped to the back of his organic ear.

"So, right now, you could tell me the state of our crystal core, even while we're at supercruise?" she said.

"I can, but to be honest, that information wouldn't come from the node, it would come from my internal computer, which is synced with *Ursula*, the same way that Zan's is. With the implant, you as a fully organic human will be able to get that information with a simple touch of the node."

"Won't be fully organic anymore after today," Helga mused, giving him a wink to let him know that she was joking.

9

Ursula was alive with activity, Cilas in the center of it with Ina Reysor, scrutinizing a holographic starmap, which displayed a region of Genesian space. Adjacent to their meeting, in separate stations, four of the new officers were chatting on comms, establishing clearances with the Alliance and local defense force patrolling Genese. Alon Weinstar was speaking to the Cel-toc, Zan, programming her to assist with monitoring the equipment on the bridge.

Helga was still getting used to her role as first officer, no longer needed at the helm. Where *Ursula* was concerned, her role was teacher and enforcer, which meant tightening up on protocol and keeping an eye on the new crewmembers as they adjusted to the ship. Gone were the cycles of relaxing on the bridge, feet up, one wary eye on the radar, and music in her ears giving her peace.

It wasn't the downtime she missed, but the freedom to be herself. Playing officer to the rates was easy; after all, on *Rendron* it was the only reality she knew. *Ursula* had been an exception in the past, since it was just Nighthawks, and she was free to be herself. Quentin and Raileo respected the chain of command, and had proved themselves capable of joking with her during off-duty hours and toeing the line when she was in uniform.

Experience had taught her that not every spacer was capable of respecting that line. With this new crew being her first chance at leadership on a bridge, she still joked on occasion, but kept things formal to keep them out of trouble with Cilas, who intended to run a tight ship. Helga's watch was at second shift, giving Ida a break at the helm if it was necessary, but typically she would walk the main passageway, lending a hand wherever it was needed.

Her schedule, for the most part, was that of a Nighthawk's. This meant preparation, simulations, and the occasional crisis drill. First shift was for personal training, working out with Quentin, Raileo, and the Nighthawk recruit, Anders. Then once the blood was flowing, they would separate to their own separate focuses. Raileo Lei would be in the range, running high-level sniper exercises, Quentin would work out some more, and Anders had a flair for close-quarters combat.

Helga spent time in the simulation room, flying virtual dropships through random disasters and scenarios, committing good reactions to muscle memory. Cilas and Quentin would sometimes spar, going over all manner of combat situations. Once personal training was done, they would go up to the galley and Chief Mas-Umbra would have something delicious prepared.

Team drills came after the meal, which were typically breach-and-clear exercises. Today Helga skipped it to see Dr. Cleia Rai'to, who had left a note on her rack to come and visit. The note had been the classical sugar-sweet Cleia, neatly wrapped and scented, despite the language being stilted. She had wanted to stay, loving the physical activity, though she remembered how just last year she would have hated these drills.

Three missions of staring death in the face had taught her to respect the readiness that repetitive training instilled. Forgetting a step, slipping on a breach, or having poor aim were things that a Nighthawk couldn't afford to do. One mistake could cost the life of another, a reality that they had all experienced.

"Helga, a moment," she heard Cilas call, and she hurried over to where he and Ina stood on the raised central area of the bridge where the large starmap loomed next to the captain's station. "Got a message from Sunny. He'll be missing this trip. Something about a trial he has to undertake to win enough favor to be in good standing with the Jumper agency. He didn't write much, but told me to inform you that he will be here with you in spirit."

Helga was stunned. "This trip? Did he mean Genesian space, or is he saying we may not see him until our return to *Rendron*, whenever that is? Um, Commander," she said, adding the title, since they were within earshot of the crew.

"Sounded mysterious, as with everything Jumpers do. You know how it is. Lamia Brafa was the same. Before you came on he would return to their headquarters on Virulia to do trials, whatever that means. Always came back better though, martially. He was the best of us, as you recall, but the Lamia you knew was a deadlier version than the man I met when we were first given the Nighthawks moniker."

"I miss him," Helga said. "Only knew him for a heartbeat, but his words and kindness bolstered me when I needed it."

"Can you give us a moment, Lieutenant?" Cilas whispered to Ina, and the redheaded lieutenant obliged. She saluted, then made her way past Helga, touching her shoulder as she headed back to the galley. "You and Sunny are close," he spoke in a hushed tone so that only she could hear. "You and Lamia were close as well. It makes me think that you've shown interest in becoming a Jumper. Is that correct?"

Helga looked around to see if anyone could still be eavesdropping, annoyed that he would ask her something so private in the middle of CIC. She flashed him a look of contempt, hoping he'd pick up on her meaning, but Cilas merely stood looking at her, his hands tucked into the small of his back as he waited patiently for her reply.

What was she to do? Tell him that she liked Jumpers because they were sworn to protect people like her? Reveal to him that she was one of those with the blood that the Geralos sought? Reveal that the only reason she was spared on Dyn was because her Casanian blood made it dangerous for the lizards to devour her brain?

How would he take it? How would their relationship change? That latter question made the truth so difficult to share. Helga the Nighthawk was a spacer, pilot, and team member. Helga the Seeker would become a protected asset. The Alliance would want to keep her safe, run tests on her blood, and treat her like something other than the Nighthawk she had fought hard to become.

"It's something else, isn't it?" Cilas pressed, still speaking low. "Something to do with your luckiness. Sunny merely tolerates the rest of the team; with you he has been like a teacher or mentor. That's why it's been bothering me. Hel, if you show interest and they deem you worthy, they will send for you, and the Alliance isn't supposed to get in the way of that. Jumpers hold a higher authority, but as you can see, their lives are complicated."

"I don't want to become a Jumper, Commander. Lamia showed me the las-sword, and I developed an interest in them. He was kind to me while everyone else jeered. It wasn't anything terrible like the cadet academy, but I felt very alone back then. When he did what he did, it crushed me, but my memories of him are all good. Those kind eyes, and the way he would correct my mistakes without making me feel foolish or hopeless. When I met Sunny, he was different. Rougher around the edges." Helga had to smile at the memory. "Despite all that, he was the same. Accepted me for who I was, showed me how to use meditation to deal with some of my stress, and told me things about the universe that only a Jumper would know. I do value his friendship."

Cilas looked at her skeptically, as if he suspected it was something more but didn't want to push the question in this instance. Helga wondered if this was jealousy, though it didn't make sense. There had been nothing below board about the time she spent with Sundown, and she had even informed Cilas, so that he knew about their relationship.

"I knew a woman, Calypso Rein, she led a rebellion on a hub above Traxis, an assignment given to the Nighthawks to quell." Cilas leaned against the back of his large captain's chair, his eyes on the deck as he summoned the memory. "She was a lot like you. Strong but tortured, extremely sarcastic, but with a penchant for jumping into fire, which I attributed to the fact that she was gifted. Our mission was to disarm her rebels and bring her back to the Alliance for questioning, but do you know what she told me when we finally caught up with her? She said, you can go ahead and kill me. I would rather die here than suffer what the Alliance will put me through if they learn what I am."

Helga's eyes grew wide, but she tried to conceal it by blinking quickly. But it was too late; he had picked up on her mannerisms. "This Calypso, she was a Seeker then? You are saying you met a Seeker. Wow, that's something, Commander, and to think just a few cycles earlier, I was under the impression that you didn't believe in them."

"I do hope to earn your trust someday, Hel. That is all. I'm no Jumper, but I hope to become someone you can trust, like Lamia. It still burns me up thinking of how I was unconscious on Dyn when you more than anyone needed me. The way you helped Raileo on Meluvia, and the way we will help Anders come into his own, that's what Nighthawks are about, and I feel I failed you somehow."

"Commander, you cannot apologize for being injured," Helga said, desperate to move the conversation away from Dyn. "Were you able to get Calypso to the Alliance?"

"No, she was taken by Lamia Brafa to Virulia. Apparently there's a secret settlement for Seekers that only Jumpers know where to find. The rest is classified, but the op was struck, so no one but me and now you knows about it," he winked. "Don't worry about Sunny. He'll be back before you know it, and I look forward to seeing what you can do with a las-sword after you're finished training."

"I am not training with a las-sword," Helga quickly objected, but caught herself early before he found a way to expose what it was she hid from him.

"I know," he said, smiling, tapping a finger to his forehead. "I just don't want you to worry about Sundown. He survived a year on Sanctuary all by himself, and while he's no Lamia, his skill is amazing. Just put it out of your mind and he will be back with us, quicker than you think. Now, I've held you long enough. Just remember that I'm here if there's anything you'd like to share. Are you off to the galley?"

"Off to medbay to see the good doctor," Helga said.

"Anything I should be concerned about?" Cilas looked visibly pale, and Helga picked up on his concern and what he was suggesting.

"No," she said a bit loudly. "I mean, no, no, this is social. I'm healthy, and there's no need for speculation where that is concerned."

"Oh, well, do enjoy your visit then," he said. Helga wanted to strangle him. Cilas Mec in the span of five awkward minutes had managed to unravel every ounce of confidence she had gained from the earlier training. Now she would be dwelling on whether or not he had known she was a Seeker this entire time, and was giving her an in to tell him.

"Commander," she announced, touching her heart before turning to beat a quick exit from the CIC section of the bridge. She thought about everything he had said to her, and though it should have made her frightened, she smiled with some relief. She wondered at the truth of the Calypso Rein story. It wasn't like Cilas to share that sort of detail about a past, failed assignment. It could have been his way to tell her that if he knew, he would choose her over duty and the Alliance.

With each step she grew happier, not for the talk per se, but for the support the Nighthawks had for each other. This wasn't a team; it was more than that, and in acknowledging this it made her heart full, for this was what she'd always wanted from the Alliance.

"Dr. Rai'to," she called upon entering the medbay, forcing Cleia Rai'to to quickly pause a holo-entry that she had been recording.

"At this rate, I am never going to get my dissertation done," she grumbled.

"Sure you will, Doc, I believe in you," Helga encouraged, hopping up onto one of the cots and playfully kicking her legs. "What're you doing?" she said.

"Working on a paper about the undiscovered lifeforms that exist on our most accessible moons," Cleia said. "It's just unfortunate that the war and the general fear of the Geralos has effectively stunted research galaxy-wide, and it is my belief that scientists accompanying units like this one are the key to jump-starting our education."

Helga recalled all the vicious fauna that she'd had run-ins with in the past. "Can't say I've met anything worth studying on the moons that I've been on. They're all *thyping* animals with a one-dimensional thought: eat humans, take a *schtill*, and multiply astronomically so that even more humans can be devoured. The same goes for the Geralos, those *thyping* monsters. What would we learn from anything like that? The dredge, brovila, those flying blood-sucking things on Meluvia, not to mention the bugs last mission. Uh, why don't you write about something positive like a half-Vestalian, half-Traxian baby?"

"We agreed that you would never bring up that subject again, Helga Ate," Cleia scolded her.

"I'm sorry, Cleia, I forgot," Helga lied, winning her a cutting eye from the already flustered Traxian. She whipped the tentacle-like ma'lesc that at a distance resembled hair, and as they settled on her shoulders, she took a deep breath and resumed her work.

"I do wish we had brought back a sample of those creatures you fought on Argan-10," Cleia said, as she puzzled over a slide with one hand on her hip, the other holding a mug.

"Szilocs," Helga said, smiling, amused by her ignorance of what they went through on the surface. "Getting samples would have made sense if we weren't being swarmed and running for our lives."

"Oh," she said, turning to Helga, her freckled blue skin becoming lighter. "I wasn't presuming anything of your mission, Helga. And..." She paused, seeming to grow more flustered. "Ray told me nothing about that moon, only that there were 'bugs as large as a man.' He said there were hundreds of them. Nothing about being chased or being in danger—Does he think I cannot handle hearing the truth?"

Oh, thype I've flown into it now, Helga thought, annoyed with herself for not playing dumb. *Now she's going to light into Ray, and I will hear about it, blamed for the fussing he's going to get later on. How do I walk this back?* "Cleia, we are Nighthawks, who are reminded that every mission is classified, even to fellow crew members. Raileo cares about you, but he took the same oath I did, and knowing you, he likely didn't trust himself to only give you partial information."

The Traxian studied Helga's face for a time before returning to her hologram, as if arguing was hopeless. "You always protect him." She sighed. "Even from me. You think that I will confront him. It may surprise you, but I never planned to bring it up. This is between the two of us, just women talking, off-the-record as you like to say. Arguing with Raileo would be me trying to change him, and that isn't my aim. I am just surprised and disappointed. You told me about the Geralos mutant, so why not the Szilocs as well?"

"If he's anything like me, he would have forced himself to forget that nightmare as soon as we boarded the *Thundercat*. They were disgusting, rabid spider monsters, and they put us all to a test that we were barely ready for," Helga admitted. "Couldn't you have pulled samples and DNA from our PAS suits?"

Cleia Rai'to shook her head slowly. "Yes, had I known that you fought a creature native to that moon. My mind was on Geralos, because that is what you all told me that you encountered."

Helga rubbed at her chin as she observed the smaller woman. "'I wonder how you'd fare in the field, grabbing your samples and patching us up?"

"You think me braver that I am," Cleia demurred, her skin flushing powdery blue. "I appreciate the confidence, but I am no adventurer. I am a scientist first, and then doctor. If I am ever in this so-called field, it will be in the aftermath, not before. I intend to live a long life, adding to the Alliance's knowledge base and traveling around the galaxy."

"Based on your species, you'll outlive all of us anyway," Helga offered, but immediately regretted it when the doctor's skin took on a deeper shade.

"That isn't funny," Cleia said. "I don't like to joke about that. I am here by myself, with no other Traxian. Everyone else is human. My twilight years will see me alone with all of my friends dead and gone."

"Okay, bad joke," Helga said. "But I have to admit, I'm surprised. It's not my call to approve you to follow us on drops, but even if it was, I would think you would jump at the chance to see a new moon and all the creatures on its surface and below."

"Of course I would, but then I would come to my senses and decline." Cleia sighed, her large, black eyes widening at the concept. "I do like that you thought of me, Lieutenant, and hope that you think of me when you're out there. You should remember to grab me samples from wherever you travel next."

"I will remember," Helga assured her. "The next thing new that tries to consume me, I will put a hole in its skull and collect some of the gray matter for your beaker."

"Now you're just being cruel," the doctor protested, though her smile betrayed her attempt at feigning offense.

A buzz sounded in her ear and Helga groaned, knowing what it was without having to answer. "Duty calls, Cleia. I'll leave you to whatever that complicated blob of glyphs and characters are that you seem obsessed with. Oh, we have a full crew now. Are you excited about getting them into your database for health check-ups and all that doctory business?" She stuck out her tongue as she made to exit.

"Already done," Cleia took a momentary pause to get the last word in. "The benefit of being on a starship is that they all had to go through steps before coming on board. One of those steps happened to be a conference with me, where I got to prod them with needles and verify their medical history. All of those little annoyances that you love. Oh, and before I forget, Lieutenant, you are due a check-up, and I've been looking through your psych—"

"*Thype*, but you're relentless," Helga said, stopping at the door to regard her. The doctor met her gaze bravely, exhibiting a confidence that hadn't been there when the women first met. She was practically gloating, relishing the power she had over the Lieutenant, her tilted smile becoming a wide grin, cute but predatory, a description that could be applied to any Traxian due to their elongated eye-teeth. Cleia Rai'to hurting anyone was a stretch, however, even for Helga's vivid imagination.

"When I come for that checkup, you better have some of that tea of yours brewing," Helga said.

"I always do, don't I?" Cleia winked, and with that, Helga waved, and was out the door.

10

Slipping through a three-dimensional wormhole at Faster-than-light, a phenomenon known as "jumping," the *Ursula* emerged in a region of Genesian space. Slowing to supercruise speed to allow the crystal-core generator to go into standby and cool itself, the blast shields lifted, and cheers went up throughout the vessel.

Ina Reysor looked over at Helga, but the Nighthawk was busy, studying a miniature starmap. On it was a patchwork of stations, scattered about the space, each holding a colony of workers living out their terms with their families. Traveling back and forth to the planet were a number of merchant vessels, some being shuttles carrying temps to work a season on the stations. Needless to say, the place was busy, and patrols were everywhere, keeping the shuttles guarded from Geralos invaders and the occasional pirate.

"This is madness," Helga complained to Ina, who had removed her restraints to lean over far enough to examine the details of the hologram.

"What are you seeing?" Ina asked.

"On the far side of the station ring, here." Helga increased the size of the starmap to point to a region near the edge. "Those flashing lights, I recognize them. It's a poor man's cloak. Something is onto us. Must've seen the rupture signal when we came out of FTL. *Uh!* This is unlucky, generator's cooling, and we barely have the power to maintain supercruise let alone juggle shields and impact power."

"Incoming hail from unknown vessel," the system announced, and before Helga could ask, Cilas was speaking into her earpiece, telling her to patch it in.

The voice of a male Genesian came over the intercom in a language Helga couldn't understand. Once he had finished speaking, *Ursula's* system translated his words, mimicking his voice close enough to have it sound as if he repeated his demand in the universal tongue. "Captain of the corvette, drop your thrusts, we will not hurt your crew, all we seek is your cargo. Allow us to board and take what we want, and you can leave unharmed with your ship."

"Is he serious?" Ina mouthed to Helga. "Do they not recognize that this is an Alliance warship?"

"All hands on deck," Cilas shouted, rising to his feet with his hands still gripping the arms of his captain's chair. "Apply full thrust and evasion maneuvers until I say differently. Get us out of this region and near that cluster of stations. Communications, hail the Genesian guard and let them know that we are here. I want an update of our status sent to Alliance command, and if there's any Navy in the region, I want to know about it."

Ina sat up in her chair, pulled on her restraints, and switched the controls into manual mode, which caused her chair to rise up and shift forward as she gripped the yoke and placed her feet up on the console. While she moved to outrun their ignorant pirate, Helga surveyed the starmap and selected a destination, which was close enough to a station to dissuade any violent action.

A thought came and went. They were running, and Cilas wasn't the type to run from anything. No matter the loadout that pirate vessel had, it wouldn't have the ordnance necessary to break their shields. Cilas could have simply ordered weapons online, and have them trace it into ribbons, eating whatever they threw back, knowing it was futile. But he had told them to run, to flee a weaker enemy, and he would have only done that if they were not allowed to engage.

"Commander, are we disallowed from fighting in this region?" Helga asked through private comms.

"You guessed it, but not for the reasons you're thinking. Things are complicated here politically, and potentially volatile if we fire first on a vessel, pirate or not. Until they initiate violence, hold your fire, and let's see if they'll chase us to the station."

"Not wise," the pirate countered, openly showing his frustration at their noncompliance.

"Not wise he says," Helga heard one of the crew members mockingly announce.

"Stow the chatter, it's all hands," she reminded him. "Keep your peepers on those readouts and your heads in the game."

An alarm went off, screeching three times, followed by warnings flooding the screens on the bridge. "Shields under duress," the system chirped.

"We have a tracer aimed at our port-side flank," Zan suddenly announced from the far side of Helga, who had almost forgotten the Cel-toc was there.

"Working on it," Ina shouted, taking the ship through a series of maneuvers to try and prevent the trace laser from focusing.

"They only have one tracer cannon, Commander," Helga informed Cilas. "And our shields are dropping rapidly. That tells me they've put all power into weapons. If we counter now, they won't have much to defend with."

Cilas stepped down from the raised platform where his chair was housed, and hopped down to the deck where he could easily access the cockpit. "What the heck is he flying?" Cilas said. "I can't make out anything up there. The *cruta* is using some sort of cloak that has our radars cracking and popping."

"Chief Weinstar is working on the issue, Captain," Zan said, her smooth, humanoid face looking the least bit concerned for the impending danger.

Helga showed him her hologram with the two blinking lights, but changed it to display simulated visuals, and the *Ursula's* computer constructed the ship. "It's a Louine cruiser, likely stolen and rigged. The ordnance is Alliance, that is our tracer, and the pew-shredders are pulled from a lizard's zip-ship. These pirates know their way around shipbuilding. Considering where we are, it wouldn't be a reach to say they hail from somewhere on one of these stations, or even the planet."

"Great, so if I clear weapons, we'd be firing on our allies. The reports to follow would get to the council, and it wouldn't be good for us," Cilas said. "Still, they're pushing it. What're shields at?"

"78%, now 77%, Commander," Zan replied, and Cilas looked up at the overhead and cursed silently.

"Come around and put our tracers on it," he finally said. "I want her crippled, not space dust. Am I clear?"

"Yes, Commander," the pilots said, and Helga found herself growing excited at the prospect of firing off the *Ursula's* row of tracers. Inhaling the air, she let it out slowly, and then touched an icon on the console to access the ship's intercom. "Engaging enemy warship, brace yourselves for a possible counter," she announced.

"Zan, bring tracers online, no change in power, reduce enemy shields, and target their engines. Disable her, expeditiously."

"Targeting enemy vessel," Zan announced mechanically. "Tracers active in 10, 9, 8…" She counted to zero, and through the port side windows of *Ursula*, the crew saw eight solid beams of light lock on to an invisible area, causing it to flash. Like a dying lightbulb, the pirate ship's failing shields could no longer sustain their invisibility, and they attempted to put on space brakes to distance themselves from the *Ursula's* cannons.

Now it was their turn to run, but they performed a maneuver to come about in an abrupt about-face, causing *Ursula* to shoot past her and allowing her space to try and beat an escape.

"Thrusters on her broadsides, of course," Ina complained. "If I was going to glue together my own little terror ship, I would have thrusters on my broadsides, wouldn't you, Helga?"

"On a ship that mass? No, it's ridiculous." Helga laughed. "Still, she's making us earn our pay here, so they get some sort of credit for that contraption."

Ina flew them after the cruiser, whose pilot was skilled, trying to stay in range long enough for the tracers to completely obliterate the shields. It was proving difficult due to the thruster situation. The pirate ship had the maneuverability of a fighter, and enough power to keep them chasing at a relatively harmless distance.

Helga thought about her Vestalian Classic waiting in the hangar, and how easy it would be to launch and pepper the cruiser's shields into nothingness before completing the job of disabling it. The problem with that plan, however, was that Cilas wouldn't go for it. The fighter was reserved for crucial situations where they had no choice but to have her risk her life. Speeding up the pursuit of a pirate would hardly qualify as crucial.

"Stay on it, I want that thing shut down," Cilas said from somewhere behind their chairs. Helga was surprised when she heard his voice, expecting him to have climbed back up to his captain's perch.

"Commander, the Genesian guard picked up our hails," announced Jun Sunchar, a Meluvian communication's officer who reminded Helga of Ina. "They would like a parlay."

"Thank you, Ms. Sunchar," Cilas said, straightening. "I will take it at my station."

Helga kept an eye on their power reserves, which were slowly building up as the engine recharged from their earlier jump. There was something else as well; it was charging faster than she'd ever seen it. Alon Weinstar was likely the reason, Helga allowed, since before him there hadn't been an engineer to bring *Ursula* up to her potential. "You've got enough for max thrust, Ida, just attempt to ram them. They will break to avoid collision, and open them up to our tracers easily."

Ina nodded and did as Helga instructed, diverting more power to the engine, until the system screeched a warning, "Attention. Collision imminent and unavoidable at our current velocity." As Helga predicted, the pirates changed course to avoid being struck, but instead of breaking left or to the right, they looped up and took off in the opposite direction.

"Arm energy cannons and target the thrusters directly," Cilas shouted. "Try to stay on her this time, Ms. Reysor. And keep firing until her engine ceases to function."

The pirates did what they could to avoid *Ursula*, whose onslaught had already disabled its shields. The energy cannons focused on the flank of the pirate vessel, ripping off sections of the thruster, eventually damaging the engine. Chunks of metal floated off in space, and the cruiser lagged, eventually losing all power and drifting helplessly along in space.

High-energy trace lasers reached across the gap to dance across the hull. Shields rippled like puddles during rainfall, as *Ursula* calculated that they were down to 20%. It was an energy race, and the pirates were losing, and the calibrations to those cannons made by Alon Weinstar during those first cycles were proved to be worth it.

"Enemy shields have been depleted," Zan reported. "Energy cannons locked on target's rear thrusters. Estimated energy cost, 3%. Permission to fire."

"Permission granted," Helga said, leaning forward to peer past her controls out the window to where the enemy vessel was trying hard to avoid them. "Someone seems frightened all of a sudden, after speaking so tough about letting them rob us. Maybe next time they assess their target?"

"Wouldn't have done much good. we look like a luxury skiff from the exterior," Ina said. "And these are pirates; likely criminals, the lot of them. This would be the first and last time they see a wartime corvette. Even ex-Alliance would have assumed we were soft. These vessels were meant for scout operations, not playing the scrapper like we're doing now."

"Captain Sho would be happy his newborn vessel's a success," Helga said. "Top marks for deception since they attacked us, expecting us to surrender, and top marks for the new cannons. Made short work of those shields, it doesn't even seem fair, and fresh after a jump working energy reserves."

"Enemy ship successfully disabled," Zan announced flatly.

"Good shooting, *Ursula*," Cilas said. "The Genesian guard has asked us to leave and make our way towards that cluster of stations. They will board that cruiser and make some arrests while we dock and make contact with the local Alliance presence."

"Welcome to Genese," Ina said. "We come into that, and we're supposed to hang about out here waiting?"

"Yeah, that was some welcome," Helga admitted before Ina raised a finger to ask her to hold while she received a message through her comms.

"That was the commander. We're to find a Neroka Station to dock," Ina said.

On approach from the *Ursula's* vantage point, Neroka Station appeared as a short cylindrical tube rotating around an invisible axis point with four other tubes of the same design. In the center of this formation was a nest of trade ships transporting goods back and forth, a wheel of sorts, or "belt" reminding the Nighthawks of Sanctuary Station. But where Sanctuary was one massive station, these were all separate hubs owned by powerful, private conglomerates, each having its own name and purpose.

The exterior for the most part consisted of gray metal paneling, broken up only by lights, transparent, cloud-filled glass, and a smooth metal strip where the name of each station stood out in bright white Genesian glyphs. This made Neroka easy enough to find among the numerous stations that formed the belt. Ina took them in through central traffic, taking the scenic route around towards the interior of the ring.

Once they had located Neroka, she brought them to the entrance of the station's tube, where there was even more activity from traveling ships. As they came in closer, Helga could see that there were miniature cities obscured by the clouds, visible on each tube's inner face. There was a clutch of engineers in colorful EXO suits tethered to the exterior glass of these cylindrical juggernauts, running maintenance and repairs.

Flying through it felt surreal, with the artificial clouds printed on the glass just above the rooftops of the buildings. She imagined that inside it would look and feel much like a planet, creating a convincing home for the families living within these colonies. She could see open plains, lakes, and mountains, amid a patchwork of smoky, industrial plazas and residential buildings.

There were even aircraft visible through the endless glass and its artificial clouds. Transports on highways, hospitals, schools, offices; despite Genese being a massive planet, they had found a solution for extending life past its atmosphere. With a roll and a turn, they were heading for the only entry into the station. It appeared as a gap inside the glass of clouds, easy to miss but for the dancing lights on the rim.

Four smaller vessels flew out to scan them, drones checking for contraband and weapons. *Ursula*, being a warship already cleared by the Genesian Guard, would be allowed in despite their arsenal. Knives were allowed, but ballistics and laser poppers were a surefire way to earn a discharge from breaking this agreement. Cilas reiterated this to the crew over the intercom, reading the Alliance's docking agreement plainly for all to hear.

Inside, *Ursula* roared like a titan as they rocketed past a cruiser twisted and leveled with the rotating ground. The skies about them were littered with industry, all manner of craft going about their daily routines. They reached the port, which could be described as a long silver saucer wedged into the side of a sunken building. Ina flew about it once to get a lay of the land then brought them down next to a row of smaller vessels.

The physics defied Helga, who expected a disaster when *Ursula's* feet touched the metal surface of that precarious platform. It should have collapsed under the weight but when it didn't she accepted that this was technology leveraging gravity and boosters. Engines were cut, lights came on, and a collective sigh could be felt from everyone who had been glued to their seats, staring out the windows.

Zan's voice came over the intercom, "Welcome to Neroka, Nighthawks and *Ursula* crew. Landing gear has been deployed and the engines are cooling, so you are now free to move about the vessel."

"Impressive flying, Reysor," Helga said, complimenting Ina's coolness throughout the chase, approach, and manual control that had brought them here. Before this assignment she had been worried that whoever they got for a pilot would be mediocre, but Ina gave her confidence. *Ursula* was in good hands, and acknowledging this removed the weight from her shoulders, though it still felt strange not being the one responsible for bringing them in.

"Thanks, lady." Ina reached over and squeezed her forearm. "I don't hear anyone vomiting their guts out, so I figured I did something right."

Helga sighed. "Another day, another port. I wonder what this one will yield? Wealthy aristocrats with only an abstract knowledge of the war, or more starving children thinking that we're Alliance saviors come to whisk them away."

"If this was your standard satellite fuel stop, I would be prone to agree with you there," Ina objected. "You saw what this was on our flyover. It's not really a station, it's more of a manufactured planet. The people who live here, or I should say, those born here, wouldn't like us referring to their 'world' as a port. It's so much more to them, and the attitudes here are bound to reflect that. This is Genese after all, the iron planet. They aren't hurting for resources."

So, it will be clueless aristocrats playing political credit games with no concern for the war then, Helga thought. "You're right, and I don't mean to leak air with my doom talk. It's just that I've been to so many ports now, and they're starting to feel the same despite the difference in planets, constructs, and people. All that aside, I wonder why we're here, really."

11

Soft music played from somewhere off in the background, and the air smelled of spices, food prepared with familiar seasonings. Fio Doro opened her eyes, expecting to be inside her apartment in the Basce City tenements. The music and scents she assumed came from a vendor downstairs peddling his wares, and, smelling and hearing it now, from her having left a window cracked from last night.

What she awoke to, however, was the aftermath of what she hoped had been only a nightmare. Losing Djesu to gunshots, nearly dying herself, and running into an ex-girlfriend who convinced her to board a shuttle to leave the planet for one of the stations. As her bloodshot eyes worked against the violation of the light, the memories rushed in like a flood, having battered a dam to the point of rupturing.

She remembered the trip, being seated amongst a crowd of travelers, telling her story in hushed tones to Zulia. It was all she could do to keep her emotions in check then, and she had been too tired and hurt to think clearly enough of skipping the incriminating parts. Once docked, the disembarking was a blur, but she recalled taking a taxi, where again they were stuffed inside the vessel with a clutch of other strangers, loud with their chatter and impatient.

The rest was fuzzy, and the only thing she could assume was that she had crashed upon reaching Zulia's station compartment. There had been an elevator and a lot of identical doors, but they had entered one near the end of a hallway, and that was all she could recall before waking up to the music and delicious scents. It felt strange here on the station, different, quiet but for the music whose volume was low and seemed to come from a vid-screen on the wall that Zulia left playing.

She lifted the sheets to find that she was naked, with freshly wrapped bandages over her wounds, and a note on the pillow next to hers, which read, "Gone to work until this evening. Left you some breakfast, but the food processor is stocked so help yourself."

Fio sat up, wincing from a sharp pain in her shoulder, surveyed the apartment and its decor, and found that it was all pleasantly cozy. For a station rental it was much bigger than her old apartment. The furniture was curious, their design like nothing she'd ever seen in the city, and it made her wonder if they were expensive. Zulia had always been one for luxury, but she didn't think a station job paid so well.

For instance, the cot on which she laid on seemed to grow from out of the floor tiles, like a raised basin of sweet-smelling cushions, and a mattress filled with pillows, soft as clouds. Above her hung a decorative light-fixture, suspended from thin metal poles attached to the ceiling. Wrapped about these poles high above her was a moisture system, comprised of thick metal pipes. These were a strange design choice, according to Fio, giving the apartment the feeling of living on a ship.

The compartment was a two-room shelter intended for temporary employees of the station. Nothing she was seeing made her feel this was temporary, however, and it made her wonder whether Zulia's job was a trial for her to eventually become a permanent resident here. It was all so luxurious compared to even the nicer flats in Basce City, and Fio felt foolish for the many times she'd turn Zulia down when she'd suggested she give up crime to come seek work on one of these stations.

Stretching lazily—which hurt—she threw her legs off the side of the cot, tried to stand and nearly leapt back onto the mattress due to the floor's sudden movement. While they appeared as solid tiles, the floor depressed beneath her feet with every step. It felt like she was walking on plaster, but with each step, she grew accustomed to it, and after a while it began to feel pleasant.

The more she looked about the apartment, the more it dawned on her that nothing of what she knew of Basce City would speed her adjustment here. First she explored the two rooms thoroughly, examining all of the strange appliances and the overall decor of the place. The room she awoke in was the central living space, being one part bedroom and one part kitchen, complete with a food processing unit, storage freezer, and a counter with a raised sink.

The adjacent space was a bathroom, with a standing shower, and a bio-extractor for all manner of waste. Zulia had it all decorated nicely, which didn't surprise Fio in the least. All walls were painted in shades of blue, with tiny, detailed bubbles near the sink, and a detailed nebula on the longest wall that happened to have the vid-screen.

Everything had its place, and Fio made a mental note to replace whatever she used while staying here. Zulia had gone out of her way to rescue her and since she was now broke, the least she could do was to remain extremely low maintenance for her friend. Station life was still a foreign concept, but she would take it a day at a time, healing, while picking up on the local culture until she found a place to fit in.

As far as she was concerned, she had two objectives, which were to find justice for Djesu's murder, and amass enough credits to repay Zulia for her rescue, accommodations, and the trip. Fio didn't plan on doing this through waitressing, but before bending any laws, she would need to learn about the station's security. She washed her face and played with the digital mirror, trying out the virtual dressing room, which outfitted her reflection in clothes that could then be ordered through a courier system.

Thirty minutes of doing this, and Fio's hunger overtook her curiosity. The breakfast left by Zulia was a cluster of sticky white pellets, covered in a chunky, brown sauce, none of which she recognized. Taking a spoonful, she found herself closing her eyes to savor the taste and texture. It was rich with spices and tasted amazing, one of the best meals she'd eaten in months, and just enough of it to sate her appetite.

Glancing at the clock to estimate how long she would have to wait for Zulia to arrive, Fio was disappointed to find the readout to be the Alliance Naval variant, which she couldn't decipher. Remembering her communicator, she went back to the bed to recover her clothes from last night. "Oh," she recalled, rubbing at the wound on her chest, flinching from the tenderness. "They *thyping* shot it, didn't they? And then we tossed it with everything I wore."

The song playing on the vid-screen clicked off, replaced by a menu of entertainment choices. Fio thought about taking advantage of this, just to pass the time. She was still in pain, and likely wanted for questioning by BasPol, who if thorough, would have considered that she had used the shuttle to escape the city. Going out now would not be a wise move by any stretch, but there was something about the forced solitude that made her desperately want to escape.

Fio knew it was irrational and absurd. Zulia's home was nothing like the Basce City Brick or living with Djesu as a child, where she wasn't allowed to leave the house. A sudden noise at the door put her heart in her throat, three knocks in succession, each of them heavier, followed by a hushed set of voices, and then someone was trying to force themselves in.

"Hey Zulia, open the door, it's Kline. I have something I need to tell you," one of them said. "You're really going to want to hear what I have to say, it's important. Open up, will you?" Fio looked around for her gun, tensing when she remembered it tucked in the jacket that Zulia had thrown out with the rest of her clothing.

The man kept trying to get into the apartment, and Fio retreated to the kitchen, hoping to find a knife or something else sharp. No having much luck with her searching, she hid behind the large food processing unit. Eventually the door slid open, and she heard multiple footsteps violating the space. "Oh, this is nice," she heard another man say. "Looks like Zul has been holding out on us, eh?"

"Yeah, she put a lot of credits into this nest. If we can grab the runt without damaging anything, that would be better for everyone," the first man said.

"So, frying her lock and pulling the door out doesn't count as damaging?" the other man said.

"You're really about to sass me, Ethan?" the first man said. "How about we find the girl, eh? Think you can handle that part at least? Hey, I know you're in here, girly. I see the blood on the bed. You can make this go a lot easier for yourself. Just come out and we won't hurt you. You know what you did. A man is dead. Make this difficult, and you'll regret it. Do you hear me, little girl? Now is the time to come out here. We won't even cuff you, I swear. You can walk out on your own."

Fio rolled her eyes at the threats and watched the floor near the food-processing unit to assess how close they were to where she hid. The two men had gone deathly quiet, and she assumed they now were communicating with gestures as they searched the apartment. She allowed herself a moment to process the information regarding these men. Whoever they were, they knew Zulia, but hadn't gotten her permission to enter the apartment.

They did, however, know she was inside, which could have been for any number of reasons, including Zulia not being too discreet when she brought her here. The man had mentioned someone dying, but why? Was she accused of murder now, and of whom, Djesu? Were these men looking to claim a reward of some sort? That's the only thing that seemed to make sense.

A reward would have come from Vray, looking to punish her for botching the job and allowing his luggage and documents to be destroyed. Perhaps she was merely a loose end, and he was protecting himself by having her assassinated. BasPol officers did double as bounty hunters during their off hours, and if the bounty was high, it wasn't unrealistic to assume they'd hire local thugs to detain one of the accused from the station.

She felt the dip in the floor before the man's face emerged. A pale, bald-headed Genesian, dressed in black tactical gear. He smiled at her evilly and then reached for her arm, but Fio stepped back, and threw herself at him, raking her nails across his face. Having fought larger men throughout her short career as a Basce City smuggler, Fio knew there was but one sure way to win, and that was to draw first blood and debilitate him, freeing his weapon to arm herself.

If he recovered quickly from what she had done, his strength would overpower her, or he could draw on her, and she would have no choice but to surrender. She had the element of surprise, but fighting was never a sport for thinkers; it was muscle memory. When she swiped his face, she made herself small by ducking into his abdomen. He had a gun on his hip and a knife in his boot, so Fio unclipped the pistol, pulled, and jumped back from him.

This all happened in a manner of seconds before she had the handgun pointed at his bleeding face. "Hold up now, don't be stupid," he said, and Fio felt the floor depress from the other side of the food processor, as the man's partner moved to flank her position. She aimed at the first man's leg and pulled the trigger, the kinetic round burning through the light-weave armor, searing flesh, muscle, bone, to wedge itself into the floor beneath them.

The other man grabbed her from behind before she could turn and aim the gun at him. She knew her chances were gone now, what could she do? His powerful arms were wrapped around her, and her feet were dangling, but she held on to the gun, knowing it was her last option to escape. "Feisty little *cruta*," he whispered into her ear. "Knew you were a murderer, but they never said you were trained, or we would've just shot you and been done with it. How's the leg, Ethan?"

"Better than my face," the other man said. He was reclined on the floor with the one leg bleeding, and a disconcerting calmness to his face.

Fio kicked and tried to aim the gun at him, but the man behind her slammed her into the wall, and then into something else, but she was too dazed to notice what it was. Blood trickled into her eye, temporarily blinding her, but she felt the gun still in her grip where she still held it. The large man placed a boot into her abdomen, but she summoned the strength to fire again, and fire once more from the floor, clipping his leg.

Unlike Ethan, this man screamed in agony from where the bullet nicked his shin. Fio fired once more, striking him near the groin where he fell, and this time he really bellowed, making her want to cover her ears. Spitting out blood and surprising even herself with the strength to stand after the beating she had taken, Fio limped over to the screamer and aimed the gun down at his head.

"You," she said, looking at the other man, "you're going to answer my questions, or I'm going to shoot your friend." The man laughed hysterically, possibly from the blood loss, but Fio wasn't in the mood to hear laughter in that moment. "Alright, he dies then—"

"Fio," Zulia screamed from the doorway, rushing in. "Daren and Ethan." She put a hand to her mouth and screamed when she saw the state of her apartment. "What is going on?"

"These two forced themselves inside here and attacked me, so I took their gun and shot them," Fio said, still waving the weapon at her whimpering victim. "Hold that thought, Zulia. Let me get us some answers." She sat heavily down on the chest of the man and tapped his lips with the muzzle until he opened his mouth for her to push it in. "You," she said, again looking to the man by the food processor. "Who hired you to find me, and for how much? Answer the questions. We don't have all day.".

"Garson Sunveil, from Basce City," the man answered slowly. "He offered us, 1,000 credits each. Thought it was easy money, but now I'm starting to think we got played."

Fio hadn't noticed before, but the two men bore a resemblance, as if they were twins.

"You came to murder me for 1,000 credits." Fio couldn't believe it. The sum was insulting. "Is that all my life is worth in your view, a measly 1,000 credits?

"No, 1,000 credits for your capture. If we wanted to murder you, we would have handled this much differently." He laughed, but Fio couldn't find any humor in their predicament.

"And you knew she was here, how?" Zulia said, stomping over to where he lay, her hands on her hip, and her neck thrust out with rage as she stared down at him.

"Daren said you'd understand, since the girl was wanted. Said if we didn't mess up the place, you would fuss, yes, but you'd understand why we had to do it. I should be the one asking you why you know this fugitive," Ethan said.

"Same old Ethan, thick as *schtill*," Zulia spat. "I'm calling your superiors to report this. Maybe I can get some sort of compensation. You can't just break into people's living space ... oh my, I bet the neighbors heard all the gunshots. I'm sorry, Fio, but I can't do this with the violence. You were supposed to just take it easy here. This. I could end up losing my job over this. Two security officers shot inside my apartment, ha. I'll never make permanent. I'll be lucky if I don't end up arrested."

Fio was incensed. "Arrested for knowing me, you mean? I could have died, but thanks, *cruta*, I will be okay. They broke your door down to attack me with guns, but you're worried about your work and your compartment. I never asked you to bring me here, Zulia. But thanks for reminding me who you really are. Please, do call their overseers. Aside from defending myself, I've committed no crimes, so really, it's okay."

She pointed at Ethan with her free hand to get his attention. "Hey you, idiot, yeah you. Why does Garson have a bounty on my head?"

"Bounty?" Zulia stopped fidgeting with her communicator to look over at Fio with her mouth agape. "You mean to tell me this is a freelance thing, and you aren't here officially?"

"That's right," Ethan said, "and we would appreciate it if you would calm down and don't make moves you'll later regret."

"You don't threaten her," Fio growled at him. "Now, answer the question I asked you. Why does Garson Sunveil have a bounty on my head?"

"Says you shot and killed a man named Djesu."

"Oh yeah?" Fio said, hardly believing what she was hearing.

"Yeah, says you robbed him of some documents, then got on a space shuttle and made your way here," Ethan admitted. "He called you an enemy of the Alliance. Sounded serious."

"The Alliance," Fio repeated, remembering the sordid details gleaned from the documents. "Garson Sunveil, the supposed Alliance recruiter hired you to kill me for having shot Djesu, the closest thing I had to family? Is that right?" She noticed the man below her stopped squirming, so she placed a finger beneath his nostrils to confirm that he was still breathing. "You call them yet?" she shouted at Zulia, who looked whipped and defeated from the ordeal. The woman shook her head in the negative.

"Well, since you all seem to know each other, I will leave you to it. When I'm safe and back on my feet, I will repay your kindness," she told Zulia, pushing herself up off the unconscious man to hover over him drunkenly, tempted to kick him the way he had done her. The anger won out, and she booted him, but it hurt her more than she thought it would, and she recoiled, wincing from all the pain.

"I was rash and I apologize, Fio," Zulia tried, and as much as she wanted to tell her where to shove it, Fio knew she wouldn't make it far walking if she left in her current condition. "I know a Marine with the defensive force here on the station. The Alliance would never send bounty hunters, especially ones that are as bad as these two. You could talk to him, Fio. Maybe he can look into this Garson Sunveil to see whether or not this is personal."

"It's personal for me," Fio said, sitting down heavily on the bed. "But yeah, call your friend. I have some things to run by him, and if it's as crucial as I think, then maybe something good can come of all this."

12

A crystal-clear expanse of water ran below the landing platform on which the *Ursula* perched, stretching out on either side as far as the eye could see. It was a wet, narrow spine, splitting emerald, green grasslands, peppered with trees and squat buildings. Like the Alliance HQ Sanctuary, it was a marvel of Genesian engineering, from the spans of factories producing algae to aeroponic greenhouses where vegetables and grains grew in abundance.

Helga turned one way and then the other, trying to find the curve of the station's cylindrical shape that would violate this spectacle. There seemed to be a brightness to the sky that concealed anything beyond the artificial clouds, sunlight and reinforced glass.

The scenery was breathtaking, and the people were just as colorful as the landscape. For the wealthy and powerful, long robes were the style of the day, bright-colored frocks fringed with gold and resplendent in gems. The dockworkers uniform was just as flamboyant, all sporting orange coveralls with yellow boots and hip packs. These brightly colored hustlers darted about the landing platform, fueling vessels, transporting cargo, and playing guide to their visitors.

After landing and going through the standard security protocol, Cilas had given them leave to disembark, but none were to go beyond the starport. Most of the crew stayed onboard carrying out their duties despite them being grounded. Nighthawks, as was the standard for stations, went shopping for supplies and munitions. Dr. Cleia Rai'to enlisted Raileo to help her grab medical supplies and additional equipment for medbay.

Ina Reysor remained on board, having had her fill of stations as a merchant ship's captain prior to the *Ursula* consignment, so Helga had taken the opportunity to stretch her legs. *Rendron* rules and to some degree the Alliance Navy, required a warship to always have an officer on the bridge. Ina wasn't a Nighthawk, but she was a former *Aqnaqak* lieutenant. With her taking the job, she had regained her rank and status, so she was more than qualified to stand in.

Two loud jets, Spitfires—what Alliance pilots dubbed "zip-ships"— flew low over *Ursula*, performing a series of stunts before vanishing into the cloudy atmosphere. Helga watched them go, lifting a hand to shield her face against the brilliance of the artificial sun.

Oh, to be just a pilot again, she thought, recalling Raileo zipping about Nero deck in his PAS, and these two reckless pilots, flying freely in this safe sandbox of an environment. Command had its perks, that went without saying, but sometimes she just wanted to jump into her Classic and fly. Since becoming a Nighthawk, she had flown just about every class of ship, short of a destroyer. She had done surface drops countless times, had dogfights above Meluvia, Sanctuary, and Argan-10.

Space-based combat came quick and often, but for some reason, it just did not scratch the itch. What she wanted was to experience flight without barriers. No rules, no duty, no responsibilities. She had thought that being back on *Rendron* would have given her the time to do this, but their six months of waiting didn't include access to her Classic. Like the *R60 Thundercat*, Helga's fighter had been parked inside *Ursula's* hangar and inaccessible during the refit.

Simulations, while a convincing replacement for actual flight, could be interrupted by someone or something needing her attention, so even they couldn't give her peace. Helga sighed heavily, remembering her promise to never complain about rank or success. She had attained both as an operator and officer, and even being here now inhaling the crisp oxygen of the station was a testament to that.

Turning away from the precipice of the landing platform, she walked below *Ursula's* belly to the far side where several crew members were speaking to the local dock hands.

"Everything going alright here, Chief?" she said to the wide back of Chief Mas-Umbra, who was in the middle of a lively discussion with a Genesian woman and a crowd of dock hands. They didn't seem to be arguing but their voices were raised, but that could have been due to *Ursula's* engines making it difficult to hear.

"Everything is great," the big man answered, turning to salute her, along with the other rates.

The Genesians seemed taken with Helga's appearance, something she'd expected so it didn't bother her as much as it normally did. She wore her dress blacks, with a blue beret sitting tilted with *Ursula's* "AWS" symbol embroidered in gold thread. The hat was a gift from Captain Retzo Sho as a show of appreciation for her service. Every Nighthawk was gifted one, but only she and Raileo chose to wear theirs.

"Getting some local recipes, Chief?" she teased him, waving casually at his guests, who stopped their gawking long enough to return the greeting.

"Learning about the station, Lieutenant. It's crazy how much they have going on here," Mas-Umbra explained. "Those farms you see out there produce enough insect-based protein to feed a tenth of the planet. Looking to get a crate of it for *Ursula*, and cans of dried fish from the fisheries down there." He waved an arm towards the opposite side of the lake from where Helga had been observing, and she saw row upon row of vegetation, some sections separated by tall metal fixtures, and greenhouses built of transparent glass.

"So that's what those are," Helga mused. "Fisheries. That would explain all the water, and factories everywhere."

"I think the good doctor will enjoy what I have in store for the upcoming cycles," Mas-Umbra whispered, inching in closer as if to share a secret. "Traxis stuffed dumplings, mock Surlem spores, and rice. It's a Traxis delicacy that I learned back on *Missio-Tral*. One of my bros from the galley was a Traxian, taught me how to make it. Just wait. She's going to flip."

"I don't know what any of that is, Chief, but knowing your talents, I expect it to be delicious," Helga said. "The prospect of Cleia flipping does have me intrigued, so when you do make it, let me know. I want to see her reaction myself."

She waved goodbye to him and made her way past the only other vessel on the platform, a boxy, merchant-class hauler, where four filthy-faced Genesian men scrubbed at her hull with long-handled brushes. All about the platform, dockworkers scurried to and fro, going about their duties. It reminded Helga of *Rendron's* hangar, which was always active with Cel-tocs and people tending to the ships.

At the far end past the ships were ten caged lifts meant for transporting people up and down to the starport's entry. Bordering them was a rail system connecting eight other platforms wrapped about the station, each with its own collection of docked ships. Helga hadn't noticed this until she saw the rail and followed it with her eyes, spying another platform off in the distance, closer to the water but much lower to the floor than theirs.

"Just heard from *Rendron*," Cilas announced from an ascending lift. "Looks like we'll be stationed at least another day. Captain Sho has asked me to meet with the local Alliance rep, Colonel Orlan Fumo. Spoke to him briefly, along with the captain, and the colonel requested a meeting to discuss something troubling. Earlier today, someone shared with him a frightening bit of intel. We might have a level three security breach."

"Level three." Helga chewed on her lip, trying to remember the top three levels of their leadership. "One's the council, two is at the admiral level, so that makes three a captain, or someone trusted with the helm of a class A warship. This is serious, Cilas. It could affect the *Rendron*—it could be the *Rendron*." It felt absurd to even consider it yet alone put the thought into words. "Do you get to meet him? The one with the intel, I mean, not the colonel."

"I get to meet her when I go to see the colonel, but I could use the company," Cilas urged. "Maybe with a woman there she will be more comfortable speaking."

"Maybe." Helga shrugged before falling in next to him. "This woman, they say anything else about her?"

"Just that she escaped here from the planet. Our talk was pretty short. Captain wanted to make the introduction and let me know personally that I was at the disposal of this colonel."

"Are we to protect her, transport her, or do something with the intel? I am struggling to see where a Nighthawk fits into this," Helga admitted.

"I can the codes, which the colonel wouldn't know, and with you along, you can verify the coordinates, and together we can see if this is a real threat. If it's real, I'll update the captain, then it will go up to the council, and they will handle it from there. If it's mutiny or a captain gone rogue, I don't know how they'd fix that. Probably send in another starship, but the point is they'd squash it immediately. We can't have leaks in the Alliance, but that isn't to say that some haven't tried."

"That we both know from personal experience," Helga said.

The lift descended through a glass tube past a layer of concrete that was the rooftop of the Neroka starport. Inside was a world of glass and metal, covered bridges crisscrossing on all sides of the lift as they made their slow descent. It was an ant nest of activity, with colorful bodies darting one way or another. Genesians moved so fast Helga had to wonder how it was that no-one tripped and fell.

"Not just a starport is it?" Helga looked up at Cilas, who seemed mesmerized by the splendor of the starport.

"Station like this, operating semi-independently from the planet. Real estate would be astronomical, so all of these companies will make the most of their space," Cilas said. "They put their hangar on the rooftops rather than have a big open field. This way, they could rent out the space inside. You see it all about us, and more where those bridges spanned up there. Over fifty different offices, including the Alliance's, all packed in this compact footprint."

The lift came to a stop and the doors slid open to a line of travel kiosks and a Cel-toc dressed in an officer's uniform, offering help to anyone who needed it. Helga and Cilas stepped onto a tiled floor which felt softer than it appeared. There were plants everywhere, sprouting up from square platforms that bordered the walkway leading from the lifts. The Nighthawks followed the signs to the Alliance recruitment station, adapting the quick stride of the Genesian residents.

It didn't take long for them to find it, a small corner compartment opposite a row of travel kiosks. Through the glass door and walls, Helga saw a man and a woman. The man was dressed like a Marine, but the woman was dressed in a tight blue skinsuit and a long white jacket with no rank or medals. Cilas pushed open the door and entered, and Helga followed him inside, surveying the place.

Behind the two occupants was a large desk with the flag of the Alliance above it, draped on the wall. Next to it were different models of spacecraft and miniature versions of the twelve major warships. Helga recognized *Rendron* and *Aqnaqak*, "the wayward lovers," and wished she had a replica of her own to mount in her cabin. The floor was painted in the Alliance's colors, red, black, and white circles, and across from the desk sat five empty chairs.

It was a cold, unfriendly place, which didn't particularly enthuse even a die-hard Alliance warfighter like Cilas Mec. *If this is what they use to recruit for the Navy, it would explain why we don't have many Genesians on the ship*, Helga wanted to say. Instead, she stood silently next to her commander as he clasped forearms with the older Marine, who she saluted when he acknowledged her.

"Welcome, Nighthawks. Welcome to Neroka, jewel of Genesian space. I heard you met some of the friendly locals out there." He pointed to the ceiling, which Helga took his meaning to be out in space.

"They weren't so friendly," Cilas said. "They reached for an easy prize and ended up cutting their hands on the blade."

"Sambe," Colonel Fumo roared, and Helga wished that Quentin was present to hear someone else use his favorite word. This wasn't the "sambe" he would utter when he agreed with something, but more of a "sambe" as in, "sambe, that's what they get for daring to threaten an Alliance warship." The office and colors were superficial, but standing before Helga was a true believer, the type of man who had fought his whole life and was rewarded for it with this office, which he likely took pride in running.

"And this is? Colonel?" Cilas inquired of the young woman who had been silently watching them.

The first thing that stuck out to Helga was just how young she was. When Cilas had told her about a local with information on a possible security breach, she envisioned a woman in her thirties, hardened from a life of crime, and likely dangerous. A woman like Domina from Sanctuary, a gangster in silk and lace, with the golden tongue and guile to match any street criminal's wit.

What she saw standing next to the man was a young woman, no older than she was. The difference between them could have spanned Anstractor's systems, however. She was small, slender, and she glared at Helga, grimacing, her lips a tight line beneath a mess of wet blue hair. She was dressed in a tight navy-colored skinsuit with a long white jacket smeared with blood. One hand caressed the triceps of the other arm, which hung limply to one side.

"These are the people I spoke about, Fio," Colonel Fumo informed her, and the young woman's demeanor softened.

"Fio Doro," she introduced herself, in a voice too big for her form. It was nearly commanding.

"I'm Commander Cilas Mec of the *Rendron*, Fio Doro," Cilas said, his face betraying the surprise he shared with Helga in hearing that husky voice. "This is Lieutenant Helga Ate. We heard you may have some information about the Alliance?"

"Oh my, a female spacer with a spice pirate's hair." Fio sing-songed her observation of Helga's undercut hairstyle and Casanian birthmarks. "What happened to the side of your head there, beautiful?"

"Is she serious?" Helga looked at the colonel, confused by the young woman's remarks. Both Cilas and Fumo remained silent, while Fio stood beaming at her as if she'd paid her the ultimate compliment. "I guess you haven't met many ESO's, have you?" Helga forced herself to soften. "Or spacers in general, for that matter. The haircut you can make fun of, but the marks are part of my heritage, so what happened was my birth. Blue hair a thing down on your planet, 'beautiful?'"

Fio grinned at Helga's barely veiled annoyance. "Nope, all me," she replied proudly, reaching up to tease it. "I wasn't trying to start a fight, sister. It's just that you're different from what we're told a spacer from the Alliance is supposed to look like."

"The Nighthawks do not have a lot of time," Fumo reminded her, and Fio stepped forward and took a breath.

"*Scythe*, system: Cyrus," she recited, mechanically, and followed it up with a series of coordinates whose pattern Helga knew to be the Louine system. It was a code she knew well from flying the Britz-SPZ as co-pilot to Casein Varnes on her first deployment to Dyn, a moon above Louine. Fio recited a few more vessels and coordinates as if they were a passage from a book she had memorized.

Helga saw Cilas's lips part in disbelief and his eyes grow wide until she was finished speaking. He either knew what she was reciting or knew the pattern, but whichever it was, her knowing it was a problem.

"Where did you learn this information?" he said, looking up at the colonel, who had an, "I told you so," smirk on his face.

Fio Doro exhaled heavily, made to cross her arms but thought better of it, a move that didn't go unnoticed by the Nighthawks. "Before I say anything else, I need guarantees," she said, straightening despite her obvious pain. "I only brought it to you because Djesu, I mean ... people have been hurt, killed, and now I'm being hunted here. What I want, need, is to get off this station, and away from Basce City. I don't care to where. You help me keep my life, I tell you everything I know."

"How about you tell us how you came by this intel, and we'll work out those logistics after?" Colonel Fumo urged. "You were involved in a shooting, Fio Doro. May I remind you that we're the only thing preventing you from being detained and deported on the next shuttle back to Basce City."

The young woman flinched at his words, and looked about the room as if she was plotting an escape. "You are all the same," she said under her breath, her eyes finding Helga's and holding the gaze with what she read as disappointment.

"You're desperate." Helga held her gaze. "But this isn't a negotiation over credits for your work. This is the commander giving you an audience to hear the valuable intelligence you have in your possession. Now, if things are as dire as they appear, judging from your wounds and the way you're barely drawing breath, you will need to trust us. If you thought we were untrustworthy then why even come here? Tell us your story and if we find that what you have poses an actual threat, the Alliance will want to get ahead of it, which means protecting you as an asset."

She said too much, at least that's how it felt from the silence that followed her speech to the young woman who still eyed her skeptically. "What are you?" Fio finally said, stepping forward to get a closer view of Helga's face. Despite her every instinct telling her to shove the blue-haired hellion back a pace, Helga entertained the study, assuming that wherever this woman had come from had somehow failed her in basic etiquette. "Thought every species but the lizards came through our ports on Basce City, but you look Virulian with spots I cannot place."

"We don't have time for this foolishness," Fumo cut in. "This is your last chance, girl, or we will go about this a much different way."

"My parents were Vestalian and Casanian," Helga said coolly. "You haven't seen anyone like me because apparently those two species aren't exactly a match when it comes to DNA. My brother and I look very different, I take after my father, and he our mother, but I haven't seen many others outside of one very remote station. I understand your hesitation; you have something valuable, and as a survivor you want to barter or risk being robbed and hung out to dry. Am I correct?"

Fio nodded, and her resolve seemed to settle a bit. "I'm so *thyping* tired of running. Man, you just don't understand. Feels like I've been running for days on no sleep, dodging bullets, and bounty chasers aiming to make an arrest. I shouldn't trust any of you but you're right, I'm at the end of my line, and I am desperate. You said you're part Vestalian. Well, my parents were supposedly Vestalian, so maybe that counts for something? Can I get some sort of guarantee that talking will not lead to my arrest? At least not from any local branch of government?"

Helga looked to Colonel Fumo, who seemed at his limit with Fio's sudden demands and resistance. "You talk, we listen, and if we determine you have actual intelligence," the older man said, "I will speak to the Alliance council about giving you the status of protected informant and getting you transported off this station and away from Genese. Now, this is your final chance. Tell us how you came by these codes and ship names."

13

Fio Doro told the Nighthawks of her meeting with William Vray. She spared no detail but for Zulia's role in rescuing her. What she told them was that she stowed away on a shuttle en route to Neroka, and how, upon arriving at the station, her old girlfriend, Zulia took her in. She told them about the break-in and how she was cornered by a pair of security guards acting as bounty hunters. She even told them about Djesu, and how he was betrayed by Garson Sunveil, the man they were to meet to deliver the documents. Her tale was thirty minutes long, but even Colonel Fumo seemed to be hanging onto her every word.

"This is serious," Cilas said to no one in particular.

Colonel Fumo looked confused. His eyes had been on his wrist-comms ever since Fio mentioned Garson Sunveil. When he felt their eyes on him, he quickly explained what it was that he was doing. "I am looking through the records of recruiters stationed on Genese, and we haven't had an office in Basce City for over fifteen years. Last one was vandalized and robbed of all its valuables. Wasn't worth the trouble or risk of having our people in such a hostile environment. This Garrison Sunveil is a fraud, or one of our own using an alias. The men that killed your father, Fio, do you remember how they were dressed?"

"Couldn't see anything. They were shooting from the trees, and it was too dark to see anything out there," Fio recalled.

"What were they firing?" Helga asked. "Was it just handguns or did they use an auto-rifle, or a pulse?"

"Sounded like handguns, light-pistols, the type BasPol carry, though there was one weapon that acted like a laser," Fio recalled, speaking excitedly. "That's what they used to burn the luggage, some kind of laser. In two seconds, it was up in flames, just like that." She snapped her fingers loudly to emphasize the quickness. "Seeing it burn let me know that if it shot me, I would be gone like Djesu, so I took off running away from it, and that's when I got on the shuttle."

"Sounds like a laser-rifle using incendiary ray, aimed at close proximity," Cilas said. "If it was shot from outside a hundred meters, it would have merely punctured a hole, not go up in flames. The shooter was next to the others when he made that shot."

"Weapon wouldn't be ours either," Fumo added. "They are either black-market issued, or something else."

Helga disliked how he tried to deflect from the idea that the men were Alliance operators shooting at civilians. Fumo wanted the reality to be hoodlums using stolen weapons to destroy the evidence. But there were too many variables adding up to this being an intelligence breach followed by an attempt to kill the person with the intel. "Any family left in Basce City?" Helga asked, but Fio merely shrugged and fidgeted, grimacing again.

Helga, seeing that she was uncomfortable, motioned for her to take one of the chairs. She looked towards Fumo to see if he would let her take a seat, and he waved to tell her to sit, his early hesitation now gone with her tale. Before taking the seat, however, she removed the coat to reveal the bloody bandage on her neck. It was an amateur application, nothing like the kind she'd receive from a clinic or hospital.

"Your friend Zulia, did she patch you up?" Helga asked, and the younger woman nodded. "She's a good friend then. Did you tell her about the documents? Are you sure it wasn't her that set you up with those thugs?"

Blue hair covered Fio's face as she sat forward on the chair, resting one hand on her knee as she stared at the floor, looking bone weary. "Thought about it," she said finally. "She and I had history, but it wasn't a bad break-up or anything, so why would she set me up? For credits? She came home to find those two losses shot, didn't flinch, and admitted to knowing them. If she was in on it she wouldn't have come home the way she did, and she would have acted much differently ... I know her. Can we just leave Zulia out of this, please? I've already got one person killed, and she's innocent. She doesn't deserve any of this."

"So, how would they have known who and where you were?" Fumo chimed in, looking up from his wrist-comms to regard them.

"It was a lengthy flight, and I wasn't exactly hiding. Bloody gash on my neck, bandaged poorly, and the black mark on my clothes from where my old communicator had exploded. If my name made the wanted ads, someone would have recognized me. Then when I came here, I was likely followed back to Zulia's. I wasn't myself, you understand? I barely remember even being on that shuttle, and she took care of me only for me to get her place raided. So, it's not her."

"What do you think, Commander?" Fumo said.

"I'll send the codes up to *Rendron*, see if we can learn its origin. The council can decide the rest," Cilas said. "We'll remain here for a time until we get our orders. Until then, I think you should come with us, Fio. We have room for you onboard our vessel. It will be safe for you there, and our physician can look into those wounds while we wait to hear what our next steps should be. Would you like to come with us? If they attacked you once there are bound to be more looking to cash in."

"Alright," she whispered, and Helga could have sworn she sensed some excitement underneath all the melancholy and pain.

"Are those bounty hunters still in custody?" Cilas turned to Fumo, who seemed on the verge of shooing them out of his office now that he'd fulfilled his part of the business.

"We had to let them go," Fio answered for him. "To make it easy on Zulia, since she sort of knew them. Can you let them off the hook? I shot them both, and like I said, Zulia's done so much for me, and all I wanted to do was get you all that message. It's what Djesu would have wanted."

"It's not up to me," Cilas allowed, but more of a warning than him wanting to pursue the idea of detaining them.

The door slid open and a spacer marched in, stopping with the stomp typical of juniors still fresh from OEC, Officer Education Camp, and saluting so hard that an audible "thump," could be heard by everyone. Helga caught herself smiling at the spectacle, recalling how she was once this green, stomping around in front of her seniors and denigrating the rates. She inhaled to compose herself, glancing over at Cilas, who was as stoic as Colonel Fumo, who nodded at the boy to give him permission to relax.

Helga, being so young an officer, was well aware that she was always being judged, either by those who envied her position or the ranks above her who suspected nepotism. Under Cilas what she had learned of leadership was to tread carefully, keeping the line taut but malleable for her fellow officers and rates. When something was off, however, it was difficult not to react immediately. This took focused discipline, despite a lifetime of living and breathing Alliance Navy rhetoric.

Cilas, however, was a master stoic; men and women at the helm were supposed to appear "icy" in the face of anything. Her commander had mastered the art since his first day as a cadet, but she still struggled with it, especially now, when she saw the boy enter and knew deep down that it would be negative. The young man handed a note to Colonel Fumo and he read it quickly before slipping it into the front pocket of his jacket.

"Thank you, Ensign, and thank the major for the heads-up," Fumo said, and the boy, taking the hint, saluted again before taking two steps backward towards the door.

"I take it that's our signal to get this woman out of this building," Helga said, looking to Cilas for their next move.

He nodded and motioned towards the door. "Get on comms and tell the Nighthawks to secure that landing platform, but remind them that we aren't cleared for violent action, so exercise good judgment. We need the lifts cleared and everyone back on *Ursula*. Let's see if they're bold enough to come take her once she's on the ship."

Helga touched the metal transmitter pinned to her ear, and a heads up display with the Nighthawks faces and vitals appeared. Reaching up to interface with the menu, still skeptical whether it would function like her PAS helmet would, she selected the option for hailing everyone and was pleasantly surprised to find that it worked. Cilas gave his farewell and thanks to the colonel, then ushered the two women out before reaching over to pluck the beret from Helga's head.

She reached up to object, but was too slow to catch him, too busy explaining the situation to the Nighthawks and *Ursula's* rated personnel. She ordered them to beat to quarters in case the men coming for Fio grew wise to their intended destination. Cilas gave the young woman Helga's beret, and she promptly donned it, pulling it low to conceal her face.

"Walk the way we do," Cilas urged. "Quick but purposeful, and keep your eyes forward. Don't be frightened; we've got you covered. Just stay calm and look natural."

Having made the call, Helga focused on her surroundings. They were walking below a wide, curving staircase, heading to the terminal to ride the lifts. The starport had become busier, and this was a stroke of good luck. Robed Genesians, whisking away on the soft tiled floors, floated from one end of the building to the next, purchasing tickets for flights. If there were troopers, Helga didn't see them, though she kept her head on a swivel all the way to the kiosks.

Twenty-four stations for ticket buyers sat in neat rows before the lifts. It was busy here as well, but only civilians from what she could tell. Following Fio and Cilas past them, she dared to hope that they would get to *Ursula* without any incident. A woman screamed an expletive before falling to the floor as a man in black ceramic armor stepped over her to grab Fio's arm. Helga, seeing this, instinctively took Fio's other arm to pull her back.

Cilas leaped into action, moving so fast it was as if he had seen the man on approach, and timed his ambush for when he took hold of Fio. Chaos ensued as Genesian patrons scrambled to get free of what they saw would be a fight. A few formed a circle about the tugging match, shouting support for the Nighthawks, though it was unlikely they knew their roles or commitment.

With two quick moves Cilas had his arms around the armored man's waist. The trooper reached for his face, but Cilas shifted his body to the man's right side, trapped his leg and took him down to the floor in a blindingly quick twist. Helga, seeing an opening, kicked at his elbow to get him to release Fio's arm. Alliance-issued officer's small soles struck their target, and despite all the armor, she managed to hyper-extend the arm, forcing him to let go.

Fio ran forward and kicked him in the face, screaming obscenities, but Helga pulled her away from him, sprinting past the gawking crowd to gain the lifts. Once they were on and rising upwards, Helga allowed herself to exhale. With no weapons and all the Nighthawks rushing back to the ship, they could have been in some real trouble if the trooper had been bold enough to bring a gun. The security on Neroka was plentiful, but she had noticed that none of them wore a gun.

"Didn't see any security on the platform, Cilas. Did you, by any chance?" Helga said, pacing about on the platform as it took them up to their ship.

"Yeah, but it's ballistic cannons, and two snipers on watch setup on one of the towers. Saw them from my cabin before we got off earlier. That at least gives us hope, right? But we can't trust them. Whoever wants Fio is likely to have people on the station's staff. So keep your wits; that goes for everyone. The mission is simple: when we get up there, we get Fio to the *Ursula* by any means necessary."

The ride to the top seemed faster to Helga than when they had made their descent to the ground floor earlier. The platform was clear but for five dockworkers diligently refueling their assigned vessels. She made out *Ursula* against the backdrop, resting atop the outstretched bridge. Below the closest wing stood the imposing figure of Quentin Tutt, dressed in his PAS suit, carrying an auto-rifle and waving them on, letting them know it was clear.

At the top of the ramp, her trained eyes spotted Raileo Lei, his black PAS nearly invisible against the shadows of the entrance. He was laying stationary behind his OKAGI "Widow Maker" sniper rifle, aiming at the location of the lifts. Weapons weren't allowed past the landing platform, and especially not inside the starport proper. Since the Nighthawks had been allowed to dock with their equipment, however, they were able to prepare their loadouts after Helga's orders.

What Helga found strange was that there were no alarms going off and the ballistic cannons sat idle despite the presence of weapons on the dock. This let her know that someone had either disabled the security system or there simply wasn't any, and the cannons were merely a deterrent. Anders stepped out from a parked vessel toting a collapsible baton. *Either he snuck that past the security sensors or he took it off one of the dockworkers*, Helga decided.

The three Nighthawks surrounded the smuggler, making themselves her shield as they hurried to the landing platform. Helga on her left, Cilas on her right, and Anders brought up the rear, walking backwards to protect their flanks. They walked briskly past the parked spacecraft, a thopter in repairs, and a handful of Genesians too busy to care. Helga took a moment to look back across the platform to the distance, where the farmland curved up into the clouds.

Everything was beautiful here, from the people to the clothes, but she felt no community, just workers and industry going about their business. What once intrigued her now felt like a prison in a sense. Despite the illusion of distance and travel, it was still limited by the boundaries of the cylindrical station. Then there were the Neroka colonists, and the looks she had received on her way to Colonel Fumo's office. Helga found she didn't much care for the people. They reminded her of the Genesians she'd met on an Arisani station, who looked down their noses at all Vestalians.

Cilas ordered everyone onboard and the hatches sealed, and Helga ran to the bridge where she had Ina bring the thrusters online in case they needed to go. She had wanted to launch where Fio could be safely away from the station, but Cilas wanted to wait out her pursuers. If nothing occurred, Fio would remain onboard, and a few select crew would be allowed to disembark and finished conducting business inside the starport.

His primary goal was to contact *Rendron*, inform Captain Sho of their status, and send to him the list of stolen codes. Then they would be made to wait for the Alliance's next order, which he speculated to Helga meant either they'd be sent after the man who owned the documents or they'd escort Fio out to another ship. With them already here and fitted to operate covertly on any order, Cilas assumed a planet drop would be the most likely scenario.

It will be Meluvia all over, Helga thought, dreading the memory of trudging through the jungle, nursing a bite from that bone-shelled, segmented monstrosity known as a brovila. Having recovered her beret from Fio, who was whisked off to medbay to see Dr. Cleia Rai'to, Helga changed out of her uniform and donned her PAS.

"What are we doing here?" she asked herself, remembering how defeated Fio had seemed once they got her onboard. She had been through a lot, that was obvious, but there was a deeper pain that couldn't have come from a shot. Helga pitied the girl, but there was something about her that made her want to keep her distance. Something about her eyes, a pretty violet, but beneath them was a dark pool of something tragic that made Helga queasy even thinking about it.

She walked to the door of her cabin but felt compelled to stop, turning to look back at the beret where it hung from a hook. There on the top was the *Rendron's* emblem, bringing to mind her captain, Retzo Sho, the man responsible for building the Nighthawks and one of her staunchest supporters. Seeing that symbol brought to mind that fateful night of her graduation when he'd taken time out of his busy schedule to speak to her—then a lowly cadet—about her father.

As with most spacers built on *Rendron*, the thought of disappointing Captain Retzo Sho made Helga anxious. She recalled his speech after their last mission, and those famous words, "We lay down our lives for the Alliance, because to the chosen, there is no other choice." That call to service made her feel proud then, and remembering it brought back the zeal she used to have for wearing the PAS and carrying out orders.

They were there because there was no one else, armed and ready to defend a woman with information that could save thousands of

Alliance lives. Helga couldn't be prouder. Being here made those younger years of rigorous discipline worth something. Becoming what she was today had made her survive BLAST, and wanting it more than over 150 other hopefuls had led to her becoming the first female Nighthawk.

14

The orders from the Alliance had come in quickly, two cycles following the rescue of Fio Doro. Commander Cilas Mec summoned his Nighthawks for a brief. They filed into his cabin, where he had chairs arranged in a circle, while he leaned against his large desk, his shiny black boots blending in with the soft dark carpet. At his feet was the Alliance's symbol of an A. The line in the center expanded to become the fighter's thruster, flying an angular halo around the letter.

On the walls were vid-screens displaying star maps of the three systems, and directly behind him above the desk was a framed painting of the council, smiling and standing in two rows as if ready to administer judgment on the viewer. The compartment was resplendent in black and red, with excellent lighting, allowing them all to see everything and everyone clearly. Outside Cilas's cabin, it was as if nothing had changed since the cycle they first touched down.

With Fio safely on board, the crew was again given leave to disembark and explore the station, but on their return, they would be subject to a decontamination process before being allowed back on the ship. This was protocol suggested by Dr. Cleia Rai'to, who expressed disappointment at the lack of due diligence by the Neroka security.

"A petri dish of galactic diseases and plague," were her words, before going into graphic detail on what it could mean for the crew and their health. She had spoken to Cilas, and he agreed that all spacers were to be scrubbed and scanned for any infections before re-entry. Spacers who engaged in physical relations with the colonists were to be quarantined and checked before getting clearance to be around the other crew members. These strict protocols made leaving the ship too much trouble for some of the crew, who chose instead to stay on *Ursula*, content with looking out from her windows.

Inside his cabin, now functioning as a briefing room, Cilas spoke to the four other Nighthawks about the orders they'd been given. "You're probably all wondering why we're being sent to the surface," he began, pacing the deck as he always did during briefings. "Well, as much as I'd love to say we're going to meet Tutt's family, this won't be for a house call or exploration." His joke was met with laughter, nothing forced or false, but a low chuckle from Quentin himself, who had made it known that he and his family were estranged. "We have two high-level targets: one, a man posing as an Alliance recruiter, the other, an individual who will be revealed to us once we locate the *thype* stealing our honor."

"Who lies about being Alliance? If you want the honor so much, have the heart to sign up," Raileo complained, his face showing the disgust he felt for someone playing the role of a spacer for their personal gains.

"Seems to be a thing across the galaxy," Cilas said, sharing a knowing glance with the sniper, who was still stewing over their target. "We're to settle in there and await orders. No identification, no PAS, and no formal titles or signals. Helga, Tutt, Ray, you know the drill. This will be similar to Meluvia. We have to go in covertly and blend with the locals. Chief Anders, this is what you trained for. Discretion is everything, am I clear?"

"Yes Commander," everyone present sounded off, their voices coming together almost harmoniously.

"Alright, here's the situation. The Alliance suspects that we have a leak in our intelligence, and someone on the ground is feeding information to the lizards," Cilas said, resulting in a chorus of disbelief from his Nighthawks. "The poser I mentioned is the man responsible for destroying the proof that could have easily identified the network that's behind this. Proof went poof, so all we have is the man orchestrating the cover-up. We seek him out and get him to start talking. Sound doable?"

"Righteous," Quentin whispered, grinning cruelly.

Cilas walked forward to stare up at the overhead, his right fist resting against the small of his back. "We have to go in silently, so we can't take the Thundercat, unfortunately. If it was to be ID'd on approach to the planet, it could have us exposed before we even get started. We'll be taking a merchant vessel, a hauler. We managed to get one for a good price from a local shipwright, loyal to the Alliance. Ate, that being your area, I know you're going to want to run diagnostics, so tonight we launch and make the pickup, and you along with Mr. Weinstar will have a cycle to check it out."

"Excellent, an atmosphere drop in a junker," Helga joked. "We'll have her checked out and ready, Commander, but there are some preliminary concerns. You never know how a ship will behave in atmosphere until you take that leap of faith to find out. With that element of mystery, I will need everyone on their game, ready to move whenever I say. When we're on board, those restraints are to remain on the whole trip. Do you hear me, Nighthawks?"

"Loud and clear, Lieutenant," Raileo responded. He was the one who was routinely scolded by Helga for pulling his restraints prematurely, and under the glare she had given him just now, it became obvious that her words were directed at him.

"Ship's not big enough to be running about anyway, and there's no artificial gravity," Cilas said. "Think of the Britz, but without the cryo-chairs, space, and local gravity. No one said this would be a comfortable ride, but as long as we get there in one piece, I will be happy. When we get to Genese, Ate will put us down inside their starport, where we are to play the part of haulers. Everyone won't be fooled. Any operator will be able to spot an ESO from a mile off. It's a risk we will take, but we should still be cautious and play our role as working civilians. We go in with our heads down, find a secure place to sleep and shore up while we gather intelligence, then when the time is ready, we pull them out."

"What about the second target, Commander?" Raileo asked. "You mentioned two: is there another poser, or someone else we haven't identified yet?"

"Yeah, our second target's location will likely come from the first, since he's prone to be at-large now that the Alliance is aware. My feeling is that it is someone powerful and connected, someone who will expect an Alliance presence coming in to investigate. He is why we are stressing delicacy on this mission. To become exposed means losing more than our lives; it could fray the fabric that ties Genese to our Alliance," Cilas reminded them.

"No mistakes then," Raileo said, and Anders echoed his words, reciting them as if he was trying to convince himself.

"We'll speak more on the way down, but for now, those are your orders. We aim to drop at the end of tomorrow's first shift," Cilas retreated back to his desk to lean against it.

"How's the stowaway?" Quentin inquired of Helga while the rest of the Nighthawks made their way out of Cilas's cabin.

"That your little pet name for her?" Helga countered. "Your stowaway's safe and healing nicely, Q. Didn't take her for your type, but I'm getting used to surprises."

"She's not," he quickly corrected her. "I honestly was curious about her status, but of course you're going to keep speculating, aren't you? Girl looked half-dead when you brought her in, and she's important to us, so I am honestly being serious with my asking."

"Your little stowaway is doing good, Q." Helga grinned. "Checked on her earlier in medbay, and she was nicely patched up, though she's going to need time to recover. Know what I mean?"

"Told me she comes from Basce City, and that was enough," Quentin recalled, growing serious. "Can't help but feel responsible for her somehow, Ate. She and I had a chat, and I felt something, like I said, some sort of responsibility, as if the planet is reaching out to tell me to look after her. What do you think they'll do to her, once we're told where to take her?"

"I'm thinking another station, or possibly Meluvia, with enough compensation for her to start over," Helga said. "This pans out, she could very well be a hero, though she only did this to save her own skin. Had she not been nosy, she would have delivered those codes, and the lizards would know the routes of several starships. That could have been devastating, and who's to say other codes aren't out there being spread by smugglers that don't open their packages?"

"Seems sort of harsh, Ate. Wasn't she about to deliver the intel freely to our reps on the ground when her father was murdered?"

"Sounds like you all had much more than a chat. For her to tell you all that, you two must have really hit it off or established a connection," Helga put a finger to her chin, tipped her head and looked up at his face skeptically. When he went to protest, Helga laughed at his discomfort, and he fanned her off dismissively, no longer willing to take part in her game. "Why don't you go see her, Q? Seriously. She's been through a lot, and could use a familiar face. Trust me, nowhere else feels lonelier than Medbay, and Cleia isn't a conversationalist." Quentin touched her shoulder in a gesture of thanks before saluting Cilas and exiting the cabin.

"Helga, hang back a minute," Cilas said, clapping Raileo on his shoulder as he walked him out. "Keeping you in the loop here, but steel yourself," he conspired under his breath when they were finally alone. "That document Fio stole was sent from the *Harridan*, an infiltrator belonging to *Helysian*. It's supposed to be scouting Louine space, but has been lingering near Genese citing urgent repairs. The thing is, it's been there for over four months, refusing aid and direct commands. Captain Sho says the council fears mutiny, and asked Captain Lede of *Missio-Tral* to intercept and give *Harridan* a chance to explain under direct presence."

"Direct presence, what does that mean in this instance?" Helga said, shocked at what she was hearing, but determined to know everything that Cilas had learned about their predicament.

"Means *Missio-Tral* will get within trace range and ask their captain for a face-to-face parlay. Apparently he's been acting strangely, and has stayed out of conflict with the lizards. One of the officers onboard has been in contact with the council secretly since it became obvious that something was off. Our spy says his captain, Jawal Kur, has had cruisers traveling back and forth to the planet. The Alliance wants answers, and since seeing those codes from Fio Doro, they've decided enough is enough."

"This is insane." Helga placed a hand over her mouth. "An Alliance capital class turning her cannons onto an infiltrator. It feels wrong even to consider it. There are thousands of spacers on those infiltrators, likely innocent to whatever schemes this captain's involved in. What about the spy? Aren't they concerned that a hero will be caught up in the crossfire?"

"If it comes to violence, I am sure that Captain Lede will choose to merely deplete their shields and rupture their engine," Cilas assured her. "We don't fire on one another to destroy, you know that. Even if there weren't spacers onboard you still don't open up on that class of vessel. No, they'll shut her down, put the Marines onboard, and drag the traitor off to the brig, while taking the *Harridan* a prize until they can vet and interrogate the crew."

"A few airlocks here, a few airlocks there," Helga sang, pretending to play a flute with her fingers in tune with the mockery she made. "All while the rest of us worry that we could be the next victims of a madman at the helm. I don't know what scares me more than the thought of my own Alliance coming against me, but it's up there with giant worms biting off my head. How is this reality, Cy? It's Captain Lang all over again."

"I know," Cilas said. "But things are already in motion; it's going to happen. Captains are people too, sometimes we forget. They can lose their faculties, though the hints I got from Commander Nam suggested that we're dealing with something else." Cilas paused, inhaled deeply, and exhaled while shaking his head. It was as if he couldn't believe what he was about to tell her. "Commander Nam believes that Captain Kur has been corrupted by the Geralos," he finally said.

Helga blinked twice. "That can't happen. That doesn't happen, it's just absurd. How does a lizard get close enough to a captain for him to be corrupted? Isn't that the point of keeping our most important assets far out of reach of their grip? The helm of a starship in Geralos hands, Cilas, hanging outside the hot zone, bouncing our messages, and—wait, didn't you say the Geralos have been busy out here? Distracting the defense force to soften the zone so those cruisers can leave unobstructed, but to where?"

"That's where we come in." Cilas patted his chest. "That's the mission. The reason behind everything I outlined in my brief. I don't have to remind you that what I tell you stays here. You're my number two, so you know what's on the line." Cilas's intense gaze bore into her eyes until she replied with a "yes sir," having finally processed those ominous words he so casually stated.

"The so-called recruiter who put the bounty on Fio, we are to neutralize him or bring him back to *Rendron* for questioning. He isn't our primary target, so we have the option depending on how willing he is to comply with our demands." Cilas's face seemed to grow harder, no longer the friendly commander but a militant enforcer, running through a briefing with his command.

"And who's our real target?" Helga asked, still stunned by the thought of an infiltrator in the hands of the enemy.

"Target's the official who gave Fio the job to retrieve that suitcase with the documents. This is going to test all of us, especially Anders. Windows will be tight on errors and *thype*-ups, so it will be a rough first drop for that man. Sort of like yours was." He cracked a smile, though Helga didn't find it amusing. "William Vray is his name. We're going to have to locate him first then isolate him. Fio's help will be needed there."

"We're taking her along?" Helga couldn't believe he would be good with a civilian on an operation.

Cilas split his hands. "No. Can't have any of us playing guardian. This is a stealth or nothing op in unknown conditions. A desperation shot relying on our invisibility. We're good, but that's a pretty tall order for an order that's already towering. We will have her on comms, and run a flo-bot when we need her to have eyes on our location. Small arms and knives, no PAS, moving in the darkness and living off the grid during the daytime."

"We do this without rousing the neighborhood?" Helga confirmed. "Genese isn't to know we're there doing Alliance business?"

"Yes, and yes," Cilas replied. "But Genese is aware, just not the goons in the local government. The Alliance representative knows and has given us permission to break atmosphere and conduct the extraction. With the local government out of the loop, we'd be coming for one of their own, so going in loud means that Nighthawks will be on the feeds fighting local security. That could cause our captain to lose face, something not happening under my command."

"It certainly will not," Helga agreed, feeling the same way he did about bringing shame to their starship. "Maybe this will be the one."

"The one for what?" Cilas looked at her quizzically.

"The one mission that plays out the way we planned." Helga grinned, though Cilas didn't find it amusing.

15

The merchant ship wasn't anything like Helga expected. When Cilas had informed her of his deal with the shipwright, she had imagined something old, with a rigged-up console and faulty controls. After leaving Neroka and exiting the station cluster, they had navigated to the coordinates given and within an hour found the ship cloaked and tethered to a defunct satellite.

It was more mining vessel than hauler, though judging from its shape it could manage any role. The hull was made from a composite of silicon and ceramic plates, molded into a compact design resembling a clamshell. Two raised seats occupied the bridge, attached to arms curving up to axles in the overhead, an outdated Genesian solution for keeping human pilots intact during extreme G-force exercises.

Behind the bridge was an all-in-one compartment that held a bio-extraction unit, a set of lockers, and seats mounted to the bulkhead. The cargo hold was the largest space, fitted with belts, pulleys, and other equipment meant to tie things down inside the ship. The hull could have used a scrub and paint job, its once blue coat a mottled gray from a long service in space without much attention being paid to maintenance. Still, she was better than expected, and after many checks for safety, and anything that could sabotage, she was taken into the *Ursula's* hangar for a thorough inspection.

Between the two pilots and Alon Weinstar, the ship was scrutinized from engine to cargo hold, revealing everything about its state and reliability as a dropship. After Weinstar wrote down what he needed for repairs, Helga enlisted the help of the Nighthawks and a few members from engineering. Two cycles later their new acquisition was ready for flight, and on Fio's suggestion, she was christened

Justice, a moniker the smugglers hoped would be the outcome of their mission.

Cilas's plans were set in motion with the Nighthawks ordered to ready their gear. This included 3B XO Suits and Infiltrator's Composite Armor, which were civilian clothes reinforced with armored weaving sewn inside the fabric. While they wouldn't stop bullets from crushing bones or hurting like the dickens, they would prevent them from breaking flesh.

A cycle later, and the Nighthawks, traveling in *Justice*, were orbiting Genese calculating the fastest route to their destination. From their current position, it turned out that they were in a favorable position to the planet's rotation and in less than an hour they would be breaking atmosphere to finally start their assault.

"How're we doing back there?" Helga asked, turning to look back at the Nighthawks from her raised chair.

"Are we there yet?" was Raileo's reply, which earned him some laughter from one of the others, but she couldn't tell who it was. Helga allowed a smile, happy to know that at the very least they were entertained. Drops could be the stuff of nightmares to spacers who weren't accustomed to a planet's atmosphere. Glancing up at the vidscreen carrying the feed from the rear, she saw Anders was the one cracking jokes with Raileo Lei.

"Sounds like it's a go then, prepare for entry," she announced, turning back to the front, leaning forward to manipulate the HUD to plot a course down to the coast of a country known as Voan. Fio Doro had shown her a way to enter Basce City without too much notice, and it dealt with finding the coast of Voan. "Orbital tracking taken offline. We're going diving. Hold for entry."

She brought the ship's nose down, slipping into the Genesian atmosphere, and switched the commands on the console over from space to air. They picked up speed, plunging through a wispy world of gray blotches that kept the ground below a mystery for a few minutes before it cleared. "Glide mode engaged while I transfer energy," she reported, applying some thrust to take them through a layer of thick yellow clouds.

Below her feet, where the canopy ended, she could finally see the ocean, sparkling, and stretched out so far it appeared as if it comprised the entire planet. These bodies of water always brought with them a mélange of emotions for the Nighthawk. They were still strange and alien for a spacer raised on a starship, unaware if she'd ever experience a moon or planet firsthand.

At times Helga would sit and think of how it would feel to live near the ocean on a water-filled planet. On prior missions she had seen a variety of wet wonders, from the waterfalls on Meluvia to the artificial lake that ran the length of Sanctuary. The worst memory was BLAST, one of two times she'd experienced the ocean and its mysterious depths. Black waters on Arbar, salty enough to dehydrate the hardiest of Traxians, had been the last "obstacle" for she and the other future ESOs to pass after a day of hell.

Seeing it now below her brought back all of those memories, especially the ones she had worked hard to forget. That strange blue deep, whose appearance changed depending on your proximity, and was its own world filled with life and mysteries that made it both necessary and dangerous. Turning to the holo-map displaying a topographic outline of their intended destination, Helga worked out how much longer she would be staring down at the abyss.

"I'm really glad Ina decided to come back," Cilas offered, rescuing her from that war inside her mind. "Not many would after going through what she's been through, but I honestly think she did it for you. From the moment you two came in contact, you've had a connection, don't you agree?"

"You really think so?" Helga volleyed back the question. She respected Ina, but didn't really feel that they were close. "It's been a little hard, to be honest, handing the controls over to someone else. All those cycles inside the cockpit, it sort of became my safe place, and I still do miss having it all to myself."

"I keep going up there to look for you, Ate," Raileo admitted. "After the third time I forced myself to stop. Lieutenant Reysor probably thinks I have a crush on her."

"Nah, Ina's pretty sharp," Helga assured him. "She knows we came from having *Ursula* to ourselves, and you're likely not the only one to have done that."

"He's not," both Cilas and Quentin admitted from where they sat behind her.

"Ina has been a tremendous help with the transition," Helga continued. "She's both brilliant and vicious, which is what *Ursula* requires in a pilot. I think we're lucky to have her, really. You all remember *Aqnaqak* and Misa having to fly us to Meluvia? I still feel guilty for everything that happened to her down there."

"Are we sure this is good conversation to have in front of our new recruit, Lieutenant?" Quentin asked. Helga exhaled heavily at the memory, recalling the ordeal they had gone through with Misa, who had been a ranked fighter pilot that Captain Tara Cor had loaned them. "I feel guilty as well for what happened. It was a *schtill* op, and we did manage to rescue her. Speaking of, have either of you heard anything?"

"When we sent out invitations for *Ursula's* crew, Misa sent a nice note informing me that she had already been promoted to CAG," Cilas recalled. "I thought I told you that."

"You did, but I always wondered if that was valid or if she just didn't want any more dealings with our team," she said, still watching the water as they continued to lose altitude.

"I believe she was sincere," Cilas said, "She did mention how she enjoyed her brief time in the cockpit with you."

"How we looking, Anders?" Helga queried the Nighthawk, who didn't look to be doing too well with all the turbulence.

"Ready to get to it, Lieutenant," the young recruit shouted, putting on a brave face.

"That's what we want to hear, right Nighthawks?" And Helga pumped her fist in the air when all but Cilas replied with a chorus of shouts.

They spoke some on old missions, recounting the good and bad experiences on different moons and planets. Anders was intrigued, and Helga hoped he wasn't expecting Genese to be anything like Meluvia, which by appearances alone was considered a paradise.

"Would it be alright to stretch my legs, Lieutenant?" Anders asked once *Justice* had dropped below 18,000 meters in altitude.

"Oh yeah, sorry everyone, you can move about now. We're cruising on autopilot, so it should be alright. Just be careful, some of that cargo back there may have gotten dislodged upon entry. Bio-extractor's off to the right there, Ray. You're just going to have to deal with the smell," she teased. "Strap back in when you're finished whatever, though. We're still up pretty high, and there's no telling what will happen once we get closer to the port."

Before she could finish talking, she could hear the straps loosening on the restraints, and Raileo moaning loudly from stretching his limbs. "Oh, before I forget." Helga held up a hand. "Welcome home, Tutt. This may be our only time getting to say it to a Nighthawk. Welcome to your home planet, big man. Being the most traveled of us all, the commander aside." She flashed Cilas a smile. "I can't think of a more appropriate candidate."

"Thank you," Quentin said, visibly uncomfortable from being called out. "Um, don't tell my family I'm here," he added, which elicited a laugh from Cilas.

"So, this Genesian woman we're protecting," Anders began.

"Fio Doro," Helga asserted, not willing to believe that after all they'd been through, he wouldn't know her name.

"Fio Doro," he corrected himself. "She was asking a lot of questions about our team, and how we decide who can and cannot become members. Seemed particularly interested in you, Lieutenant. I think you've got yourself a fan."

Helga smiled. "You're also an extremely optimistic person, I've noticed, Anders. Remember we still need to give you a call-sign. I'm leaning towards Saint, but I'm going to wait to see how you perform on the ground. As to Fio, poor girl's likely fishing for ideas as to where she can dock her lonely escape pod. She's had the treatment dealt pretty heavily these last few cycles, and judging from what little I know of her past, I know if anything, she's a survivor."

"Do we ever take in cadets that old?" asked Raileo Lei, as he stumbled out of the bio-extraction unit.

"I hope you cleaned those paws," Quentin groaned.

"Why bother when they're just going to get bloody?" Raileo clawed at the air. Helga made to laugh, but with Anders present, she thought better of it, though Raileo mimicking a cat tickled her immensely.

"It's never too late to serve the Alliance. We start off young, so we have tools in place and ready when we're old enough to don a uniform," Cilas informed them. "Depending on her condition and skill level, a woman like Fio could be right here with us if she's a one-percenter. Haven't seen many of those though, and from what I know of Fio, she isn't interested in our life. If I was to wager a guess at that line of questioning, she wanted to know more about you, Chief, or our Lady Hellgate."

"That's enough of that, Commander." Helga felt herself starting to sweat. She couldn't understand the reaction but couldn't qualify if it was embarrassment or the thought of someone that wasn't Cilas wanting her romantically. She knew what she had. Accepting that she was attractive to others had come early so it wasn't that. It was that Cilas, who was her chosen partner, was joking about it casually.

"That's odd," he said suddenly, causing her to stop and look at him incredulously, surprised that he wanted to press the issue. "I just got a message on my HUD telling me that a *Helysian* channel is open. Outside of this op, we shouldn't have any presence here. What in the worlds is going on? Hey, Nighthawks, cut the chatter, I need to bounce a message to *Ursula* for *Rendron*. Hel, get me any information you can on the vessels in the area, especially spacecraft or multipurpose."

"Aye-aye, Commander." Helga spun around to face the console. The ship was silent but for Cilas's hushed voice below the squeaks and groans of the engine. It remained this way for a long time until the ocean gave way to the coast. Now, the expanse of blue and green that had once unsettled Helga was identifiable as lakes and forests, with the occasional break where swampland added variety to the canvas.

An hour later and Cilas was off comms, his relaxed demeanor replaced by a sudden urgency. "Nighthawks, we have a traitor," he announced. "And to most of you here, that is no surprise considering the sort of missions we've been given in the past. Traitors are a part of every war, and there's always more than we like to admit to, but what we're dealing with here is a possible mutiny, and an attempt to cover-up the things we've discovered. The signal I received is Alliance, *Helysian* to be exact, having been deployed by a rogue infiltrator to find anyone involved with Fio Doro. Basce City is in chaos right now, and the locals believe it's mercenaries warring with the gangs. This isn't accurate. BasPol, what the local security force calls themselves, have deployed a task force bolstered by our own *Helysian* Marines."

"No." Quentin exhaled suddenly. "I refuse to believe it. Marines?"

"Last time it was an ESO," Helga reminded him.

"Exactly," Cilas agreed. "Those aren't our Marines any longer, Q, they're our enemy. Mission's still on, but this complicates things. Threat level has been raised. They will likely have ordnance that will match anything we brought for covert operations. Now, as much as this should be considered a warzone, there will be civilians present so no shooting unless we're certain."

"Call your targets and wait for clearance," Quentin quickly added, unable to stop himself from assuming a sergeant's role.

"You said a channel just came open from *Helysian*, Commander?" Raileo queried. "Wouldn't that mean they could track us as well?"

"Outside of a certain class of officers, channels are regulated through our consoles," Cilas explained. "It's how the ship's system knows not to set off alarms when an unfamiliar but friendly vessel shows up locally. For captains, our personal devices are given the same update as our ships. We can communicate beyond the computer to identify threats that may be exploiting a breech in our defense. It's also a good way for us to know if there's support available at our immediate vector."

"While you were on your call, Rend, I studied the radar, ranging back to about the time you picked up that channel," Helga updated him. To show what it was she meant, she activated a prompt on the console that she had saved to show him once he was off his call. The screens above her changed from the feed of the interior compartments of the ship to a series of rings, each becoming wider as they spread.

Helga, through a sequence of gestures, focused the view on a cluster of blips, expanding them as much as it would allow, until one morphed into a rectangular blob which she knew would still be unclear to everyone. "If you don't recognize the shape from this poor illustration, I will let you know it's one of our cruisers, an SOS Phoenix to be exact. One of those vessels could transport an entire platoon to the surface. It looks like we're about to have our hands full."

"*Thype*," Quentin groaned. "Where do they get the balls to break atmosphere in a Phoenix dropper? Wouldn't Genesian air control be all over this?"

"Not if they've been given clearance," Anders chimed in, though somewhat meekly. "We got clearance through the Alliance, and local government wouldn't know the difference between them and us." This assertion was met with a long silence as every Nighthawk considered the implications of what they'd just heard.

"Well done, Anders." Cilas's voice cut the thick, troubled air. "We now know why they're here, and we cannot allow it, because as you said, to the people in charge down there, all this *schtill* will be seen as the Alliance. Our advantage is in our position. Based on that radar, they're ahead of us, possibly have been here raising hell for days. They don't know that we're here or that we have a resident on comms ready to act as our guide."

"Better get strapped in. We're coming up on Basce City in approximately 45 minutes," Helga announced, unsure now as to what awaited them.

16

The iron legs of *Justice*, the Nighthawk's converted merchant ship, came in contact with the tarmac outside of the half-moon shaped starport of Basce City. The sky above was packed with all manner of craft drifting along on virtual lines in the night sky. When they made their descent, it had been to a cityscape resplendent in twinkling lights and spotlights lasing the dense fog in the sky.

Despite the tension in the air, Basce City's splendor was not lost on the younger spacers, who only knew cities from simulations and vids. Helga had done her part in playing the clueless pilot. When prompted by the starport's system to give some identification, she had sent over their false credentials and cleared landing with the air traffic controller, who had informed her that they would need to be searched before being allowed into the city.

Fio Doro, who had briefed them on what she as a smuggler would do to avoid detection, had given them the words to say to the controller to initiate a bribe to bypass this. To Helga's surprise, the controller accepted the offer of one canister of fuel, which according to Fio was worth a small fortune on the black market. The controller rerouted them to a separate hangar once the deal had been made, and *Justice* was given a station out of sight of the regular travelers.

On the side of the runway where they settled down, the only other vessels parked were a luxury jet and a space yacht whose shape reminded her of the R60 Thundercat. When the landing gear settled and the thrusters made to cool themselves, Cilas reached into a pack and started passing out matching coveralls for the Nighthawks to wear.

"Listen up," he announced. "Now I have to remind you that here we are on a first-name basis when we're out in public. Nicknames are allowed, but stow the titles, salutes, and Navy protocol. We're supposed to be haulers, civilians having stopped for a few nights of rest, so let us act like it."

They threw on tattered hooded cloaks over their clothes, made of a thick, water-resistant material to guard them against the freezing rain and wind. To conceal their Alliance-issued boots, Cilas had suggested they cover them in plastic. The weather, despite being absolutely miserable, especially to the space-born boomers who knew little of the cold, had turned out to be a benefit to the mission. It would allow them to cross the slick, wet airstrip on foot without having to worry about onlookers seeing what it was they were carrying.

Cilas lined them all up inside the cargo hold, scrutinizing their appearance and running checks on what each of them wore. When he was satisfied with their readiness, he released the airlock and gripped the handle, waiting for the system to give him an "all clear." With a twist and a push, he swung the hatch open, drowning out their thoughts with the sounds of aircraft, spacecraft, and wailing from the wind.

To his surprise, at the bottom of the loading ramp stood a pair of uniformed Cel-tocs waiting with a hovering luggage cart. To keep up appearances, they loaded the fuel onto the cart, covered it with a cloak, and fell in with the androids, who took them to a covered walkway leading up to the starport's entry. Upon arrival, Anders, being the rookie, was made to carry Quentin's gear so that the Genesian strongman could hoist the heavy fuel canister up onto his shoulder.

Inside the starport was a hub of activity with all manner of people, their identities evident by their dress. The Genesian residents almost all wore robes or cloaks, adorned with colorful fabric and gems. The few Vestalians they saw were in uniform, but nothing that clearly signaled Alliance. Green-haired Meluvians were in attendance as well, all too busy to notice the five cloaked newcomers hugging the walls to make their way around to a waiting attendant.

The woman, who Helga recognized from Fio Doro's description, held up a hand to greet her when their eyes met. She was a dark-skinned, bald-headed beauty, with silver chains linking a large ring in her nose to the pair on her ears. Gray eyes widened happily when she saw Quentin toting the canister.

"Is that my juice, Captain?" she asked Helga, her Genesian accent throwing the Nighthawk for a bit.

"Yes, your juice, and your guarantee that my ship will not be tampered with, or our identities shared." Helga reminded her of the deal that had been made. "Do we have your guarantee?" She leaned forward so only the pretty attendant could hear. She pulled her hood close to conceal her spots, which she feared would make her stick out more than she already did.

The woman busied herself with a handheld tablet, touching and swiping, her dark fingers dancing deftly across its surface. While she worked, a large, uniformed man came over to take the canister from Quentin, who the woman acknowledged with a nod, after giving the Genesian Nighthawk a suggestive wink. Helga saw her do it, though it may have been missed by the other men. Five minutes later she exhaled heavily, put the tablet down, and looked at them expectantly.

"Anything else?" Helga asked, wondering what else was needed. It hadn't taken long for them to make the exchange, but the longer they remained inside with such a heavy crowd, the more she worried that someone would notice something that could make them.

"All set," the Genesian attendant sung, her face all smiles after confirming the contents of the canister. "You're free to enter the city now; you've all been checked and cleared. We have cars for rent, sale, or you can take the mono into the city. Lots of options there. Thank you for choosing our starport." This time it was Helga's turn to receive her wink. The woman leaned in close. "You tell that little blue-haired hellion that this doesn't count for even half of what she owes me," she informed Helga before sitting up straight and announcing loudly to the others, "Enjoy your time in Basce City, friends, and when you're ready to depart just ask for Nyora Ohn. Everyone knows who I am."

She waved them along mechanically, her eyes still locked with Quentin's, who seemed more than interested, Helga noted.

"If there is ever a next time, *thype* the fuel, we should hand her Q," Raileo commented, as he followed Helga out into the even busier ticketing area then out onto a lot where a variety of transports sat parked, ready for rent.

Outside of a set of glass sliding doors was another lot, this one lined with cars, each tethered to a kiosk where travelers could deposit credits to take one, or a bank ID if they had credit with the city. The rain was really coming down now, a blessing in disguise for the Nighthawks, for the lot was now for the most part empty.

Cilas, cloaked in all black, determination overtaking his façade, took the lead and made his way out towards a large utility vehicle. It favored a cruiser on wheels, with six seats in the front and an open cab, large enough to hold all their equipment. The reinforced sides, hard angles, and gated bumpers gave it the look of a military transport that had been retired and repurposed as a civilian vehicle.

Helga thought it posed a risk, them being who they were driving around in a transport that screamed, "Killers on board, violence impending." Typically, she would make a lighthearted joke to nudge her CO in the right direction, but Cilas had not been himself since learning about the *Helysian's* involvement. Second-guess him now and who knew what could from it; nothing short of taking her head, she assumed. Now was the time for her to be a loyal Nighthawk, which meant falling in line, and taking the wheel when he beckoned.

When the credits had been deposited and everyone seated inside the rental, cloaks were removed and thrown in the back with the rest of the gear. Helga turned on the heating system to help fight back the chill. A few prods and pokes at the console and a quick perusal of the manual, and they were rolling off the property and onto a side road leading out to the city.

"What's our destination, Cilas?" she inquired, looking over at her commander. He was seated on the far side of Anders, who sat shivering between them.

"Just take us up there for now." He pointed to where several elevated highways crisscrossed one another, only breaking for the occasional exit, linking to another. "Take your time. I'm going to contact Fio to see if there's a place we can use, or if she has any suggestions."

"See if she knows any good eateries as well, Rend," Raileo added from the back.

"*Ursula*, this is Rend, do you copy?" Cilas spoke, prompting them all to become silent once again. "Zan, is that you? Could you patch me through to our guest?" He waved his hand before his face, probing the air with his fingers and opening the comms so they all could hear. Helga drove them away from the starport, onto a road lined with tall trees, floodlights, and signs giving directions out from the starport to popular destinations in the city.

"I'm here," Fio said after a minute had passed, her low husky tenor coming through clearly over comms. "Are you in Basce City?"

"Leaving the port for the city now," Cilas replied. "Know any good places where we can lay low?"

"Yeah, my old apartment in the stocks, but it's likely to have some of Sunveil's thugs watching it to see if I will come back for my things. You all can take them though, I'm sure of it," she encouraged.

"What about your neighbors though, Fio?" Helga said, "Do you trust them that much to think that they wouldn't be watching as well? Since you have a bounty, what's to stop them from trying to collect?"

"The fact that they're like family, and even if they do, you all are Alliance with armor and guns." Fio laughed. "We're talking rat poppers, shivs, and maybe the occasional semi-auto against your elemental rounds and bomblets. Hell, you could walk into anywhere down there, show your strength, and what choice will they have? The stocks respect strength."

"Fio. Not to be in your business, but have you been in the wine, by any chance?" Helga asked, exchanging looks with Cilas.

"Why, because of my joke? Get off it, you think Miss Blue Pins and Needles would let me get close to anything that isn't one of her teas?"

"Miss Blue Pins and Needles?" Raileo repeated, deadpan, clearly unimpressed with Fio Doro's nickname for his girlfriend.

Helga muted her comms. "It's likely the painkillers are making her into a bit of a *cruta*," she whispered, hoping that explanation would satisfy the hot-tempered sniper.

"Heard that," she sung. "But back to your question, Commander, I think using my place would be easiest, wouldn't it?"

"She makes a good point," Quentin said. "It's an actual home, which means shelter, berths, possible rations, and the best part, desperate *thypes* milling about it who we could question to locate our target."

Cilas gave it some thought, rubbing at the back of his head, and looking around for any objections other than his own. "It's a good suggestion, Fio. I just wonder if it's wise, since we are to maintain a low profile."

"Commander, we're dressed like refugees," Anders reminded him. "We're wearing secondhand coveralls and toting baggage. We'll get a lot of eyes, sure, but how are they to know what we are? I've been looking at the uniforms here, trying to identify who is security, and I am having a hard time. I see nothing but mercenaries in out-of-place tactical uniforms. They look like civilians playing at ESO, dressing up in their worthless, expensive gear."

"The rookie's right, they look like fakers," Quentin added, clapping Anders on the shoulder to show his support.

"When you run into BasPol, you will know them from the mercs hanging in the starport," Fio informed them. "Their uniforms are distinct, so there's no mistaking them. Listen, when you reach my building, Nighthawks, watch the skies, that's how BasPol does its policing. Avoid the drones and it won't matter who calls to report you entering. They don't care what goes on inside the stocks unless it deals directly with them."

"But aren't they the police force?" Raileo asked. "Better equipped, backed by government, and by extension the military?"

"Where you're going, believe me when I say this," Fio spoke softly. "No one comes into our neighborhood unless we let them. That includes BasPol, mercs, missionaries; it doesn't matter. I was joking earlier. It doesn't matter how good you are at killing, come in uninvited and you will leave in a body bag. The gangs and their runners are who police the stocks. Lucky for you, you're with me, and I will give you someone to call to make sure no one stops you from using my apartment."

"Who is this someone?" Cilas asked.

"He's a powerful man who owed my father a favor. His name is Derrin Blackstar, but everyone calls him Thrall. I'm sending you the address to my building, and Thrall's contact. Call him and tell him that I hired you to take revenge on the men who murdered my father. That should be enough, but if he needs proof, tell him that the name he used to call me was Blue Bird."

"I don't like this, Cilas," Helga complained. "We're working with gangsters now? They're unpredictable, and who's to say they haven't been purchased by Sunveil?"

"Do you have a better idea, girlfriend?" Fio cut in, already annoyed with Helga's opinions. "Want to book a hotel instead from a pervert eager to sneak into your room after knocking you out with sleeping gas? Or would you rather I point you to the farmlands where you can camp out? I hear they're pretty empty this time of year."

"That's enough," Helga nearly shouted. "I don't find any of that funny."

"She thinks I'm joking." Fio chuckled under her breath. "Just take my advice and take your spotted ass into the stocks and use my apartment. Tell me, did you land on the public strip or did you talk to my friend?"

"Your friend," Helga admitted, still shaken at the thought of someone drugging her while she slept. "She gave us a private strip and cleared us through customs. That was extremely helpful."

"So, you're already working with gangsters then," Fio laughed. "Though I have to admit, not many have a smile as sweet as Nyora's."

"So, you're already working with gangsters then," Raileo mocked her from the rear, which earned him a look from Helga, who was just as annoyed with the smuggler, but ready to get going.

"Send me the information, Fio, and while I have you on comms, how are you managing?" Cilas asked, his tone making him sound genuinely concerned for her wellbeing.

"Food's good, and everyone's being nice to me ... except for the cyborg; he stares a lot. I'm doing better, though Pins and Needles wants to submerge me in some sort of tank. Is she mad? Won't I drown?"

"Take it from someone who's been in one, you want to do it sooner rather than later if you don't want to bear visible scars on your skin," Cilas advised the young Genesian. "You've been through a lot, Fio, and you're tired. The drugs may feel good now, but they won't be enough when your memory starts to haunt you, and they will. Last thing you need are those war wounds to keep your trauma present. It's a few cycles of sleep and you wake up feeling as if you'd been reborn."

That, and you'll want to thype anything that gets near you, Helga recalled. "Just give it some thought, Fio, it doesn't just make you feel better, it will keep you at the top of your game. There's going to be a life for you once we are done here, and you will want to take advantage. May as well get healed," she added.

They were on the highway with other transports, a six-lane road of twists and turns, bordered on the sides by poles anchoring force fields to keep the vehicles contained. Since leaving the starport they had been on the dark road bordered by trees and the occasional building, which eventually became a ramp leading them up to the highest expressway.

Helga saw loud, speedy racers slipping past everyone, with little care paid to the traffic's direction or their lives. A fleet of massive tankers hauling everything from processed milk to fuel brought the traffic to a standstill, while flying hovers zipped by, avoiding the congestion of the hard roads ahead. The rain was really pouring now, and there was a mist. The sun, having set, put everything under a sleek, red-colored haze that could be deemed beautiful or ominous depending on who saw it.

Cilas was back on comms with Fio, having moved past trying to convince her to get in a tank to picking her brain on everything she knew about William Vray. Helga listened in, but became distracted when the mist cleared enough for them to see the hills on either side of the highway. The hills were covered in buildings, stacked so tightly together they appeared to have been carved out of the stony foundation that held them.

"Maker," Raileo whispered.

"Is that where we're going?" Anders inquired, and Helga quickly consulted the map to see their destination.

"That is where we're going," she confirmed.

"You must have found the Stocks," Fio mused. "You all sound so shocked. That is the real Basce City you're seeing there, what most of us consider our home. Oh, just wait until you're actually inside it, smelling the rot." She laughed.

"Never again will I speak down on the condition of hubs," Helga muttered. "How does a planet as resource-rich as Genese allow such conditions to persist?"

"Not just resource-rich, but credits-rich," Anders chimed in. "This is the Iron Planet. They build starships the way we built paper fighters as cadets. There's no shortage of anything here. I can see why the Geralos wants it. They have everything here, but from what I'm seeing, only a select few get to take advantage of it."

"It's not as bad as it appears," Fio tried, but her voice made it sound like a plea rather than an objection.

Cilas, who was the only one not bothered by what he was seeing, turned to look over at Anders, who paled, thinking he had offended the commander somehow. "Geralos," he repeated. "The Geralos want in here, where they're leaking secrets about the location of our starships. Do you all see the importance of this mission now? Why failure isn't an option? Why we must find the source and snuff it out?"

"Loud and clear, Rend," Helga acknowledged, joining the chorus of similar sentiments responding to his pronouncement. From the little she knew of surface life, it was hard to imagine what awaited them inside that gauntlet of stacked homes and misery. This brought it back to Fio Doro, the survivor, who had escaped to bring them information that could potentially save millions of lives.

Looking out at all that poverty and depression, Helga, hearing Fio's voice informing Cilas, considered that the Genesian was no different from the Vestalian refugees displaced from their home planet. In essence, she decided, this made it the Nighthawks' business to set things right. Find the traitors, plug the leak, and secure Basce City from the Geralos. That in essence was the mission, even if they were only five.

"Everything alright, Ate?" Quentin asked, ever the big brother showing his concern.

"No," she admitted. "I'm angry, as all of you should be. Now, let's go find this *thyping* apartment and get it done."

17

The Alliance Starship *Missio-Tral* emerged from a jump through hyperspace to assume a position against the backdrop of distant Genese. One of six Genesian-built capital class starships, she was a champion of over 1,000 battles. Home of 3,500 Marines, whose hard-earned scholarship earned them a place in most Special Operations across the Alliance, *Missio-Tral* had developed a reputation as an indomitable force.

Like her sisters, *Rendron*, and *Helysian*, *Missio-Tral* was built as an answer to the Geralos battleship. From system to hull, her role was that of a warship intended to be at the vanguard of a fleet. Hosting a loadout of 320 kinetic energy cannons, and 30 torpedo launchers stacked at varying levels on her broadsides, *Missio-Tral's* offensive potential made her a formidable opponent for any vessel.

Able to deliver a continuous stream of ship-destroying energy, either from her cannons or the four trace-laser beam emitters installed on bow and stern, her shape was unmistakable, even as a shadow of nothingness against the distant stars. 560m of tapered hull, building itself into the reality of this new region of space.

From the bridge of the *Helysian* infiltrator, *Harridan*, the warnings of an "Incoming Extra-Dimensional Shift," had sent the crew scrambling to take emergency measures. But the system had lagged, or had been blocked, and a mass of black nothingness replaced a segment of space. Hands beat to quarters, cycles of drills and muscle memory, sending her spacers scrambling to mount some sort of defense.

Her captain, Jawal Kur, had not been warned of another Alliance vessel approaching their vector, and no Geralos ship had been reported on radar. He stood frozen, hands behind his back, his bald, gaunt, 183cm frame staring up at the holo-screen rendering the

STEEL-WINGED VALKYRIE

activity outside his ship. From the time the first alarm had sounded he hadn't moved from his position, but the crew knew better than to interrupt him.

What he was witnessing was something unheard of: a potential ambush from a capital vessel on an ally of significantly less mass. There had been infighting before—in over 600 years of war it was inevitable—but those handful of occurrences had been starships firing on starships, performative combat, nothing significant beyond the crippling of shields, and nothing as drastic as this.

Whether it was fright or deep consideration of what to do next, Captain Kur was frozen. His frustrated XO, Leon Anu, a handsomely bearded Meluvian, recognizing the crew's need for guidance, took the initiative to order navigation to stand down from plotting an exit jump. He too had recognized what ship it was, but what confounded him was why it was here, and why they hadn't been warned cycles in advance.

He had questioned his captain on their decision to remain in this system despite their orders to jump out, but after numerous arguments and threats to his position, had given up. Now, the bridge was in a state of wonderment, and from the feeds, he could see that the hangar deck was abuzz with activity. This was an Alliance starship, but its proximity was a threat, and they needed to be ready to move to avoid a collision.

On *Missio-Tral*, the mood was very different from the panicked decks of the *Harridan*. Uniformed officers seated in stations about the bridge chatted away on private channels, prepping suggestions for their captain, Felan Lede. Above them, on a raised platform, where a more active set of officers darted about scrutinizing holo-maps, a young Vestalian woman cleared her throat to address the *Harridan* using the captain's private channel.

"*Harridan*, this is *Missio-Tral*. Captain Lede would like a word with Commander Kur," she said, then waited patiently for a minute to pass before looking over at her Virulian commander, who acknowledged her with a nod of his head. He in turn looked down at the XO, who raised his hand with two fingers held high, a sign that the *Harridan* was to receive a final warning. The message was relayed, and the communications officer spoke again. "*Harridan*, this is *Missio-Tral*. We must ask you to respond to our summons, or we will assume this as a sign of non-compliance with a capital ship."

The bridge went silent on *Missio-Tral*; even the computers seemed to quieten. All eyes were on their captain as he leaned over the tall, central war table glaring at a hologram of the *Harridan*. He stood up straight and swiped at the interface to transform it into a view showing *Missio-Tral's* proximity to the rogue infiltrator. With a graceful turn, he surveyed his crew and lifted the communicator to his dark, cracked lips.

Like an orchestra waiting with bated breath to perform a soul-moving symphony, the crew of *Missio-Tral* stood frozen in anticipation of the command they knew would come next. "All hands," Captain Lede growled. "Beat to quarters." And like a conductor bringing in the allegro, *Missio-Tral* came alive with the activity of over 1,000 seasoned spacers.

Marines made their way to the hangar to be in place for boarding dropships, and pilots took to the cockpits of Phantoms, prepping engines for launch. In engineering, practiced hands pulled crystal cores from their cells, replacing them with overcharged reserves. *Missio-Tral's* cannons came online, and her tracers began their charge, as the tactical officers on the bridge worked at picking out targets to cripple the *Harridan's* engines.

It wasn't every cycle that an officer witnessed the ordnance of his allies aimed at him. For Commander Leon Anu, watching phantoms launch to take position about the *Harridan*, it confirmed many months of suspicion that his captain had indeed done something foolish. Their lengthy stay in this remote region alone, the merchant vessels supposedly transporting ship parts from the planet.

He had asked questions, but every time there had been legitimate manifests, and reassurances from his captain. What could he have done, he wondered, more than ask around, which he had done, multiple times. Short of mutiny, he had been powerless, having no evidence of Kur's underhandedness beyond intuition.

Now their crew was being confronted by the deadly effective *Missio-Tral*, a rated warship whose sheer mass was easily three times that of their own. One well-timed torpedo to their failing shields would split them in half if they were lucky enough to maneuver their stern out of the way. "This must be how it feels to be a lizard," he mused, which earned him a look of pure venom from his captain. "What are your orders, sir?" he tried again, hoping to hear something of a plan of action if he was truly refusing to speak to Captain Lede.

The man went back to staring forward, doing nothing, still frozen in disbelief at the situation, Leon could only allow. There was something different about his demeanor, an arrogant sneer at the image of the starship etched against the stars. Was he welcoming this? Leon couldn't qualify any part of his behavior. Surely this was the same Commander Jawal Kur, who he would have gladly followed into anything prior to Genese and his sudden change.

"The bridge is yours, Leon," the older man said, turning to leave. "I have to speak with the Alliance council in my cabin. Hold him off will you, old friend? Give me some time to find out what this is all about." He was already leaving the bridge before the young executive officer could react.

Leon was dumbfounded but he wasn't alone. Puzzled looks came from all corners, nothing directly, but enough to be noticed. One ensign even went so far as to reach around her station to take the hand of a petrified cadet. Knowing glances were passed between officers, unsurprised at Captain Kur's reticence.

Rather than dwell on his captain's failings, Leon picked up the communicator and took a moment to collect himself. "*Missio-Tral*, this is *Harridan*, Commander Leon Anu, Executive Officer. We are willing to comply with your demands."

"Why am I talking to the XO, and not the captain, Commander Anu?" Captain Lede said.

"The captain had an emergency that he is tending to. It's unfortunate timing, but I hope to answer any and all of your questions, Captain Lede," the anxious commander offered.

"Not good enough. The Alliance has questions for your captain. Does the emergency prevent his lips from working, Commander Anu? The Alliance has tried numerous times to reach your captain. What is going on here, man? You have forty-five minutes. Get him to this ship, alone, and ready to talk, or we will be forced to take command of the *Harridan*."

While the captain spoke with Leon Anu, a *Missio-Tral* navigator saw something register on her holo-map near the *Harridan's* starboard dock. One second something appeared there and the next it was gone, as if a glitch had just occurred. Trained to question everything untoward, particularly when it came to holograms, she rewound the time, scrutinized the anomaly, and enlisted a handful of others to help sort it out.

It took a lieutenant, her predecessor, seeing the playback to identify what it was. A vessel had launched from *Harridan* under cover of cloak, using the port opposite their vector to avoid detection. "Commander, we have a runner, cloaked," she shouted into comms, and the XO, Cecil Bo-Antar, ran over to her station to verify the information. It didn't take long for him to confirm, and he rushed back to the captain to whisper in his ear.

Captain Lede was incensed, hanging up on Leon to address the spacers on his own ship. "Launch all fighters, and bring our cannons online. If *Harridan* so much as engages engines, I want her FTL taken offline through violent engagement." He got off the intercom and turned to his XO. "Commander Cho, get Commander Horne up to speed, fast. I want that vessel disabled before it can coordinate a jump."

"We have an incoming EDS," an officer shouted, and the bridge went red with spacers scrambling and the holos from every computer sending out warnings.

"Proximity?" the captain asked coolly.

"It's within range of our tracers, Captain. 8.4km to be exact and charging weapons," a small-framed ensign nasally reported from the communications platform above them.

Captain Lede consulted his holographic starmap, where he saw the new outline of a Geralos destroyer. Cecil Bo-Antar walked over to join him. "This can't be happening," he muttered, walking around the table to get a better view of the massive warship.

It was a bulbous mass, reminiscent of a potato, the hull's material seemingly organic, with cannons stacked in five rows, and launching pylons mounted around what would be considered the stern. What it lacked in beauty it more than made up with the fear it evoked in every Alliance vessel. Destroyers against any ship less its mass was an instant death sentence, and they were strong enough to hold their own against starships fighting alone.

Bo-Antar mouthed a curse and tightened his fists.

"It will be coming out of shift where our stern is exposed, but we're already arming our cannons." Captain Lede indicated with his hands for Bo-Antar, and two other officers that had come up to converse with him.

Commander Homerus Cho, *Missio-Tral's* officer in charge of tactics, kept hands tucked behind his back while he inclined to scrutinize the incoming Geralos vessel. Chief Engineer Chrystal Ma-

Ren thrust a finger at the static from whence the destroyer had emerged. "Coming out of shift, they will be low on energy and have to recharge before they can fire anything stronger than ballistics," she informed her captain.

"Low shields and delayed tracers," Captain Lede considered. "This gives us advantage, but the *Harridan* is compromised. That leaves us exposed if we focus our attentions on the lizards."

"A team of Shrikes and Marines aboard a pair of cruisers is all I need to penetrate *Harridan's* defenses," Cho added confidently. "Our fighters can work at weakening her shields, distracting her cannons and induce some panic. If that's the captain on the fleeing cruiser, the crew may not be as willing to keep up his defiance. With all that going on, the Shrikes can be secreted to a hatch while the Marines storm the hangars. Distractions everywhere, with limited casualties should the Shrikes gain the bridge."

"And what about our runner?" Cecil Bo-Antar asked, ever the skeptic whenever it came to Commander Homerus Cho, whose confidence he viewed as youthful naivete.

"Horne's Blood Wraiths have already launched, Commander," Cho explained. "The cruiser is cloaked, so the shield is exposed, making them easy for our squadron to disable. My only concern is that the cruiser is heading for the planet or to another warship, which could put our fighters in a vulnerable position."

"You think that the crew isn't complicit, Mr. Cho?" the captain asked, looking directly at the tactician, who shook his head in disagreement. "And you, Cecil?" He gave his second a measuring look. The humorless Bo-Antar may have thought his second-guessing of Cho had gone unnoticed, but Felan Lede, ever observant, did know.

Bo-Antar confirmed. "I agree with Commander Cho, Captain. The spacers serving on *Harridan's* decks are most likely hostages, unaware of what's happening. If we can reach them, we can take that ship. Their XO did seem unsure, didn't he?"

Captain Lede had to agree. "Let's see where their loyalty lies then. Commander Cho, carry out the plan, and Lieutenant Ma-Ren, I want that lizard jumping back out of this space. Cecil, we need reinforcements sooner than later in case this is the first of a fleet of lizards coming for this prize." He stopped to wipe at his brow, where he'd started perspiring from the intense light coming from the table. "Communications team, patch me through to the *Harridan* on a secure channel."

"Patching you through now, Captain," a voice said, and in less than a minute he was back on the line with a frazzled Leon Anu.

"*Harridan*, you are suspected of mutiny," Captain Lede informed him. "You were offered a chance to explain your behavior, and what do you do? You launch a cruiser, cloaked, while talking compromise to placate me. Not only that—" He cut Leon Anu off, who kept trying to proclaim their innocence. "A Geralos destroyer appears within range of our tracers. Hell of a coincidence, Commander Anu? Now, you have one last chance. Stand down, and allow our Marines to board without any interference."

While the captain spoke, *Missio-Tral's* engines came online, and she turned in such a way to angle her broadside towards the destroyer. This put her stern out of range of their weapons, as a squadron of phantoms raced out towards the enemy ship. Kinetic cannons came online, starting to bark as explosive rounds soared across the soundless vacuum to whittle away at the shields protecting the destroyer's hull.

As the Chief Engineer had predicted, the ship's depleted energy hurt its defenses to the point where it had to commit everything to its shields. This rendered the ballistics nearly worthless, but the fighters were already adding their own ordnance to the attack. Without the energy to go evasive, the Geralos launched their own zip-ships as a counter, and brought their ballistic cannons online to volley bullets back at *Missio-Tral*.

Missio-Tral, however, was loaded with energy reserves, and a crew of spacers who lived for destroying Geralos vessels. Her helmsmen kept her coming about until she was lined up perpendicular to the destroyer, presenting a smaller target for the Geralos cannons. She would turn one way, presenting enough of her broadside to unload a salvo before shifting back to become a thin target again.

Back and forth they peppered one another, lines of tracers from *Missio-Tral* swiping back and forth across the destroyer's hull refracting harmlessly from the still-intact shields. The squadrons flew wide arcs out of range of the crossfire, and collided with the zip-ships buzzing about the mothership, playing at defense. Two cruisers loaded with Marines launched from a private dock, reserved for VIPs and the captain's vessels. They crossed the space to the *Harridan*, escorted by five phantoms from the squadron.

From the bridge of *Harridan*, Commander Leon Anu tried to keep his composure as he watched the vessel approaching against the backdrop of the warring ships. He thought back on the past, the madness of the captain, which had only gotten worse over time. First it was the command to stay in this region of Genesian space where nothing was happening: no trade, no Geralos for them to fight, and no missions from *Helysian*.

For an infiltrator whose role was to hunt the enemy, that command had struck him as odd, but he let himself think that the captain had a reason. The cruisers transporting ship parts, trading for fuel with a shipwright who operated directly from the planet. That too was odd, but when he had brought it to his captain's attention, he was threatened and accused of insubordination, a night where he believed his career as an officer was finished.

With no communication coming from *Helysian* in months, *Harridan* had become a small empire with an authoritarian ruler in Jawal Kur. Leon Anu had been a part of it; he had been complicit, so why should he deserve better from the Alliance than Kur himself? Whatever his captain had done, he would be made to answer for it, and as the XO, he couldn't use ignorance as a defense. "This is my last chance," he mouthed the words so that no one in his vicinity could hear.

"Commander, we have seven vessels on approach to our hangar," a voice announced over comms. "Two armed cruisers and five Phantoms. They are asking for permission to come aboard."

"Let them in," Leon Anu snapped, suddenly irritated. "It's the *thyping Missio-Tral*, what else would we do, take on a starship? I will follow orders and meet with Captain Lede, but first have master-of-arms Morin get me the names and ranks of every spacer that has visited Genese since our arrival. This includes officers and Marines. Send the information to my personal mail, and tell Major Virden Josk that I need to see him on the bridge."

18

Since their first day of construction, the Basce City tenements had been given a variety of names by both those who were forced to live there and those who looked down on them from the spires above. Streets strewn with refuse, spice vials, and filth of every variety, were the playgrounds for children, whose destiny was limited to two paths: become an enforcer or someone that had to be enforced.

Stacked, tiered housing made privacy near impossible, and the narrow roads too dangerous for the security force to chance. Due to this, the gangs became the law of the districts, a role respected over time, even by the government, who entertained some of their demands in order to keep the peace. Wanted criminals, out of favors and credits for bribes, would be turned out of the zones, where BasPol could make an arrest.

This was the system, a nefarious partnership, unknown to most but the men and women who lived at the top of the tenements. Those crime bosses with small armies at their beck and command, and penthouses that could rival those elites who paid them to smuggle in vice. Violence was a way of life in Basce City, so for the citizens born within her walls, seeing armed patrols was so normal it gave no cause for alarms.

The Nighthawks had been cleared by Thrall to enter the tenements, and had arrived in the middle of the night to the tightly set facade of multi-tiered buildings. There were hundreds of these settlements, similarly constructed, though rundown to the point where some were literal ruins. Stone stairwells and iron lifts gave access to the upper floors, some climbing as high as eight stories with bridges spanning the rooftops for convenient access.

Every door was a business, or a former home made into something else, and every tier was its own plaza of shops, apartments, and entertainment. Signs were painted on wood for most of these enterprises, but there were a few who spent the credits on more decorative signage using lights.

Even at night the streets were filled with people going about their business, some milling about with drinks, winding down the day with their friends. Helga had seen that despite their attempts at dressing down, they still stuck out amongst the brightly colored hair, loose-fitting clothing and masked faces. There were chemicals in the air, a sweet pungent addition to the sewage and aromas coming from the carts that several vendors were manning.

Here was society the way it would have once been in Vestalia, ignoring the dilapidated state of everything. When they arrived and parked, a trio of teens—two boys shouldering rifles— introduced themselves as "runners for Thrall," sent to make sure they wouldn't be bothered by the residents. Despite a few knowing looks among themselves at the absurdity of armed children protecting Nighthawks, Cilas and team fell in with the youngsters.

The parking lot had been outside the tall wall that separated the stockade, or stocks—as the natives named it—from the free-standing buildings and beach that bordered the property. Once inside, it became a market, and outside of the smell, no one dared try to speak or approach their party. Children were everywhere, running and laughing when they weren't crying or screaming from some mischief.

It all rang similar to the hubs that Helga had experienced, and though she stayed guarded, it just didn't feel as ominous as it looked from a distance. The adults looked hardy, and the gangsters became evident to the Nighthawks once they realized that they were the best dressed, and the only ones brave enough to stare. No BasPol presence was felt here, unless they were out of uniform to mask their identity.

It all seemed like just another night for the residents, without any of the violence that they had been told to expect from agents of William Vray. The Nighthawks walked in silence, bowed in cloaks against the drizzling rain, which didn't seem to bother the residents. Eventually they reached Fio's building, a six-floor stack with a busy, open market on the ground floor. Fio's home was on the third floor between a hair salon and a gun store.

"Who are you?" a child's voice shouted, and Helga looked up to see a bundle of limbs and rags drop from above, though their guides didn't seem too concerned that they were being attacked. It was a boy, no older than 11 years old, with a shock of red hair, freckles, and a ratty brown raincoat that had seen better days. He had stuck the landing masterfully, bounded up and walked towards them, unafraid of the two armed boys, and the strangers draped in cloaks.

The shorter of the two armed boys stepped forward to intercept his path, mumbled something unintelligible, and the boy stopped his approach to mumble something back. "This one knows Miss Fio," the boy relayed to Cilas in a broken attempt at Universal Vestalian. "He is, what's the word?" he asked his taller partner, who made a sign with one hand before falling back dutifully to watch the upper tiers. "He is a lookout, you understand? Fio's friend. Maybe you speak to him?"

"Is this really necessary?" Helga muttered. "We're completely exposed out here."

"Exposed is why he's on us," Raileo explained over comms. "Like a hub, these stocks aren't exactly safe for anyone, even if you grew up here. Fio likely pays the neighborhood children to be her eyes and ears. This little man is only doing his job. Could be useful actually, if we can convince him that we're with her."

Cilas pushed back the hood of his cloak and approached the boy, who shrunk back hesitantly when he saw the Nighthawk's tired red eyes above his rawboned, unimpressed visage. "Fio hired us to come because she's in trouble," he relayed flatly. "She cannot come home until the bad men are gone. We will be here for a few days, waiting, so when they arrive, they have us to deal with and not her. Understand?"

The boy looked over at the Genesians to get their cosign, and when they gave it, he stepped back and bowed. "I will watch too, for Fio," he responded dutifully. "I live upstairs, but come down using the pipes." His grin was a child's grin, full of mischief, shattering Helga's icy defenses when she realized he was trying to be brave for his friends.

"If anyone comes, we would prefer you stay inside," Cilas instructed him. "There will be—"

"BasPol," the boy blurted out. "They come before, for Fio. This is why she hired you, I understand. My name is Aquilo, I can see far from up there." He gestured to the floor above Fio's level. "I saw when you come in, I warned everybody. I will do it again when they come tomorrow. You can count on me. Hey, I gave you my name, what is yours?"

"Cilas. I am Cilas, and those four are Helga, Ray, Q, and Anders. You say you live upstairs, with your parents?"

The boy shook his head hesitantly as if he worried that in admitting to having parents, he had somehow compromised his family. "

When you see them coming, Aquilo, you and whoever you live with need to look out for yourselves. Do you understand?" Cilas opened his coat to expose the shiny black auto-rifle hanging from his shoulder, and the young lookout's face lit up with amusement.

"I understand," the boy said quickly, scanning each of their faces with a newfound respect.

"Give us a moment." Quentin's deep voice brought their attention around to where he shambled forward towards Cilas and their new friend. He knelt on the wet floor to level his eyes with that of the child, and started talking to him in a language that Helga did not understand. "We can go in now, he does understand the situation," he finally said, touching fists with the young man, who was astonished to find that one of their number was a fellow Genesian.

Cilas tipped their guides and let himself in using Fio's door code. Inside was a tiny, three-room apartment with cream-colored walls, soft black carpeting, and humble furnishings. It was all so normal and neat that Helga had to reassess her thoughts on Fio Doro, and how she knew next to nothing about their resident fugitive. They placed their packs near the door and laid their wet cloaks and boots on top of them. It was cold inside the apartment, but Raileo located the heating unit and soon they were comfortable.

"It's a shame she had to leave all her things," Helga said, reaching down to pick up a baby doll that seemed to have been waiting for her owner. There was a handgun wedged into the cushions below it, prompting a nod of appreciation from Quentin Tutt.

"That Fio's no fool," Raileo said, plopping down next to Anders, who looked ready to pass out at any minute. "She had us come here to collect her things. Shelter's just our payment."

Cilas seemed to find that amusing. "I was thinking the same thing. Look at this place. She must have worked years to have it look so nice? Compared to all the *schtill* she's made to live in."

"Can you imagine living down here?" Helga said. "Stuck between that vast ocean and all of this *schtill*?"

Raileo raised his hand sheepishly, followed by Cilas, and Anders, though reluctantly. All three had been born on hubs, the spatial equivalent of the tenements. She felt foolish and exposed, wanting to reel back time and lock her lips. Of course, they could imagine this miserable life; it was the reason their parents had sent them to the Alliance. Her story was different. She was the child of a Marine and an architect. There was no poverty, just loss, and she had been practically raised on a starship.

"Well, guess who looks like an ass now," she surrendered, rolling her eyes. "Q, a little help? You see me bleeding out here?"

"I don't think the lieutenant is questioning the conditions so much as the fact that there's no access to space," Quentin tried, earning him a chorus of boos from the three men.

Helga threw up her hand to get their attention. "I'm just trying to say that I admire Fio," she explained. "I admit it, I underestimated her. Thought her to be just a lucky survivor who needed protection. Being here really gives me perspective on the reality of her situation. You can say it puts the story together. We don't get to pick the conditions of our birth; I get that. The majority of our recruits do come from hubs. I just want you all to know that's what I meant."

"Well, I agree with you that imagining life here is hell." Raileo shrugged. "I'm not going to act like it's a badge of honor coming from *schtill*. I think the thing we all agree on is that we made it out of it. That could include Fio if it all works out. So don't feel bad, we're just giving you a hard time. It's funny when it gets all awkward like that."

"This whole thing is a disgrace, let's be honest," Quentin added. "This city is known for its exports, but the people here are living worse than any hub. That's insane."

"No argument here, brother, but it isn't our concern." Cilas waved an authoritative ration bar at them. "Let's keep our heads in the game. You make this personal and you're going to leave yourself open. I want us to go in, unseen, and get the hell out with the two *thypes* responsible for selling out the Alliance. If we can ground those Marines, that's the cherry on top, but we're not here to overthrow their government."

"Do you know what I hate?" Raileo blurted as if he hadn't heard a word that anyone said. "I hate being a Boomer."

Helga was sure this was the beginning of a joke. "What's wrong with being a Boomer?"

"People think you're limited, and they're not entirely off-base. We're not ignorant, but the look they give you when you admit to it, as if they pity the poor little star child, it's so condescending."

"Hmph," Helga said. "Never looked at it like that. Now I feel bad."

"Why? Aren't we all Boomers here?"

"Nope. Some of us were born on a planet but were taken too early to remember it," she said, reaching for her pack to look inside it for another ration bar.

"That label has more to do with who you know than where you were born, Ray," Quentin advised him. "We all are boomers. Everyone here grew up on a starship, learning how to aim straight. You shouldn't feel bad about them giving you looks. It's not like the Alliance cares where you were born, and even if they did, wouldn't they favor their spacers?"

"The lizards don't care," Anders drawled.

"I like him." Quentin pointed at Anders. "You hear that, Cilas? The lizards don't care. See, that is what I'm talking about. Here we have a Nighthawk with his head in the game."

"Hey, before we relax, I have to do this," Cilas said, prompting the other four Nighthawks to look at him, confusion reflected across their tired faces. "I need to give you the identification of our target. You should see him appear within your view if you're still wearing your lenses, which you really should not be removing when we're deployed. Do you understand?"

They all agreed in a garbled blend of, "Yes Cilas," "Got it, Rend," "Oh, it's right there," and, "I see it," not realizing how silly they appeared, moving their hands around in front of their faces, playing with the interface. Before them was a holographic information card displaying the resume and computer-generated likeness of Garson Sunveil.

His information was sparse, but his occupation, Alliance recruiter, made Helga want to laugh out loud.

"Think this 'recruiter' ever served on the deck of even one of our lite cruisers?" Helga asked.

"This old man has only ever ridden shuttles up to Neroka and the other stations, and not as a recruiter," Raileo offered.

"Ray's right, Helga. When I asked Colonel Fumo about him, he said that there were absolutely no recruiters on record in Basce City," Cilas added.

"I remember," Helga said, wondering if he had forgotten that both she and Fio were there. "Why impersonate a recruiter? It isn't like a luxurious position, or one with any power. What is the benefit?"

"Do you really want to find out?" Anders gloomily asked her. "It won't be anything good. This *cruta* is the same one sending bounty hunters for Fio, isn't he? He's not a good person, and he's using our name. That to me is enough to warrant trial then execution. All these poor souls in places like this all over the galaxy look to the Alliance for hope. Men like Sunveil erode that, and without the Alliance, why would humanity have any hope?"

"That was almost poetic." Raileo tilted his cup towards him, with a straight face to show that he actually meant it.

They talked for hours switching between subjects, from where they were born to their thoughts on the mission, never staying on a single topic too long. Helga participated but it all felt forlorn, like this could be their last night together. She exchanged glances with Cilas, who looked to be thinking the same thing. It was getting late, so he suggested they all get some sleep.

Helga being both the smallest and the highest rank after Cilas, was given Fio's bedroom to sleep where she could have some privacy. The other Nighthawks slept in the living area, Cilas taking first watch to secure the door until the start of what would be the equivalent of the Navy's third shift.

Inside Fio's chest of drawers Helga found a treasure trove of contraband. All manner of weapons, stimulants, spices, and bejeweled clothes unlike anything she'd seen before. The bed was small but still managed to occupy two-thirds of the space, and on the ceiling spun an orb projecting images onto the walls. They were of people, photographs from Fio Doro's past, giving Helga an idea of the woman's journey through the years.

There was a young, innocent Fio, standing between a man and woman who she resembled. She was no older than eight and looked to be happy. Another showed her seated on a hover bike with a girl behind her armed with a rifle. The Fio in this photograph looked to be thirteen but the innocence was gone, replaced by a hardness to her eyes.

The last photo was her with a much older man. She was standing in front of him brandishing pistols pointed at the viewer. Helga put her at about sixteen years old. She wore a scowl and her eyes had gone from hard to happy again, and there was a caption. "Wherever you go, whatever you do, I will always have your back. Love Pops." Helga's hand came up to her mouth when she recalled Fio mentioning her father being killed.

The remainder of the images were posters of fashion models, each in a different style and variety of dress. The bed was comfortable despite its looks and Helga passed out as soon as her head touched the pillow. She woke up to shouting, and thinking it was coming from the front of the apartment, she quickly pulled on her gear to rush out and join them.

All four Nighthawks were at a window, each in a different state of undress. She crossed to see what had them so curious and heard more shouting coming from the street below them. "What is going on out there?" she asked.

"Good you're awake," Cilas said. "Aquilo came earlier, warning us that BasPol, which is the local security force, is kicking in people's doors searching for Fio."

"Change of plans then?" Helga pressed rhetorically, letting her eyes roam over the rooftops of the stair-stacked buildings in the distance. It was dawn and dry, the sky awash with all manner of colors, and the sun was on the rise, revealing the filth along the sides of the streets and in the alleyways. People were up and starting their day, but some were being questioned by what appeared to be an armored militia. "They look pretty damned geared and loaded to be police."

"They're thugs, and like I told young Aquilo, he and his people need to hunker down, and when they finally come to this apartment, we'll give them hell," Cilas said. "One is bound to know where our target is located, so they're doing us a favor by coming here. You see how splintered they operate? One or two per building as they canvas the area. We wait them out, take them down, and get one talking to get a name or some form of location."

Somewhere in the distance, Helga heard the chattering feedback of an auto-rifle, and that was when she saw the source of the chaos. On one of the tiers directly across from them, a BasPol officer was having a shouting match with a woman. He wore black padded armor, thin enough to be form-fitting with red stripes down the sides of his arms and legs. The woman turned to leave, and he reached to pull her back, but his partner walked up and stopped him, waving her away.

Cilas stood up and walked over to the side of the door where he waited expectantly as they all turned to eye him curiously. "I am going to guess that they were the same men who were tearing up half the city searching for Fio last night," he suggested. "We were warned about them working for the enemy, remember? They likely left before we arrived, and came back this morning with numbers to cover more area. Which means that they'll probably be coming—"

The door flew open and Cilas stepped out from the side, grabbed an intruder by his chest plate, rolled backwards, and threw him over his head and into the table, shattering it on impact. Quentin sprang forward to take the second man, grabbing his arm to send him crashing into his partner and then the wall behind him. He checked outside for more but found none so he barred the door.

Helga went inside Cilas's pack, took out some cuffs and bound their prisoners, securing both their ankles and wrists.

"Way to respond the hard way, Rend," Raileo said, "But what are we to do with them?"

"I don't know, Ray," Helga responded before the commander, placing her boot on one of the men's chest. "The way they roughed up all those women, we can start by cutting out their tongues."

"Easy, butcher," Cilas said softly, touching his temple to remind her that an officer should remain calm even in this instance. He then crouched over the other man, the one he originally threw and who was now up in a seated position. "Whoever you are, you're going to answer all of my questions. Are we clear? First question. Are you two really BasPol officers?"

"No," the man answered, too quick for any of them to believe it. Cilas put a hand over the liar's mouth then slammed his knife into his shoulder between the armor plates. Even with his mouth covered, the man's scream of pain could be heard just as clear as day.

"I'm going to ask you again. Are you BasPol?"

"Yes," he shouted, staring at the entrance as if hoping help was on the way.

"Good," Cilas responded. "You see now I don't have to hurt you. Keep telling me the truth, and you may actually get out of this alive. My brother Quentin there will take your friend to the other room, and he will be asking the same questions. I don't have to tell you what happens if the answers don't match in the end, right?"

The two men were surprisingly forthcoming when they realized that they were dealing with professionals and not gangsters from the neighborhood. The Nighthawks learned about Garson Veil, and how he had told them that a traitor from the stocks was looking to smuggle intelligence out to the Geralos. BasPol wasn't being paid for their involvement; these had been orders passed down to their chief by an official, William Vray.

This information corroborated most of what they knew, and helped to clarify why the city's police force was working against them.

Cilas got the information on Garson Veil's estate, and was pleased to hear it could be accessed from the stocks. The men knew nothing about Vray, other than he was a councilman who was over the district, and known to have some dealings with a few smugglers.

"The Marines," Quentin said to his man, when Cilas was finished with his own interrogation and crossed over to check on him. "The Alliance Marines that are in this city. Why are they here?"

"I don't know," screamed the man, who was cuffed and hunched over on the carpet. "Wait, did you say Alliance? Oh, I remember now," he quickly added, after Quentin pulled a knife from his boot and threw it into the air, catching it skillfully in a reverse grip. "They are investigating something, and we were told to either stay out of their way or help them. They don't want our help, though. A few of them went up to Sunveil's compound. Since he's Alliance, we figured he's hosting them."

"And who do you think we are?" Helga asked from behind Cilas where she had been studying the man's face to see if she could tell if he was bluffing.

"You're obviously mercs, but for who? The *cruta* that owns this place?" The BasPol officer laughed. Cilas and Helga exchanged looks. Despite the questions they were asking, he hadn't picked up on the fact that they were the same Alliance their captive claimed that Garson Sunveil was a part of.

"We ask the questions, not you," Quentin reminded him, driving a big boot into his chest. "Keep this up and you'll make this next part easy. What do you say, Rend? Does his story match up?"

"It does," Cilas admitted, though he stood frozen, looking down at the man, one hand rubbing at his chin while the other gripped his unmarked sidearm. "What do you think, Hel?" He turned to regard her, and Helga felt her jaw tighten and her patience run out. Something told her that this man was simply delaying them by being difficult rather than giving it all up like his partner.

"I think he's stalling, and won't give us anything useful," Helga injected, her voice gone level and cold to reflect her patience having run its course for these men. "He doesn't know who we are. If he did, he would know that these games are useless. We didn't come here to play. How about we hand them over to Thrall as a gesture of appreciation?"

19

With two officers missing, BasPol quickly exited the tenements, a move which meant they were likely to return with the Marines in tow. For several long hours inside Fio's apartment, the Nighthawks busied themselves with preparation for an evening raid on Garson Sunveil's compound. From the location given by the BasPol men earlier, the compound was located north of the tenements, close enough for them to walk.

They each took turns watching the door, weapons live and at the ready. The others passed the time training or staring out the window at the crowds surrounding the market. With BasPol gone, it was all back to normal, the only shouts coming from the vendors hocking their supplies. Cilas called *Ursula*, updated Fio, and spoke at length with Ina Reysor about the status of the crew.

When the sun went down, its light replaced by streetlamps, they were all geared up in their composite armor, concealed by their wet, hooded cloaks. The loadout was auto-rifles and sidearms, but Raileo Lei brought his OKAGI "Widow Maker" Sniper.

On the streets, the rain picked up once again, and brought with it a wind that chilled them to the bone. Cilas took them off the main road into a tight alleyway and onto another that was identical to the first, though with much less people and lights. Hunched close together, they stuck to the sidewalks, every head on a swivel, with hands tucked below the flaps of their cloaks, gripping their weapons.

Many of the people they passed were curious, but not enough to impede them. Helga expected to see Thrall's runners shadowing them to keep them safe so their boss could make good on his word. She realized they hadn't been there earlier, and wondered if they had been the ones shooting it out with the officers. Cilas moved like a man possessed, and her short legs were struggling to keep up with him and Quentin Tutt.

"Some sort of party going on up ahead," Quentin reported, his tall frame giving him a vantage above the crowd. There was the sound of broken glass, shouts rising above the music and rain, an explosion followed by gunfire, and the familiar uniforms of BasPol flanked by soldiers dressed in Alliance Marine armor. Cilas grabbed Quentin before Helga could reach him, the two of them knowing he'd fly into a rage at the treachery of those men.

"Take this alley," Cilas instructed, shoving him to the side of a once-busy bar, whose blue sign illuminated the surprisingly empty alleyway. Looking up, Helga had a moment of reflection, seeing the exterior walls of the buildings that sandwiched them, stretched up and up, seeming to go on forever. Twelve stories of cracked, concrete plaster with bridges, wires and pipelines crisscrossed above them, obstructing the rain.

Raileo ran forward to work at opening the lock, and the other four Nighthawks hugged the building's sides, watching the entrance. The Marines were still shooting. It sounded ominous, and not three times did Helga look to see if Cilas noticed it. He was in a mood, driven, which had been amplified earlier when BasPol kicked in the door.

"We're in," Raileo whispered, pulling open the gate and waving a hand for them to run on ahead.

Helga made to move but Cilas stretched out his arm to stop her, then signaled for the others to do the same. Before them stood a concrete courtyard with a fountain at the center filled with wet refuse. Enclosing it was a tall wall, brown from a combination of wetness and the low light. During the day Helga imagined it would have been more ocher, with its surface covered with graffiti, names, and territorial gang signs.

"What in the worlds is this?" Helga groaned.

"Our northern wall," Cilas replied, walking around the wall, slowly examining the surface. "When BasPol isn't here terrorizing, I imagine that children of the tenements come to this circle to play. I'd even go so far as to say it's a special place, considering the treatment. Maybe for worship, study, who knows? For us, it's the barrier that separates us from Sunveil's compound. I assumed there'd be an entrance over here."

Helga looked for Raileo to chime in with his off-color humor, but the Nighthawk was already pulling himself up onto the barrier.

Reaching down, he held out his hand, but she had to run and place a foot against the wall to gain enough height for him to pull her up beside him. Cilas helped Anders in the same way, but Quentin slapped away his hand. With little effort, he leaped up and grabbed the edge, pulling his large frame up to theirs without missing a breath.

"Oh, to be tall," Helga quipped. "A man your size shouldn't move like that. How is it even fair?" Quentin slapped her backpack playfully before walking around to where Cilas perched looking out at what lay ahead. "Sunveil sics his dogs on the tenements all while he sits comfortably in this compound living off them," the big Nighthawk commented.

"Alliance, my rear. This crook has it coming. He deserves everything we're about to give to him," Cilas added.

"Just look at this place," Anders remarked. "One man owns all this?"

Spread out below them on the other side of the wall was a tremendous garden, filled with all manner of exotic plants, wide-branched trees, and a manicured lawn. It stretched on for 50 meters, stopping at a wall of bushes, trimmed in such a way they appeared as an impenetrable wall. From where they surveyed, a walkway made of stone bridged the garden to a gap in the bushes, behind which the Nighthawks saw buildings, squat and unremarkable, like a prison or barracks.

Above it all, faded in the backdrop, sat the manor of Garson Sunveil. This they saw plainly, even above the highest branches of the trees. A two-level marvel of unrestrained creativity and architectural execution. Giant concrete cubes, stacked at odd angles, like ice cubes fused together inside a tall narrow glass. Each floor seemed to collapse into the one below it, with no visible supports, only the marvel of physics defying what they knew of gravity.

Tiny sparks flew about the top—that's how they appeared to Helga, who after some time realized they were drones. She always thought Reapers resembled miniature fighters, winged and aerodynamic in design but for the disproportionate cannon on their bellies. They were absolutely menacing, silent on the approach and deadly accurate with their aim.

"You know what this reminds me of?" she asked no one in particular. "Stories from old Vestalia. How the enlightened, instead of sharing knowledge, used it to exploit the masses to accumulate wealth."

Cilas bristled. "This is Sanctuary all over, they just aren't willing to hide it. Whoever this Garson Sunveil is, he's set himself up as tenement king, building his corrupt empire where they can all be reminded of it."

"Silly king to impersonate an Alliance recruiter," Quentin said. "No one here to set that *cruta* straight, and he's backed by *Helysian* Marines. Am I awake, Rend? Is this really happening?"

As a unit they crossed the lawn at a sprint, boots crushing flowers and carefully manicured hedges. They scrambled from tree to tree, sticking to the shadows. Lights for the property were provided mostly through lanterns and floodlights mounted on tall posts, but a large portion of that green field remained shrouded in the blackness of the night. This was how they remained unseen, crossing the field to a wall of bushes separating it from a gravel road that wound about the compound.

The bushes were low, so the team hunkered down, waiting on Quentin, who crept forward to peer through the leaves to see what was waiting over there. Like Helga and the others, he had his heads-up display visible, where he could receive messages and feeds sent discreetly by the other operators. It wasn't his PAS with a screen capable of night-vision, but it had many other features to help with communication.

"Contact," Quentin whispered. "Solo sentry at the gate, armored, holding an auto-rifle. Shot is clear, just awaiting your call, Rend."

"I have eyes on two reapers making their way over to our location," Raileo informed them. "We may want to seek cover below something or take them out."

Cilas glanced up at the night sky. "*Thype* the drones. What can you make of the sentry? Anything that identifies him as Alliance?"

"Think I see a patch, and he's holding an ASR blue-shell," Quentin reported, describing what was the Alliance Marine's preferred auto-rifle. Cilas tapped Raileo on the shoulder, and he and Anders crawled past Quentin to aim up at the drones flying over towards the garden.

They all raised their guns and aimed, holding for Cilas's command, and Quentin brought his knife up to his chest and took a breath. Jumping through the gap in the bushes, he struck like a viper uncoiled. The sentry, who had stopped for a moment to scan the air in the opposite direction, could not have seen the big Nighthawk coming.

"Stay back," Quentin shouted, his knife still buried in the dead man's chest. "Sentry's a Cel-toc, I'm in the *schtill*. This is some kind of—"

"No," Cilas exclaimed. "Ray, Anders, take out those drones and get to Tutt."

Anders took a shot at his reaper, striking it dead center, causing it to fall to the asphalt, crackling where the rain struck its now mangled and exposed wires. At the same time, Raileo struck his where he knew them to be the most vulnerable, in the belly, directly above the gun. The drone he shot came apart from the bullet, raining bits and pieces all over the lawn. Helga and Cilas were already up, sprinting past them to join Quentin where he crouched.

"If it was rigged you would be dead already, and Ray cleared the rooftops. The only thing left were those two reapers," Cilas explained.

"We should hurry," Helga urged. "This is a road, and something could pull through at any minute. Drag that body inside and hide it. Anders, collect what's left of that reaper, and grab that ASR. It's Alliance property."

As a unit, in stack formation, they advanced to the rear of the nearest building. Here it was dark and would provide cover if any more reapers came by. "Get airborne, Nighthawk," Cilas directed Raileo, who broke off from the line to run back the way they had come. He would look for a suitable rooftop to scale and establish a secure position to guide them from the top.

The ground was flooded from the downpour, forcing them into puddles that came up to their ankles. To keep up their stealth they moved slow, stopping at every break in the building to check for enemies. Helga kept an eye on the rooftops, searching for snipers. The buildings were so rundown they resembled ruins, and if they were ever housing for people, it would have had to be in a past age.

Deep down Helga knew they had been a part of the tenements prior to the construction of the wall. She guessed that the people who once lived here were run off or killed so someone could take their property. It would have been fairly recent, so she filed it away in her mind to ask Fio about later.

After the fourth house, Cilas took them back west, towards the main pathway leading up to the manor. There was a wide gap between the ruined buildings with a large, blocky reservoir in the center. Water spilled out of it making a pool about its base, the downpour steadily adding even more liters. Helga saw something move in the distance, but it was too dark for her to make out what it was.

"Place is like a ghost ship. Eerie," Raileo commented from somewhere above them on the rooftops.

Thump-thump. Cilas fired his handgun, and Helga's lens registered the target, outlining a corpse slumped behind the reservoir. He appeared to be another Marine with an auto-rifle and an assortment of Alliance weapons. Like before, they disarmed him; dead men had no need for guns. Helga upgraded her sidearm with his heavy pistol, a practical cannon in her hands. With the guns reclaimed, Cilas picked up the pace.

Another overflowing reservoir with a much larger building loomed before them, but as they made to start towards it, a pair of black clad men rushed out at them. Anders opened up his auto-rifle, cutting one down before he could make it to any cover. Helga fired at the next one, aiming for his torso but she underestimated the kick of the pistol and hit him in the shoulder, where it struck his armor and ricocheted off a wall and into his head.

"Don't move, Nighthawks," Raileo whispered, and then they heard the unique sound of his Widow Maker firing two blasts at the distant building. Helga saw the window shatter and a body fall, landing in a sickening crunch where it broke apart like ice. Cryogenic rounds were Raileo's favorite, so the people he shot would be frozen, thus cutting off their screams. "Sniper down," he reported. "I'm seeing incoming transports behind us on the road."

"They'll find our dead Cel-toc, so they will know we're in here," Cilas commanded. "They don't know who we are and what we're capable of, so at the very least we're still a mystery and that lends us some advantage. Our only recourse now is speed to make it to the main building. Mercs, Alliance, BasPol, it makes no difference what we come across. From now on you have one directive, outside of our target, you're to neutralize anything toting a gun."

The wind picked up and the rain was cascading sideways, the sound of thunder crashing like explosions. They worked their way past the large building where Raileo killed the sniper, and started running towards the manor, staying crouched behind the ruins, fallen columns, and disabled transports. They only slowed for Raileo to catch up after he shot another reaper patrolling the grounds.

They made it to the courtyard without further incident, and hunkered down inside an abandoned house. Helga was feeling the fatigue of their lengthy trek to make it there, her quadriceps burning from the constant squatting, and the anxiety making her testy. "I see three armors having a chat north of our position," Quentin reported.

"What's with all these transports? They look functional and there's footprints all in the mud," Helga pointed out.

"Five reapers making the rounds," Raileo reported.

"This looks like an important meeting. That's why he has all the security," Anders said. "We chose a bad night. Our target's entertaining guests, the type of guests that require armed guards and Marines-for-hire. Who do you think we're likely to find inside there?"

"Stay on walls and mind your cover," Cilas urged.

"Maybe we'll get lucky and find both our marks in the building together," Helga offered with a shrug.

"Regardless of what's in there, we have to make it across this courtyard to find out, so cut the chatter," Cilas hissed, with enough finality for all four members of his team obey.

Now that they were inside the perimeter of the property, Helga fully understood why the layout had been confusing on every front. The garden at the border to the tenements had been the original beginning of Sunveil's lavish setup. The citizens, annoyed though powerless against the official, had struck back by lobbing trash over the walls, and that had forced Sunveil to reconsider.

With the garden constantly under assault, he had instead built northward on the other side of a barely used road. Buildings were razed, hence the ruins that remained, and the bricks were reclaimed and used on his residence, which still appeared to be unfinished. She imagined that in the end, once it was fully completed, the remaining buildings would be flattened, or at the very least reclaimed. The muddy soil would be tilled, grass would be planted, and the compound would morph into a thing of beauty.

What still confounded her, however, was Sunveil's lie that he was an Alliance representative. It was obvious that he was a man of wealth and considerable power, so why would he have need for such a facade? Did it have anything to do with the Marines helping? Was Sunveil a former Alliance figurehead, long since removed, but holding on to the amenities and reach of his former office?

The answers would be inside that manor, she hoped, though whether or not they would have the opportunity to search was unknown. They slipped back into the shadows, timing the reaper's patrols to advance on Sunveil's home. Armed men stalked the entrance, and the lights on the neighboring buildings shone with the brilliance of miniature suns. Helga saw a myriad of uniforms, hinting at something nefarious.

Quentin spoke softly where his voice would only carry through comms. "Without knowing our mission details, what does this gathering remind you of, Cilas?"

"A briefing," Cilas answered. "Local militias meeting an Alliance impostor to plot something against their government or its people."

"Clearing that building is going to be necessary if we don't want bullets in our back," Helga suggested. "All of these barriers and walls everywhere; it's going to be a maze if we stay on the ground. We'll be at a disadvantage, and Ray alone won't be able to pick them off with reapers complicating things. I say we find a way up into that structure and neutralize every target that gets in our way. That's how we'll maintain our speed and what's left of our cover now that they're coming."

"Ate's got a point, Rend," Quentin added. "It's much too quiet, and if Ray hadn't spotted those snipers, we'd likely be loud right now with our target in the wind. Why don't we take the high ground, using the rooftops to travel to ... whatever that building is supposed to be. Sunveil's house? *Thype*, what a waste of resources."

"Good thinking, Nighthawks, let's do it." Cilas urged them forward towards the closest building.

20

Alliance starships are built for war, but function more as floating cities for conscripted warriors spending their lives to train and prepare for enemy engagement. Built in space, these vessels doubled as both refuge and enforcer for the Vestalian people, displaced for over a millennium by the Geralos.

Recognizing the importance of these ships as representatives of the lost planet, the Alliance council recommended that its captains leave the fights to vessels built exclusively for engagement. This meant infiltrators, cruisers, assault ships, and fighters leaving the starship to act as a defensive juggernaut, orbiting the Allied planets to keep the Geralos off.

Missio-Tral's captain, Felan Lede, had never agreed with the council on this. In his mind, the starship was their strongest weapon against the Geralos, and in keeping them out of fights, it had only extended the war to where it now seemed endless.

When he had received word of a potential traitor at the helm of an Alliance infiltrator, he had reached out to Captain Abe Rus of *Helysian* to ask him what he intended to do. *Helysian* was stuck on the far side of the planet, serving as a deterrent to Geralos invaders. Abe Rus let Captain Lede know that if they jumped out to reclaim the *Harridan*, it would leave the space exposed to Geralos invasion.

That wasn't good enough for the hot-blooded captain, who informed Abe Rus in so many words, that he would volunteer to "clean up his mess." Now, as he watched as his *Missio-Tral* softened the destroyer's shields for his primed torpedoes, Lede felt somewhat vindicated for his sharp admonishment of *Helysian's* captain. Even his commanders had underestimated the importance of stopping this mutiny. Overkill, they had termed it for him to bring *Missio-Tral* instead of their new infiltrator, *Inference*.

Had he followed the advice of those thrust heads, *Inference* would have been sucked in by the *Harridan*, all to get savaged by the Geralos destroyer. Thousands of lives would have been lost, and he would have been blamed for sending them off to their deaths. Now, because he had come personally to remove the traitor, *Harridan's* treacherous captain was no longer at the helm, and her crew would be escorted back to *Helysian*, where there would be a court-martial and proper refitting.

"Tracers have come online," a tactical officer reported.

"Already?" Captain Felan Lede reached into the hologram which still displayed a diagram of the three ships exchanging ordnance. With a practiced motion, the image changed into that of the destroyer, with a visible shield. A caption appeared above it: "Overcharged shields at 40%," it read.

He looked down at his wrist-comms, where the dark glass screen held all the readouts from *Missio-Tral's* systems for him to scrutinize. Her shields were still at 70% despite being on auxiliary power, and a tracer focused could bring them down to 53%, but in that time, they would respond, and the Geralos captain, knowing that, wouldn't gamble on his life.

"What are you playing at, you scaly *thype*?" he muttered below his breath. "Mr. Cho, why the trace?"

"It isn't intended for us, Captain," Homerus Cho said as he walked about the table surveying the ships. "I think it means to strike the *Harridan*."

An explosion of panic went off in the captain's brain and he brought his wrist-comms up to his lips. "Alert the *Harridan*," he roared into the intercom, too frustrated with himself for not having seen it. "Lieutenant Banks, put us in the path of that tracer, double-time now, make it happen. We may not catch it in time, but we must try, Maker save us. All fighters, focus your fire on the destroyer, missiles are free, unload it all. Do you hear me? Give them everything."

He shifted the hologram back to the engagement view, where he could see at various angles where the bow of the *Harridan* was exposed to the destroyer's trace laser emitter. He slammed his fist into the table when it became clear that neither ship could move fast enough to avoid what was coming.

From the bow of the destroyer, a thin line of white light split the blackness to then vanish off the exposed end of the *Harridan's* hull, stretching beyond it like a line cast into pitch black water. The line thickened and shimmered, becoming a laser, blindingly hot, and stretching on from the tip of the emitter out beyond the location of the *Harridan*. It grew as it moved, destroying any fighter unlucky enough to be in its path when it came on and intensified.

The tracer struck *Harridan* mercilessly, obliterating her shields nearly instantly, then tearing a line through the hull, killing 43 spacers instantly who had been huddled together watching the bout. The galley was ruptured, taking with it another 26 spacers dining together or working their shift preparing the chow. All of them died horribly but quickly, bodies seared, broken apart, or evaporated under the energy, while the lucky ones were frozen and sucked out into the vacuum of space.

When it moved to destroy engineering, *Missio-Tral's* starship-rated shields refracted it harmlessly away off into the distance. Her tracer was on the destroyer now, whose beam was powering down, having exhausted its energy, while the pair coming from the Alliance warship had barely started its path.

Captain Lede pushed away from the table angrily and nearly collided with a junior officer, who had shown up to deliver a personal message from communications. The old man bit down and inhaled steadily, this practiced move appearing as stoicism to the downcast eyes of the frightened teen.

"Urgent message from the Shrikes, Captain," the boy nearly shouted, causing the old man to cock an eyebrow to remind him that the message was private. Luckily for him, the boy lowered his volume to the level appropriate for a one-on-one conversation. "Captain Kur's cruiser was located and they're currently in pursuit. They wish to know how to proceed, sir. Through stealth to discover where he's running to, or should they disable the ship and take him captive?"

"Disable the ship," he replied, decisively. He was here to take out the trash, not follow it about the galaxy wasting valuable time and fuel. In the hands of a psych, Commander Kur would tell him everything they needed to know about his mutinous actions. The council had made it permissible to capture and detain the rogue captain of the *Harridan,* but there had been nothing said about what he could do to him.

He glanced over and saw that the awkward boy was still waiting, frozen at attention, eyes looking forward into nothing. The old man glanced at his nameplate and reached forward to place a hand on his shoulder. "Thank you, Ensign Lark," he said softly. "You may return to your station." Then he turned and approached a large bay window, where he could see the shadowy form of the destroyer behind ripples of energy depleting its shields.

"What are the chances of hooking her before she burns line?" he asked Homerus Cho, who was back at his station though well within earshot of his animated captain.

"Impossible, Captain, not unless there's an idiot at the helm willing to risk staying longer than the little time they have. But no scenario I can think of makes that a gamble worth anything short of death," he reported, crossing over to stand next to his captain. It was something he often did when they spoke, though it annoyed Lede, who despised the way the man was so eager to please.

"Got word from the *Harridan*, Captain," his XO, Cecil Bo-Antar, reported over comms. "They have many dead or injured. I also got word from our Marines, and they are safe. *Harridan*'s XO Leon is complying with your orders to stay on the cold side of our hull where the tracer can't reach. One more thing, Captain. They're requesting medical assistance. Should I shuttle over a Cel-toc with a medkit and escort detail for them? They've lost all access to both medbays. It has to be unpleasant in there, sir."

"Of course, send them help, man," Lede growled his acknowledgment, "I need that thing gone." He held up his wrist-comms, which revealed the Geralos destroyer's shields having dropped to below 30%. "Put me in a Phantom with a torpedo launcher, and I will give you thirty," he whispered, remembering days when he was in the cockpit of a Vestalian Classic.

"Captain, their FTL drive just came online," Homerus Cho reported after receiving his own update over comms.

Run, coward, run, Lede thought, glaring at the destroyer with extreme malice.

In the space along the 8km distance between the warring starships, the Phantom pilots of *Missio-Tral* saw the Geralos zip-ships suddenly break off to beat a quick exit back to the destroyer. Already at risk of falling prey to the blast of an energy cannon or trace-laser, the only pilots who dared to pursue were the ones whose sparring partners were close to their doom.

Flight commanders rallied their squadrons back into formation, applying heavy thrust to return to *Missio-Tral* through practiced routes to keep them out of the crossfire. The destroyer was turning to calculate its jump, still firing its cannon as more of a deterrent than any real attempt at crippling its foe.

Though it faced no real threat of disablement, barring malfunction or sabotage—two issues that could be accounted for the majority of their losses to Alliance vessels—the Geralos knew when a fight was lost, and wasted no effort in beating a quick escape whenever they could. This frustrated old warlords like Captain Felan Lede, whose pugnacious reputation was widely known across the Alliance Navy.

He watched it go through the motions via the holographic simulation, which took the great distances, invisible ordnance, and varying heat signatures of space combat and made it all very visible to him. Some captains relied on the more intelligent mathematicians, scientists, and engineers to go through the motions, only chiming in when the intangibles needed addressing. This was Captain Felan Lede, however, a pilot turned captain, who treated the complex strategies of capital ship warfare no different than he did fighters dueling.

They had won, and he should have been happy, but as he stared into the blackness—as if he could see the details of the destroyer with his naked eyes—he muttered a curse at the method in which they had won it. Having another lizard force them to expend energy only to tuck its tail and run when they were halfway through its shields? How could that not be unsatisfactory for a man who once took great pleasure in disabling several zip-ships in a line, just to watch them come apart under the force of his energy cannons?

He shot his cuffs, suddenly feeling the restriction of his jacket, and all the eyes on the bridge scrutinizing his mannerisms to see if he would again vent his frustration on their duties. He knew his flaws, his tendency to lash out at the closest thing when things weren't controlled the way he liked them. The cadet from earlier had looked ready to melt, not from the difference in rank, but because of his infamous temper and reputation. The boy had been frightened.

"Captain." Cecil Bo-Antar again materialized at his side, breaking his inward study and putting an end to his reflecting. He chose not to look at him because surely if anyone was to feel his temperament, it would be his XO, the second most powerful person on the bridge. "Captain, a transport cruiser from *Harridan* has come aboard with a handful of our Marines and Commander Leon, " he reported, seeming to dread his role of being the messenger for this sudden turn of events.

Now Captain Lede looked at him. "Leon is here?" he asked, and when the younger, hawk-nosed officer made a bow of acknowledgment, Lede looked back out at the stars and smiled knowingly. "Must be urgent, him coming so fast with the lizards still scratching and clawing from their backs. I hope this means he has information worth our time, Mr. Bo-Antar, or his already difficult cycle is about to become positively nightmarish."

"Aye, Captain Lede," Bo-Antar agreed. "He did relay to me in our ongoing correspondence, however, that he has been wary of things on the *Harridan* for some time, but was rendered practically helpless by his captain. The details on this he wished to express in our confidence, with the understanding that he too is under suspicion of violating his oath, and could wind up in stasis cuffs, awaiting a trial if we find any reason to detain him."

"Good," Lede confirmed with finality, turning to walk back from the window towards his war table. "I want you there with me, Cecil. It is important for the Alliance council that any interviews with the command of *Helysian's Harridan* have no less than two senior officers present."

"Is that a precaution, Captain? I don't follow," Cecil Bo-Antar admitted.

Lede stopped to turn and regard the man. "A ship has gone rogue, Cecil. A powerful Alliance infiltrator. You and I both know how stringent an application for helming a warship is. The *Helysian's* a premier starship, and the *Harridan* has done good things up until this. Must I outline to you what this says about the sudden change in behavior of their captain?"

Cecil Bo-Antar froze, seeing his meaning for the first time, and understanding why a second was necessary. "Corruption, captain?" he whispered. "But we've never had one so close to—"

"Understand now?" Lede coached, placing his hands behind his back as he stepped up to the holographic display. They spoke more on Lede's suspicions that captain Jawal Kur's mind had been invaded by the Geralos and was now on his way to one of their ships, bearing Alliance plans, locations, and secrets. His tone was no longer speculative, Cecil Bo-Antar noticed, as he drove home their need to capture Kur's cruiser or risk annihilation by the enemy.

Minutes later, with the destroyer having fully charged its engines and powered down its canons to leave the system, Bo-Antar updated his captain on their guest being taken to his quarters for their meeting. He reassured him that the commander had been treated respectfully since coming aboard. Despite a senior officer being one of the accused, it was the Alliance way to afford them all the allowances befitting their rank up until they were convicted and removed from the role.

Captain Felan Lede was a believer in protocol despite whatever feelings he had on *Harridan*. Hearing the report actually pleased him and set his mind at rest. Leon being confined to a compartment with what he knew would be a full Marine escort meant he no longer had to give it any thought until he was ready.

Never one to miss the sight of a Geralos ship fleeing into the bridging dimension of a wormhole, the captain scrutinized the holo for nearly an hour until the destroyer was but a memory, leaving them alone. Even when it was gone, he took the time to personally grade the ranks on their performance. Only then did he and his executive officer leave to make their way out to his office.

The captain's quarters, like most on a capital starship, was a large compartment, with dark-red paint on the bulkheads, over which were installed numerous frames and vid-screens bearing honors, memories, and renderings of old Vestalia. On one side towards the bow of the ship sat the captain's berth, lounge, and an expansive collection of spirits from every known planet. Above his bed hung several weapons, former tools of the trade long retired now that their master was at the helm.

On the other side sat a large desk and three high-backed chairs, one behind it and the other two mounted to the deck at catercorner angles. A massive Alliance flag showcasing the twelve planets about a shattered crystal sat above it all, draped behind the desk where Lede's visitors couldn't miss it. More replicas of a long, multi-faceted career were evidenced here, along with a tired Leon Anu who stood up to salute as soon as they entered.

"You can remain seated. Do make yourself comfortable, Commander Anu," Captain Lede instructed, after turning to relieve a young master-at-arms who had been waiting with their guest. The short-haired Meluvian saluted crisply before exiting to the passageway where six waiting Marines stood guard, ready in case of anything. Lede sat behind his desk and Bo-Antar took the remaining seat, facing his impatient captain.

"Let's get to it, shall we?" the older man said directly to Leon Anu, as if this whole exercise was a waster of time and a test of his patience.

"From what I can remember, Captain Lede, everything started when we first arrived in Genesian space," Leon relayed through a steady but hesitant voice. "One of our fighters tracked it, cloaked, whilst conducting a routine patrol 50km out from the Karace Colony, where we intended to get repairs. At the time, the ship's signature wasn't recognized, so we approached sending hails. None of which were answered, so we fired a few shots across her bow to get her attention. Standard operating procedure. Still, her helm wouldn't answer our hails, so we traced her, effectively removing her cloak to expose her as a first-generation assault cruiser. One of the older, full-sized sloops."

"Very interesting," Cecil Bo-Antar mused, crossing his legs and massaging the top knee methodically, as if this was a casual chat among old friends. "A ship that old still intact and fully functional?"

"Yes, indeed," Leon confirmed, "We were intrigued, but not our captain, who was convinced that it was a Geralos prize with human captives on board needing help. We disabled her easily, with still no answer to our hails, so we sent our Marines aboard to investigate. They found and neutralized a dozen lizards, and as the captain suspected there were prisoners: twelve Vestalians, and over thirty Genesians. Captain Kur went along with the Marines personally to see what he could glean from the cruiser's records. He was gone for a long time—became driven, dare I say, obsessed. He sent back most of the Marines. He stayed with a handful acting as bodyguards while he locked himself inside the quarters of the cruiser's former captain. What should have been a cycle turned into weeks of his absence, while we of the *Harridan* waited, preparing for a possible ambush. See, we were no longer in Alliance space, but just beyond it."

Leon became distracted, pausing his report to raise his near-empty mug to his lips. "When he returned, he was different," the commander continued after a long, heavy-chested sigh. "He ordered the cruiser destroyed, claiming corruption rendered all of her parts unusable, which at the time didn't make a whole lot of sense. We did as was ordered then jumped out to a more remote region of Genesian space, here. This is where we've been since then, Captain. We've kept our thrusters on standby and our fighters grounded while Captain Kur held private correspondence with the Alliance."

"Strange, since our council sent me here because your captain refused to answer any of their summons, be it on comms, holo, or virtual mail," Captain Lede commented. "Your starship *Helysian's* captain, Abe Rus, hasn't been able to reach Kur. Have you spoken to him?"

"Briefly, sir," Leon quickly admitted. "He reached me directly to check on the status of our crew, and to inquire why Captain Kur had been absent. I reported what I could to him, but you understand that I couldn't relay my suspicions, not at the risk of undermining my lead, when I had no real proof to support any of it."

Lede crossed his arms and tucked his chin into his chest, realizing now that it was in fact Abe Rus who had set things in motion to liberate their wayward infiltrator from Jawal Kur. He wondered how he would reconcile with the man after thinking him somehow complicit, or just worthless, letting a rogue ship exist within his fleet. "What about the Marines who went on the ship with your captain?" he asked, deciding to mull it over later on when all of this was finished.

"They too acted strangely, Captain Lede. We started getting reports from the rates of some unrest which involved some of those men. One who was detained ended up stabbing the officer who was trying to counsel him. Many strange things started happening with them. They were different. Stranger still was when Captain Kur sent some of them to the surface as 'ambassadors' for more private correspondence. I objected, but was overruled, and threatened with the brig for insubordination. It wasn't long after this disagreement that *Missio-Tral* appeared, followed by the destroyer."

"What about the hostages, Commander Leon? Are they still in your medbay?" Cecil Bo-Antar pressed.

"All have died from their wounds, Commander," Leon responded morosely. "The lizards weren't just biting into their heads as we expected. They conducted experiments, butchered them, fused them with things that, if you saw, you could never forget."

"And in all this time that your captain exhibited such strange behavior, Commander Leon, what did you assume was really happening?" Captain Lede asked, looking not so convinced of the younger man's tale.

"To be honest, Captain, I assumed he'd gone mad from something he'd seen inside that compartment. He allowed no one else in there, and had us destroy the vessel once he'd come back aboard with his detail."

"Aside from pleading your innocence to this entire fiasco that has exposed us to the lizards, Commander Anu," Captain Lede growled, suddenly impatient with this meeting, which was presenting nothing more than what he already knew. "Is there anything else you would like to tell me?"

"Yes," Leon Anu said quickly, and Lede noticed that despite his tone, the ever-professional Leon Anu had maintained his composure. "Gentlemen, the ship my captain left in was an '05 Exalt multipurpose cruiser."

"We know of it. Go on," Bo-Antar urged, already wary of the growing impatience within his captain.

"It has no FTL capabilities," Leon continued. "So barring it docking with a capable vessel, it is still in this system. I—I hate to admit this, Captain, but I came immediately to inform you and the commander in confidence that I had trackers installed on all of our light cruisers once I became suspicious. The following are the codes you can use," he said, leaning forward to place a small tablet on the desk, displaying myriad cryptic codes and symbols.

Captain Felan Lede almost cracked a smile, surprised for once that some good fortune had finally fallen their way. "Cecil," he said, looking at his number two, who too had perked up at the sight of Leon Anu's gift. "Get Commander Anu some accommodations. He'll be staying with us until I can verify this intelligence. *Harridan* is tethered?"

"As of thirty minutes prior, Captain," Cecil Bo-Antar replied, eager to get moving on something.

"I need to get back to my bridge and coordinate some actions with the Alliance to prevent the former captain from escaping." He stood up suddenly, walking over to place a hand on the shoulder of Leon, who had gotten up with him. "This turns out to be what you say, Commander, you will have earned some of my trust, despite having planted these trackers through speculative means."

"Thank you, Captain," Leon Anu nearly shouted, looking somewhat relieved.

"Sit tight. We're not out of the muck yet; not until we catch him," Lede continued conspiratorially. "We'll see how far he can run with local Alliance intelligence on the lookout."

21

In the streets of the tenements, armed militias rolled through in armored transports, hopping out to harass any and everyone who they believed had knowledge of Fio Doro. The gangs, having no payment to account for the invasion of armor and uniforms, struck back with a vengeance, sniping the invaders from rooftops and lobbing firebombs into their transports. Some corners turned into war zones, with bullets being lobbed back and forth all through the night.

BasPol was involved, but only the bravest or the ones on the take were available to strap up and ride into the tenements. For the mercenaries, Alliance Marines, and otherwise thinking this would have been an easy shakedown of their careers, they were met with forces just as vicious as the most committed Geralos with an honor debt. Buildings were on fire, and people were trampling one another to find refuge from the gunfire.

Both sides suffered injuries and many losses, but the citizens, mostly gangsters, were losing five to one. This wasn't the worst of it. With the distraction of the violence happening, and people feeling helpless, more than a few of the Marines took advantage. Kicking down doors, they took what they wanted, having their way with people who believed they lacked any power to stop it.

Every vid-screen and holo-projector showed the footage of this violence, no matter if you were stuck in the tenements or had a miniature mansion in the hills overlooking the skyway. People saw BasPol, Alliance Marines, and unmarked mercenaries firing high-powered weapons into this residential area. Calls to officials prompted help from neighboring cities, and the governor announced that the Genesian Guard was on their way to institute martial law in the tenements.

While this went on, the Nighthawks made their way to Sunveil's tribute to deconstructivism, using the rooftops to speed their approach until they were close enough to reach out and touch it. On the backside of the structure, there was a frame set up with a ladder to allow the builders to gain access to the unfinished top floor. Here the bricks were stacked high, lending enough cover for them to time the reaper drones and climb the three stories up to a precipice.

No sentries were present when they crossed to an empty balcony that was scattered with fallen bricks from an unfinished wall. They worked their way through the naked frames to a door that opened to a small, dusty room. Soaked and tired, Cilas allowed them to take a few minutes to catch their breath. Cloaks were rolled up and autorifles broken down and placed inside of backpacks; loadout was strictly muzzled handguns and knives.

Things hadn't gone perfectly with his plans. They had made contact on the approach, which meant bodies would be found as well as the remains of the drones no longer patrolling. They were now inside the dragon's lair, but tracks had been left behind, and even with their speed, reinforcements had been called and security would be bolstered, meaning more fighting.

What made things worse, Helga realized, was that Cilas had yet to mention plans for an egress. Would they sneak out, dragging an unwilling Sunveil to the tenements, or would they keep him here, waiting for local support to evacuate them? She looked at Anders, their effective rookie, and the young Marine gave her a nod of acknowledgment. He had impressed her, and she found herself getting used to the idea of him being a Nighthawk.

Quentin was up and pacing, prepped and half-cocked as always to get to the action. Raileo Lei stood next to the sole window, peering out at the tenements through the raindrops. Last night's conversation about hubs had remained in Helga's mind, and seeing how forlorn he appeared, she could only guess at what he was thinking in this instance. Was he thinking of his past, or his Traxian girlfriend inside her med-bay, stressing over his and their survival?

"Can I speak to you for a moment, Cilas?" Helga crossed the room to approach her commander, who was waiting by the door while they got dressed. He was drenched in sweat and had the smell to go with it, but they were all similarly disgusting from their slog through the mud.

"What's on your mind, Hel?" he said, low enough to keep it between them.

Helga crossed her arms and rocked back on her heels, flexing her aching soles. "What do we know of the Marines from *Helysian*, exactly?"

"Having doubts?" He smirked, scanning the others to make sure none were listening.

"We've neutralized several mercenaries and a Cel-toc," she recounted. "Each was armed with Alliance weapons, but nonidentifiable as ours."

"Of course not," he said confidently. "Traitors or not, I really don't expect to see Alliance Marines guarding this bio-rot's property."

"But you asked Q to look for identification on the first man," Helga reminded him. "And you seemed as surprised as the rest of us that it was a Cel-toc dressed up to be a Marine."

"Speak plainly. What are you asking?"

"I want to know if we're certain that the Marines we saw in Basce City are aware that they're violating their oath to the Alliance. I want to know that when we engage, they deserve everything that we throw at them. I just don't want to regret what we've done here once the sun comes up in the morning. I still have doubts about Meluvia, and you promised us that you would do your best to steer us clear of ops like that."

Cilas made to answer, but caught himself, shutting his mouth to mull over her question. "I was told there would be no Alliance presence here; outside of us, that is. We're not here officially. Any other Alliance here neglected to inform the Genesian council. Only one reason they would do that."

"So, their crime is coming here unofficially then?" Helga pressed.

"Do you want to hear my theory? They're here for the credits, selling weapons the same way Wolf did in Meluvia. There's a good chance they have nothing to do with the stolen intel."

"How does that vindicate them?" Cilas became impatient. "They're freelancing as mercenaries. Selling, using, and placing Alliance weapons into civilian hands is a violation worthy of the airlock with no honors. Helga, our information is being sold to the lizards, we cannot afford to take chances or we could end up losing part of our fleet."

"Thank you, Comm—I mean, Cilas, I just needed to hear it." She exhaled.

"Have I ever steered you wrong?" he countered, and she felt suddenly embarrassed for questioning him. "We about ready?" He looked past her to where the other Nighthawks were waiting. "Let's go," he announced, and nudged the door open with the barrel of his handgun. "Looks clear," he whispered after checking both ends of the hallway, though Helga heard music and lively conversation coming from below.

They had come in on the top floor, and this was evidenced by the vaulted ceiling, with a thin column of yellow-tinted glass running horizontally near the top. White walls and an assortment of saucer-shaped floating lights hung above them, and a statue of a black, crystalline consistency displayed a life-sized Genesian, bald, robed, and regal. Silently and methodically, they walked the floors, clearing several adjacent rooms, looking for Sunveil or some sort of evidence.

"What is this place?" Anders asked at one point, after their fifth breach and entry with no results. He more than anyone had been taken with the splendor, straining his neck to view the paintings and trailing his fingers over the surface of the sculptures. Helga assumed it was his newness to planetary things, but she hoped it wouldn't prove dangerous, him being enthralled with everything.

"This is what you build when you have too many credits on your hands and too little morals to fix the city you live in," Quentin grumbled.

"It's a resort of sorts," Helga guessed. "Every room has a rack, a bathroom, and some form of entertainment. The more I see of this place, the more I believe it to be commercial, something like a hotel. It's unfinished, but from the security and the collection of transports parked out there, he already has guests paying him to live here."

"Guests?" Raileo scoffed. "I wouldn't call them guests. How about Alliance traitors, politicians, and gangsters? The transports I saw ranged from armored cars to multipurpose hovers. Do you hear all that laughing from below? Guests wouldn't all be participating in whatever is happening. I think Sunveil's hosting a meeting."

"This isn't his home then?" Anders puzzled.

"I believe it is," Cilas added. "Now, let's kill the chatter and get our heads in the game."

They descended a set of stairs, stacked single-file, guns pointing down, ready for anything. The stairs were unconventional like the rest of the building; rather than angle down to the next floor, they twisted and wrapped several times before ending at a door with a camera mounted above it. Raileo did something to silence his rifle and fired on the camera before it could reveal them.

Cilas crouched by the door, listening for movement, then carefully cracked it open, stepping inside and motioning for the Nighthawks to follow. They emerged behind the bar of a lounge, empty, but recently occupied, judging by the half-filled glasses on the counter. Beyond the tables and plush silky cushions on sofas, a panoramic window displayed a stormy view of the distant gardens. Helga, being the last one to enter, slid the door shut behind her, noticing it blended with the wooden texture of the walls. She shared a look of appreciation with Anders before joining the others at the window.

"Q and Anders on the doors," Cilas commanded. "If you see someone coming, back out, and we'll use the bar for cover if there's cause to engage them."

Raileo stayed crouched behind the bar, typing away at something on his wrist-comms. He had been doing it on and off, and Helga hoped he wasn't sending messages to Cleia. She looked out at Sunveil's property, though the rain and mist made it difficult to see. She brought up her holographic HUD from Weinstar's implant and looked through the options to see what was there.

"Hey, I didn't know our lens came with night vision," she said, excitedly.

"Comes with a few useful modes actually," Cilas commented, but his eyes remained glued to the window. "You see that there in the distance? Showing a lot of activity out there."

Helga followed his finger using her night vision, and saw a clutch of armed individuals searching the grounds. Through her lens they appeared as highlighted human-shaped blobs, running about as if they were searching. The shriek of an alarm went off, and several reapers started flying towards the building, causing Helga and Cilas to back away from the window.

Suddenly, Raileo hopped up from behind the bar, running over to join them as if the reapers were of no concern to him. "Found the network controlling those bugs and rerouted them to the starport." He laughed, presenting his wrist-comms to show a spattering of glyphs that Helga couldn't decipher what they meant.

She looked helplessly at Cilas, whose expression remained blank. Raileo, annoyed at their inability to appreciate his genius, pointed to the window where the reapers were flying off into the distance. "No more drone cover for these *thypes*. They have to meet us head on," he explained.

"That was you?" Helga was intrigued, though the alarm was still blaring, loudly.

Quentin jumped back from the door, pistol raised to eye-level with his offhand gripping the knife. "Contact," he whispered, motioning for them to look for cover.

The door came open before they could move, sliding to reveal an Alliance Marine in full battle dress uniform. He was so close to Quentin, it would have been natural for the Nighthawk to start shooting before he could react. The Marine wasn't alone, however, and Quentin reacted appropriately, bringing his close-quarters mastery into effect.

Rather than retreating, he stepped forward, utilizing his speed to shove the muzzle of his handgun into the man's chest. His free hand came up to grip the top of it near the slide, removing any chance of his victim disarming him. He fired three times, the proximity rendering the light armor plates useless, and with a shove of the elbow up under the man's chin, sent him sprawling back through the doorway.

Helga, who witnessed this happen in real time, was already firing her pistol, killing a second Marine behind his comrade. Anders, without concern for his safety, stepped up with his own gun raised, shot through the door at the others, rushing in to assist their friends.

"Anders, find cover," Helga hissed at him, confused by his apparent recklessness.

"You see that?" Quentin said, causing Helga to turn to catch him looking at the ceiling. She made to follow his eyes but was suddenly thrown onto her face from what she could only guess was a bomblet, since her ears were ringing and smoke was everywhere, stinging her eyes.

Helga tried to stand, but a wave of fatigue kept her anchored. It was a laboring effort, though she made it to a knee, but a bout of disorientation left her unsure. It felt as if her brain had performed a barrel roll, with her consciousness as an unwitting partner. She knew intrinsically that she was kneeling inside a room with shots buzzing all about, but what she was experiencing was a nauseating imbalance.

"Get back here, Anders. Stay with, Ate," Raileo could be heard shouting, but everything else was muffled nonsense.

"Ate, get down," Quentin urged, and she looked to her right where she could barely make out his silhouette.

Something punched her in the chest, at least that's how it felt, and the spinning ceased, replaced by a bright light, and she was up on her elbows, prone, coughing again. The world steadied enough for her to get an inkling of reality, and some feeling returned to her limbs. Her right arm felt heavy, but she pushed past it, lifting her heavy pistol to reach up and support it with both hands. She felt underwater, weighted down, and every attempt of movement was obstructed.

"Don't bunch up," Cilas shouted.

Helga blinked to clear the tears from her eye's natural defenses against the smoke-filled air. Anders went down cursing, and Raileo ran forward to drag him back out of the line of fire. Cilas and Quentin backpedaled past her, auto-rifles chattering away, sending back death through the smoke and chaos. Helga felt two strong hands grip her shoulders from behind, and it was her turn to be dragged back into the lobby.

Bullets whizzed back and forth above her head, and despite her state, she hoisted her own sidearm and started firing at moving shadows through the blinding yellow smoke. "Bang," one of her shots nicked one of a shadow's legs forcing him back into a sitting position. "Bang-bang," she hit him dead-center, and he fell back into the smoke, replaced by another spraying an auto-rifle, blindly countering before he too went down, lifeless beside his friend.

Helga knew she would die, but the programming from a lifetime of service replaced her fear with words like sacrifice, heroine, and glory. *To be the second Ate immortalized in the Rendron's Hall of Honors, that was worth all of this, wasn't it?* she pondered. The line of Ate would be cut short, but she'd proved herself worthy of remembering. Fear fought for a place in her mind, however, but Helga still had enough fight left over to keep on denying this was her end.

She felt even more fatigued, her limbs rubbery and heavy, like fuel lines attached to her aching frame. It became an out-of-body experience for her, seeing a new round of bullets striking the floor near her legs. She looked up to see the shooter fly back suddenly, a line of red light revealing the shooter to be none other than Raileo Lei.

Her consciousness waned, and she could no longer hear anything. Fading in and out, she could make out action, Nighthawks exchanging bullets while someone dragged her all the way. Smoke gave way to night sky, rain, and the moon above Basce City, peering down with its unblinking judgment. They were now somewhere on a balcony, one she recalled seeing on the third floor from the outside, wrapped about the building.

    Helga's eyes rolled back suddenly, taking awareness with them as the scene faded. The last thing she would remember was the balcony shifting, and then the sudden sensation of falling before…nothing.

22

Cilas Mec knelt peering over a collapsed section of flooring where the balcony had exploded moments before. Below, the ever-reliable Raileo Lei was pulling Anders Stratus from the algae-filled water of the fountain. Sprawled out to one side was Helga, pale and unmoving, her meticulously maintained undercut now a damp, grass-filled mop. Anders too looked to be a corpse, but Cilas wasn't able to accept that he'd lost his Nighthawks to an ill-timed bomblet.

So many thoughts, fears, and suppositions zipped through his mind as he stared at them, feeling helpless. *Not like this*, he thought, wishing he believed in the maker to send up a prayer for the lives of his men.

A brief survey of the grounds revealed the gravity of the situation. Raileo Lei had survived his fall, but there were reinforcements inbound and he'd be vulnerable even with his and Quentin's help. There may have been hope for the other two, but it was hope they would need to win for them. Sunveil's men were now on the offensive, and the best he could do was use the vantage to hold them off.

"Ray, how we looking?" he asked through comms, and was met with a high-pitch whine, followed by static, and then nothing.

"*Schtill*, he's not answering," He looked at Quentin, who turned to give his commander a shrug. After the collapse—which the two of them narrowly avoided by being on the far side of the balcony—Cilas had killed the Marine who threw it, while Quentin covered the ground to hold them off. Now, sprawled out below them in deep shadows and blackness was the courtyard where Sunveil's enforcers were rushing in.

"Contact," the big man reported, but Raileo Lei was already aware. The sniper positioned himself behind a robed statue in the center of the pool, sending laser-rifle fire into the blackness.

"Ray," Cilas tried again, and this time he could hear the Nighthawk's labored breathing.

"Commander," he managed. "Ate's alive but unconscious. Anders is too, but he's going to need a doc. We're exposed. If we could get some cover, I can drag them into the ruins where we have a better chance of surviving."

"Already happening, Ray, but are you wounded?" Cilas chanced a quick glance at Quentin, knowing he too would be concerned for their man. The fall had been enough to knock the wind out of anyone, and even though they fell into water, Raileo could be working on borrowed time, adrenaline numbing his pain. There was no answer, so he tried again. "Ray, do what you need to do, we'll cover you from here. Do you copy?"

"Yes, Commander," he replied, with a finality that spoke volumes coming from the marksman.

"We can't afford to lose momentum, not now when we have them all hunkered down on the third floor," Cilas continued, already feeling himself coming down from the shock of the firefight earlier. "Never thought there'd be this much resistance on the inside, but it makes sense considering how easily we got here. Ray, I'm going to need you to be honest, are you still effective, can you watch them until Q, and I are out? We're going to collect the target, but only if I know I'm not sending you off to your death."

"Breathing, whole, and mad enough to clear this place if you tell me," Raileo replied dutifully. "Ruins are everywhere, and I'll find something with only one way in and out. We'll wait for your update, Commander. Still effective, don't you worry. Still a Nighthawk."

"Sambe," Quentin shouted all of a sudden. "Let's *thyping* go." He leaned into his auto-rifle and started firing. Cilas, surprised by his outburst, had no choice but to join in. The big man was spraying to keep the incoming hunkered, so he took his time to aim down the sights and put a round into the helmet of an outlined head. "*Schtill*, Ray," the big man groused. "Anders is *thyped*. Get the lieutenant to safety. They're coming from the north; pull her to the south side."

Cilas saw what he meant, and Raileo complied instantly, despite the bullets volleyed back at his location. He crawled out from behind the statue, picked up Helga, cradled her close and ran back into the shadowy ruins. Two armed figures materialized in the location where he was running, and Cilas feathered the trigger at a stroke, perforating them.

Meanwhile, on the north side, the enemy picked up on what they were doing and aimed their weapons at the balcony instead. Cilas placed a hand on Quentin's rifle, wordlessly telling him to stand down and take cover behind the stone balcony. "We'll come back for Anders," he promised the big man. "Hopefully they assume that he's dead and start searching the grounds while we go get Sunveil."

Quentin pulled back his rifle and ducked below a solid section of the balcony's railing, shouldering the auto-rifle to arm himself with his sidearm. Cilas Mec chanced another glance down to where Anders lay half-submerged in the pond, like a creature from the depths in its final death throes. The armored Marines surrounded his body, one kicking him hard in the side which resulted in him recoiling, hacking up the filthy remnants of the drink.

The kicker signaled to the others, and two of them rushed forward to pull him out onto the grass, where they started questioning him violently while the others stood guard, some scanning the balcony above them. Cilas cursed under his breath. "We need to move." He signaled to Quentin, and together they leaped the gap to return to the door leading back to the hall in which they had been fighting earlier. "Q, that first doorway opens out into a staircase leading down to the first floor. We need to seal it in case the target tries to run."

"There's also an elevator. Managed to see it through the smoke on our way out," Quentin reported. "No one rushed out before the bomblet. You think there's a chance they're still in that room up here?"

"If they weren't, we'd have seen them down there," Cilas guessed. "Not unless they went down a floor just to hide, which makes very little sense."

"I'll jam the elevator and seal the door to the staircase then," Quentin informed him, and Cilas dropped to a knee, raising his auto rifle up to eye-level. The hallway was surprisingly empty but still had the lingering smoke from the earlier bomblet, limiting his vision and forcing him to cycle through a variety of filters on his contact lens.

He saw someone emerge from a doorway in the distance, armed with a rifle and slinking blindly towards where he knelt. One of Cilas's shots struck him in the chest, the other through the faceplate, killing him instantly, and the Nighthawk exhaled slowly, trying to maintain control over his nerves. Two bullets had punctured holes in the wall near where he knelt, and he realized just how close he had come to finally meeting his death.

"Doors are jammed, I'm on my way back out," Quentin reported before another shadow followed the first, firing erratically at Cilas. A bullet struck the Nighthawk in his chest plate, painfully, but the composite weaving prevented it from penetrating. Cilas took his time to aim steadily, and set the shooter to screaming with a bullet in his abdomen.

Quentin materialized next to him. "Both doors are permanently sealed," he said. "Heard your weapon report, with no call for contact. Looks like you're hit. Are you good?"

"Golden, and we're *thyping* live alright." Cilas grimaced. "Now, let's go get this *cruta* and be done with this hell."

They moved quickly down the hallway to the second of four open doors. Inside was a large room with five small windows letting in the moonlight. Random folding chairs were scattered about, and the ratty tan carpet was dotted with splotches of garnet-colored blood from one of the men Cilas had killed. Moving in carefully, they came upon a cracked door, which was fortunate since it too blended in with the wall that held it.

"I won't ask what they do in here," Quentin commented as he stepped to one side, aiming down his sights. Cilas mouthed a countdown, yanked it open and ducked out of the way. When nothing jumped out, they stepped through to a set of stairs leading down into blackness. Cilas turned on his night vision and through a practiced signal urged Quentin to do the same.

"Got a line on the third step: booby trap. How do we play it?" Quentin said.

Hidden room leading down to the first floor where they can sneak out. Cilas analyzed the situation in the span of a few seconds. "I neutralized their lookout, so they know at least one of us is up here. Two intruders wouldn't give Sunveil cause to run off just yet. We still have time, but we need to move fast. Trip the bomblet and we'll use the element of surprise to rush in."

"On your command," the big Genesian responded, still aiming down the staircase.

"Now," Cilas whispered, and Quentin triggered the trap, causing them to nearly collide when they scrambled back up the stairs to avoid the shrapnel. "Are you good, Q?" Cilas whispered, and when he gave the sign for okay, the two of them rushed back down the stairs. It wound down to another landing, this one covered in rubble from the explosion, then even more stairs leading to what Cilas assumed would be the basement.

"An underground compartment," Cilas mused, while Quentin took point, probing for more surprises. When they reached the bottom, they found a space illuminated by a solitary light bulb. Another lounge, from what it appeared, this one much larger than the first. On the carpeted floor squatted several Genesians hiding below tables and assorted furniture. Another bar in the back revealed one carefree member who sat sipping at his liquor as if he had no fear.

It took a mere second for Cilas to get a lay of the land, and even less for Quentin Tutt to step up and aim his rifle at two shadows attempting to flank them. No words were exchanged, Quentin just started firing. Crouching to a duck walk to avoid the response, Cilas crept behind a table and placed three bullets in the side of the bar where the drinker had ducked to retrieve his weapon.

One of the bullets struck home, and the man stood up to escape, but a fourth shot threw him back against the wall where he slumped down, lifeless. He had been the last of Sunveil's guards, so Cilas ordered the civilians to gather in the center of the room where they could be questioned. He counted eighteen, all having the appearance of pampered diplomats unused to being on the receiving end of the violence. They were ordered to lay prone with their limbs outstretched.

Cilas picked out one of their number, a mustachioed dandy who looked about as close to what he'd imagine an official from Basce City would look like. Snatching him by the collar, he dragged him away from the others to stand by the corpse of the man who had pretended to be there drinking.

"Garson Sunveil?" Cilas asked, but the man kept staring at Quentin, seemingly petrified.

The big Nighthawk did look frightening, even through the night vision, covered in the rubble and blood from the night's ongoing conflict. Out of patience and worried for his Nighthawks outside, Cilas stepped forward and struck him in the jaw with a closed fist, sending him backwards into the bar. He slid to the floor, holding his face.

"Garson Sunveil?" he tried again, and when the man wouldn't talk, Cilas knelt down and pulled his knife, placing the tip of the blade inside a bloody nostril. "Closing your eyes won't stop me from lopping it off. One more time, are you Garson Sunveil?"

"I'm Garson Sunveil," someone announced from the people lying prone in front of Quentin. Cilas snatched up the man he had been questioning and shoved him back towards the rest. He then walked over to the one claiming to be Sunveil and placed a boot on his back to prevent him from moving.

"If you're really Sunveil, then give me the name of the woman you've got your goons from BasPol tearing the tenements apart to find," Cilas demanded. "There's a lot of people in here, and one of you is bound to be our target, so either answer the question or Quentin there will start shooting. Do you want a demonstration?"

"No," the man said quickly. "What is this about? Did Djesu's little girl really hire you to come after me?" He seemed more intrigued than frightened now, despite the environment.

Cilas shot the prone man in his leg, aiming at the fleshy part of his outer thigh. The kinetic round hit its mark, but ricocheted off the tiles to strike an area of the ceiling where a shower of dust came down on their heads. Garson Sunveil screamed out in agony, prompting the commander to step down harder on his back. "You have one minute to convince me that you are who you say you are, or the next one goes into your head."

"Fio Doro is a smuggler," Sunveil said quickly. "She fumbled a package that put a lot of heat on some important people over the tenements. The residents hid her, so we were forced to resort to violence. You mercenaries or whatever you are wouldn't understand the sort of hell that will be unleashed if we don't turn her over to our government. Think BasPol was bad? You haven't seen anything yet. But if you let my guests go, I will be willing to talk."

"You'll tell us everything whenever and wherever we choose, *cruta*," Quentin barked, his muscular jaw clenched so tight he looked menacing. "This is no longer your game, unless you haven't been paying attention." Sunveil could only manage a momentary glance at him to see that he wasn't bluffing. "Feels like stalling, brother, what are your orders?" Quentin asked of Cilas, who happened to be thinking the same thing.

"He says he's our man, so let's just collect him," Cilas instructed. "Even if he isn't, he's bound to know something, even if we have to cut it from him." He looked up at the guests still sprawled out prone on the floor. "The rest of you don't move a *thyping* muscle until we tell you," the Nighthawk commander told them.

Removing his boot from the injured Sunveil, he flipped him over and placed the muzzle on his chest. Using his free hand to thoroughly search him, Cilas discovered a small handheld communicator with a name on its face. "Garson Sunveil," it read, with an accompanying image of the man who lay bleeding out below him. Despite himself, Cilas had doubted they'd find him. A part of him believed Sunveil had already escaped the property.

"Mission accomplished, brother," Quentin assured him, and Cilas allowed himself a brief moment to appreciate those words and their meaning.

23

Prior to every mission since leaving the nightmarish moon of Dyn, Helga would stand before a mannequin bearing her PAS armor and make herself a promise to never again be taken prisoner. When the Geralos had her, she'd been subjected to countless horrors being dealt to her fellow captives while waiting day after day for it to be her turn. Barely conscious throughout the days that she hung from a hook waiting, she couldn't have known everything they did to her back then.

When Cilas eventually found her, she had been inside a room by herself, naked—which she hadn't been able to remember happening—with tubes running in and out of her body. Later, a Louine physician had informed her the tubes were for a transfusion so the Geralos could find a way to bite her safely. She was a Seeker, having the gift of sight that the Geralos harvested and massacred millions of her fellow Vestalians to find, but she was also a Casanian, a species whose blood was dangerous to ingest.

She hadn't been the same spacer since her capture, and the only person to understand had been Cilas. His support, along with her learning of her gift, were the only things that kept her among the living. Many drunk nights inside her cabin, lonely and fearful, she had contemplated the worst to end the pain. Cilas and Joy pulled her back from the precipice, and ever since then she had started the ritual of making promises to her mannequin.

Helga came awake to darkness, noise, and confusion. The world was spinning, everything ached, and it tasted as if she'd made a meal of dirt prior to her fall off the balcony. The fall hadn't killed her, and she could barely recall what caused it when her eyes came open to a dim light shining.

High above her was a ceiling with a gaping hole, through which the rain was soaking her through and through. As her vision cleared, she began to recognize Amberle, Genese's solitary moon, whose off-white, cratered face defied even the clouds. She assumed the cold wet rain had roused her, and she split her lips apart to allow the droplets to collect inside her mouth.

Turning her head to face a muddy pile-up, she spat the remnants from her mouth. Just that slight movement was enough to send a wave of unbearable pain throughout her body, so she stopped and closed her eyes to try and remember where she was. Helga was inside one of the ruins, this she could tell from the holes in the wall letting in the floodlights, and half her body was buried in a mountain of rubble, with a generous sprinkling of broken glass.

How am I here? she wondered, flexing each digit on her hands and feet, methodically. In doing this exercise, she could determine if any part of hers was damaged to the point of needing a splint. Fingers were stiff, but curled on command, toes as well, though the restriction of her boots didn't give her confidence. *I guess we will know once I attempt to stand.* She surrendered to fate, moving on to attempt to bend and unbend her knees and elbows very slowly.

The poor light from the moon proved insufficient for truly scrutinizing the damage. Helga reached up to examine her chest, where she was sure that a bullet had struck. But while there was a depression, the kinetic-resistant fabric had held. She breathed a sigh of relief of not only being alive, but to still be clothed in her composite body armor. Though much of it had been damaged, her having it on meant she was not in fact captured, but had survived the explosion and consequent fall.

She reached down for her belt, pushing a pile of rocks out of the way, probing for the tiny hip-pack holding essential medical supplies. Pulling it open, she dug inside for an emergency resuscitation transmitter, commonly known among the Alliance Navy as a revita-shot. It was a form of processed spice, highly addictive and illegal without consent from a medical professional. Dr. Cleia Rai'to had shown it to them, and urged Cilas to make it a requirement for every Nighthawk to carry.

Helga placed the tip of the needle against her neck and made to push it in but hesitated. She was suddenly aware of her surroundings, the dead comms and the rain's rhythm pattering all around. Where were her Nighthawks? She looked about frantically, ignoring the pain.

The room was small, busted-up, and windy, with muddy debris everywhere, but there were no Nighthawks aside from herself.

"He's on the rooftops," she heard a man shout, startling her, followed by a laser-rifle's whine and a loud, blood-curdling scream. The unmistakable sound of Raileo's Widow Maker striking an unsuspecting target.

No stranger to pain, Helga worked herself up to her elbows and felt around in the rubble for her backpack. *Come on cruta, earn your name*, she thought, biting down hard as she worked to get up to a sitting position. It felt as if her muscles were being torn off the bone, but she eventually propped herself up using the back wall for support.

The next effort was to gather her bearings and work out how she'd wound up here without her Nighthawks. Was she in immediate trouble? Did the enemy drag her in here to die, or had she managed to do it herself? Gunfire was an indication that fighting was happening, but the Nighthawks would never have left her, making her predicament even more confusing.

Remembering her implant, she touched her ear, and through the dry, caked-up blood and mud, she located the cold metal surface of the controller for her lens. Tapping at it gingerly to trigger the interface, Helga exhaled with some relief when the HUD appeared before her eyes, brilliant blue lines hovering before her, forming a menu of options for her to interact with.

"Ray, can you hear me?" she managed before an itch in her throat sent her through an uncontrollable wave of coughing to expel the gunk.

"Ate," Raileo breathed into his comms with relief. "Oh, thank the maker, you're awake. How are you feeling now? I was working my way back to get you. Can you move?"

"More or less," Helga admitted, though he spoke so fast, she was still trying to process what he said. "Are you with the others, Cilas, Q, and Anders? How long was I out?"

"It's been a few hours. Cilas and Q went to get our target and I've been out here trying to locate Anders," he reported. "We got you to safety, but then all hell broke loose. I think they took Anders captive, and the commander ran off with Quentin. Told me to watch over you, that was my job, but they started sniffing about here, so I had to let loose. Wait ... sorry ... I have to go silent, Ate. Hold tight and I'll reach you. I'm almost there."

"You find that, *thype* yet?" a gruff voice called from somewhere behind the wall where Helga slumped.

She remembered her promise to never get captured, and it steeled her, pushing past pain, disorientation, and the need to use her one and only revita-shot. Desperate fingers rifled through the rubble beneath her boots, turning this way and that to see if she could locate where her backpack and guns had gone. Eventually she surrendered. *Raileo would have taken it,* she decided. *To protect us from being identified while he cleared us an escape.*

Lightning struck, illuminating everything, and a piece of timber caught her eye, as thick as one of her arms, and long enough to serve its new purpose as a club. Reaching out to grab it, she used it to assist her getting up to a kneeling position, though the sudden movement made her waver at the edge of collapsing. "Oh, *thype* this," she whispered and jammed the needle into her neck. Hot fire exploded through her veins, numbing the hurt but allowing her to stand, still unsteady but no longer fearful of passing out.

She hobbled over to stand near the sole doorway, feeling stronger with every second, senses focused, and her heart rate slowing, bringing with it a calm. Someone had come into her hideout, and despite the feedback from the gunfire in the distance, she could hear him sucking in breath as he conducted his search. His large boots crunched wet glass, and rotten timber as he explored the rooms, looking for what, she could not know.

Finding a place in the shadows off to the right side of the door, Helga waited patiently for him to come in. She didn't have to wait long before the muzzle of his rifle pushed the door open and a man stepped inside, aiming at each corner skeptically. Down came the timber on his hands, unbalancing him just enough to take the brunt of the upward swing that followed directly in the chin.

Crouching while he struggled to get his balance, Helga pulled a knife from his boot, and slammed it into his groin where the armor couldn't protect him. This rendered him nearly helpless, and she ripped into him like a tigress. Abdomen below his vest, his neck, were just some of the places she struck until he was no longer moving. She shouldered his rifle and took his radio, sidearm, the bloodied knife, and an Alliance-branded ration bar, which made her feel vindication for savaging him.

She heard boots in the mud, Raileo's laser-rifle, and hushed voices sending instructions, bearing down on her location. Cat-walking through the adjacent rooms, which were just as barren as hers, she eventually found an open window facing away from her pursuers. Feeling fitter than usual, pain forgotten, and adrenaline pumping, Helga scrambled out and up onto a low roof, ran across and leaped to another.

Getting to her stomach, she quickly scanned the skies, praying that a reaper wasn't close. Nothing but the moon and the rain was visible, and off in the distance, Sunveil's mansion, where she could see the missing section of balcony from which she fell. It was a long way down to fall, but there had been a pond right below it, deep enough for them to survive the fall.

The voices were now becoming clear.

"We don't leave here until every last one of them is dead," she heard, peering off the edge to see five black clad, mercenary-types skulking about the area. The whine from Raileo's rifle cut the silence, and the resounding scream got them moving faster towards Helga's old building. Lying perfectly still for them to pass her hiding spot, she was ready to get up and jump when a weak splash made her pull up short.

One of Sunveil's thugs was standing directly below her, fiddling with his equipment, confident that he was safe below the concrete overhang. Without her PAS helmet to pinpoint enemy location, Helga had to rely on her senses and intuition. Soft steps from behind and she made out another man who had fallen well behind the rest. Had she struck prematurely, she wouldn't have seen him coming up on her flank while she neutralized his friend.

Helga exhaled heavily; things had become difficult. When she made her escape, she was counting on contact, but one or two soldiers, not a whole unit. Reaching down to her belt, she grabbed a bomblet she had taken off the man from earlier. She primed it, got up into a crouch, and waited for the man to round the corner before she threw it near his feet, where it exploded into a brilliant cloud of sparkles.

"What the *schtill* was that?" the man below her shouted, walking out slowly to investigate the sound.

He was lightly armored, wearing only a vest, and several meters out from her position. Helga looked for the original four who had walked past her, couldn't find them, and this made her anxious. Her heart started beating like a generator on overdrive, fueling her adrenaline-run engine. Without thinking, she leaped, landing on his shoulders to drive her knife down between the neck and shoulder-blade.

She was up and rolling away from him before he choked out his ghost in one last gurgling breath. Slinking back into the shadows, the mineral stench of his blood in her nostrils, Helga tried in vain to catch her breath. "They are massacring us," someone in the distance shouted. "No amount of credits is worth this *schtill*."

Raileo's laser rifle responded to the sound, which caused Helga to cover her mouth to suppress a laugh at the timing. Switching her lens to night vision, she climbed through the window of another building, choosing to use its hollowed-out interior as a source of cover from any stray reapers. Outside a window she saw another solo wandering, waving his weapon around like an amateur playing at operator.

She placed her rifle on the windowsill and leveled the sights at his chest, breathing lightly while brushing her fingertip across the trigger. It was an ESO trick to let off a single round from a weapon meant for suppression and automatic firing. A bullet flew out, striking the leg of the clueless amateur, knocking him down where he lay screaming for his friends.

Having laid her trap, Helga hopped out the window and made for an adjacent building, scrambled to gain the roof, which proved to be a challenge since it was wet, angled and slippery. Once atop it—thanks to the grips of her magnetic boots—she used its angular design to her advantage, lying near the apex where she could peer over it at her wounded man.

The four from earlier came running, rifles pointing everywhere, flashlights forcing her to lay flat to avoid detection. One tended to the wounded amateur while the other three issued several loud threats. This was a mistake, which they learned immediately when a beam of red light touched one of their helmets. The marked man fell over backwards into the mud, followed by the familiar whining of Raileo's rifle recharging its laser.

Another man, this one of the more athletically built variety scrambled to get out of range of the sniper. He slunk around to Helga's side, and she tried to slide off using the slickness from the rain to land behind him. Unlike the one she'd shot earlier, this man had an operator's instincts. He responded as if he had known she was there, spinning to fire on her with a heavy pistol, clipping the left side of her vest.

Helga fell backwards while letting the auto-rifle loose, perforating his body from boots to shoulder. At so close a range her bullets punctured his light armor, leaning him awkwardly against the building's exterior wall, his face frozen in a look of surprise. Raileo took out a bigger Marine who was already moving on Helga's position. She sprinted south past another building, slid down behind a stone barrier and sat with her back to it, listening.

"Silly me, thinking that you would wait for my rescue." Raileo laughed over comms. "You don't come looking for Lady Hellgate, Lady Hellgate comes looking for you."

He fired again and another of the enemy went down quietly. The last of them walked right in front of Helga, missing her small body leaning against the stone. It was dark and where she slumped was shrouded in shadow but still, she couldn't believe he wasn't checking his surroundings. She raised her handgun, aimed down the sights, and shot him twice in succession, one in his chest, and the other in his head, silencing him permanently.

"Hard to believe these were ours. They don't fight like they've had a day of cadet training, yet they're wearing our uniforms and carrying our weapons," Helga complained.

"On your flank, Ate," Raileo announced himself, and slid in to sit next to her, handing over her pack. Punching his arm playfully, she gripped his shoulder to show her appreciation, then reached inside the pack for her cloak. Raileo kept staring at her. "Are you sure you're alright, Ate? Your face is as white as the stone," he said, his eyes reflecting his concern.

"I'm alright," she tried to convince him. "Where did you see them take Anders?"

"Back south to the gardens. There's a whole army of BasPol transports at the entrance," Raileo said. "We need Q and Cilas, Ate. My rifle's overheating, and you look like you're seconds away from collapsing, if I'm being honest."

"Anders is alone, Ray. You know this cannot wait," she said. He reluctantly agreed, and they set out together with him taking point, substituting his rifle for a heavy pistol, and Helga close behind him, checking the sky for reaper drones.

"Don't worry about those drones, Ate, I took all of them out earlier, remember? So, what's our plan?"

"Distraction and confusion. Sneak out there, flank them, find him, and then the three of us can return to meet up with Cilas."

"You say that so confidently," Raileo returned. "You, the woman who looked half-dead when we pulled you out of that pool. You still look half-dead now. With respect of course, Ate, I just don't like the idea."

"That's the plan." Helga made it final. "Anders needs us. If we wait for Cilas and Quentin to return, we may be too late, and that isn't a chance I'm willing to take."

24

According to Raileo, while Helga was unconscious, he had questioned one of the mercenaries, who complied under the threat of death. Anders had been taken to what he termed headquarters. There, they would question him to learn the nature of his business, and then he would be airlifted out to the BasPol Corrections Facility.

Unfortunately for his capturers, however, the Genesian Guard had come to bring peace to the city, and instituted a no-fly zone over the tenements and surrounding properties. Any aircar or flying shuttle would get grounded and the driver arrested if they violated this warning. What Raileo gathered from that news was that Anders would still be alive, and was bound to still be somewhere on Sunveil's property.

Helga followed his lead through the remains of the demolished buildings, some so far gone they no longer had ceilings. More spotlights had come on, so bright it was nearly as clear as daytime, and without the cover of darkness to help, the Nighthawks were forced to travel via these decrepit structures. Earlier it had all been shadows, with the sparse lights giving Helga the impression that they were still being used somehow.

What she saw in the new light, however, was a sad foreshadowing of the tenements and its people. All it would take is one powerful person's greed and Fio's home would be reduced to ruins, just like this.

"Down here," Raileo whispered, pointing off to his right, where a depression—once hidden by the shadow of a two-story building—ran down to become what she thought was a cave. Switching to night vision, it was revealed to be a tunnel, the walls reinforced by concrete, and it looked to go on forever. Could this be where they had taken him? She didn't bother to ask. Though the eternal rain made tracking impossible, something told her that they were on the right path.

Most of the mercenaries not loyal to Sunveil had fled the tenements, and they wouldn't have done so with Anders. The loyal ones had to keep him, and where would be better to keep a prisoner than a subterranean cage? Once inside, Raileo quickened his pace, and Helga stayed close on his backside, boots sloshing through wet mud, refuse, and some form of fabric. These walls too had scribblings, graffiti, and the signs of a different age, when they served as hospice for the residents of this city.

The floor angled down before leveling off once more and eventually ending in a set of stairs leading up. Helga's heart was racing and she felt good despite the mildewed, musty scent of the tunnel, and the nagging thought in the back of her head that she could crash at any minute. Having never taken the revita-shot before, she wondered at the aftermath and the side-effects. Cleia wouldn't have given them something without instruction or warning, but she recalled the day they received their syringes, she had been in a playful mood and not really paying attention.

One hand on Raileo's back, she followed him up, and like the staircase inside Sunveil's manor, these stairs wrapped four times before opening up into the interior of a large, windowless room. The space reminded Helga of the subterranean caves below the moon of Dyn, where she and the former team of Nighthawks had come in contact with the dredge: a species of giant, flesh-eating worms.

There were four square walls and a ceiling, caked with dust, and though no rain had made it inside there, it still reeked of mold and wet soil. They stopped at the top of the stairs, checking the shadows for anyone hiding, and as if on cue, a shower of dust fell from the ceiling above the sole exit. Raileo aimed up into a corner, fired, and a shadow fell.

Helga leaned into her auto-rifle and let off several bursts, aiming at the area where she knew he would land. Two bullets further damaged the already far-gone wall in the corner, but another three struck their target, and their would-be ambusher was dead. "Contact," Raileo announced, aiming his heavy pistol at the darkness of the doorway, where another merc was rushing in, only to regret it when laser fire tore into his chest.

While that man toppled to the ground, Helga ran past Raileo, sliding behind a concrete pile-up near the exit. From this vantage, she hoped to see what lay ahead for them through the door. It was how they trained, one person on cover, the other advancing carefully, then the roles would be flipped. Another came through firing at her, but she had seen him on approach and dove behind the rubble. Raileo killed him easily, and joined her at the doorway when it appeared that no more were coming.

They entered another half-destroyed room, with wall sections broken in half, more graffiti, and on the floor was what could be best described as concrete pews. "Temple of some sort?" she asked Raileo, though still alert as ever for anymore ambushers.

"Watch out." Raileo used an arm to keep her from advancing. "The floor has holes, and where you were about to step seems ready to go. I agree, this is a temple. We're probably inside the big building next to the manor, the one where I cryo-shot the sniper."

"Bingo," Helga whispered in agreement. "Move." She pulled Raileo down with her to crouch behind one of the pews. Two armored men had come in, which she had picked up on immediately. There was no explaining how she knew they were coming, but she was grateful to have followed her instincts.

A loud shot struck the concrete, tearing a chunk out of their barrier. Helga shouted "Covering fire" and raised her rifle over the pew, volleying several bursts back at them. Distracted and shifting to find cover to respond, the mercenaries had wrongly assumed that they were only dealing with one man. Raileo's long night of sniping had many of them thinking he was a solo enforcer from the tenements.

Scrambling from what they believed was one man's response, they missed Raileo raising up to aim and deliver precision shots with critical effect. A quick glance at the Nighthawk revealed to Helga just how frightening Raileo Lei really was. The normally jovial and playful operator wore a mask of icy aloofness as he slid back down to a sitting position, one hand clasped over the charge to suppress the whine while he monitored the temperature gauge.

The cadet academy, Marines, pilot school, all had given them the tools to be effective, but BLAST had changed them all into killers. Helga, like her fellow Nighthawks, had grown to accept this fact. Along with the powered armor suit and passport to the galaxy came the death of a part of themselves that was considered civilized. They were charred in BLAST to withstand anything in the war with the Geralos, but in reality, what they routinely killed turned out to be other humans.

As if reading her thoughts, he met her eyes and shrugged. "Endless *thyping* night," he commented, and got up to his feet. Helga could see that his glove was smoking from where he had held the base of the barrel to force it to remain silent. She wondered why he hadn't given it to Quentin to modify on *Ursula*, since the big Marine was an expert at tinkering and had modified her own handgun. Pride, she decided. "Laser Ray's" Widow Maker was special.

With no other contacts after taking a minute's rest, Helga chanced a peek through the hole in their pew, and was able to see over the rubble that the far entrance was still clear. She made to stand, and her legs felt rubbery. *Thype, thype, thype,* she cursed inwardly, incensed at her body for failing her now before they had Anders. Stubbornly, she shambled forward, gripping the concrete with her left hand, swinging the auto-rifle around with her right to aim at the exit.

She saw Raileo watching her struggle, conflicted with helping her—and provoking her ire—or pretending he didn't see it, which could become disastrous if she fainted during combat. Shifting his gaze forward while he remained kneeling behind the concrete barrier, he reached into the pack on his belt, pulled out his syringe and handed it to her. Helga felt weak and pathetic for having him do this, as they both knew the risk of spice and its addiction.

Snatching it, not out of malice or anger, which she hoped he understood, she jammed it into her neck, bearing the pain. *Why not?* A part of her felt she deserved it. The familiar fire tore through her veins, and she felt it travel to her heart to bring false life to limbs pushed beyond their limit. She took the lead and shouldered her auto-rifle. "When this is over, and we're back where we belong with your darling Cleia, you stay on my rear about getting this *schtill* out of my blood," she said.

"Exactly what I was thinking, Ate," he admitted softly. "We're here for Anders. Whatever it takes, like you said."

Despite the risks, Helga had to admit it felt amazing getting lifted again. She could be thrown into the midst of the opposing army and her only concern at that moment would be the heat sink on her weapon. Raileo fell in behind her and a little off to her right where his aim would be clear. Stacked and ready for anything coming between them and reclaiming the Nighthawk recruit, they cleared the doorway and stepped into a hallway with a metal door at the end.

Raileo was the marksman, so the decision on the breach was already established. Those cycles of repetitious training made kicking down doors one of their most common exercises, and muscle memory accounted more for their actions than any thought. There was a problem, however; neither of them had a clue as to what the layout was inside, and with no flash-bang bomblet to disorient the enemy, they would be at a disadvantage.

The other issue was the gunfire. They had been loud on their push to clear the building. Whatever awaited them inside would be ready with counter-fire or booby traps, and if they weren't lucky this could be the end for them. They exchanged looks of understanding, one second's glance communicating their appreciation and care for each other as not only Nighthawks, but as friends. Helga took up position on the left side of the door opposite Raileo.

Comms came alive. "Nighthawks, this is Rend Mec. You copy? What's your status? Ray ... Hel?"

Helga, surprised, felt her insides lurch with a bout of anxiety. The timing was ridiculous, and any hesitation could mean death for she and her two Nighthawks, for surely on discovery of who they were, Anders wouldn't survive past this instance. Ignoring her commander, Helga nodded to Raileo, who—like her—knew the risk of getting on comms in their position.

With the butt of the rifle, he broke the door handle off and kicked it open. With one step he was back in position, protecting himself with the wall adjacent to the doorway. Helga meanwhile was in the other corner, ready, and when the door flew open to the expected ambush, she was prepared. Instincts, credited from her Seeker genes or the revita-shot, gave her a split-second advantage to react.

Inside were three Marines, one holding Anders at gunpoint, the other two behind fallen rubble, firing out at the direction of the door. She hit the one holding Anders, putting every ounce of pressure that could be applied to the delicate trigger of her auto-rifle. The kinetics lifted him, throwing him into the wall behind him, while the other two fell from the Widow Maker's trace.

Anders, no longer supported by his captors, fell forward into a chair with a heart-wrenching crunch. For a moment, Helga thought she may have shot him on accident, but when he rolled onto his back laughing hysterically, she let out an audible sigh. Three men had held him, and from the look of the place, it was meant to be his prison for a long time.

"This is Ate," Helga reported on comms, motioning for Raileo to keep watch on the door while she stepped over the rubble to get to

Anders. "Rend, you copy? I'm here with Ray and Anders. How are we looking?"

"*Thype*, it's good to hear your voice," Cilas admitted. "Did I hear that right? You're with Ray and Anders? Righteous. What's your status?"

Helga studied Raileo's mannerisms while he crouched near the door, realizing that since escaping, she hadn't bothered to ask if he had any injuries. The Nighthawk had been alone and exposed for hours while she recovered in that building. His breathing was labored and every other second, he winced, making her suspect that much more was happening beyond fatigue. Anders had fallen unconscious, and even with night vision, she could see the blood pooling near his legs.

"Ray and I are still dangerous, but Anders isn't good. We need to get him to a hospital sooner rather than later," Helga reported. "How are you doing? Did you secure the target?"

"We found our man," Cilas confirmed. "Gave us a lot before he lost consciousness. He was our variable, but we chose a third route. We're turning him over to the Genesian Guard."

"I know the Guard is technically Alliance, but can we really trust them?" Helga asked.

"No choice. Alliance says work with the guard. That's the only way we were allowed to break atmosphere here. Sunveil practically begged us to shoot him instead of turning him over. That made it even easier for me to decide. Is your location secure? Can the three of you make it back up this way to the big house?" Cilas sounded winded, which made Helga wonder if he too carried wounds that he wasn't divulging.

She looked to Raileo for an answer and the Nighthawk looked back at Anders and shook his head. She understood what he was thinking. Staying inside here, they were hidden, and moving Anders now could be a mistake. There was also the fatigue after a long night of ducking and shooting. She was running on fake energy from Raileo's revita-shot, and he looked about ready to collapse. Helga wondered at their chances of even making it back out of that building.

Cilas came back on comms. "Q's going to find us a transport. I'm coming to get you. What's your location?"

"We're in the building where Ray chilled an ice cube," Helga joked. "There's a tunnel below it. Should be already cleared. Ray and I will retrace our steps to meet you outside."

"A bit of good news, Nighthawks. *Missio-Tral* caught up with the rogue infiltrator, *Harridan*. Now that we've found the source of our stolen documents, our duty here is done. Stay on comms, eh? I'm leaving now."

Helga took a breath and hoisted her rifle, crossed to Raileo and took the lead out to reverse course back to the tunnel. It was nearly over, at least that was what she kept telling herself, though a nagging doubt lingered in the back of her mind. Hadn't they come for two targets in Basce City? Sunveil was supposed to be the lesser option, the one to reveal the location of the second. She wondered what happened to change their plans.

What bothered her the most was the way he said, "our duty here is done." It could mean the target was already dead, or apprehended by another team of ESOs, which would be a real punch in the gut. Perhaps local government, or the worst scenario, he had managed to escape.

25

It was early morning on the Nighthawk's third day of being passengers aboard the *Velecrance* hover-carrier, the mobile airbase of the planet-based arm of the Genesian Guard. After the events of Sunveil's compound, Cilas had them transported to the carrier where they could deliver Sunveil and get on a secure comms directly to the *Rendron* for formal instructions.

While there, the Supreme Lord of the Guard, Siraj Tat Sunfleck, had his medical staff tend to the Nighthawks, which ultimately extended their stay due to the number of injuries. Helga was found to have two broken ribs, multiple contusions, and shrapnel from a kinetic round stuck inside her abdomen. The fall had resulted in a concussion, and then there were the revita-shots, which she couldn't have known was on the verge of giving her a stroke.

She like the others had been treated and given a space to themselves with bunks, and enough amenities to keep them self-sustained. Helga's treatment hadn't been lengthy, and she, Cilas, and Quentin had been allowed to move freely about the vessel. Raileo had two gunshot wounds, one in his right thigh, the other in his chest. Both of them non-lethal, thanks to his armor preventing them from penetrating, but he had sustained enough of it to require surgery.

Cilas made it out in one piece, but had many superficial injuries which caused him discomfort, even from standing. Anders was still questionable; he had been beaten and tortured for information that he wouldn't surrender. The physicians did their best for him, but in the end found it necessary to shuttle him off to a hospital. Discretion was typical of anything dealing with the *Velecrance*, but Quentin Tutt had gone with him, and Cilas, already low on trust, had reluctantly agreed to it.

So, for three days they were at the mercy of the surgeons treating Anders, and the Alliance going over the information Cilas pulled from Sunveil. They passed the time reopening wounds, by thinking themselves above the human limitation of giving wounds time to heal by remaining sedentary. When they weren't exercising, they were arguing over mistakes, and when they weren't doing either of those things, they would watch the feeds detailing an ongoing riot in the tenements.

The first night after Quentin left on the shuttle, Helga and Cilas had gotten into an argument, and resolved their differences with an hour of awkward, bruised-body sex. Nighthawks were sworn to always, "finish the job," so while each did persevere, they agreed to wait before attempting this again. Now this was day four, if she was remembering correctly, and Cilas had left her alone and was outside the compartment having a heated argument.

Cilas shouting; that was so alien a concept, it made her worried. The door slid open and he walked in, dressed in full infiltrator's body armor. When he saw her sitting up, he crossed to her quickly with a frown on his face. "Sorry to wake you, but the equipment is *schtill*. The damn engines are so loud outside that I couldn't even hear myself. I have our orders, but I have to wait to share. Will brief the team when Ray and Q are back with us, and then we can get back to the *Ursula*."

"I've never known you to lie so brazenly, Cilas. You were shouting out the words, 'how is this fair?'" Helga scolded him softly. "Whatever it is, you know you can talk to me. I won't react if you just want me to listen. I just want you to know that I am here. Is it really too classified to tell me?"

"No," he returned, quickly, embarrassed to have disappointed her with losing his cool. "I was told to leave Anders behind. Not only by his doctors, but the captain. He wants us off this planet as quickly as possible. Seems everything we got involved in is about to explode, and Basce City will not be keen on seeing Alliance Navy for some time. Our primary target, Vray, was seen two nights ago on a station near Neroka. It's now up to the Genesian Guard to catch him."

"We're to leave Anders here." Helga was incapable of finishing her thought, too appalled at the very suggestion.

Cilas sat down on the bunk next to her, leaning forward to rest weary elbows on armored knees. "Moving him now would do more damage, that's what they're telling me. It wouldn't be permanent; we'd just end up having to return here to collect him. We don't leave our people, Helga, you know this. The ones still buried on moons that I couldn't reclaim, it's like their ghosts haunt me whenever I sit still."

Helga reached over to rub at his back, but he stood up suddenly and exhaled, seemingly frustrated.

"You may be here one day, sooner than you think." He jabbed a finger down at his boots to indicate his position. "If there's anything you remember when you're there, remember, no matter how right you try to do by those around you, the Alliance will find a way to make you disappoint them. We've known each other long enough for me to speak clearly with you, Helga. This isn't cynicism, and it's not me wavering. It's the truth, and the sooner you accept it, the better you will be for it."

"I've never heard you sound so gloomy," Helga whispered. "It's like you always say, Cilas. Shrug off the inevitable and focus on what you have control of. Attitude, dedication, and execution. Trying to change what you can't will only lead you to madness. All things you've said to us at one time or another. We're all miserable here, and you're still very tired."

"You're calling me cranky," he acknowledged, smiling.

Helga threw her legs off the side of the bunk to try and summon the energy to stand. "Cilas, how did Anders get captured?" she asked. It was a question she had meant to ask, but never got around to it.

"When the bomblet went off, it cracked the stone beneath our feet on that balcony. Q and I were barely out of the hall, so it merely stunned us. The three of you collapsed with the ledge, falling into a fountain—thank the maker for that—but no sooner had Ray pulled you out, they got Anders. We cleared the hall, tried to give you cover from what was left of upstairs, but there were too many of them in the end. So I made a decision to finish the mission, leaving Ray to watch over you until we could meet him. As for Anders, leaving him isn't an option for me. I just want you to know that," Cilas assured her.

"I know." Helga was forced to agree, "Still would prefer him to be in our own medbay when he recovers, where familiar faces are waiting, not a bunch of Genesian strangers."

Cilas looked distracted for a moment, turning his attention to the vid screen hanging above the doorway. "What is this you're watching, Hel?"

There was a reporter on the feed speaking to a family whose humble tenement dwelling served as a backdrop to their discussion. It was nothing like Fio's home, which had all the amenities of a successful smuggler with enough credits to live comfortably despite being surrounded by squalor. A man in the background sat staring past the reporter into the viewer's eyes, a long-ranged stare Helga recognized from spacers traumatized, unable to stay in the present.

"I'm watching the aftermath of the two days of *schtill* visited upon these people by our so-called brothers of the *Helysian*. I—I just have no words, Cilas. They keep referring to them as 'Alliance Soldiers,' as if this represents us. As if we're all capable of—" She shut her mouth and shook her head, too upset to complete her thoughts. Cilas, recognizing this, increased the volume to focus on what was being said.

"None of this is new to us," a woman was saying. "We are used to it. This is what they do every time there is an election, or someone important decides they want to see the slums. BasPol comes in, makes a big show of it, roughing people up, but nothing ever changes once they leave."

"The Alliance were with them this time," the older of the two men added. "They beat and murdered innocent people. Even our children."

"Even our children," one of the younger women agreed. "We were lucky because we ran. They had big guns and armor, just to shoot people who have only their fists to fight back."

Helga was disgusted. "These *crutas* made the trip all the way down here to terrorize our allies. How deep does it really go, Cy? What is happening with our Navy?"

Cilas visibly deflated. "Nothing's going on with our Navy, Hel. This is what happens when you have an undisciplined group of spacers. You know it, I know it, we all know it. This is tragic, and *thyping* embarrassing, not to mention dangerous for every Alliance spacer station in Genesian space. The council is aware of it, and the local Genesian leaders seem understanding of what went on. To be clear, they shoulder as much of the blame as we do. They allowed a segment of this city to rot, unsupported, and allowed criminality to take hold, growing so powerful they began to interfere with our war. That is how this happens. Those Marines deserve what's coming to them, but they stopped representing the Alliance when they boarded that cruiser."

"Tell that to the family whose home they tore apart and used," Helga countered. "Tell that to their daughter, now missing, possibly an unwilling participant to maker knows what. If I could go back to our time in the manor, I would have begged Tutt to burn it down with every one of those *thypes* trapped inside. They better pray I don't get clearance to bring the Thundercat local—"

"You won't," Cilas interjected softly, "But knowing the council, anyone not having clearance to be here will no longer have a home on an Alliance deck of any kind. I know it won't make you feel better, Hel, but without a home they'll be stuck here, and these families, many of them, at least we can hope, will hunt each of them down to execute them."

Helga shook her head, still staring into his eyes, unflinching. "You're right," she said, "it does not make me feel better. We were welcomed into the stocks as friends of Fio, and they knew us to be Alliance. A day later here comes the thugs, wearing our colors and aiding BasPol in bringing terror. Why would anyone here trust us ever again?"

Cilas shifted his gaze back to the vid screen, eerily quiet for a long moment. "Here's the truth." He spoke without looking at her. "It's likely they won't trust the Alliance ever again. Basce City will be hostile to any Alliance member from this day forward if we continue to cover this up the way we've been doing. Unfortunately, that will never be up to us unless one of us somehow gets called to sit on the council."

"Question for you, Commander."

"Commander?" Cilas repeated the title, turning to see what she wanted. "What's on your mind, Lieutenant?"

Helga stood up from the bunk, having had enough of the chill from the ventilation, hugging herself to rub some warmth into her exposed, sinewy triceps. She kept them there to cover her bosom, which didn't leave much to the imagination beneath the thin undershirt she had been using as a nightgown. "Are we stuck here or are we allowed to leave at any time?" she asked.

"Only thing holding us here is our injuries," Cilas replied, walking over to their stacked-up gear to retrieve a jacket from her backpack. "Once Ray is up and about, which could be as soon as tomorrow, we can leave if we want to. Why? Is there something you wish to do before we depart?"

Helga took the jacket, thanking him wordlessly, and pulled it on, relishing the feeling of its insulated warmth. She crossed to the sole window and stood to the side, looking down at the city. The clouds obscured much, but she could see the ocean twinkling beneath the sunlight. A fleet of ships, no bigger than specks, were leaving the shores to embark on their journey to what she could only imagine was a distant land. It brought to mind Ina and the crew of the *Ursula*, somewhere above them, awaiting their return.

"I would like to return to Fio's apartment to collect some items. While we're there we can ask around and get the real version of what went on while we were at Sunveil's. I feel this could be important to our cause to find out. I don't trust BasPol or any of Basce City's officials, for that matter, and the guard won't know the type of information necessary to get the Alliance to act."

She expected Cilas to inform her that what she suggested was madness, but he remained silent and walked over to take a turn at looking out at the city. "I will be honest," he said. "Q and I discussed going back while you and Ray were being treated for your injuries, but then he had to go with Anders, so I killed the thought. What he and I aimed to do, though, was much different."

"What was the plan?" Helga turned to face him.

"Get on that dropship brought here by the traitors and pull what we can from the logs, maybe tap into their comms to see who was sending them commands. With Vray gone, there still remains a lot of questions, and the corrupted captain behind all this has managed to slip the *Missio-Tral's* squadron."

"Of course they did," Helga quipped sarcastically. "Even the almighty *Missio-Tral*, solver of all Alliance problems, let slip a lizard agent intent on destroying us from within. Maker forbid something going our way in this whole debacle. For all the spatial superiority the Blood Wraiths love to tout themselves as having, I can't help but feel a little bit of pleasure at that fumbling this up."

"Yeah, well, they don't have our Revenants or Lady Hellgate," Cilas returned, causing Helga to study his features, wondering if he was being sincere. "We're already here and technically still cleared for action by the Alliance," he continued, "so my thought was for us to take the initiative and get back down there to dig some things up."

"Sambe," Helga whispered in agreement. "Knowing Q, what he wanted was to find a few of those rogue Marines and hyper-extend their arms until they spilled everything they knew. That and make them give up their uniforms and weapons, all while begging his forgiveness for violating their oaths."

"There was no discussing his plans, Helga," Cilas confided. "Just told me he wanted to make sure Anders was good, and what could I say to that? No? Even now, a part of me wonders if he hasn't slipped past the hospital's attendants to hunt down all those *thypes* on his own. We both know he's capable, and I won't sit here and pretend that I would be surprised if that's what he chose to do."

"Very capable, but without leave from his commander to run off and play vigilante killer, he would risk everything we've worked for," Helga thought out loud. "Though thinking about it now, that doesn't amount to much, does it? We managed to capture one target of the two we were sent to neutralize, and the other is in the wind, leaving a city in flames with our Alliance as the scapegoat."

"None of that is ours to fix, Hel, and Tutt respects the chain of command. Let's not assume he's suddenly gone rogue." Cilas scrutinized the room, rubbing at the stubble on his chin. "You can't stay in here scheming," he decided. "Things are still fresh in our heads and that's where this need to do something urge is coming from."

Helga agreed quietly. Perhaps he was right. He normally was. She had been helplessly laid up for days, and though spacers were used to confinement in tight spaces, the guilt from the feeds were eating her alive. "Maybe I should get some fresh air," she offered, still looking out at the clouds. "The topside is open, isn't it?"

"Yep," Cilas confirmed. "It's where they have their fighters—"

"Fighter jets," Helga corrected him.

"Fighter jets," Cilas repeated. "You should have yourself a tour. Stretch your legs and clear your mind of all these negative thoughts. I have a call with the captain, but while I do that, I suggest you get dressed and take yourself topside. Visit Ray if you like, that's if he's up, and when I'm finished we can talk some more. It may not be out of the question for us as a unit to return to Fio Doro's."

Those last words filled Helga with joy, remembering the holo displaying the memories of Fio Doro's childhood. It was something she lacked, something they all lacked, hard memories of a life outside of the 'forever war.' She didn't know why it meant so much to her. Fio Doro wasn't family or someone she considered a friend. It felt like vindication, however, something right to come from all this mess.

"That would make me very happy," she said, meeting his eyes with something more than gratitude for considering her request.

"We'll talk later, but until then, try to take your mind off the tenements," he said. "I'll let the captain know we will be delayed on our egress." Cilas touched her shoulder, and she straightened up to reach out and in turn touch his.

26

The sun was out, a rare occasion in Basce City when the rain didn't accompany the bone-chilling cold, which wasn't letting up even with the change of weather. Its bright white disk blurred against the clear blue sky—clear being a stretch, considering the smog, which was Basce City's toll on its populace for hosting chemical factories whose pollution altered the atmosphere.

Three bedraggled strangers to the tenement stocks made their way through once-busy streets, now barren, but for a few brave souls running about. The raiding party from the night before had locked horns with the Genesian Guard, and the evidence of their minor war was everywhere. Buildings, already well-past their date of repair, now hosted new perforations from kinetic rounds, and burn marks from bomblets and homemade firebombs.

As expected, the Genesian Guard had put an end to the terror with superior firepower and veteran tactics. The rogue Marines had been forced to flee north to what remained of Sunveil's manor, where more of the Guard would be waiting to trap them. The BasPol forces involved with the terror were rounded up and taken into the city where they would be tried and eventually convicted for turning their guns on the citizens they had sworn to protect.

On every corner the guards patrolled, the Nighthawks were stopped and made to verify their credentials. Despite this annoyance, it was still too soon after the conflict for them to relax. Their trained ears could still hear gunfire chattering in the distance, those last Marines carrying out their final order, which was to not get taken alive on the surface.

It was both sad and inspiring, seeing an already broken city invaded, only to show so much resilience in the end. On the walk up the steep road that took them from the gates to Fio Doro's tiered apartment building, it had been a much different experience from earlier. Elderly residents, too seasoned to let the violence keep them from enjoying the rare glow of the sun, sat out in front of their residences, eying the trio skeptically as they hustled along.

"Keep your head down and act like you belong here," had been Cilas's only instructions, and in doing so, the Nighthawks made it through several checkpoints of vigilant street enforcers playing at guardians for their tiers.

Helga had worried that coming in geared would have people mistaking them for the Marines from *Helysian*, but Cilas had assured her that the way they were dressed was more Genesian Guard than Alliance. Before setting out, they had ditched the cloaks, whose purpose was to shield them from the rain and windy environment. They still wore the form-fitting body armor, all-black and unmarked, with backpacks loaded with their gear and racked weapons.

Raileo Lei had been released early, cleared by the *Velecrance's* head physician, with a warning that he needed rest to fully recover from his wounds. He, Cilas, and Helga had been taken directly to the tenements by way of an armored aircar, courtesy of a Corporal Josh Jo-Lin, who was a friendly fellow with family members serving on the starship *Missio-Tral*.

The mission was retrieval, grabbing the rest of their gear and whatever else they deemed valuable from Fio's apartment. The young smuggler could never return home, and knowing how that felt, Helga was determined to bring her the holos of her father and friends throughout the years. She stopped to adjust her pack higher up onto her back, thumbs tucked into the straps as she leaned forward, watching Cilas approach Fio's door to unlock it.

"Aquilo," Helga sang, cupping one hand as she repeated his name, confident, though in truth hopeful, that he was lurking somewhere.

The young boy's face stuck out from the overhang leading to the higher tier, where he'd told them he lived with his friends. "Get down here, scout, let's have a look at you," she instructed him, cheerfully, though she did notice his manner was much more reserved. Gripping the overhang, he threw his legs over his head, tumbling forward to hang above them by slender arms, before dropping to the floor before them.

"Why didn't you come back to help us when we helped you?" he accused Cilas, ignoring Helga to stare up at the commander with a look of defiance.

Cilas met his gaze evenly, stoic as ever, but to the two who knew him, he looked very annoyed with the question. "The person who did this to you," he said. "We left to stop him and make sure he can never do this again. You understand? I am sorry this happened to you and everyone here, Aquilo. Had we stayed to fight, they would still be here hurting innocent people, but we made sure that didn't happen. Are you alright?"

Aquilo softened enough to survey the three of them before focusing on Helga, who had recognized his struggle with being brave in the face of so much tragedy. "Hey, we came to get Fio's stuff. Is there anything you'd like for me to tell her when I see her again?" she asked the fidgeting urchin, who responded by shaking his head in the negative.

"Tell her when she comes back home, I will own this building, and she can have her house back, for free," the boy stated firmly.

"Righteous," Raileo remarked. "Here's a gift to help start your ascent." He leaned past Helga to hand Aquilo three MRE packages and a fistful of chocolates. This brought a look of surprise to the boy's forlorn face.

"I believe you will do exactly as you say," Cilas offered, reaching into his own pack to grab the remainder of his MREs, which he combined with Helga's to add to the bounty. "You did look out for us, boy, and we don't forget our friends. If you don't find opportunity in this city, just remember, there's always a place for you up there." He pointed up to the sky where Aquilo's filthy face followed, struggling to understand what he meant.

"When the time is right, you'll know what he means," Raileo assured him. "Now, get back to your people before they think something happened to you out here."

Aquilo kept looking up at the sky for a moment, then looked at Helga, eyes dropping to scrutinize her gear. He turned to examine Raileo's, then Cilas's, before turning back to look at the sky, thoughtfully. "Is Fio up there now?" he asked.

"She is," Helga replied, hoping he wouldn't start asking for details on where she was hiding.

"Goodbye," he offered meekly, clutching the stack of MREs to his chest. He turned without saying more and jogged on bare feet to a set of stairs leading up to his tier, where he could stash them for later consumption and selling.

"Breaks my heart," Helga muttered. "Let's get what we came for and leave before I do something stupid."

"Can't save them all," Cilas reminded her as he entered Fio's apartment with his pistol primed. "Clear in here, let's go."

"Isn't that the point of this war, to save them all?" Helga countered, itching for an argument to help suppress her sudden feeling of helplessness. But Cilas didn't bite. He simply ignored her, and started reaching for things that belonged to Quentin and Anders to stuff inside a bag.

"Everywhere we go, we see glaring examples of the powerful taking advantage of the weak," Helga pressed on, making her way back towards Fio Doro's bedroom. "The greedy and selfish do everything in their power for credits, including selling out their own to the lizards. They get their boon and retire to the mountains of Meluvia, Casan, and wherever they think they can hide from us."

"Places like here," Raileo added. "They come to places like here, where they can become Garson Sunveil, profiteering off the tenements where no one above him will ask any questions. You get so rich, even if they catch you, you'll never be made to pay for it."

"Oh, he will pay," Cilas assured him. "You don't touch our property and live freely once we're onto your scent. Finding Vray and his ilk is precisely what the Alliance has ESO operators for. If not us, then the Jumper Agency will put someone on him, and you know as well as I do that they don't fail. Vray would've been better off staying here and taking our questions."

Helga shrugged dismissively. "Sunveil's just a tiny atom in a universe of treachery. That *Inginus* captain has an excuse. Like Lamia Brafa and Bira Sun, his mind was likely stolen by the Geralos. A part of me wonders if this was how we lost Vestalia. The lizards, seeing how self-important humanity was, invaded the minds of our leaders, who in turn made our troops stand down until it was too late to push back against the invaders."

"From the archives I've seen, that is exactly how we were defeated so fast," Raileo confirmed. "Vestalia's leaders sat on their hands when the dropships came, many telling their people the lizards were 'friendly visitors,' despite all the warnings from Meluvia. We were lost before the first of their dropships broke atmosphere over Vestalia."

"And here we are again." Helga spread her arms dramatically. "Trusting a few powerful humans to stick to the mission of winning back our planet. Sometimes I feel like our little team is the only thing stopping a system-wide implosion of our fleet. Captain Retzo Sho's enforcers. Maker take us if the old man was to ever become the unthinkable."

"That happens, he would find a way to airlock himself," Cilas said. "That, I can say is a fact. Same goes for me. They corrupt my mind, I would expect one of you to do me the honors. No Nighthawk can afford to cross over, you understand this?"

"Of course we do, Commander," Raileo said. "Think I want to face any of us with a lizard at the helm of that mind? *Thype*. Raileo Lei as a lizard; that's enough to give myself nightmares."

"I just wish we could do more." Helga sighed. "Something other than hunting these one-offs. Something bigger, and more meaningful. Something like hitting the generator on one of those elusive lizard battleships. Disable even one of those and the lizards would be forced to play at defense, indefinitely. But what do I know? Those are my thoughts anyway ... a pilot's solution, as you always tell me. I just want to make a mark in this war, not just go through the motions."

"Every little bit counts, Hel," Cilas assured her. "The only thing missing for you to understand this is acknowledgment from the greater Alliance. We Nighthawks are known by our council. Captain Sho gets his direct orders from them, not the Admiralty. That is how we ended up on Sanctuary. You won't hear it while you're out here in the muck, but in those warm cushy offices where the big decisions are made, we're one of the game pieces. None of this is unimportant."

"Well, that's pretty good to hear," Raileo said, though Helga wasn't entirely convinced.

She tampered with the orb projecting the photographs of Fio's memories until she figured out how to power it down. Then Helga faltered, becoming lightheaded, her legs no longer able to keep her standing, falling face-first onto the bed. Outside Fio's room, the other Nighthawks kept talking about the Alliance, unaware of her state, and her voice being gone, Helga found that she couldn't call for help.

No pain, just silence, and the inability to move her limbs. Vision blurred, then it all went white, and before she knew it she was unconscious, though to an outsider it would appear that she had simply fallen asleep.

She dreamed of being in the same starport as before, staring down at the black tops of her boots against the filthy checkered floor below them. Looking up, she saw a Marine dropship that wasn't the standard Britz-SPZ, but the older Genesian R20-Lodestar, the same model she had seen transporting the *Harridan's* Marines to Basce City. Recognizing this, Helga felt the dream had concocted this scenario using her fractured memories from the past three days.

Lucid, but unable to move fast enough to override this manifestation in her mind, she was forced to play passenger along for the ride. She looked up and recognized the sky, too perfect to be real with its soft clouds against the backdrop of a colorful skyline imitating sunset. Several panels projecting this holographic facade glitched erratically, killing the illusion, and letting Helga know this wasn't Neroka but another colony or privately-owned station.

The dropship was an eggshell color, streaked in *Helysian* blue on her bow, wing tips, and landing gear. These details made it different than the one they'd planned to liberate to take back to *Ursula*, if she was truly asleep. Looking around, she noticed for the first time that she was among strangers, very official-looking Genesians in robes, bordered by their personal guards wearing the same armor as the mercenaries from Sunveil's compound. Armed civilian professionals.

A hatch opened below the dropship, and a ramp descended, from which an imposing Alliance Marine emerged to descend and wait at crisp attention as twelve other men poured out to form lines before him. A tall Genesian was the last to emerge, in a black formal suit with a short cape, a lighter grey like his buttons, cuffs, and sideburns. He was no Marine, but they showed him deference as he hurried out towards Helga, glancing about worriedly, as if he expected some trouble.

"Welcome home, Councilman," a Cel-toc barely got out before being shoved to the side by the Genesian, who was obviously in a hurry.

"Can you verify that it's him, Ate?" Ina's voice came through her earpiece, snapping Helga's attention away from the retreating man.

"It is him," she replied mechanically, though she didn't know who she was referring to, or why she lied to their pilot Ina Reysor. Then the scene faded to nothing, and she opened her eyes to the off-white walls of Fio Doro's bedroom, where Cilas Mec came into focus, leaning against the wall near the doorway.

"All finished in here?" he asked, and she sat up quickly, nodding her confirmation, though too confused to qualify any of it. Past the tingling of her scalp and the memory of the nightmare, she worried that something was wrong with her brain, a possible side effect of the revita-shot, or the stims she had been given during their brief stay on the *Velecrance.*

"I'm sorry, Commander, I must've passed out," she whispered, making to stand, but petrified with the thought that doing so would cause her to collapse, leading to him questioning whether she was capable of flying in her condition.

"The commander's absent at the moment. It's just Cilas, Hel. We're actually alone, if you can believe it." He walked over to sit next to her on the bed and placed a warm hand over one of hers, gently squeezing it.

"Where's Ray?" she asked, sitting up and inwardly celebrating the fact that she accomplished this without any signs of discomfort.

"Said his wounds were hurting him and he needed some fresh air. He's exploring the tier while we finish up here, and when you're ready we can just reach him over comms."

Helga smiled. "You know he's full of *schtill*, right? How long was I out for?"

"Half an hour, forty-five minutes, I'm not sure," Cilas replied, reaching over to brush gently at her hair.

"Are you alright?" She met his eyes, showing concern for his state. Even now, despite his attempts at playing the doting boyfriend in this strange room, she saw a pain behind his eyes that had remained since the raid.

"We're all tired," was all he would give her, looking away quickly to mask the reality of his mental state.

"We're all *thyped* up," Helga corrected him, wanting to explain that she hadn't been napping, but had indeed collapsed which led to a dream, or "vision," as Sundown would call it, of a station somewhere she had never visited. How could she tell him this, however, without going into the deeper explanation of what she was? This simply was not the time or place, and with the time Ray had gifted them, it didn't feel fair to Cilas, who she could see was inwardly hurting.

In one quick motion she pulled him down next to her, climbed atop him and started working at the straps of his armored vest. "Whoa, slow down," he tried, but she placed her left hand over his mouth to silence him. Her right hand reached down to undo his belt, and then his pants, which she dragged down to fully expose him to the lights.

"The longer this takes, the longer Ray waits," she whispered, still holding his mouth shut as she worked at her own gear to accelerate their coupling. Strong hands found her hips, the commander no longer objecting but moving to assist like every Nighthawk had been trained to do whenever an action was in play. He moved to get started, but she shifted her hand up to his forehead, pushing his head deeper into the mattress.

Rolling to the side, she pulled off her boots, and then the pants, while he sat up to do the same. He was barely out of his first boot before she threw a leg over and gripped him, guiding him home as he held her hips firmly. Groaning audibly as they completed their union, she reached down to grab both his wrists and pin them above his head. Cilas surrendered to her willingly, and she threw reservation to the wind, moaning, no longer concerned for who might hear.

Selfish urges won out over anything romantic, and with his fire stretching her, pulsing, she ground her hips into him, bucking savagely, sending waves of pleasure up her abdomen. Jaws slackened, toes curled, and eyes rolling from the sensory overload, Helga Ate cried out like she couldn't cry out before when they were sneaking into crawl spaces and into each other's berths on *Ursula* while the Nighthawks slept.

Her strong fingers pressed into his wrists, and it was a wonder their skins didn't chaff, as she would not slow down or let up. And Cilas, she could tell, was near his limit. She too could feel her climax rising, and there would be nothing that could stop her from getting it. She rode him even harder now, too focused on bringing them home to worry about anything else.

Cilas began to warn her that he was at his limit, but she covered his mouth with one hand while keeping the other firmly gripped on his shoulder like the controls of a descending dropship. Galloping even harder now despite his objections, she felt the core hit the tip and then it was happening. Absolute euphoria resulting from her urging, shooting bolts of energy down her legs and up into her brain, arms, and fingertips.

Mouth agape and muscles tensing, she bucked her hips with every quiver of pleasure, no longer aware of who was below her as she shook uncontrollably, feeling him expand and add his own groans of pleasure to the mix. She could no longer see him, due to her eyes remaining shut to ride out the climax, but she could hear him mutter something before going still. Then her energy gave out, that sweet apex having been achieved, and she fell forward limply onto his chest, no longer moving.

"Are you alright?" he managed, and she nodded slowly, unable to stop her body's tiny convulsions.

"Are you alright?" She echoed the sentiment, though she wished he'd shut up and let her touch down in silence while savoring this rare moment.

"When I'm with you, always," he whispered, and those words added yet another pleasant element to Helga's free fall back to normalcy.

Basce City was hell, but they'd survived it, and she felt closer to him now than she'd ever felt since Dyn. She closed her eyes and allowed her thoughts to rest, relishing the safety and love she felt in this small instance. It made her feel wanted, and despite being Lady Hellgate, it was a feeling she hadn't realized she'd needed.

27

It was still a bright day, though closer to evening, and the skies were no longer as clear, rain clouds, having made a comeback from wherever they'd gone earlier. The three Nighthawks, Cilas, Helga, and Raileo Lei, returned to the starport to investigate the dropship from the *Harridan*. Getting there was the easiest part, since Corporal Josh Jo-Lin had waited for them outside the tenements and flew them to the strip in his armored aircar.

Once there, Helga found a security guard and dropped the name of "Nyora Ohn," the woman who had cleared them upon entry. The guard became immediately friendly with the mention of that name, even volunteering to drive them out to where the dropship was waiting. Though they had him outnumbered, Helga kept him under a watchful eye the entire ride on a hovering shuttle used to transport travelers to their waiting ships.

Being associated with the rogue Marines painted a target on their backs from the very people they were fighting to protect, and she had seen his eyes go wide when she mentioned the dropship as their destination. The ride out came by way of a series of tunnels, dipping lower into an underground section of the starport, which opened up into a massive hangar.

This arena-like hiding place explained to Helga why they hadn't seen the Marines when they had landed, and hinted at just how deep the connections were between the powerful Genesians in Basce City and the traitors from *Helysian*. It had the look of a starship's dock, and enough space to park the *Ursula,* along with a handful of cruisers. Aside from the dropship, which was an R20-Lodestar, there was only one other vessel, an aircar, black all over and as sleek as an aerodynamic racer.

Paying their guide handsomely, with a promise of silence Helga knew he would break, they approached the vessel cautiously, weapons raised just in case there was someone onboard waiting. They circled to the thrusters, where Helga placed a hand on the hull, taking note of how cold it was and the lack of vibrations from the generator.

"She's been parked for a while without cycling its energy," she commented, scrambling up them nimbly to gain the top. Auto-rifle resting snugly against her shoulder, she walked the length of the ship from stern to bow until she reached the glass of the canopy, where the cockpit could be seen. Nothing was visible, even with the assistance of the lenses she wore, and when Cilas and Raileo confirmed the same, she hopped back down to join them.

"How do we get inside?" Raileo asked, still scanning the windows with his rifle primed for any movement.

"Watch and learn, Chief," Helga boasted, scrutinizing the various hatches for one to break into. She chose the access ramp which that would have no pain-to-crack airlock compartments or coded blast doors to crush one of her hands should she fail. Like she did as a child exploring the outer hulls of cruisers on the *Rendron* when the docks were less crowded than normal, Helga nimbly scaled the landing gear, up into the space where the ramp had detached from the lower hull.

The gap was big enough for her to crawl until she found a hatch that was meant for granting access to the cargo hold. The door was flush with the rest of the hull, only made visible through gaps, revealed by the dirt caked up on the metal, the result of transports rolling over puddles from the polluted rain. Helga jammed her knifepoint into the corner of the access panel, prying it open to reveal the interior. Cutting two lines, she crossed them, biting down against the pinching sensation of the short to twist them together.

The hatch made a whining noise before popping open, giving her purchase to slip her fingers in and coax it open. It always felt good to find that her tampering with ships as a cadet had been worth all the disciplining that came with it, since now she could employ it as a Nighthawk. Touching burned fingertips to her tongue to soothe them, she slammed the panel shut, and hopped back down to the floor of the hangar.

"Nicely done, Lieutenant," Raileo offered.

"A compliment from our resident slicer? I'll take it," she responded with a wink.

"Look alive," Cilas announced suddenly, his gun already raised as he placed one foot on the ramp to start his way up into the vessel. Armed and stacked, Helga and Raileo fell in single-file, focused eyes searching for any movement past the hatch sliding open. Together they entered before separating to search and clear the ship. In less than ten minutes, they were back together on the bridge, confirming that it was indeed clear of its owners.

"Clear?" Helga confirmed with Cilas.

"Clear," he agreed, letting his auto-rifle sag, then removing his backpack with one arm to start digging into it. He was about to say more when he regarded Raileo standing up straight to examine the sniper with some interest. "That dark stain on your shirt there, Ray. Is it blood?"

Helga followed his eyes to a dark, wet stain on the left pectoral of Raileo's charcoal-colored, padded long-sleeved shirt. Mouthing a curse, Raileo removed the shirt and turned around slowly so they could examine him. Helga was intrigued, The Genesians were known for their industry, but medical sciences? That remained a mystery. The tenements and general condition of the city had made her skeptical of being treated on the surface, but she had hoped whatever bolts and screws they'd used to put Raileo together would at the very least hold up until their return to *Ursula*.

What she saw was a lean, tanned torso, lined with veins rising defiantly past the valleys and plateaus of his sculpted shape. Outside of a few shallow scars from knives and former patchwork, there was black mesh bandaging where new skin had been grafted to mend the bullet wound on his chest. One side of the mesh had been ruptured, possibly from the morning's activity, but blood was now running freely from it.

"Patch up as best you can for now," Cilas advised him, satisfied with what he had seen.

"Dr. Rai'to is going to lose her *schtill* when she sees us," Helga commented while removing the largest bandage available inside her medkit. "I can already hear her voice. *Thype*, you would think she was my CO or parent. I'm actually concerned."

"You?" Raileo breathed, suddenly stoic at the mention of Cleia Rai'to. "You'll maybe hear a comment when you go for your tea or whatever together, but I will hear about it for at least sixty cycles."

Helga glanced at Cilas to see how he was reacting to Raileo's situation, but the senior Nighthawk was distracted, staring up and out of one of the windows, but at what? She couldn't know. While Raileo turned around to dress, she stepped closer to the commander, curious at what he found to be so interesting. The view was of a wall of the hangar, though far back enough for them to catch a glimpse of a few spires from the city's tallest buildings.

"What are you looking at, Commander?" she asked.

"I think Anders and Q are in one of those high-rises," he said. "That's the actual city, and I was getting one last look at the architecture, so when I record my message for the captain I can be thorough. Every port, every planet, moon, whatever, gives me a chance to see different worlds, so I focus on something that I can remember on each of them. Everything else we've seen here has been ... foul, so I'm going to remember those buildings. They remind me of old vids from Vestalia."

Helga looked back at Raileo to see if he too was enthralled with the cityscape, but he was in the middle of pulling on his 3B XO-suit. She began to understand Cilas's poetic explanation of why he stared off into the distance. He had been Nighthawk team leader even before she graduated from the cadet academy, and after over thirty separate operations, it would be difficult for him to remember them all without a souvenir, tragedy, or memento.

She thought of the missions she had been on, and the memorable elements of each, though she would pay high credits to forget everything of Dyn. Meluvia was just a beautiful planet, and she had been there on two separate occasions. If she was only allowed one thing to remember it by, however, it wouldn't be the colorful mountains or the gravity-defying building architecture, but its friendly people. Oh, how she missed their brief time on that island, seeing so many strange, alien things, and eating real food. Nothing since could compare, especially not this seaside city with its corruption and chilly weather.

"You see that?" Raileo inched in close to them to whisper. "Even the commander's done with this place."

"Indeed," Helga concurred. "Now that you're dressed, let's see if I still remember how to override the ID scanner on a Lodestar."

Cilas turned to eye her skeptically. "No need," he said. "You're with an Alliance commander, remember? I shudder to think what mischief you got up to as an unsupervised cadet."

"Oh, I was supervised alright," Helga said as she walked away from them towards the cockpit. "I stayed in trouble, but when I had the chance to escape, I was finding my way onto fighters, cruisers, and assault carriers. You name it, I've gotten into it. Even been a stowaway on a few occasions." She sighed as if it was the most wonderful memory. "I just really look forward to being dry again. This forever dampness from the rain is the absolute worst."

"Hey, wait," she exclaimed suddenly. "You mean this whole time you could have given us access and you just let me break in? Next time I'll know better," she quipped, no longer proud of her earlier display of roguish excellence. "You knew, didn't you, Ray?" She turned on him next.

"No ma'am," he quickly said. "I too didn't think that a commander could override access."

"I can't for hatches, but an emergency override to a Universal Alliance system is different," Cilas corrected them. "What you did was necessary to get in, Helga, but I can override the system. Just point me to it."

She led them into the cockpit, where she climbed into the pilot's seat and scrutinized the console, offended by the grit of its appearance from lack of care.

"What's the verdict?" Cilas asked after several long moments of silence from his normally talkative second-in-command.

"This wayward little vessel?" she said. "She's no different from any other Marine Extractor."

"Hey, come on," Cilas whined, offended at the slur. Sometimes she forgot that their Commander's career had started as a Marine.

"I'm not saying all third-rate dropships are extractors," Helga quickly explained, "but this one squeezed out Marines aiming guns at Genesian civilians. "Plus, as we always say, present company doesn't apply so let me continue. Once Ray overrides the system, she's ours in every way possible. So, what's the mission, Commander?"

Cilas leaned up against the edge of the canopy and exhaled, looking unsure of how to answer that question. "Give me a moment. I need to think this through," he muttered under his breath, two fingers massaging divots into his temples.

"Of course," Helga said, forcing herself from offering up some advice. They should follow through with their orders, but leave the planet in the *Harridan's* dropship rather than the merchant ship they arrived in. Quentin knew enough of flying civilian ships to get it into space, where *Ursula* could retrieve them. It was a good plan, allowing them to get moving on pursuing Vray, while Anders had time to heal with Quentin Tutt standing watch in case their location was leaked.

What Cilas was concerned with, she knew, was the fractured report he would be forced to give to Captain Retzo Sho. Her eyes came up slowly, taking in the tall trees and buildings about the starport. In the distance behind it she could see the spires of the city, and behind them some countless meters away, was the raised terrain of the tenements, gray and forgotten behind a thin veil of polluted, smog-filled air.

"Maker, it's about time," Raileo exalted when the console came alive, followed by the crystal-core generator to power on the engine. They ran inventory for the third time since the morning, accounting for everything they had brought along: the items taken from Sunveil's home and Fio's apartment.

Raileo joined Helga in the cockpit, happy to be seated in the comfortable co-pilot's chair, while their commander, ever-brooding, opted for some alone time at the stern, where there were over thirty empty stations for him to choose from. Helga worried for him but was happy to have some time with Raileo. His positive attitude and sense of humor was always welcome on the dreariest of days.

"Is it bad that I'm becoming neutral to the thought of killing humans?" Raileo said all of a sudden, causing Helga to turn on him with her mouth agape. "Not all humans," he corrected. "I'm talking about the traitors, predators, and corrupt animals who we routinely get sent to kill. Used to bother me something fierce, Ate. I can't even explain it. That Meluvian mission nearly did me in."

"Don't talk to me about Meluvia," Helga said, staring forward. "We were all there, and no, it's not bad that you're neutral to it. That's just how your brain chooses to deal. It's when you start liking it that you have to worry. You're a good person, Ray, everyone knows it, but these traitors and mutineers we go after? Someone has to neutralize them, or we get attacks on civilians using our weapons and ships."

"Righteous," the young Nighthawk responded, leaning back in his chair. "I know what we are, and I do try to do right by everyone. Maybe that will count for something when it's my turn at the business end of a Widow Maker's gaze."

Helga slapped him on the knee, causing him to sit up and look at her, surprised. "You sit up here, you don't do this," she counseled. "You be the Ray that I know during down times, I don't want to hear any more about Meluvia, killing humans, or any of that *schtill*."

She glanced back at Cilas to make sure that he was seated with his restraints in place, then looked over to check on Raileo, who was already strapped in. "Going to take us straight out, so strap in tight and keep your comms online. We're going to be pulling at least 4 g's of thrust to achieve escape velocity."

"Like we did on Meluvia?" Cilas offered.

"Yeah, but back then, she didn't give us any warnings." Raileo laughed.

"We've both flown with you multiple times, Helga. You don't have to give the same warning every time," Cilas complained.

"Alright," Helga muttered. "But don't blame me if your experience this time is a little bit rough. These ships don't come with balancers; it's why they replaced them with the Britz-SPZ. Prepare for launch."

She brought the thrusters online and waited for the system to run its checks on Cilas's rank and status. Blue lights signaled, go, and Helga reached forward to grab the yoke and pulled it towards her groin while keeping her feet planted on the deck. She missed the pilot's seats on the *Ursula*, which were not only comfortable but flexible as well, allowing her to put her feet up on the console while gripping the detachable controls.

The R20-Lodestar did shake a lot, and the reactor droned on miserably, as if it was being made to work against its will. Helga showed no sympathy to its plight, however, putting the thrusters on standby while overcharging the crystal core to near critical levels. The trick was to store up enough energy to divert it to the reactor for the power necessary to rocket them into space.

They shot upwards towards the clouds, gaining altitude steadily, while Helga monitored the radar and radio for any surprises. The system seemed to go out momentarily as the energy generated from the crystal core was transferred to the engine's reactor. Lights flickered and the console came to life with a million warnings, and then the three Nighthawks were thrown back in their chairs as the dropship soared up towards the atmosphere.

"Goodbye Basce City, hope to never see you again," Helga managed to comment, but it likely wasn't heard by Cilas, who blacked out on the sudden change in g-force, leaving her to whisper an, "I told you so," to herself.

28

Having dedicated spacers on *Ursula* made everything feel so much different than when it was just Helga, Raileo, Quentin, and Cilas Mec. Walking the passageways now, the feelings of "my ship" had morphed into "our ship," and Helga just didn't know if this was a good or a bad thing. Ownership had come from her multiple roles, which placed the *Ursula's* every operation on her shoulders, especially with abstract decisions that required breaking protocol and baked-in tactics.

Now, although she remained first officer, despite Ina's rank as a lieutenant, it didn't help the way she felt. *Ursula* had been transformed into a formal warship, serviced by not only the Nighthawks, but a host of spacers, freshly graduated from the cadet academy. There were pimple-faced petty officers at once-vacant stations on the bridge, career Marines anticipating action from being on a ship with Cilas Mec, and midshipmen looking for a fast track to a lieutenancy.

Each of these youthful hopefuls seemed to love *Ursula* as much as she did, but it still didn't give her ownership, not the way it did when the decks were vacant. What couldn't be argued, and this she was forced to acknowledge, was that their new crew was efficient, even in their absence.

As with all deployments, now that they had crew and officers to keep the *Ursula* capable, the Nighthawks not named Cilas were given a cycle of personal time before returning to formal duty. Helga, her mind still on Quentin and Anders, who were still on the planet somewhere, stayed inside her cabin to mull over everything that happened: from falling off the balcony to running the grounds with Raileo Lei.

She missed Sundown, her mystic mentor, who in times like this would be schooling her on the secrets of the universe, and her supposed power to see beyond the veil. A power she still didn't understand because to her they were merely dreams. There were so many questions now that she needed him to answer, but he was off redoing the trials to prove himself worthy of his rank with the Jumper agency.

A familiar chime brought her attention up from cleaning her PAS helmet, and she stared at the door wondering at who could be waiting outside. Cilas would be busy playing catch-up with the *Rendron's* captain, and she doubted Raileo would be able to pry himself free from Cleia Rai'to. *Alon Weinstar, perhaps?* she mused, hopping up to pull on a robe over her tank top and shorts combination.

Helga cracked her door slightly, peering out to see who would bother her on an off-day. The first thing she noticed was the blue hair, before the slender young woman stepped forward to get a look inside her compartment. "Your room is no bigger than mine back in the stocks," Fio Doro commented, pushing past her to enter, uninvited, then turning to face Helga, who was annoyed at the intrusion but intrigued.

"Fio Doro," Helga announced, flatly, pulling her robe close and crossing her arms to regard the smuggler. They were the same height, though she was skin and bones where Helga was Alliance Navy tempered musculature. "How may I help?"

"I came to thank you, actually," Fio replied, still scrutinizing the compartment. "The soldier, Ray was his name? Told me you were the one who grabbed my things from the apartment." She seemed to be struggling with getting the words out, as if speaking gratitude was somehow thick and disgusting to her taste. Helga chalked it up to a native Basce City Genesian's struggles with the universal Vestalian tongue. "Wanted to tell you personally. I won't forget it. You all have done much for me, and I know it's because of the leaks, Vray, and the government, but this you didn't have to do, so, thank you."

"You're quite welcome." Helga forced a smile, despite feeling that the gratitude was but a lead-in to another request. She wanted to ask what she had really come in here for, but this wasn't Ina or Cleia who knew her well enough to be questioned without assuming offense. "Why don't you sit down, Fio, you look like you have some questions," she insisted instead, and the blue-haired woman complied readily, plopping down into the chair mounted at her desk.

"Can I ask a question? I don't know how to phrase it without it sounding offensive, so know that isn't my intent," Fio tried, grinning nervously.

"Alright," Helga said, tying her robe before sitting across from her on the edge of the bed.

"What are you, exactly? No offense, but I thought you were Vestalian or off-world Genesian, but you have those spots." Fio ran a hand down her own face to indicate her meaning.

"Vestalian father and a Casanian mother." Helga recited the same explanation she had been giving people her entire career. "Sort of a super-rare pairing, I guess, and most of us half-breeds either come out looking completely Casanian or human, but I wasn't so lucky."

"Wasn't lucky? You're *thyping* gorgeous," Fio admitted. "Couldn't take my eyes off you from the first time I saw you on Neroka with Captain tall-and-angry."

"You know his name. It's Commander Cilas Mec, Fio, come on now," Helga scolded her, still shocked at Fio calling her gorgeous after coming unannounced to her compartment. She decided to change the subject. "Did Ray tell you we met a young boy playing guardian to your apartment? He was the cutest little thing, all fight with nothing behind it, like a freshly minted Alliance cadet."

"Oh, Aqui, my little man," Fio gushed. "Wow, so the tier really did welcome you in. That's what I like to hear. Thrall owed me one big, whopping favor, so it's good to know he did right by you. Guess he and I can now call it even."

"I have to apologize, Fio, our presence there likely had something to do with the BasPol raid on the city," Helga confessed.

"Pfft, I doubt it. Raids aren't new to us," Fio said. "You get used to it. This is what they do routinely, whenever there is an election and someone important makes the stocks their target. BasPol comes in and makes a big show of it, roughing up everyone too dumb to avoid them. Feathers get ruffled, some end up dead. Most get thrown into the bricks—"

"Bricks?" Helga puzzled.

"Sorry, it's a Basce City thing, what we call our jail," Fio clarified quickly. "Same old thing every year. The gangsters like Thrall do what they can to fight back against the BasPol thugs, but nothing ever changes. The powerful still do whoever, whenever, with whatever gets them off, and the people of the stocks go back to living. I'm just glad you all were able to see it. Now, maybe someone in your Alliance can expose what is happening to us down there."

Helga made a face, and Fio shrugged with a casual familiarity that wasn't the response the Nighthawk expected. She was tempted to ask her about that, but knew it would only serve to further douse what little flames were left in the once blazing bonfire of her smuggler's soul. "If it helps," she tried, "we delivered one of the key conspirators to the Genesian Guard, but that's all I'm at liberty to share. He had a big, fancy house to the north."

Fio's face immediately brightened, and her eyes went wide as she studied Helga's face, looking for the lie that wasn't evident there. "I know the house but not who it belongs to," she admitted. "I do know they are connected to the raids and the pressure on the stocks, so if you truly got that *thype*, my people are forever in your debt. I don't expect you to understand the complications of our politics, but you all have earned my respect."

"Been to many stations, Fio?" Helga asked, seeing an opportunity to corroborate the details of that strange dream she'd had about a *Harridan* dropship.

Fio Doro shook her head in the negative. "Neroka was my first trip off-planet, and I only made it there because of a friend."

"The one whose berth was raided by the bounty hunters you shot?" Helga confirmed.

"Yes, if by berth you mean home," Fio corrected her. "She's an attendant for one of the shuttle companies, so she's seen all the stations. Me? All I knew was Basce City up until a week—is it weeks up here to you people? Feels like about a week, but who knows. Everything's just been fast, *thyped*, and inconvenient. Why? Are you looking for something?"

"No, it's stupid," Helga began, but thought better of giving it up, deciding instead to at least try her. "If we can get you contact with your friend, could you ask her about a starport with tall, vaulted walls and a checkered floor, firm like the floors on the planet, not adaptive paneling like the ones on Neroka? There has to be hundreds of starports I know, but this one seemed to have heavy traffic judging by the state of the filthy deck. Limited workers, large hangar, checkered floor, and the biggest clue would be a uniformed presence. The locals would assume they're Alliance."

"Is that all?" Fio asked "And what are you going to do for me?" Laughing when she saw Helga sit up straight. "It's a joke, relax. I owe you for getting my stuff, and speaking to someone who likely hates me now is the least I can do to repay you. Where did you get that description anyway? Sounds about as vague as *schtill*. I'm not so confident you'll get an answer."

"Footage I saw on a vid long destroyed," Helga lied. "Uniformed men, not Alliance but dressed in our armor, exiting a dropship similar to the one you saw us arrive in. The floor was checkered in red and white, and I could tell that this was a port beyond a planet. I don't expect much, but I want to at least try. Do you know what I mean?"

"I do," Fio admitted, beaming at her now. "So, you and the commander," she whispered, her eyes full of mischief and wonder.

"What about us?" the Nighthawk asked innocently, eyes still locked in with Fio's, robbing her of the reaction she anticipated.

"Come on; I have eyes. You're on a small ship full of good-looking people, young, no doubt randy from all the long trips. Better to have someone to keep your mind off it, right? I picked up on your energy the moment you two walked into Fumo's office, barely able to resist holding hands."

"That's *schtill*, and you know it. Your radar needs calibrating," Helga cracked, disbelieving Fio's observation. There was no way she and Cilas were that obvious, especially now with a full complement and observant rates on the ship.

"So, you're saying you two are not together?" Fio pressed, her eyes softening to reveal something behind the questions.

Is she asking because she's interested in me or Cilas? Helga had to wonder. She took a measured breath and looked off towards the bulkhead, her eyes finding the helmet gifted to her by her best friend, Joy Valance. She could hear her now, "Spacers *thype*, Helga, who cares? If it doesn't upset your work or your ability to take orders, who gives a *schtill* whose bunk you wake up in?"

The thought of the fiery, brown-skinned beauty throwing care to the wind and passing it off as advice brought a smile to Helga's face, which confused Fio further.

"That good, huh?" she remarked. "He doesn't seem like much, honestly. Don't get me wrong, he's an amazing person for rescuing me and taking on Vray's thugs, but as a mate he looks as boring as they come."

Helga rolled her eyes unconsciously. "Cilas is ... complicated," she had to admit, "but he's also caring, reliable, and loyal to a fault. As you said, we're a small ship, and I was the only woman for a long time. It's a position I've known my whole life. I'm sure that you know it as well, doing what you do with smuggling, but *Ursula* isn't a good example because of the Nighthawks. On *Rendron*, our mothership, it's like a city, so you get all types. It was never safe to be alone, not if you're small and vulnerable. You have to know who has your back, and who will come for you when you call. Cilas, Raileo, and Q have proven to be my brothers, but over time we all grew closer. I'll leave it at that."

Fio burst out laughing. "All of that runaround to avoid saying you chose the commander to *thype* out of all these blokes. Is that it, though, nothing more?"

"That's all you're going to get, you nosy little *cruta*," Helga quipped. "I don't even know why I gave you any of it, but repeat it to anyone and I will airlock your skinny rear faster than the span of two blinks, and inform the others you were screwing about and did it to yourself somehow."

Fio made to counter, but then an alarm began to blare, and Helga hopped up to her feet, beckoning the blue-haired smuggler to follow her into the passageway outside her compartment.

"That alarm signals incoming, Fio. Get back to your quarters, quickly, and strap yourself in," she instructed. "We can finish our chat later, but for now do as I tell you, and no matter how much you're tempted don't go roaming about the ship. I will talk to you later." Helga's comms was already chirping from Ida and Zan giving her updates on what was happening.

A Geralos dreadnought had come out of cloak, close enough to be picked up on radar, and was now coming about to engage them. Cilas, Ida, and Helga received an immediate summons to the bridge, where Zan was already priming weapons for the engagement. Helga got on the intercom, leaning over the console as she issued her commands. "All hands, beat to quarters. Non-crew find a station, strap on your restraints, and do not move about the ship unless instructed. This is what we all trained for, *Ursula*. Hurry to your posts. This is not a drill."

Cilas stepped up to his post behind her, standing behind his high-backed chair. Helga and Ina stood up to acknowledge him, saluting with the rest of the crew on the bridge. The commander walked around and took his seat, staring forward through the viewport past the pilots' heads at the tiny white speck that was the dreadnought. He leaned over to scrutinize a simulation of the *Ursula* and the incoming ship.

The dreadnought was close in mass but bulkier in shape, though its design was Louine, revealing it to be a convert. His computer gave him a series of details ranging from its weapons charging to its identification being that of a Geralos. This was all he needed. He gave Helga the nod of approval to go forward with carrying out their defense plans. No words needed to be exchanged, since the *Ursula* conducted drills weekly to simulate these situations, and she in turn gave Zan the go-ahead to run out their batteries at the enemy vessel.

Heavy caliber kinetic bullets soared across the 9km space to weaken the shields of the incoming warship. It in turn sent back a volley of bullets, which the *Ursula* shook off with its overcharged shields and armor. "System is screaming for us to take evasive maneuvers," Ina warned, but Helga, whose flying style had always violated the safety protocol of ships' systems, was so used to the shrill objections that she hadn't even noticed until Ina had said something.

"Hold course, and let it come in close," she commanded. "She assumes we'll turn, which would be the smart thing to do, but our cannons will obliterate her shields before any form of collision can occur."

"I guess we're jousting then," Ina commented, overloading their foremost shields by transferring energy away from the thrust.

"Brace for impact," Helga shouted into the intercom. "If you're not in a station by now, find the closest one and strap-in." She rolled her eyes at the need to remind them, but Fio Doro was a civilian who needed to hear it. Alliance spacers were trained to get locked in and restrained on engagements, but she couldn't assume the few drills would have been sufficient.

"What's the status on our tracers, Zan?" she asked the ever-busy, multi-tasking Cel-toc seated on the far side of Ina.

"Tracers are charged, Lieutenant," she informed her.

"Good, now hold until I tell you," Helga said. "Break away towards our port side when she's 3km or less, Ina. When I give the command, Zan, you put all tracer focus on the near broadside."

Ursula grew silent with anticipation, each spacer's eye on a monitor, holo, or vid-screen. Many did brace for impact, not having seen direct combat before in a mid-sized warship. Some whispered prayers, some became angry, others wished they could do more, but were stuck waiting to hope that they had signed on with a competent captain. Cilas Mec's face was stony anticipation, but there was no hint of hesitation, or any doubt of them calculating wrongly on this strategy.

The ship grew closer, but something was wrong. Helga felt the change but couldn't verbalize it. A shrill, screaming whine came from *Ursula's* alarms, warning of a loss of atmosphere from where a section of the hull had become ruptured from several hundred bullets getting past their shielding. The artificial gravity faltered, and the vessel shook, resulting in a chorus of gasps and groans, injured spacers who in the chaos had forgotten Helga's warning.

"How are we breached when our shields are still at 80%?" Helga shouted. "Ina, transfer power back to thrusts, and prepare to break. Zan, let fly our tracers, I don't care if you overheat them. This is survival now."

The redheaded pilot did as she was commanded and Zan activated the tracers, sending four long lines of laser energy into the dreadnought's hull. As predicted, their shields balked, nearly failing outright, but some of the tracers got through, cutting their own holes into the enemy and sending no less that ten Geralos spilling out into the vacuum of space. The dreadnought, not anticipating the *Ursula* staying the course to lash out so aggressively, reversed thrust to slow its approach, presenting to its broadside to turn away from the lancing tracers shredding its hull.

"They're coming about, the stern's visible," Ina exclaimed excitedly, but then the dreadnought vanished from what they could view through the windows and was nowhere on radar, starmap, or simulation. Helga unlocked her restraints, stood up, and started studying the logs from the recent engagement. Surely there would be an answer there for not only the disappearance that had come without a warning, but the bullets that had struck them, resulting in the alarms that continued to blare.

"Tactical, engineering, bridge, report. I want updates on our damage, not system readouts, mind," Cilas growled, scanning the faces of the petrified officers chattering away on their comms. "I want to know who we lost as well as what's being done for repairs. Helga, where did that dreadnought go?"

"Still finding you answers, Commander," Helga informed him. "I assumed it used energy reserves to somehow cloak, but that doesn't make sense. We should still have some awareness of where it is, considering our system was locked onto it. The only logical explanation I can think of is an Extra-Dimensional Shift."

"With no prep and a ruptured hull to boot?" Ina cut in. "No way that's what just happened. The lizards don't have that kind of technology."

"Yeah, but the Louines might, and that dreadnought started out as a Louine ship," Helga corrected her. "Look, they may be considered neutral, but there's a reason the lizards go out of their way to savage and take prizes from their fleet."

"Launch a probe," Cilas ordered, impatient with the banter and lack of answers from his leads. "Find that vessel, and in the meantime, keep batteries hot and ready to fire as soon as we locate it."

29

The bridge became thick with a silence that Helga found maddening, the only chatter now coming from CIC to the rear. Communication was an unintelligible drone of hushed voices discussing strategy, their suggestions in text form, littering hers and Cilas's wrist-comms, too many to keep up with.

Commander Cilas Mec, a newly minted captain with his first command over an actual crew, not just the Nighthawks, faced a dilemma that no simulation could have anticipated. A vanishing ship capable of dishing out as much as it could take, armed with cannons firing payload that shredded energy shields like a blade through paper. Technology he and his officers weren't familiar with.

The probes were launched, and Ina Reysor put what little energy reserves were left into the shields. Helga sat silently staring through the glass at the empty space before them, where she felt the dreadnought remained cloaked, keeping enough thrust to avoid detection from the *Ursula's* system. The cylindrical probe darted about, then a second was deployed to help canvas the 4km area about the *Ursula*. On the bridge and off, the crew did as they were ordered and kept their discipline.

"Let us recap what just happened," Helga said, while still staring out into the blackness. "If we were at the helm of that dreadnought and we saw *Ursula* and tagged her as an Alliance ship, what would make us close instead of running? We split them on first salvo, so they should have known they were outclassed before they engaged."

"In a ship of that mass?" Ina mused. "Good question. You would think they had a death wish. If this were a fighter, well, you know the strategy. A basic heart-check maneuver for rattling newbies, frightening the target into doing something foolish, like coming about in attempt to give chase."

"Clip close and cloak," Helga recited. "Yeah, basic *schtill*, but a ship of that mass? That's just insane."

"Perhaps they were desperate. We showed up on their radar, and them being crippled already thought they could rattle us into evasive maneuvers, giving them enough time to get away. Helga, you're the one that's been out here, sparring with them, while I was happy transporting cargo in my retirement. This is beyond anything I've personally seen. What are you thinking? Is this a new tactic for the lizards?"

"No, but that is one reckless captain," Helga said. "*Ursula* was a scout class prior to being upgraded to the mock-infiltration assault class that she is today. Our radar should pick up vessels, even cloaked, once we've exchanged energy. I'm as confused as you are, Ina, but there has to be a logical explanation for this." Helga leaned across the right arm of her chair to get the woman's attention. "How many lizards do you think are on that dreadnought, and do you suppose those cannons are automated?"

The red-haired Meluvian placed a gloved finger on her chin as she pondered it. "Similar mass, Louine construction. If I were to wager a guess, I would say no more than a hundred crewmembers. I don't know much about the Geralos power structure, but I do know they tend to pack loose to make room for their captures. The cannons ... judging from their action during that fight. I am prone to believe they're automated. The tactician chooses the target, and they do the rest, just like our Zan." She turned to wink appreciatively at the Celtoc, who was still facing forward, staring out into space.

"Those guns that ruptured our hull, I am going to call them shredders for now until we learn what they are, exactly," Helga said. "I agree those weren't automated, but if they were all we had to contend with and not the other thirty-odd cannons, we could overpower it, couldn't we? Since shields would be worthless, we could shunt all our power into a tracer, then split the *cruta* in half with one swipe."

"What are you thinking?" Ina asked her directly.

"When we find it, and we're back swapping energy with our shields doing naught, if we could knock some of those cannons offline, we could do like I said before and transfer energy from our shields to weapons, trace the engine and watch the fireworks go off within its core. I'm telling you, Ina, it would be as simple as that. Her shields have failed, and with cloak applied they can't charge, but I know Cilas wouldn't agree to it unless the cannons were powered down, and I have an idea to do just that."

Ina studied her face for a time, looking for a punchline that wasn't coming, then averted her gaze for a second before facing her again. "You're thinking one of us plays decoy, pulling the cannons off *Ursula*, and while that happens, we power everything down and hit it with all we've got?"

"Bingo," Helga whispered. "If I can get close with my fighter and make a bit of noise, the system will be forced to go into self-defense mode to try and stop me."

"A fighter? Why would it bother?" Ina wondered. "The most you can do is damage some of its hull, but not enough to distract it from *Ursula*. And if the captain is smart, which he's already proven, he will know that ridding you of a ship to return to means that your tiny pin pricks are worth ignoring."

"You would be right if I was to act like a rook and jump out there to fire at its hull, but if I get close, I can pull off at minimum three passes, putting everything on those energy cannons and a few will go offline," Helga explained, using her left hand to manipulate the hologram to show Ina what she meant. "Launch out, circle back wide and come in near the stern, skimming the shields close."

"Lieutenant, are you really considering that?" Ina's face had changed color, reminding her of Dr. Cleia Rai'to, who would flush different hues of blue depending on her moods. Ina's skin however had lost a shade of color, and though her face showed no emotion, her eyes had gone wide.

"Lieutenant Ate's skill with vessels is rated superb, Lieutenant Reysor," Zan chipped in, deadpan, her eyes still focused out through the viewport to a region of space. "Her suggested tactic, though considered reckless, has a high probability of succeeding, should she survive leaving our hanger to approach the enemy ship."

Ina sat back heavily and exhaled while running both hands through her hair. "And we barely just reunited, you and I. Now you want to run off and get yourself killed. I don't like the idea, Helga. You're first officer. The commander couldn't accept it, even if he wanted to," she said.

"You're right, he won't," Helga admitted. "But if it comes back, uncloaks, whatever, and we're looking ready to lose it all, I am going to get inside that Classic, and I am asking you to back me up."

"Back you up, how?"

"The same way Zan just did, by reinforcing confidence in my ability. Cilas knows what I can do, he doesn't stop me, and I've done crazier *schtill*, trust me. He would be in agreement with Zan. The lieutenant and first mate thing, Ina… I honestly hope that when it comes to making a decision as to whether it be me or everyone else on this ship, our commander makes the right decision and sets me free."

Ina took a long moment, hands clutching tufts of hair as she stared up at *Ursula's* overhead, while beyond her Zan continued communicating with the system. After what felt like a minute, her shoulders relaxed, and she turned to face Helga, her face a mask of gravity. The Nighthawk could imagine her in that instance as an icy captain at the helm of her own ship. The friendly pilot was replaced by the seasoned lieutenant who had taken time to ponder her reckless suggestion.

"I apologize," she said, surprising Helga. "I forget myself because everything about *Ursula* has been so refreshingly casual. The way you and the commander behave, it is easy to forget that you're Extraplanetary Spatial Operators. I will have your back when the time comes. It's the least I owe you for everything. Die and it will break me though, Helga Ate, and I won't be the only one. I've seen and heard enough to know how much everyone here adores you."

"Yeah, well, that's the paradox of ESO life, isn't it?" Helga commented. "Our good times are really good, and I wouldn't trade the galaxy for them, but I signed up for this knowing the risks. Death is a possibility always, but the reason I'm out here is because I can take these risks and have a good shot of surviving. Thank you, Ina. With you and Zan backing me up, Cilas will be forced to consider it rather than shutting it completely down when I suggest it. Now, let's find this *thyping* thing."

"Captain," came the husky voice of Chief Engineer Alon Weinstar. The tall cyborg had just come onto the bridge looking more miserable than normal, which for him was such a feat it revealed his injury. Helga got up from her seat and walked up the angled deck to where Cilas was standing, eagerly anticipating Weinstar's update.

Together the three of them met before the large orb-shaped starmap, which was a globular mass of lights representing the Genesian system and ships within it. Already present was the Marine, Master Sergeant Gideon Rue—a muscled, soft-spoken man—and the clutch of officers from the tactical group who had been pitching potential strategies and outcomes to their channel.

Weinstar was hunched over, breathing heavily, gripping an emergency handhold to hold himself steady. A young midshipman hurried to help him, and Helga—after a second of hesitation with seeing the older man look so feeble—moved to lend him a helping hand. Weinstar politely bade them to stop by raising one large mechanical hand. He paused to suck in some energy, wincing as he stared up for a moment at the overhead, whose hexagonal shape mirrored the deck.

"Thank you for your concern, Lieutenant, but time is of the essence, and I am okay. There was damage done to the engine, but repairs are underway to stabilize our thrusters. *Ursula* put blast shields about the section of engineering that lost atmosphere, but we haven't been crippled or stalled, maker save us. However, evasive maneuvers at this time would prove a challenge." He said this while directly looking at Helga. "We are effectively without a rudder for a while."

Voices became loud from the stations about them, a melody of panic, affirmations, and bravado that forced Helga to turn and glare at them, though the desired effect took longer than she wished. Weinstar continued, "We found some shrapnel from one of the rounds, and are analyzing to see how it managed to slip past our shields. Lieutenant." He turned to Helga, his eyes pleading. "We need time to repair and see to the injured. Right now, our priority is on the engines but there's still the access to the galley, medbay, and stores that have been cut off to isolate the rupture." His eyes shifted to Cilas. "We're working as fast as we can, Captain, but I fear—"

"Thank you, Cheng," Cilas cut him off quickly, knowing he was about to speak negatively about their situation, thinking it to be important facts. "As soon as we're clear, have Dr. Rai'to look at your injury. Did we lose anyone?"

"Still inconclusive, Captain, but my three engineers were accounted for before I made my way here," Weinstar responded, so low that Helga could barely hear.

"It's back," someone shouted, and everyone sprang into action, rushing back to their stations.

Helga walked with Cilas back to the center of the bridge, where he finally took a seat and pulled his restraints before sneaking her a wink. "We'll get through this yet," he told her confidently, "Though much of it relies on you, Zan and Ina. Whatever it takes, let's get that thing."

Saluting with a bow of acknowledgment for the charge she had been given, Helga practically sprinted down the decline to the open cockpit.

The dreadnought was visible through the viewports, moving away using reverse thrust to present their bow to *Ursula* where it couldn't easily trace its most vulnerable areas. On the tactical terminal she saw that its cannons were back online and already firing, whittling down their shields. She counted twenty kinetic blasters, arranged in a V-shape on the dreadnought's belly, with the point being below her nose, the rest running along her narrow, aerodynamic hull.

What struck Helga as odd, however, wasn't how well armed she was—though for a dreadnought she would admit to it being intimidating—but how she was armed precisely. This broken example of Louine technology had an assortment of extra batteries near her bridge. "I believe I found our weapon." She transferred the diagram of the dreadnought over to the central holo-display where Ina could see. "I don't know how they're doing it, but those aren't energy cannons."

"Never seen the like," Ina said. "I'm prone to agree. Our rudder is *thyped*, so we're going to have to get creative with avoiding those guns while powering our shields."

Helga got up and walked over to where Zan was seated and leaned past her to point at the image of the warship. "Put our tracers on those cannons, Zan. Disable them all then focus everything on the bridge. They will be forced to flee, at which point we'll prime a torpedo, knock out FTL and then reduce her to debris."

Zan complied, sweetly, as was her way. Cel-toc androids had the luxury of appearing human without the weaknesses in battle of worry and fear. She merely looked up at the lieutenant, who had always treated her like a person, smiled confidently as she confirmed. Ina applied some thrust and accelerating towards the tilting dreadnought, who appeared to be looking for an exit while its pursuer traced the first of the four firing batteries.

Another alarm went off from the bullets getting past the shields again, this time placing massive dents into the armor protecting the stern. *That wasn't random*, Helga thought. *Whoever is on that ship knows all of the critical points to strike on our ship.* Touching her wrist-comms and turning to leave the bridge to find the lift that would take her down to the dock, she took a measuring breath before contacting Cilas on a private channel.

She knew that he was at his limit. He had been in command most of his career, but that was on ground assaults and reconnaissance, not delegating action out to spacers managing a corvette. From the time they learned *Ursula* would be theirs, this had bothered her, but she believed with enough small victories his seasoning would come, and he would take full command of everything. Duty, however, had not given them time to grow into a proper crew of *Ursula's*. They were still Nighthawks who happened to own their own ship.

Now they were here, facing off against a Geralos captain who felt emboldened enough to rush them. Cloak and cannon tricks aside, he had employed standard tactics a wartime spacer would have seen plenty of times, but Cilas's greenness in this area was evident, and now they were all a bad decision away from dying. Shutting her eyes against reluctance, she reached up to her ear and opened a private channel.

"Commander, this is Ate. I have a suggestion and you're not going to like it, but please hear me out."

She told him of her plan to launch the Classic and distract the dreadnought while they armed a fully charged torpedo to shut its FTL down. To her surprise, Cilas listened silently, no interruptions, no "are you crazy," just silence while she ran through everything she'd discussed with Ina. When she finished, he was still silent, and she had to confirm that he was still there, by pointedly asking.

Another alarm went off from the cannons having struck the rudder again, and now even if they wanted to try and run, it would be a problematic maneuver that could end with them losing everything for momentum, most importantly the FTL.

"*Thype* it, go," Cilas commanded. "Just do as you've always done and go at it with everything you've got. But if I tell you to pull off ,Helga, it will be an order. Tell me you understand."

"I do, and I will, Commander ... Cilas. You know I can do this, and we're not in a spot with time to consider alternatives," she reminded him. Feeling the weight of her words and his silence in that moment, she did as she always did and joked, the words coming out before she could reconsider them. "If I don't make it, let Fio know she can have my compartment."

"If you don't make it, I will find and destroy the planet Geral by myself," Cilas swore, without any hint of humor in his voice.

"Then the lizards better hope we win," she said, smiling to herself, touched by the sentiment no matter how ridiculous it was in reality.

Cilas was a man capable of anything he set his mind to, and that she had known since she met him. Destroying a planet, though, that goal set the line of extreme when it came to promises. It was his way of telling her he cared for her, and she knew it, and to make one more trip with that in her heart, she couldn't think of a greater motivation.

She gripped the railing tight and squeezed her eyes shut, trying to come down from the excitement. The *Ursula* was being torn apart, and even now as the lift cleared the bridge deck to descend on the docking area, the fear of this being their last trip clouded her mind and made it hard to think. It touched down sooner than she expected, forcing her to snap out of her meditation and face reality. *Here we go,* she thought. *Let's get it done, Nighthawk. You've got this.*

30

Bam-bam-bam. Helga heard the bullets from the dreadnought's railgun striking the hull behind the section of bulkhead she knew to be the location of their energy generator. It was a disturbing noise that had her imagining being inside a fuel canister drum while someone from without swung a hammer trying to break inside. She ran back to her berth, peeled off the uniform, wormed herself into a skintight black 3B XO-suit, then pulled on over that the insulated pilot's uniform.

Unlike her PAS suit, which she wanted to wear, the flight suit could be donned quickly, though the protection it gave was minimal in comparison. She picked up the helmet, quickly scrutinizing the oxygen reserves. It hadn't been charged since the last time she'd been out spacewalking on the hull, but still had enough to last two hours, which she decided would be enough.

Many things ran through her mind as she prepared. Mainly, the thought of getting captured—always a possibility when dealing with the Geralos. For this reason, she decided to bring a small pack containing her sidearm, two ration bars, an additional wrist-comms, and a data card containing her information for the Alliance to ID her body in the event she died.

Helmet donned, emergency pack clipped to her black flight suit just below the waist, Helga completed her pre-flight ritual by stopping inside her doorway to observe all that she had, committing it to memory. Spacers were conditioned to have a small footprint of the decks of their ships, even within juggernauts like *Rendron* and *Missio-Tral*. What she owned could fit inside a backpack, and meant the worlds to her, but always with the thought that they were temporary.

STEEL-WINGED VALKYRIE

Playing in the flames of battle came with harsh consequences at time, and while death was always looming, getting captured or boarded would mean what was hers would end up taken or sucked out into space. Her eyes fell on the old helmet that her friend Lieutenant Joy Valance had gifted her, back when she flew with the Revenants. Though she missed her friend and sometimes mentor, what the helmet gave her in this instance was renewed confidence.

From graduation up until now, there had been plenty of situations where Helga Ate should have died. She hadn't, and Joy, an ace among aces, had admitted to Helga in one of her rare, complimentary diatribes that the Nighthawk was one of the best, not only from *Rendron* but the Alliance. She could do this, and she knew it, but doubts had seeped in after taking that fall back off Sunveil's balcony.

Bam-bam-bam-bam-bam. The shots sounded as if they were within *Ursula's* belly, striking the bulkhead on the far side of the passageway where Helga stood collecting herself. "Sambe," she whispered to herself, using Quentin Tutt's famous word to get motivated, and strangely enough it inspired action as if the big Nighthawk was there, shouting it at the top of his lungs.

Lengthy strides took her past the doors of the adjoining compartments owned by the Nighthawks and their resident Jumper, Sundown, who she too wished was in place to offer words of wisdom as he always did. Past the crew quarters, where she saw a multitude of spacers, their faces masks of horror as they waited helplessly while the dreadnought's cannons continued to punch holes through the hull.

Seeing her dressed for action inspired cheers, and that too helped to lift the clouds, and she showed her gratitude with a confident nod before picking up her pace to gain the hangar. Before she knew it, she was pulling herself up the ladder to the cockpit of her Vestalian Classic, surprised it had taken less than fifteen minutes to prepare since getting the approval from Cilas. All the anxiety from before dissipated, leaving her blank and ready to fight to keep the *Ursula's* crew safe.

Bam-bam-bam. The lights went out in the hangar and alarms blared, summoning the three dockworkers who had done as instructed and sat themselves at a station. One of the shots had cut through the hull, striking the cage they had set up for shooting. *Raileo is going to lose his mind when he sees that*, Helga thought before a crashing sound snapped her head around to where an emergency blast door sealed off the breach.

"Zan," Helga spoke into comms. "All checks are a go, and I'm ready to depart. Give me a countdown then open the launch hatch at section C, where the Vestalian Classic is parked."

"Good luck, Lieutenant Ate. Prepare for launch in five seconds, starting ... now, with five, four, three, two—"

"One," Helga whispered as the hatch opened below her, sloping down into a form of ramp. The Vestalian Classic, being an older model of fighter—prompting the "Classic" in its name—had wheels on its landing gear for landing on the surface of spaceship decks, carriers and landing strips. With a little thrust, Helga had it rolling down and out past the forcefield and into space where it drifted away from the *Ursula* until she tilted the flight-stick and rolled its mass away.

It felt so good to be inside the Classic, and she relished the feelings that came along with the whole experience. She maxed thrust to get out of range of the crossfire, and though the dreadnought was still over 4km away, the ship's system could still track and destroy her if she wasn't careful. A few hundred shots still managed to clip the Classic, and her shields were failing rapidly, forcing Helga to put everything into thrust to get away.

How embarrassing would it be to suggest this insanity of flying solo distraction on a dreadnought, have your commander actually agree to it, only to die before impacting anything?

Once in the clear with shields recharging, she exhaled to ease some stress, for she'd really thought she wasn't going to make it out alive back there.

The fact that she would have been destroyed had the dreadnought used its shredders sent icy tendrils down Helga's limbs, and she shook uncontrollably with fear. Never had she felt this lucky since she took her first flight and narrowly survived her dogfight with another cadet. Existential paradox flashed through her mind, coupled with fears of falling victim to those mysterious shield-piercing cannons.

What was I thinking? This wasn't necessary, was it? Couldn't we have just initiated a jump once we'd realized we were outclassed by this ship? Is this ego? What am I to possibly do?

"Get it together," she screamed, slamming her fist down onto the console. "They are relying on you." She forced her mind to stop sowing doubts and to stay focused on the task at hand.

She brought the Classic about, flying a wide arc to try and reach the dreadnought's dead side. Shields were back to 60% and climbing, enough for her to take the risk on approach. Through the mask of her helmet, the Classic's computer displayed an outline of the dreadnought in the distance after she had completed her turn. She came under fire, but again from the energy cannons and not the shield shredders. This made her think that they were being manually controlled since it would have been easier for the shredders to target her. Which meant no matter how much trouble she'd give them, they would continue to aim at the *Ursula's* hull.

Being out alone on a diversion run meant she couldn't employ the tactics of a squadron to be effective against a larger ship. Her Classic was nothing to that dreadnought, just a loud mosquito looking to be swatted once the *Ursula* was disabled or destroyed. They would ignore her, but not if she could help it, not after surviving that first salvo to be given this second chance.

Helga fiddled with the computer, quickly analyzing the specifics of this peculiar class of dreadnought. She saw a vulnerability, a flaw in the design, and a chance to make a significant impact on this fight.

"*Ursula* command, this is Lieutenant Helga Ate, do you copy?" she reported, dipping and twisting the Classic to avoid the shots incoming from the few cannons that were locked in.

"Ate, this is Commander Cilas Mec. Are you alright? Maker, what were you thinking? What's your status, over?"

"Still here," she nearly shouted. "Commander, I think I see a way to cripple this vessel and force them to power down their cannons to jump away. But I am going to need a distraction, something to force their tacticians to panic, buying me time to approach it safely to do what I can."

"Helga, you were nearly destroyed, and if something were to happen to you, I will be forced to live with the fact that I agreed to it. Rudder's been repaired, so we need you back on board so that we can safely jump away to get repairs. When we're out of range of the cannons, I would like you to dock. That's an order, Lieutenant. It was a noble attempt, but we're not prepared for this kind of ordnance."

"Once you're out of range, I will make my way back to dock and return to my duties," Helga promised, slamming the thrust forward to speed her approach of the dreadnought.

She saw *Ursula* moving, circling to keep her stern away from the Geralos, while tilting ever so slightly to present her topside to the shredders. Aside from Cilas's cabin, there were no important compartments up there, and the reinforced plating would do a better job of stopping the bullets from piercing the hull. This new move forced the dreadnought to engage its own thrusts to match the circling or risk exposing its own stern, where a well-aimed torpedo could wipe them out.

This new dance favored Helga, who, as she assumed, was ignored by the dreadnought's mounted cannons. She came in hard but leveled out with its hull, careful not to make contact with the invisible energy shield. Clip that, even slightly, and it would send her flying out into space with disabled controls. The hard part was over, thanks to the *Ursula* being back up to form to reposition on her enemy.

Staying tight to the hull, Helga was able to avoid all the cannons while she added her own energy blasts to its shields. She flew down the length of its belly, nose angled down to allow her guns to maintain their accurate aim. When she reached the stern, she pulled up, barrel-rolled to one side and then slammed on her brakes, forcing the Classic to reverse its trajectory. This sudden change in motion always came at a sacrifice, as she felt her consciousness wane, nearly causing her to black out.

She flew back towards the bow, now on the port-side hull of the dreadnought. From her vantage she saw the energy cannons in rows before her, firing on the *Ursula* somewhere off in the distance. Friendly fire peppered the shields all about her, from the volleying return of the Nighthawk's corvette. Putting it out of her mind, she launched a missile into the exposed base of a cannon sticking out beyond the shields.

The projectile imploded on contact, crushing it into a harmless chunk of debris drifting off into nowhere. Helga fired more missiles into the rest of them, knocking most of them out in just one go. Since she flew belly-to-hull, splitting their rows, it made it impossible for the cannons to stop her barrage.

Her computer showed the dreadnought's shields to be failing, but it had already increased thrust, and she was unable to keep up with it, so she was forced to pull off. She took a wide arc to come about, curious at what the dreadnought would do now that it was vulnerable. A part of her feared that despite its cloaking, the Geralos may be committed to disabling their ship.

For what end? That was the part missing from this doomsday theory of hers, though it kept nagging at her as if it were real. A loud pop startled her so badly that she released the flight stick, and another pop and the console was going haywire. She experienced vertigo and before she could react, the canopy opened, and she was ejected out into space. Small boosters on her seat's back responded to a set of controls on the pilot's armrest.

Helga, still disoriented, had enough forethought to activate them, launching herself away from her beloved Classic, which was now permanently disabled while the dreadnought continued to fire on it. She wanted to see *Ursula's* response, but she had started twisting, and getting the chair to right itself was a skill she hadn't mastered. How could she? Would she have believed as a cadet that she'd one day be stranded outside of her fighter, awaiting rescue?

She was so angry she could scream but no one would hear her; she wasn't even sure if they realized that she had been hit. Looking down, she saw that the flight-suit had expanded itself to become an EVA space suit, providing her some protection, though she questioned whether her helmet had been sealed properly. She fumbled for comms, hoping she wasn't too far off for someone to pick her signal up. Then she heard some chatter.

"I see her vital signs and she's alive. Though how, and where?" Cilas was saying.

"They could have taken her prisoner, Commander," Ina Reysor offered.

"Not the lieutenant, she would bite off her tongue before she let the lizards take her in," Raileo countered. "If she's alive, she's somewhere out there, and we're going to have to find her, fast."

"Thank you, Ray," Helga croaked, suddenly exhausted, which she translated into something being wrong.

"Ate?" Raileo shouted.

"Yes, I am ... have a malfunction. Follow my tracker. Come and get me, Ray."

"We're coming to get you, Helga, just you hold on," Cilas said, and she smiled at hearing his voice. For some reason it made her feel confident that there was a chance she could make it. When Raileo acknowledged her, she had seen the flash of the dreadnought's reactor imploding from a torpedo. It was a beautiful sight, and for a moment she had thought to herself, that for an exit out of this dimension called life, that view would have suited her.

Lady Hellgate, dead, but she took a dreadnought with her to the grave. She had been ready, but Cilas's voice made her consider that perhaps it wasn't time. She studied the readouts on the glass of her helmet, where it was warning her that oxygen was low, from what she had guessed, her Classic's helmet. No pilot expected to live to perform a forced exit from a fighter. Many had tried; after all they were trained to use it, but most died before they could clear the ship, or were hit on the way out by the strafing bullets.

She was alive, and though oxygen was low, she had this strange sensation of being reborn, sure of much but pragmatic about her impending death. It felt freeing, but deep inside, a part of her was frightened of her having lost something with the destruction of the Classic. That ship had represented her in so many ways. Losing it, and knowing no other vessel could ever replace it, burned a hole inside her heart. She sat silently, staring out into the blackness, fighting back the tears.

"Can you fly that thing, Ray?" Cilas inquired, and it took her a while to realize they had been trying to reach her for some time, but she had been blacking out and distracted with her own thoughts.

"I'm out here. Come, I activated my tracker. Come," she whispered, shutting her mouth stubbornly. Talking was likely taking away from her oxygen, and so she shut up. *Tracker is on, come and get me*, she thought, smiling mischievously. *Maybe my Seeker powers will allow me to send them my thoughts through their comms.* That elicited a laugh. *No, laughing might be bad*, she thought, then shut her mouth and applied a little more thrust from her chair.

"Yes, sir, but Zan should be the one to fly it," Raileo was saying, but Helga couldn't make out the rest as she drifted in and out of consciousness. They were so far away now, Cilas's voice, Raileo's care, and she thought of Quentin Tutt, and how he would have found a way to reach her before Cilas could make a plan. Then it was vacancy, nothing, the deep black that could swallow outer space. Helga Ate was off to the dimensional void, where dreams and nightmares keep the unconscious entertained.

Several kilometers away, the dreadnought drifted, no longer shooting off her cannons or trying to beat an escape. She had been declawed, her teeth removed, and her heart crushed under the weight of an energy torpedo fired with precision timing. She was dead and her crew along with her, but it all started with a Vestalian Classic that had dared to take her close. It had been destroyed, but before it did it took out thirteen energy cannons and sent the crew into a panic.

Helga Ate had done that, and the dreadnought lost, despite having cannons that cut through shields and advanced cloaking technology that defied everything known about energy manipulation. And now she slept, unknowingly, dreams askance, her lips still turned up into a smile of mischief, the low-oxygen warning beeping every other second.

31

Though the *Ursula's* hull looked as if it had been put through a shredder, it still had more than 50% shields remaining. The shredding railguns had ruptured more compartments and stations, bringing the death toll up to seven for Commander Cilas Mec. The dreadnought, however, was down to armor and an FTL working overtime to charge as it maxed out its thrust to get away.

To a man, *Ursula's* crew was of a mind to disallow the Geralos from escaping; the butcher's bill had been too high, and they all wanted their revenge. Desperate to pull away, the dreadnought again went into cloak despite being low on energy reserves, which should have been impossible. Cloaking wasn't technology that played well with others, however, so for the time it worked at convincing *Ursula's* system it was no longer there, its cannons were not firing.

Four charged torpedoes shot out from the corvette's launchers, aimed at an area of space where Zan had calculated the ship would be. They struck with brilliant effect, tearing open the dreadnought's hull to explode inside it. The massive vessel flew on, but with no obvious control, indicating that its navigational system was damaged. The FTL drive was no more, the crystal core generator becoming unstable, which spelled doom for any survivors on the ship.

While this went on, Raileo Lei, with help from Ina Reysor, took the R60-Thundercat out to rescue Helga. She had been tracked from the time she'd ejected, so they were able to find her, though it was still challenging due to the weakness of the signal. Once collected, she was placed in the care of Dr. Cleia Rai'to, whose large black eyes looked to not have slept in many cycles. Eight of her beds were occupied with injured spacers, including Helga Ate.

Cheers erupted throughout the ship from the spacers watching the dreadnought implode throughout, her once frightening cannons now unmanned, never to fire again. Helga would have loved to see it, the first duel of the Nighthawk's warship, and how they had managed to be victorious despite a new Geralos weapon that could have done them in.

She missed hearing her name, spoken by no less than ten crew members, praising her for her bravery and sacrifice. She missed seeing the crew become closer, conquerors and survivors both, living out the adventures they had been told to expect when serving with the Nighthawks. And she missed Cilas visiting her daily, cycle after cycle as they sped back to the Nusalein Cluster to meet their contact and get the *Ursula* repaired.

"You were out for a while. How was the afterlife?" she heard a voice she recognized as Cilas's. He had known she was conscious even before she did, it seemed, and she was still trying to get her bearings.

"Dark," she replied, pulling herself up to a sitting position and opening her eyes. The lights were low, and they were in the medbay, where she saw that every rack had a body in recovery. "Where's pretty blue and cranky?"

"I asked her to take the shift off," Cilas explained. "She was going on 48 hours and on the verge of passing out. After looking over the credentials of several crew members, I was able to find her some help. So, that being said, Helga, I would like you to meet Chief Irena Falco. She's been giving you great care in Dr. Rai'to's absence."

He stepped to the side to reveal a young female officer who cradled a tablet on her forearm, similar to the one Dr. Cleia Rai'to always held.

"Welcome back, Lieutenant Ate," she effused, touching her heart in a casual salute. She was petite with the voice to match, and a shock of white hair cut low like a Marine recruit. Enormous brown eyes, bright and curious, seemed to twinkle in the medbay's bright lights. The way she regarded the Nighthawk should have been off-putting, those large, piercing eyes peering into her own, unblinking.

"Thank you, Chief," Helga commented, breaking away from Medusa's glare. It was likely she too had stared; her mind was still trying to process another officer in charge of Cleia's medbay. It was a temporary post, but yet another reminder that the *Ursula* she knew was now a long past reality that could never return. Seeing the three other blue uniforms tending to the injured made her think how overwhelmed Cleia would have been in the aftermath of the fight.

"I will leave you now, Commander, Lieutenant," Irena Falco said, making a slight bow before turning away.

Helga watched her go to another bed, survey her tablet and then lean in to start a conversation with its occupant.

"Is Cleia in her compartment, do you know?" she asked Cilas, thinking now that she was awake, she would take the lift down to the lower deck and look in on the doctor before returning to her own comfortable rack.

He let out a deep sigh then snapped his head around to face her, as if he'd just realized she had come awake. "She's in the galley now, eating with Ray and Mas-Umbra. Hey, I bet you can't guess where we are?"

Helga smiled at how easy it would be to win this game. "Let's see," she said. "The generator's powered down, and it's all quiet, so I am going to go with us being back at Neroka, and if not Neroka then a neighboring station. We got hit, so we came back to get repairs." When he raised both eyebrows, she knew that she had guessed correctly, and she bobbled her head smugly at him. "Wait," she said, becoming serious. "That means I've been out of it for how many cycles? Five at least, I'm guessing. *Thype*, what happened?"

"You really don't remember?" Cilas was surprised. "Helga, you did something to disable the dreadnought's cannons, but you took damage on exit when you attempted to pull off. You ejected and we found you already unconscious from hypoxia. Something happened to your helmet, it was leaking oxygen, but luckily we got you in time." He reached down to take her hand into his. She reached up and cupped his strong jaw, running her fingertips over the stubble on his chin.

"I was out that long from passing out?" she said, suddenly remembering where they were and pulled back her hand.

"No," Cilas said quickly. "Dr. Rai'to ran some tests and found that you were underweight and some other medical term for starving. I gave her permission to keep you under while you were treated, to give your body some well-needed rest and force-feed you some food. What's going on Hel, why are you skipping meals?"

"I'm not. It's just that I'm never hungry, and I'm just not going to force it. Plus, Cleia complains about my weight all the time. It's just her excuse to mother me and get me to take my meds or whatever. You fell right in with her plans," she complained.

"Yeah, but I bet you feel amazing and healthy now, don't you?" he challenged, stepping up closer with his hands behind him, puffing up his chest.

"How many did we lose?" she said, no longer able to ignore the groaning spacers in the racks next to hers. Cilas shook his head in the negative, looking to the side to indicate that he didn't want to discuss that in the company of injured men, worried that they too would join the dead. "Sorry, Cilas. That wasn't wise, and I know it. What about *Ursula*, how bad is she?"

"She's like us, Hel. Takes more than cheap tricks to break her, but it was close. She gave all of us a scare. Weinstar lost some people, and he himself was injured pretty badly. He and all of our seriously injured people have been transported to a hospital. You and everyone else here remain because of several factors, the main one being that Dr. Rai'to wants to treat you personally."

"I really don't need her to any longer though. I feel fine," Helga said.

"Ah, see, you admitted it right there," he teased. "You feel great, and it's all because I made the right order."

"Any word from Q and Anders?" Helga grew serious, still watching the door, expecting at any time Cleia would waltz in to scold her about her health.

"Spoke with Q. He and Anders are set to come back, though he still hasn't fully recovered from everything they did to him. The Genesian Guard offered to shuttle them here with one of their units, so they don't have to fly that junky merchant ship all the way out to here. We'll be seeing them soon. Under a week's time I'd wager, maybe less." He stood up straight, still holding her hand.

"Cilas, Commander, wait," Helga said suddenly, remembering her dream about the stranger and the unfamiliar starport. "Our second target, Vray, do we know whether or not he owns property on one of these stations? Perhaps even a station itself? I know he's rich and connected, but owning a space station, well I wouldn't know what he's capable of … uh. Do we know whether or not he has property in this space?"

Cilas studied her face for a long time, his mouth slightly open as if she'd guessed a mystery that had gone unsolved for a lifetime. What she read in his paralysis, however, was him being surprised that he hadn't thought of it before. If Vray had property he could pay his neighbors to remain silent while he waited out the Alliance to eventually give up on the search. "I … what makes you ask, Helga?" he managed to spit out after a painfully long pause while their eyes jousted.

"It just makes sense to me that a man with that much power would only run if he knew there was a way back. If all he had was his position in the Genesian government then he would fight back through the system, sanctioning assassinations and paying whomever to discredit Fio Doro and clear his name. This one ran, so I am thinking he left temporarily to let Basce City cool off."

"You can be a thrust-head at times, Hel, but when you try at being an officer, you're downright brilliant, do you know that?" Cilas said, grinning out of range of her punching or kicking him for the backhanded compliment. "I do have to go now, but I'll be back to check on you when I'm finished. We'll discuss your theory later. Happy to have you back." He took two steps backwards to hide the wink he sent her, then turned to acknowledge one of the injured, who had sat up to salute him as he went past.

Helga, seeing him in this moment, felt guilty for the doubts she'd had before when the dreadnought was damaging them. He was meant to be a captain, and it was so clear to her now in this moment. When he left, she felt alone again, despite the other patients trading conversation back and forth across their racks. All of their voices became like so much white noise against the peeping and tick-tacking of the attendant's fingers on the screens of their tablets, giving updates and receiving them.

Thirty minutes into this, Helga had had enough, but when she made to leave, Fio Doro entered, dragging a stool over to sit next to the Nighthawk. "What are you still doing here?" she asked the ex-smuggler turned fugitive. "I thought you would be out with everyone else, stretching your legs and exploring the port."

"Ask him." Fio gestured toward the doorway, which Helga knew meant Cilas, since she would have likely had seen him on her way in. The casual manner in the way she addressed him, however, was still somewhat jarring to the Nighthawk, who was used to a certain level of respect observed by spacers serving in the Alliance. Fio's casual familiarity was a constant reminder that she was a civilian guest temporarily assigned to them.

"I'm not exactly free of the *schtill* just yet." She shrugged helplessly. "I still have to wait for an interview with your council, whenever that'll be. Last time I asked, Commander Cilas told me they'll only tell him when they're ready, and until that time, I'm under his protection. All that to say, 'If she goes out, she must have a Marine escort, with no less than two sentries.," Fio recited. ""No further than the port. So, here I am, protected but bored out of my mind, Hellcat."

"Helga," the Nighthawk corrected her, wondering if it was the Genesian's Basce City dialect that had her butcher her name into Hellcat.

"Hellcat." Fio Doro doubled down on the moniker.

"Hellcat?" Helga arched an eyebrow, curious at the source of what was bound to be another nickname she did not want.

"Hellcat is what we call the craziest *thypes* in the speed circuits back home. The way you fly, you remind me of one of them in the stocks. I mean, Basce City," she said, her voice trailing off as if she just remembered the city of her birth.

"Oh," Helga commented quietly. "Guess I must've earned that." She still wasn't fully clear in her recollection on what she had done to the dreadnought, and wasn't ready to relive it through words, vids, or memory. A part of her knew she wouldn't have been proud of it. She was a lieutenant and first officer on a ship with a newly minted crew, responsible for saving this woman's life, and she had violated the commander's order to return when her shields had been decimated.

He hadn't seemed upset with her, but Cilas was the master of masks, hats, and any other metaphor for role switching. In this instance he was the doting boyfriend, but she wondered at the discipline that awaited her once she was back in uniform, formally taking the helm.

"You don't like the name? It's literally a compliment," Fio assured her, scooting her stool closer to the rack.

"Hellcat is fine for you, but only you," Helga told her. "I don't need another title thrown around by the rates.

"How is it that you're a Nighthawk?" Fio asked, pointedly, causing Helga to stop and work at an answer. She was still on the Hellcat name, coming around to liking it more than she would ever admit to, but here was a serious question coming from an outsider to not only Alliance Navy life, but to the war. "The Commander has the look, as well as Quentin, and I guess the rest of them, but you're so—"

"Female? Small? If I had a year of survival tacked on to my lifeline for every time this question comes up, I would live long enough to see a world without the Geralos and the need for an Alliance," Helga muttered half to herself, but Fio Doro overheard what she said. "Take a look around, "Helga spread her arms for effect, to indicate the entirety of *Ursula*. "Every one of us is different, but there are similarities, right? Figure those out and you know what makes a Nighthawk."

"That isn't so clear," Fio said. "Plus, you are nothing like the rest of them."

Helga wondered where this was going. Did she somehow inspire Fio Doro to take an interest in the Alliance, and would she have to be the one to tell her that becoming a Nighthawk was near impossible for someone her age?

"You thinking of signing on?" she tried.

"Oh no," Fio replied on time, as if she'd anticipated the question. "Wake up at the wee hours just to make my bed, eat protein bars, and run until I want to puke it back up every day? No thanks, sister. What I want to be is rich, and away from all this drama ... the war, BasPol, Vayle, all of this *schtill*. Give me a seaside home in Lowarn or Ficant Harbor, and you will have one happy girl, fishing and whipping about on a hover, good and retired."

"You know, I saw the photographs inside your room, and they told me a lot," Helga said. "The commander does the recruiting, but as far as statistics go, had you been born elsewhere, as a boomer, or to parents who were Vestalian patriots, you could have very well ended up here. Many of us hail from hubs, er—satellites, refugee satellites, high crime, never enough food. You know what I mean?"

"You're saying that me coming from the stocks makes me something of a candidate?" Fio tried, but Helga shook her head in the negative.

"Just give it a try, Fio. Think of every Nighthawk that you've met. If I just gave you the answer, what will you learn from this discussion? Nothing but a rigid list of traits that hardly represents this team."

"Alright, here goes," Fio said, sitting back suddenly. "You're all capable in a fight or you wouldn't have made it back here to Hellcat that alien ship into oblivion like you did. I already see that you're the pilot, that's how you can be small, and I bet you have a killer aim, so you qualify. That does beg to question what you said earlier about me being born a spacer and making it. You haven't seen me fight, so how would you know?"

"Call it a gut feeling," Helga offered. "I have to admit you said some things that I haven't really considered before concerning my role. The commander told me the stocks are similar to the hubs he and Raileo came from, and they both felt a level of kinship with your people. There is a reason they're Nighthawks, just like me, Quentin,

Anders now, and whoever comes along in the future. Anyone who lived through hell will view BLAST as a walk in the park."

"BLAST?" Fio asked quizzically.

"Basic Land and Space Training," Helga said. "It's the first level or test for becoming a member of Special Forces. Think of it like a dangerous obstacle course on an alien planet where you can die if you fail or get lost during a week's worth of hunger and humiliation. When the commander looks for recruits, he studies their backgrounds, taking into account their history. What he aims to find is moments when the candidate had every right to give up, but pressed on regardless. A Nighthawk has no quit inside their heart, Fio. We take this post knowing that on any hiccup in an operation, we can die. When you pass BLAST, you get invited to a team like ours, and we take you on a mission to see how you work, how you hold up under pressure, all those things. We evaluate your performance, reliance, whether or not you're a fighter or a just a poseur with bad nerves. Filling our ranks is important, but your quality must be measured before you join us."

Fio shrugged. "It doesn't sound much different from a street gang. Everyone wants the toughest soldiers with the addition of them being loyal, so they set up crazy missions where you prove to them how badly you want in. Never liked gangs, though. The thought of one loser telling me how to live my life ... no thank you. I would rather rough it alone than live like that."

"You wouldn't like the service then," Helga responded, disappointed.

"Did your parents give you up to the Alliance?" Fio asked, and Helga shrugged, a practiced reaction to that line of questioning, but she couldn't bring herself to be offended at someone who was new to everything Alliance Navy. The young woman was obviously trying to make friends with her, and why not? She was the lone civilian on a vessel full of spacers. Helga had seen something in the way Fio looked at her, and chalked it up to admiration for her rank, position, and moxie.

She decided to try sharing her story, but keeping it short and sweet without details. "Lost both my parents when I was eight," she started in a low, measured tone. "My father was an Alliance Marine, so they sent me to his mothership, *Rendron*, where I was taken into the academy, and trained to become what I am today."

"Pops, I mean, Djesu, is the reason I'm even alive after taking that *schtill* job," Fio recounted to Helga. "He died trying to do something good for the Alliance, even after I practically begged him to take the credits instead. He would have liked you ... all of you, for all his talk of Alliance heroes and whatnot. I bet he's smiling right now seeing me here on an Alliance ship, talking to a Nighthawk. He's likely hoping some of your rhetoric will rub off."

"Was Djesu former Navy?" Helga asked, trying to recall if the name had come up in their original brief before landing in Basce City to start searching for Sunveil.

"I never asked. Never really cared, to be honest. He did have a lot of Alliance stuff about the house though. Posters for recruitment, digital archives of stories, the allied planets; he really was obsessed with that *schtill*. When I wanted to gift him something, it was easy. All I had to do was look for something Alliance-related." Fio grinned at the memory. "You would have thought he'd won enough credits to retire on, he was so happy to receive any of it. Could you find out somehow if he was Alliance at one time? His full name is Djesu Mar, but if he was forced out it's likely to be an alias."

"We can check," Helga offered after seeing the struggle taking place behind Fio's words. She was holding it together, but like a vessel without shields another tragedy would likely pull her apart. "I don't know if it helps to know this, Fio, but what you and Djesu did makes you heroes of the Alliance. He will be honored, and you will be taken care of. How exactly? That'll be up to the council, but you're with us now, and we take care of our own."

"What I wish was that I was there with you all when you got Garson Sunveil. I wish that I had the chance to face him and make him answer for murdering Djesu in cold blood. I wish I could have seen the life leave his eyes while he pleaded with the girl he tried to have killed. Everything you said was nice, Helga, and I do appreciate you giving Pops his honors, but what I want is blood."

"Knowing the commander, you may not have been there to execute him, but Sunveil would have gone through some things before they turned him over. If there's any consolation, know that his hurting one of our own would have guaranteed him a long, painful transition to the Genesian Guard," Helga offered, though she knew it wouldn't help much. "Just hang tight, Fio, justice is coming. For now, take this as a vacation with friends, and new possibilities on the horizon."

32

It was obvious that the architects of Nova Mar station weren't interested in aesthetics or tricking its residents that they were on a planet or moon. Walking the passageways leading away from the docks, Commander Cilas Mec let his eyes wander upward, tracing the iron bulkheads up to the overhead 12 meters above. Everything was large on the station, the path he walked so wide you could fit twenty spacers in a line across it.

Robed Genesians sauntered past him in groups, their voices little more than a whisper, none of them seeming to notice him or care, despite his out-of-place uniform. Genesian Guards were present as well, dressed in close-fitting armor similar to the Alliance Powered Armor Suit. Most were armed with assault rifles, a strange sight on an industrial station, though with the Geralos circling, Cilas wasn't surprised.

From small grates near the bulkhead, a thin white plume of smoke rose up from someplace below. It stank of sulfur, but no one seemed to notice, though the smell was so intense at certain points that Cilas would reach up and pinch his nose. He wondered how long of a walk he would be taking before he reached the Alliance recruitment office where Commander Alwyn Star, his Nova Mar contact, was supposed to be waiting.

His wrist comms vibrated, and he glanced down at it, seeing a message received from Captain Retzo Sho by way of Commander Jit Nam of *Rendron*. It was brief, as was Commander Nam's way. "Stay on Nova Mar until further notice," it read. "Mission details coming." It was as cryptic as the man who sent it, but led Cilas to believe it was related to their Basce City adventure. Perhaps Vray had been spotted on the station? He dared not hope. Conveniences didn't come regularly, and the Nusalein Cluster had many other stations Vray could have gone to.

"Commander Mec," someone called, and Cilas stopped to follow the source of the sound, which had come from the far side of the passageway where a tall, dark-skinned Vestalian officer in a spotless white uniform stood smiling at him as if they were old friends. The man reminded him of an older Raileo Lei, since they both had that charming smile below predatory eyes whose glare spoke of a long history of violence. He liked him immediately.

The two men waded past the passing station dwellers to greet each other, and the stranger introduced himself. He was Commander Alwyn Star, the Alliance recruiter on Nova Mar station, and the person responsible for adding over 250 cadets onto the Navy roster. A number he was proud of. "One Alliance," was all Cilas could manage after Star had given him his credentials, since his record as a Nighthawk recruiter was nowhere close to that number, and included deaths and injuries that he still blamed himself for.

They spoke as they walked, Commander Star leading the way to his office, which fortunately for Cilas was on the same deck as the hangar. "Let me ask you a question," the Nighthawk commander said after some seconds of silence. "This station appears to be a part of the Nusalein cluster, but it's nothing like Neroka, or what I saw on the vid screens there of the other neighboring stations. Is there a reason?"

Alwyn Star chuckled. "I was waiting for that question. Nova Mar station is a proper hub. We repair ships, and handle imports and exports from not only the planet but from the other colonies. No goods come into the cluster without going through processing here. This is how we limit smuggling, particularly human trafficking, which is rife in this part of the galaxy, sad to say. Smugglers from the planet find their way through, but once caught, they come here to get processed and tried for high crime. Everyone living here is here for a job, since the governing council limits us coming and going to a handful of times per year—barring provable emergencies."

"What made you take up this post?" Cilas queried. "Given your rank and track record, you could be at the helm of your own infiltrator fighting the lizards."

"Not for me." Alwyn Star laughed again. "I'm like you, Cilas. I may have been born on a deck waking up to charging generators and rotating energy stores, but I wanted to be where I felt my work meant something. You go at the lizards directly, you and your Nighthawks, keeping them on their scaly toes. Whereas, for me, I want to find more Alwyn Stars and Cilas Mecs to fill out the ranks of our Alliance. That is how we will win, I am sure of it. Putting the poor unfortunate orphans of the galaxy on vessels where they can strike back at the very scourge who placed us here."

Now it was Cilas's time to laugh. "Pleasure to meet you indeed, Alwyn. You were made for the role, it appears. Every word out of your mouth is a slogan. If I were a boy again, stuck on a hub such as this one, I would happily have signed up just from one of your speeches. Seems you've done your homework on me and my crew."

"I hope you aren't offended," Star returned. "Old habits are hard to break, and as a recruiter, I need to know the people I am to meet with, not just from what their captain relays, but from their files, legends, personal records. For covert operations, however, you need no introduction, brother. Spacers across the entire fleet know of the Nighthawks. I regret that our meeting has to do with this mess that has come out of the greed from Basce City's corruption."

"Any word on that?" Cilas asked. "We left roughly a Vestalian week past, and I wasn't given any information outside of docking here immediately and meeting with you to discuss things."

"Following the shootings and threats to your lives on Neroka Station, the Genesian Guard has shut down access to the colonies. There won't be anyone coming and going until they finish looking into things, and considering the loss of credits from this change, the Genesian government is bending over backward to help get them answers fast. Every colony in the Nusalein cluster has agents watching the stations. As soon as Vray or any identifiable citizens from Basce City tries to enter a starport, they will be held for questioning by an Alliance representative."

"What an absolute disaster," Cilas said with a shake of his head. "A city burned for five Genesian days, and for what? For the ones behind everything to make it out, leaving their colleagues to be pressed for answers, of which they'll likely be clueless. Alwyn, in your honest opinion, what are our chances of finding Vray up here?"

"He will be found. That I can tell you definitively. Why am I so sure?" Star leaned in and whispered conspiratorially, "The Alliance reached out to the Jumper agency, and they've agreed to go after him. No one escapes the Jumpers' reach, but I don't have to tell you what they're capable of. No, Vray's time is up, though he likely doesn't yet know it. Who we're concerned with is Jawal Kur, the former captain of the *Harridan* infiltrator. He's managed to slip capture despite having a tracker planted on his vessel."

"*Missio-Tral's* Shrikes are exemplary," Cilas started to offer, but caught himself mid-sentence when he remembered that Jawal Kur was corrupted by the Geralos. "Then again, the old captain is likely corrupted, so who knows where he could have gone. If he boarded one of their vessels, he's no longer in this system."

The passageway opened up into a large, circular deck filled with kiosks, vendors, and an assortment of doors with colorful signs advertising what each had in store. While Cilas took in the spectacle, letting his eyes roam upwards to where several landings and bridges offered even more traffic, Alwyn Star unlocked the door to his recruitment office, which sat below a large billboard showing a Marine with his boot on the skull of a Geralos.

"In here, Commander, before they notice your newness and swarm you with offerings of liquor and flesh," he said, still smiling as if life was an endless pleasure for him. "There's liquor enough in here if you need, without the premium on credits, and the chance of gut rot from some Genesian's home brewed recipe." He shuddered dramatically as if to show that it was an experience he'd had and didn't recommend.

While he loved hubs and cataloging their differences inside his memory banks, Cilas was ready to get down to business. He was surprised that, despite the difference in station design and population, the layout of Alwyn Star's office was similar to that of Colonel Orlan Fumo's, who had been their contact on Neroka station. Alwyn grabbed two chairs and offered one to Cilas, and then scurried back behind his desk to retrieve an unmarked bottle of something dark. He poured a quick tip into two gold-rimmed snifters and handed one to the Nighthawk commander.

"To our Alliance." He offered a toast.

"To the warmth of fellowship and to the corrupt feeling the chill after an airlock," Cilas ad-libbed.

Commander Star seemed to like that, his grin getting even wider, and he knocked back the drink at the same time as Cilas, who struggled against the thick hot syrup that made its way slowly down his throat.

Alwyn Star noticed and his face grew solemn. "I apologize," he offered. "Sometimes I forget myself whenever I have visitors from the Alliance. Having been here so long, I forget that the liquor is unlike what we have from the other planets. Genesian liquor takes some getting used to. A positively *schtill* experience consuming it, but Commander, you will love the results." He winked and stacked their glasses neatly to one side of the squat, smoking bottle.

The thyping bottle is steaming, Cilas screamed inwardly, wondering how he'd managed to miss that important detail.

"Now that we're alone." Star leaned in as if he suspected someone might be eavesdropping on their conversation. "Message came in from the Genesian Guard, to be delivered to you, and to you only, Commander Mec. I am passing it onto you now. Will you acknowledge that my duty has been done?"

He stretched out one arm, peeled back the sleeve and unclipped a thick black bracelet. He removed a small panel on the underside of the band and extracted a miniature disk. Examining it closely, he took a breath and handed it over to Cilas, who took the object and placed it on the flat face of his own wrist comms. It reacted by revealing a cluster of hovering white glyphs, an encrypted message from their local allies.

"Commander Mec, this is Captain Torkel Aton of the Genesian Guard, I hope this message finds you well and clear in these dark times of sabotage and treachery. In response to your earlier query about properties owned by Councilman William Vray in the Nusalein Cluster, on Lestrat Station, Vray owns a considerable share of investment property located in the business sector. Starport surveillance showed him arriving three days prior to your departure. I went ahead and researched your rights as a galactic agency in collecting criminals from the colonies, and according to our law, fugitives are not eligible for sanctuary if their crimes involved treason. This extends to the galactic war."

Cilas felt energized. He hadn't dared to hope his Nighthawks would get another chance to fulfill their mission. Vray hadn't fled the system as he suspected, but had stayed, which was a crucial mistake. Thinking dockhands and engineers he paid off would have been enough to keep his movement obscured, he had underestimated the rage that the attack on the tenements had caused. He wondered if Vray realized his time was up, or if he was too insulated to know when he was exposed and out of favors.

"He's all yours, Commander," Captain Torkel Aton was saying when Cilas's focus was brought back to the present where he was hearing the good news. "The location of the property and blueprint details will be coming in momentarily, so please be on the lookout. Other than that, I wish you good hunting, and may his eventual demise bring peace to the citizens who've fallen victim to his greed for credits."

Cilas looked up from his wrist-comms at a curious Star, who had been trying unsuccessfully to disguise his eavesdropping on the message. Cilas jabbed a finger at the desk's surface where a two-dimensional diagram of the station clusters could be seen. "Lestrat Station, where is that exactly?" he asked, barely able to contain his excitement.

"Directly next to us. Well, not really, but yes, it's the next station over from Nova Mar," Alwyn Star informed him. "Are you needing to visit Lestrat Station?"

"I am," Cilas admitted, "But only after my Nighthawks return. If this intelligence is sound, we'll have plenty of time to go there and do what we have to do. If we can get Vray, the Jumpers can focus their search on Jawal Kur, and his lizard puppet masters.

"If it's like you say, and he's no longer one of us, a, um ... human? Then I will pray that he was with the crew of that dreadnought you vanquished, and permanently out of commission," Star offered optimistically, placing a fist above his heart for added effect. "The longer a corrupted human draws air, the more risk we take of having it expose the host's knowledge to their lizard leadership."

"We'll get it done," Cilas said confidently. "But things like these, inside jobs, they get messy when it comes to extractions. People tend to look out for their own, and if Vray is considered one of theirs, they will make it difficult for us to go in and bring him out. Anything else I should know, Commander?"

"Just more bad news I'm afraid," said Alwyn Star. "But with a somewhat happy ending to it all. *Scythe* was ambushed by the Geralos while patrolling Louine space."

"That sounds familiar," Cilas added, recalling Fio reciting the information that had been leaked by William Vray.

"It's our worst nightmare realized," Star said, becoming serious. "A pair of battleships leading five destroyers jumped in on their vector, so precise her crew should have been left helpless with no FTL options. Thanks to the action of your team, in acquiring Sunveil to corroborate our suspicions, we were able to get *Scythe* a warning that the lizards were on their way. Unfortunately, the message was received late, after they had been disabled and boarded—"

"Boarded?" Cilas nearly shouted, unable to believe what he was hearing. Geralos boots had made it onto a starship's deck. "If they board a starship, they can claim her, and the thousands of crew. Sorry, didn't mean to interrupt, but tell me this ends with our boys and girls rallying to remove them from their decks."

Alwyn Star nodded. "This is the *Scythe*, brother, have some faith. She's the last surviving starship from the first conflict. Now hear. *Inference* was close enough to support them and chase the lizards back into deep space. Lots of casualties though; you don't want the number. As for Admiral Hal, that old war dog, the Alliance is suggesting he retire to Sanctuary, where he'll be honored as a legend while their doctors repair the hole inside his chest."

"Admiral Hal is injured?" Cilas couldn't believe what he was hearing. "How bad is it?"

"My contact was forbidden from giving out details, I'm afraid," Star said with a wave of disappointment. "Admiral Hal caught shrapnel from a console exploding on his bridge. A zip-ship's lancer cut through the soft hull once their shields had depleted. That did the old man in. He has been in stasis awaiting surgery ever since. They suspect it wasn't accidental. First the leaks, then an admiral taken out."

"Now I know why we're calling in the Jumpers," Cilas muttered. "They got to one of our best, and cracked a champion starship. Just now we came up against a vessel, the dreadnought if you recall, and it was using ordnance that ignored our shields to tear apart my hull. Mission after mission we're seeing the evidence that we've been infiltrated at every level."

"Let's not go down that road, Cilas. That road leads to cynicism, and you more than anyone should know how it affects you as a spacer, and as an officer. The evidence is there though; I'm not blind. It's been there, and this situation with Vray has it incorporating civilians. It isn't cynicism to recognize that we have to end that immediately."

"What are you saying?" Now it was Cilas's turn to look around for watching eyes or strangers straining an ear to hear their conspiracies.

"I'm saying that you were called in here, not only to repair but because this is where they likely suspect our runaway councilman to be. Your Lestrat Station, the one Vray owns. I have been sitting here puzzling it through. Why bring the ESO team to the colonies where they will be vulnerable when there's an Alliance fueling station less than a jump outside of here? I believe we will find out soon enough if he was foolish enough to escape to his colony."

"That or arrogant," Cilas said, standing. "The way Fio made him sound, I wouldn't be surprised if he doesn't get the weight of what he's done, and how every spacer in the galaxy wants to end him. Man like that will think small on the repercussions. He will think us getting Sunveil and not him will be the end of our searching since we got some sort of justice."

"An interesting character study." Star nodded his agreement., standing with Cilas to see him back to the doorway. "We're glad you're here, Commander. We Alliance are few here, and things are about to ramp up for all of us. I'm putting in for additional presence even on this station."

"When we find Vray and squeeze him, he will give up all of his co-conspirators and whatever lizard is in on the deal. I don't see anyone involved with this getting out, even if it takes us fifty years to find them," Cilas promised. "I hope you're right and we get the mission on Vray, but for now I'm worried for Admiral Hal and the crew of the *Scythe*. They managed to get us, Star. They got inside."

"May be time to make some examples for future Vrays, don't you think?" Alwyn Star gripped his shoulder with a vicelike grip, his eyes flashing their wicked intent. "Do they all get to have a comfortable stasis cell, where they can drag out the process until their hearing? Hundreds, no thousands, have lost their lives for this man, and the snakes within our Alliance who bought into it. If you happen to, I don't know, find him dead, would anybody mourn his passing?"

"We'll see how it plays out," Cilas offered, alarmed at how brazenly this commander was sanctioning murder despite the orders to detain him.

"For the Alliance," Star said, his shoulders sagging, as he physically came down from his earlier excitement from plotting justice.

"For the Alliance," Cilas repeated the phrase, happy to have found a knowledgeable colleague with as much passion for the conflict as he had.

33

A slender hand, pale and warm, caressed the smooth back muscles of William Vray, millionaire, mogul, and former Basce City council recently retired. He was seated on the edge of the bed, staring out at the endless rows of algae farms through the large glass walls of his bedroom. His thoughts were on the deal of a lifetime going to *schtill*, all because he outsmarted himself hiring an amateur to transport those Alliance coordinates.

Had she succeeded, he wouldn't be living on one of his properties; he would be on a yacht above Louine, licking cream-flavored urka dust off bountiful blue fingertips. Now he was a fugitive, stuck inside a glass tube pretending it was a world, and no matter how much he stared out at his wealth he couldn't help but feel like a prisoner.

What made things worse was the news cycle. They were using his actual name, accusing him of being involved with the fires in the tenements. As if he would have anything to do with that wretched blight on an otherwise futuristic city. The thought of the blue-haired smuggler having something to do with it haunted his every thought. Oh how he had wanted to press her when she asked for three times his offer, but greed had won out and he had decided to go along with the fleecing.

Had he known it would end up with Sunveil's vaults emptied of all their recorded correspondence, he would have taken everything he wanted and tossed her corpse out onto the rooftops of those tenements. If time was but another dimension to manipulate like interstellar travel, he would give an arm to return to that evening, lure her in, and snuff her out.

Months of planning, ruined, and for what? Sunveil's committee keeping records and playing lords of the slums in their fancy compound. He had been warned off doing business with spice dealers, grifters, and pimps, but he wouldn't be where he was, even in a place such as this one, if he hadn't dirtied his hands for the extra credits.

What is wrong with me, I'm losing my grip, he thought, feeling the warmth of that tiny hand on his back helping to push some of that anger down into the furnace that was his stomach. He was technically ruined, having crossed a line they all swore not to cross. Interfering with the war, becoming accused of being a traitor, not just to Basce City and Genese, but to every human being across the entire galaxy.

"With flowing robes and bearing arms they lift me up to praise me, all so my actions are on display for all to humiliate me," he quoted.

"That's beautifully morose," said the Arisani woman, her face barely visible beneath the sheets. "What does it mean?"

Vray glanced back at her, struggling but determined not to reveal to her the cauldron in his bowels singeing his insides. He was no stranger to sharing his bed with women, but they usually were paid for and gone before he opened his eyes. Minoru E'lune being here now was due to the stress of the last few days, *and that thyping dress that barely concealed anything on her tall, slender shape*, he had to admit.

He fought back against the fear that she'd seen the news feeds and would share his whereabouts as soon as she left the property. Perhaps she'd already done so, and there were agents on the way to make an arrest. *Stop with the paranoia, councilman*, he scolded himself. *This is your world. You paid for it with your own credits.* It wasn't an exaggeration; he held the most stakes in the station, so technically as majority owner it was his.

Every Cel-toc was coded to be loyal to him, from the dockhands at the starport to the pleasure models walking his gardens. This was his fortress, and despite having to stay put for a few years, there would be a time soon in the future when he could return to Basce City. Until then, why not enjoy the time with the senator, whose cruiser was stationed at his port getting repairs? She was generous and submissive, everything he wanted in a mate, and then there was more; she was Arisani, exotic to a Genesian for multiple reasons. He was winning, and though it didn't feel much like it now, he hoped sometime soon in the future he could feel some appreciation for his success.

"William?" Minoru's thick accent cut through his thoughts, sounding genuinely concerned as she sat herself up behind him and placed her other hand on his abdomen. He could feel her naked breasts pressed against his back as she pulled him into her, kiss-nibbling him gently on the neck.

"It's an old Louine poem, translated badly," he said, realizing that she had been waiting while he sat there brooding. It made him feel exposed. "Somewhat appropriate for the way I've been feeling." He turned around to face her, fingers finding her long silver hair, and then he placed a kiss on her plump, blue-tinted lips. This was pleasant, this was ... happiness? How could he neglect the time with this beauty to stress rewriting history?

He felt himself growing from her proximity, and the thoughts of worry, sorrow, and rage subsided quickly, replaced with carnal urges. He wanted her now more than ever, and not just to get a few minutes of pleasure leading up to that majestic release, but to use her as a distraction for as long as she wanted to stay with him. Surely the property, the servant Cel-tocs, and all the amenities measured up to the privileged life she enjoyed as an Arisani ambassador.

She decoded the kiss, worming herself around to his front, long legs wrapped about his waist, with her arms resting on his shoulders, clasped behind his neck. Once again, she welcomed him, wrapping every part of her about him, whispering commands in his ear using Arisani words he would never understand. Gasps turned to moans, then growls, obscene commands as she took the reins, assuming control.

Despite the performance and the fantastic feedback it solicited, he couldn't shake his fears, and what should have been a brief dance of happiness became a lengthy chore with no end. He just couldn't finish, and he was spent, exhaustion forcing him to stop, followed by the disappointment of having failed her and himself in the attempt.

For several long moments they lay in each other's heat, embraced, backs to the soft but firm mattress, staring up at the lights recessed in the ceiling. He wondered what was going through Minoru's mind. She wasn't the type to let things lie; that he had picked up back when they merely flirted and spoke on mundane things like shipping cargo on and off the station. He chanced a glance at her, and caught her staring with what appeared to be concern on her smooth, milky-white visage.

"Oh, tell me what's wrong, William," she urged. "You've obviously got something on your mind you can barely resist, and it's been eating at you since you woke up. Was it a nightmare?"

He turned to stare into her large, almond-shaped eyes, trying to read the setup if this was it. Arisani faces were always the hardest to read, even for someone who had lived with them. Still, she seemed genuinely concerned, her warm hand resting on his cheek, complicating his feelings. "Just something I saw on the news feeds from back home. I'm sure you've seen it," he said.

"I'm afraid not. What was it?" She sat up suddenly. "Was it the Geralos?"

"Even if it was, why would you care?" Vray snapped at her suddenly. He was irritable, and he knew it, but couldn't check his tone or his words as he kept saying them. "At least your people are distinct enough not to be mistaken for Vestalians. Genesians are rounded up and eaten with the rest of the freeloaders, so we have no choice but to join the Alliance."

"I'll have you know, I have family in the Alliance. I grew up on Ilerance Station, not Arisani. Nice attitude, Councilman. Was all of the tact, charm and wit from last night just an act?" She stuck in the barb before scooting herself to the side of the bed to quickly get dressed.

He grabbed her hand. "Don't run off. That all came out in a way I didn't intend it," he quickly said, unwilling to release her until she'd given him the time to explain.

She hopped up, twirled, a spiral of fabric following her as she spun, resulting in her tall, slender body being wrapped in an elaborate toga-styled dress. Long, ring-adorned fingers danced behind her skull, pulling her hair back into an even more complex ponytail, and she was gone from the room in a stomping huff, sliding the door shut manually so he could hear it crashing into the grooves of the entryway.

Vray sat stunned, refusing to let it bother him. Doors could easily be replaced, and with his wealth and status, she like the rest would be the one to apologize to him when she eventually remembered her place. He heard the door click and looked up expectantly, surprised at the speed in which she emerged, which only meant she was ready to argue her position to him.

What stood before the doorway, however, was neither Arisani or attractive. It was a composite armor-adorned hulk with an automatic rifle. Several more stood behind it, and there was no sign of Minoru E'lune, though they appeared to have come from the same bathroom she had gone into. He dove for his pillows, looking for the sidearm he kept there for protection in case of something like this.

The armored man was fast, however, and anticipated his actions. One massive leap and he was on the bed, pulling Vray after him onto the floor where he placed the muzzle of the rifle against his head.

"This you?" the voice boomed, and the intruder's free hand shot forward to reveal a holo-emitter bearing his likeness. It was from the BasPol database, not a mugshot, but a census rendering, accurate in copying his features despite being an image generated by artificial intelligence.

At first, he shook his head in the negative, thinking there was another way out of this, but the giant only became angrier, even going so far as to slap him with a backhand when he denied it. He swapped the image to an actual photograph of him in a starport exiting a shuttle, and he recognized it. This was on Basce City, taken with surveillance on the same night everything had gone south with his plans and Sunveil had put a number out on that thieving smuggler's head. *This couldn't be about that,* he mused before chiding himself internally for being paranoid and ridiculous.

"Alright, alright, alright, hero, you have me, no need to rip my arm off," he protested. The masked figure spun him around to place him in an armbar, foregoing stasis cuffs to bind his wrists in what felt like wire cutting into his skin. "Are you with the agency? BasPol? Alliance? If you let me get to my office, I can get you whatever you need, for whatever this is ... this, misunderstanding," he pleaded.

The large figure moved to face him, put a hand to one ear and swung it laterally, striking him hard on the other side of his face. The blow robbed him of his hearing from that ear and robbed his conscious for a split second, causing him to wake up feeling disoriented with four, no five figures standing over his crawling form. One of these figures was his lover, Minoru E'lune, and to his surprise she wasn't bound or detained.

Did she? He thought, no, there was no way he had fallen for such a simple trap. A beautiful stranger on his lonely, remote station, and an ambassador to boot, one with the credentials of a mover and shaker' he had verified this himself. Why then was she standing with the others, looking down at him suffering from that stolen blow thrown by an intruder?

The intruder pulled off his mask to reveal the hard, raw-boned features of a man born and bred for war. Low-cut blond hair covered his scalp, but for one side where the Alliance tattoo stood out prominently below what appeared to be a knife wound above his ear.

This was a Marine as they were reputed, all size and rage contained in a vessel barely holding that storm at bay. That storm looked upon him as if he were the foulest bio-extraction slime. If death had a visage, it had to mirror this man's.

Vray wracked his brain, looking for answers. Did he recognize this Marine from a deal in the past, or did he favor someone he'd conned in the past? With the way he conducted business, he would never know. "What's this about?" he tried again, crawling backwards on his elbows and heels to get as far away from Quentin as he could.

The crawl took him to the feet of another masked man, this one much smaller than the first, but just as agitated from his profile. He reached up and removed his mask, revealing a young, pretty face with black makeup around her eyes and a shock of bright blue hair. This wasn't a male Marine. This was the girl, the start of the problems that led him here, where he was stuck hiding out.

"Fio Doro." His words were a curse, but her face was twisted into a mask of rage similar to the bigger man, but crueler in his intent, and he knew he was in trouble.

"I think you owe me 500 credits, Vray," Fio Doro said, thrusting her hand out at him.

"Is that what this is all about then?" he asked. "You hire a team of thugs to collect your chips?"

"You also owe me a life. Djesu Mar, the man you had your goon Garson Sunveil murder in cold blood to keep your secret. Return him to me and I will call off my thugs, as you put it. Do that then, and my 500 credits, and we'll hop back on our shuttle and leave."

William Vray looked for a logical advantage in Fio Doro's wants, barring the impossible task of resurrecting the dead. "How about 500,000 credits? You can erect a memorial, even become the next mayor of Basce City. With that many credits, you could buy your own luxury liner and retire to the stars if you wanted."

"Since we're making deals," another of the infiltrators offered, pulling off his mask to show his face. This one was another hard-faced male with a similar hairstyle. Instead of glaring angrily, however, he had a calm to his demeanor that was chilling. "Over 50 civilians killed or injured in the Basce City tenements, a combined number of 1,200 more on vessels across the galaxy. All hit by the Geralos, thanks to the intelligence that you sold. How many credits do you think would cover that?"

There was no right answer and Vray knew it. These weren't hired mercenaries, they were Alliance Special Forces, but it didn't explain the girl. His eyes met hers. "They're with you? You made contact with the Alliance." His tone was accusatory but beneath it all, William Vray was impressed. Basce City was cut off from everything but the local colonies, yet this young woman somehow had found a way to reach the dreaded Alliance.

He felt his options slipping. The two men were obvious killers and one looked so cocked to explode, he could sense the end was coming. Then there were the other three masked figures behind them, armed statues watching him wallow, though he could feel the weight of their hate as they looked upon him. "If I talk, what will that win me?" he inquired of Cilas, who he assumed was the leader of this masked Alliance company.

"The more you cooperate, the more likely it is you will survive this encounter, and onto Justice Station where you will undergo a trial and pay for your defense," Helga informed him. "For us, considering all you've done, we would rather take you apart slowly and let your screams lull the souls of the spacers you got killed."

William Vray pulled himself up to his elbows, wiggling backwards against the side of the bed until he had worked his way up into a sitting position. The effort took a lot out of his already racing heart and distracted mind trying to calculate an escape. A splash of warm, slimy wetness struck him on his left eye, which he realized was spittle once he reached up to wipe it from his vision. Helga was pulling Fio backwards, and though they made no noise, he could see the rage on the blue-haired woman's face. It was then that he surrendered to his helplessness. There would be no escape, and the only way to keep his life was to admit to it all, and bring down anyone involved who he personally knew.

"Let me start by saying that I don't consider myself a traitor," Vray said, his voice dropping in volume, revealing that even he now questioned whether or not that statement was correct. "Last year in the first cold season, I met an officer from the Alliance. He was visiting Basce City, he told me, and he wanted to set up a recruitment office with a focus on intelligence, something that an investor could profit from."

"What was his name?" Cilas queried.

"Labi Solstice O'lan, a fellow Genesian and an Alliance lieutenant," Vray said softly. "Labi had a lot of credits and didn't seem busy for an Alliance officer, but we didn't care to look into any of that. All we saw was opportunity for the city. The offices went up, paid for by our donations, with the promise that those of us who put the top percentile into the pile would be made partners in the venture. So, I bought in, and it really did pay off. We would send children to the recruitment offices, and it would earn us credits, legal credits, and so much of it."

Helga glanced at Cilas, who in turn had been looking her way when Vray explained the business of Alliance recruitment. If any of what he said was true, it was disappointing to think that money was being exchanged for their service. Someone had been paid for them to become cadets, and the whole time in Helga's mind, it was the parents sacrificing what little they had to win back Vestalia, even if it meant their children. Her head felt heavy, her body light as she tried to process this information.

"Then one day Labi ended up dead, his throat cut inside his penthouse, and suddenly we had a new Alliance representative running the Basce City office. That was Garson Sunveil. We knew he wasn't Alliance; he was the biggest gangster the tenements has seen, and we've have seen hundreds of these types. But he laid out a plan to us for more credits if we could do a bit of smuggling for a captain in the Alliance. I thought it was all above board, so I covered the legal end to allow the transfer within the city limits, collected the package and paid a runner to get it onto a shuttle going out to one of the stations."

"Where one of the lizards posed as a Genesian would collect it and share it out to their fleet, who would use it to massacre numerous spacers, unaware that they're jumping into a trap," Raileo added. "That sound about right, Councilman? But you don't care, do you? You get to buy station property and entertain beautiful Arisani women." This rewarded a look from Minoru E'lune, which went from skepticism to amused acceptance, and culminated with her blushing from the compliment.

"We never considered that," Vray admitted, sighing heavily as he found it increasingly hard to breathe.

"Verdict?" Quentin asked of Cilas.

"Lock him in stasis cuffs and get him onboard for transportation. We did our part, now the council will do theirs," Cilas relented, earning several groans from Fio and Quentin. "He'll get his time, and eventual punishment, but we don't get to decide that, not when he's cooperating. Come on, Nighthawks, let's be done with it. Scrape this *schtill* off the floor and onto *Ursula*."

"We got him," Helga said to Fio, who stood staring at Vray with murderous intent. "His life is over. The council will pull everything out of this *cruta*, and he will never know freedom again. What do you say?"

"It's not enough," Fio Doro replied as she dabbed at a rebellious tear. "Djesu deserved better, but thank you. Thank you, Lady Hellgate, for everything."

EPILOGUE

It was late, the station equivalent of an hour to midnight. Most of the population was in their bunks, racks, or hammocks sleeping, while the night owls ate, watched vids, or smoked spice to relax. Helga and Cilas were seated at a bar, Cecily's Oasis, one of the only businesses still open at that time of night. She nursed a fruity Vestalian cocktail, and he was on his second shot of rum.

"I have something to ask you," he said, sounding serious. This after hours of jokes and light banter. Helga had known he had something on his mind, but Cilas was a closed book who she still struggled to understand on her best days, so she expected he wanted to end things, or he was promoting her. One could never know.

"Ask away, Commander, I'm sure I can answer whatever you throw at me," she said, steeling herself.

"When you asked about Vray owning property here, it wasn't a hunch, was it? You knew, but you didn't want me probing so you pretended it was merely a guess. But I know it in my heart, somehow, Hel, you knew where to find him. My question is how? Is Sundown leaking you information somehow, some sort of Casanian intuition, or am I going insane?"

Helga's pulse picked up and she inhaled, letting the breath out steadily as she considered whether to lie to the closest thing she had to family. She thought about all they had been through, the way he remained so delicate and considerate of her. Even when she was being her bratty self, he would show that he was willing to be patient.

She hammered a fist into the table, cursed at her bad luck, then pulled her knees up into her chest and rested a cheek on them, looking away from him.

"It's not only that, Hel, but I had a long conversation with Sundown before his reassignment. He seemed really concerned with your welfare, beyond the concern of a brother, if you know what I mean. At the time I was worried that you and he were, you know? But that didn't make sense, so I thought about Jumpers and their obsession with Seekers."

"You think I'm a Seeker?" Helga asked, turning to face him. The line had been crossed and there was no going back.

"Helga, I know you're a Seeker," Cilas surrendered. "I've known it in my heart since I found you in that isolated room back on Dyn. I thought to myself, why are they doing all this to her? Is it because she's Casanian? Why do all this when every other species would have just been tossed out and killed? On the *Sur*, I asked the doctor about your condition, and he wouldn't talk to me, citing patient, physician trust or some nonsense. Please tell me I'm not going crazy."

Helga exhaled heavily and stared up at the overhead, wondering what was going to be sacrificed with their relationship once she admitted to being what he suspected. "When we were at Fio's and I took a nap, I had a dream about a dropship landing on an unfamiliar station. Vray and his entourage emerged, and he was an ass like I assumed, but in the dream, Ina called me to confirm he was our target."

"Wild," Cilas whispered, inching in closer to her. "Ina was the lead in your dream? As in Ina being a Nighthawk?"

Helga nodded, "I confirmed blindly that it was Vray and then I was awake, looking up at Fio's holo-gallery. The vision was still on my mind, so I took a shot in the dark and asked you whether or not it was possible for Vray to own property on a station. Far from prescience or local dimensional shifting." She smiled. "Are you worried that I'm a Jumper-hopeful that you'll lose off the team when Sunny finally recruits me?"

"Don't even joke about that, Helga. It's crossed my mind as well. It's a Commander's nightmare to lose good team members to the Jumper agency. I know it's part of the deal, and we're not to stand in the way if it happens, but it isn't ideal, and especially not you, not when I—well, I cannot imagine the team without you, Helga. Just the thought of it leaves a vacuum in my mind. But I'm beginning to realize that you may really be too important to be a Nighthawk. You're one of the chosen few and we've thrown you into the fire so many times, and for what? ESO missions? You should be in Sanctuary helping to steer the war instead. You have the sight, and we have you on a team getting shot and blown up."

"And that is why I've never told you." Helga sighed, still reeling from him saying he loved her in the most roundabout Cilas way possible.

"You don't want that, and so you kept it to yourself," Cilas tried. "Just like being with me you worried for the preferential treatment. You again being an outcast with attention being brought to your unique gift instead of your actual accomplishments."

"I love to fly, Cilas," Helga explained. "I would rather be shot, blown up, or torn to shreds fighting for the same thing my father and all his ancestors have done since the lizards stole our planet. Being a Seeker means I get dreams, so what? I have faster reactions, yes, and it does give me a bit of an edge, but do I not train twice as hard as any spacer on here and *Rendron*? Do I not spend countless hours honing my craft to help our success?"

"And you shouldn't have to qualify that, ever." Cilas raised a hand to cut her off before she became even angrier. "You're a Nighthawk because you're talented, intelligent, and a BLAST graduate. No one can ever rob you of that. You're my first mate not because we're *thyping*, but because you've proven yourself to me, and two other very, very talented and intelligent operators. Again, that's you, you did that, and me finding this out doesn't change any of your accomplishments. If anything, it lets me know that I've been holding you back somewhat."

"So now that you know, what will you do with me?" Helga asked, her hard eyes still staring into his.

"To be honest, Hel. Nothing. This is your private reality and while I am expected to report it to the captain, we both know what comes with that, and the last thing I want to do is bring you misery after everything we've shared. You make me fear the lizards more now though, that I can say. I fear them capturing you and completing whatever they attempted back at Dyn. I know we've promised each other before, but now it feels different. More dire, perhaps?"

"You mean us promising to kill each other rather than be taken in by them again?"

When Cilas nodded, Helga grinned, remembering the Louine ship that rescued them, and the two of them barely conscious, in pain, and making death promises. "I meant it, though. All I have special about me is that my dreams tend to skew real, at times showing me glimpses of someone else's life or future. Sunny and I aren't together romantically; he was using his Jumper training to show me how to unlock my gifts."

"What other visions have you had?" he asked, hopping off his stool to stand even closer. He threw his arm around her shoulders, which she accepted readily, leaning her head against his chest and closing her eyes.

"My accident, losing the Classic. I didn't envision it exactly, but I did dream of losing oxygen and dying alone without any warning, just the reality of being helpless without any communication. I've dreamed of my parents, back when they were younger and trying to have babies," she recalled, smiling. "I've been on Casan, fighting wars against the lizards, which felt real enough, but I'm hoping that really isn't something somewhere ahead of me."

"And Sunny helps you do this?" he asked, confused as to how dreams could be taught to someone.

"Jumpers are trained to look for Seekers. Their charge is to protect us with the greater goal being the destruction of the Geralos since they pose the biggest threat to our survival. He knew what I was from the moment he saw me fight," Helga reminisced, smiling when she remembered him calling her out. "Kept my secret easily, but wanted to train me regardless. I don't even think the agency knows, or else they would have already exposed me to the Alliance."

"You do things in space and air that I didn't think were even possible, Hel, even I knew something was up," Cilas whispered. "Sundown's quite the character, no short of surprises with that man, and now I learn he's something of a mentor to one of my Nighthawks. Will you be using las-swords any time soon? Please say yes."

Helga laughed. "I'm good, but not even I have the skills they require to be a Jumper. You've fought alongside them. Sunny is impressive, but Lamia was a wizard of some sort with his movements, and I'm sure there are others who make even those two bad asses look like rooks. No sir, I am merely a dreamer with some reflexes I guess as a bonus, but I'm no Sunny or Lamia."

"Funny how under the wisecracking hot shot pilot is a humble monk downplaying her abilities," Cilas joked. "Just remember us little people when you're an important member of the Alliance council representing either Casan or Vestalia. Helga Ate, ESO, Ace Pilot, Jumper-trained Seeker, Heroine." Cilas mimed the rectangular outline of a marquee as he threw out her titles in this imagined future where the galaxy would honor her service.

"Oh, get off it, you're famous right now, and you're no Seeker. Anyone gets to be on the council, it would be *Rendron's* future captain, not the hot-headed, half-alien lieutenant that follows him everywhere. My place, until I'm no longer able, is at the tip of the spear, helping to drive the lizards back to Geral where they belong," Helga said before reaching for her glass and knocking back the last of its fruity lukewarm remnants.

"Guess they will need to look elsewhere for new council members." Cilas shrugged dismissively, causing Helga to smirk at the change that had become evident in her commander.

"Is it enough to be fighting for a better future though, Cilas? Men like you, you may be humble, but I know you're ambitious and well on the way to being on the bridge of a capital ship. We don't get to have normal lives like our ancestors. Up here we're owned, first by the Alliance, and then what we've been told we owe our species. All we as Vestalians have is service, and individual needs never factor into that."

"So, what are you saying?" Cilas sat up to face her, his fingers still interlocked with hers.

"I'm saying that we shouldn't label or limit our time together, or weigh its importance against my role as a Seeker. We go into every mission knowing it could be our last, or we will lose someone we love and care for violently. How is this any different, except I've shared my deepest secret with the man I *thype* on occasion, who I also am made to salute?"

Cilas actually laughed at that, a loud laugh of relief, and she could see him deflating from his earlier worries. "You got it, Ate. This stays between us until you say differently. We will carry on the mission," he swore. "It's the Nighthawk way."

"It's the Nighthawk way," she repeated, and they shared a long stretch of silence, nothing uncomfortable, but something deeper, an unspoken bond between lovers that no words or glyphs in the galaxy could convey.

Made in the USA
Las Vegas, NV
06 March 2023